The Witch of The Valley

Michael E Reusch

A Novel

Author's Note

This work is intended for mature readers. This is a work of fiction. Names, characters, places, and incidents either are the product of the author's imagination or are used fictitiously, and any resemblance to actual persons, living or dead, events, or locales is entirely coincidental.

Cover photo by Michael E Reusch
Rear cover photo by Sue Reusch
Cover Design by Michael David

There by the grace of God go I

Thank you to my family, especially my wife Sue, who made this possible.

A special thanks to my son, my editor, My Zles, Michael David. Whose fine editing, constructive criticism, notes, ideas, long talks and great discussions throughout the writing process brought out the best in me.

iv

For my mom, Judie, who instilled within me the love of reading. She always wanted to be a writer, but never got around to doing so. She was always too busy taking care of someone, or something…or reading.

Table of Contents

Chapter 1

Introduction

I often think of a story that my grandfather, Clyde Younger, told me over the course of many years when I was a boy. I would help him doing odd jobs and working with him on his farm. I was intrigued by his stories about friends and acquaintances that he was blessed to have known throughout his life. He ended up outliving all of them. He had many stories to tell. But the one story that I wanted to hear—the one that I could never get enough of—was the one about the witch. A story from the days when he was young.

I would prod him to tell it again and again. Reluctant to retell it, from time to time he would collect himself, take a seat, and find a way to do so. He always needed to sit when he told me the story of the witch. And he would never look at me when he did. I didn't realize at the time how old wounds can be ripped open anew by simple words. Every time he told it some new tidbit of information would bubble up, and I soaked it up like a sponge.

The story went on about this nasty old witch that terrorized the community. My grandfather was the town constable at that time. He heard the confession of Hazel Dill, who the townspeople grew to call *The Witch of The Valley*.

He eventually refused to talk about it, my grandfather. He kept the story to himself. But the reach of the Witch's tale was wide, and it left its scars on the people of my hometown of Valley Center, Ohio. The story itself grew into a bit of an urban legend amongst those some may call superstitious, and while they have many details askew, they're not wrong. Out of everyone I've come to know, the only person who even came close to the level of knowledge my grandpa had about this tale was Peter Ertz.

Peter Ertz was a reporter for the local paper, The Valley Center Visitor. He was a friend to both my grandpa, and my dad, Ben Younger. Before I left for college, I fixed a hole in the roof of his house. While in the attic of Pete's house I found a trunk that was full of newspapers and notes. The Visitor, as it was known, was a periodical that was printed when they had enough news to write about. I called down from the attic to Pete and told him about the trunk. He said to bring it down. We sat in his garage, and he opened the trunk.

The top newspaper had the headline: "The Witch of Valley Center Confesses." It sparked memories of what my grandpa had told me and renewed my curiosity in the story of the witch. He let me have the trunk. It contained a treasure trove of information that he had gathered. From official transcripts to interviews of members of the community who were living in The Valley at that time. Every time I saw him, I would ask him to tell me more. I knew there had to be more.

There were interviews of Hazel's sister Elsa, her brother Skid, my grandfather, my good friend Mike Muller's grandfather, Johnny Muller, who we both affectionately call Grandpa Johnny, Art Gunther, and various other town folk that I will introduce. One of which is the eldest son of the witch, Luther Dill. My talks with Luther and the notes from Pete's interviews were key to me figuring out the true identity of The Witch.

I will unveil to you what happened in The Valley. It's not so cut and dried as everyone seems to think. There's more to the goings on in The Valley other than the evil doings of one person who was thought to be a witch. There's more to it than meets the eye. There is something in the air. There's a man behind the curtain. The devil is in the details.

I should know, I was born and raised in The Valley. My generation is the fifth generation of Youngers to be born and raised in Valley Center. My grandfather saw things that his father never saw. My father saw things that my grandfather never saw. And I have seen things that my father never saw. I have seen things that defy any logical explanation from the physical realm in which we live. My grandfather knew a lot of the story. My father knew more. But I know the whole story.

My name is Mike Younger, I'm the youngest Younger. And now that I'm no longer young, I understand why my grandpa had to sit when he told the story of the witch. My Grandma Anna once told me that in order to make something out of an old tangled up ball of yarn, you must first unravel it. I unraveled the yarn a long time ago, but it took many years for me to be able to put the story to paper without my head spinning and causing me to fall to the ground. Even the fanciest Afghan quilt had its humble beginning from one end of a ball of yarn. Take up a seat as we start from the beginning. Let me tell you the whole story, of The Witch of The Valley.

Chapter 2

Early Life in The Valley

From the Valley Center Historical Society Archives; and Interviews of Clyde Younger, Johnny Muller, Ben Younger, Jake Muller, and Peter Ertz

Valley Center, Ohio is an unassuming small town. If you blinked while driving through it, you'd miss it. It came to be from the humble beginnings of an encampment near a salt mine. The salt mine was at the northernmost tip in an expansive valley to which the town of Valley Center was thusly named. A river cut through the valley, leaving the salt mine on the west side while bountiful, fruitful land was found east of it.

A tribe of Native Americans, the Potawatomi, were settled on the west side of the river, laying claim to, but refusing to inhabit the area of the salt mine which they called, "Myanakiwen Siwen," or, "Ground that is rough and sour." The land on the west side of the river almost seemed alive, occasionally it moved and made croaking noises whenever it shifted its terrain. The only desirable part of this land was its consistent dryness and its nearness to the river.

Walter Gunther, an aspiring frontiersman, wanted that patch of land. The Potawatomi warned Walter that the land was evil, and he either couldn't understand their warnings or didn't care. He was persistent in his pursuit of that particular chunk of land. He offered the Potawatomi 6 pieces of silver for it. For that price, they gladly moved down river and out of the valley where they easily found better places to build their wigwams. With the purchase, Walter Gunther became the first white settler to own land on the west side of the river.

4

It didn't take long before Walter discovered white gold underground when he was digging a well—salt. He said that he first named the patch of land, Salt Holler, because he kept hearing the salt hollering for him to come get it out of the ground. He reckoned that the sounds he heard coming from the ground were the rocks shifting and settling, like heavy branches that squeak and moan in the woods as they press against each other.

Other settlers flocked to the site to claim land near the salt strike. There was a bony, sinewy substance binding the rocks together that contained the salt. On occasion a faint smell like the malodorous stench of a slaughterhouse would waft up when digging out the rocks. No one cared too much about it, and they didn't seem to mind, they needed salt.

Everyone had big pots they used to boil the salt out of the sinew from their diggings. First they boiled it, then the bony sinew was sifted out and discarded. The remaining water was boiled away, and what was left in the pots was salt.

Salt was a necessity for preserving and seasoning food, as well as curing hides. It was bartered with as a means of exchange. In those days a bushel of salt was worth a cow and a half. Especially in those days where you would otherwise have to mine the salt yourself if not bartering for it.

It was grueling and arduous work extracting salt out of the rocky ground. It was said that two tons of rock would have to be extracted from the mine to scratch out a bushel of salt from the sinew. The worthless rocks would be dumped into the river not far from the mine. This led to the river being named Rocky River.

As the camp of Salt Holler grew the miners called it *Salt Hollow*. This came to be from the miners hearing Walter Gunther say, "Holler." To them it sounded like he was saying, "Holla," which to them was Hollow. That, and due to the mining process of extracting rocks that made the ground hollow underneath, the encampment became known as Salt Hollow.

A massive salt vein was discovered under Lake Erie. Then, along with railroads, the Erie Canal, and ever-increasing and better roadways for trading, salt became cheap and easily purchasable. Soon after that ice in ice boxes became widely available to store food with. There were more and better things to attend to than busting up rocks for a few shakers of salt. You were considered cheap or poor if you kept mining for salt. The hard scrabble to attain salt ended abruptly. Salt Hollow turned into a ghost town. Few families still mined for salt. Hazel Dill's family was one of them.

As time progressed the people in The Valley got together to plan a town. They concluded that in order to attract people and businesses, a town center was needed. The area that was decided upon was in the center of the valley to the south of Salt Hollow. That's how Valley Center got its name. The small town of Valley Center is what I call Valley Center proper. The Valley is what I call the whole area of the expansive valley. This is how I distinguish between the two. Nowadays, when someone says Valley Center they mean the whole kit and caboodle.

There were many trades and businesses that sprouted up in The Valley. There were two general stores, Frank's General Store and Valley Center General Store. There were two blacksmith shops, two gristmills, three cheese factories, and three sawmills. A foundry that produced plows, well pumps, and flatirons was east of town. The Salty Dog Saloon was a great escape from the grind of life. There were tanneries, a cloth manufacturer, a tin shop, and a gun shop. At the time that county lines were drawn in Ohio, Valley Center was the horse-trading capital of the state.

It was during this era of exploding growth in which the Marks family moved in to Valley Center.

Chapter 3

The Early Life of Hazel Dill, a.k.a. The Witch of The Valley

From Interviews of Hazel's Teacher, Her Classmates, Johnny Muller, Clyde Younger, Skid Marks, and Elsa Sauer

Hazel Dill was born Hazel Eris Marks on the Marks' family farm a mile away from the salt mine in Valley Center, Ohio on October 31st, 1882. Hazel was the middle child of the 9 children raised by Johannes and Sarah Marks. The only two that cared to associate with Hazel were her older sister Elsa, and her kid brother Gordon, who everyone called Skid. Elsa was the mother hen who cared for her younger siblings. Skid had gotten his nickname by slipping and sliding on wooden floors. Whenever he walked on ground he was fine. But when he walked in the house or on the wooden barn floor, he would slip and slide across them. He left skid marks everywhere.

The Marks children were a decent-looking crop, save for Hazel. People from this era had a roughness to them, with having to work so hard to get by, but the only photograph of Hazel from her childhood paints a clear image. She must have been near ten years old, but she wore the face of a woman well beyond her years who had seen plenty of hardship. This picture was of the whole family in front of their home, and Hazel was poised off on the far end, the nearest member of the family to her was Skid, and even he stood a few feet away from her with the rest of the family huddled together.

Skid got along just fine with Hazel despite that photograph. He would work with her on the farm and tag along with her and their father on the salt gathering runs to the mine. He fondly remembered how he never had to worry about the pack of wild dogs that would come chasing after him on their trips to and from the mine when Hazel came with them. He was scared to death of those dogs, but those dogs were scared of Hazel. If any of those dogs dared to bark at her, she would bark back and chase them off.

He never saw Hazel as all that smart, but he thought she was a hoot because of these strange ways of hers. In the cold of winter, the boys would pee off the porch instead of making the trek through the snow to the outhouse. They would have a contest to see who could pee the furthest. Hazel liked to porch pee, too. She would challenge Skid and always outdo him. She would hike up her dress, latch onto her unit, twist it just right and let it fly. Skid wanted to be like her. But he was too shy, and she was too forward. She would always blurt out whatever she was thinking and didn't have a care what anyone thought. He respected that.

Their father was for the most part a mild mannered, quiet man. Hardworking goes without saying, everyone had to work hard in those days, or you didn't eat. It seemed the only times that he got riled up was when he had to deal with Hazel and her antics. Which reportedly was most of the time. He would tell her to do something, and she would do the opposite. He would give her a whoppin' and tell her not to do it again, and she would do it again, right away, and get another whoppin'. He eventually came to think that she only felt loved by him when she got a whoppin'. Mr. Marks just couldn't stand the fact that his daughter was different in some way. He couldn't quite put his finger on it. He was the man of the house, and he demanded control. Hazel simply refused to be controlled, and that got under his craw.

Her mother was an old-fashioned pioneer woman. She was as tough as they came. She could skin a deer, cut it up, store it, cook it, and even make leather out of its hide. These were the necessities of life that the salt mine was laid there to accommodate. Sarah was a hard-looking woman, but she had a soft side to her. She would do needle point, knit, and crochet. She was a wonderful cook and could bake award winning pies that she would get blue ribbons for at the annual fair.

From an early age Hazel learned to be a darn good cook from her mother. But she was a better farmhand. Hazel was built to work on a farm. She was a hard worker from the time that anyone could remember. Her favorite part of farming was taking care of the animals. Feeding them, watering them, and even shoveling their leavings. She loved all the animals. But people? Not so much.

8

Hazel's brother Skid described her to Peter Ertz. He said, "She held a sour demeanor. She had a permanent scowl on her face as if she needed to take a good dump. She spit when she spoke. She was as angry as a hungry bear, rude like a rattlesnake, with the temperament of a junkyard dog, and she was meaner than a nest full of riled-up hornets. That was the Hazel that I liked. But when she grew up, she turned crazier than a loon."

Hazel's only breaks from being treated like a farm implement were school, which she despised; church, where she loved to sway and sing; and the salt mine, where she met her best friend. The salt mine was a much easier place for her to get along. For the most part, adults were there extracting the rocks, scratching out the sinew, and bagging it to be taken home and boiled down to extract the salt. Everyone left her alone as she was just another laborer trying to make ends meet, and a good one to boot.

But in the depths of the mine, the deepest, darkest part of the mine, was where she really liked to go. That is where she would talk with her best friend. A familiar friend that no one could see, her own special best friend forever.

What Hazel longed for the most was a friend. She had no luck making friends, especially in school. When she first attended school, her teacher knew that Hazel was different from any child she had ever known. The original schoolhouse that Hazel attended sat where the current Valley Center Elementary School sits. In 1905 the little schoolhouse was moved to the side of the property to make way for the brick school building that was built in its stead.

On the first day of school, according to my grandfather, the teacher asked if any of the children ever went hunting with their fathers. Hazel raised her hand. The teacher called on her and asked her what they hunted for. Hazel proudly said, in a strange drawl, "My dad shot a tomater, onced." The other children broke into rapturous laughter, and she refrained from raising her hand again or even speaking unless otherwise spoken to.

Hazel hated being at school and she could not be reached. In school she was mistreated by all the other children, including my grandfather. He regrets the way he treated her then, thinking it may have contributed to how she turned out, in the end.

He told me that in church the Marks family sat in the pew in front of my grandfather's family. Hazel liked going to church, he could tell. She would sing away as the congregation sang hymns. Deep down inside of her was a majestic child of God with a lonely, tortured soul. A soul longing to love and to be loved. And she would even be willing to trade that soul away even to just feel the love she had to give but for a moment. Lord knows she didn't have that at home and nothing close to that could be found at her school, either.

School was only attended through the 8th grade in those days. Skid recalled Hazel's delight of being through with school when she was twelve. But he missed her not walking to school with him. Skid said, "Once Hazel didn't go to school anymore, she developed a love to wander in the woods at night."

Have you ever walked through the woods of Ohio—all alone? There's a spooky, eerie feeling that one gets while walking through them. As one walks among the trees, it feels like there is something watching you, following close behind you, not wanting to be seen. It comes creeping up behind you in its stealthy manner. It feels not as if it's the wind, but rather one of the whispering revenants of the woods, who are not among the living. It follows along, looking over your shoulder, wondering what it is that you are looking for out here in the woods—all alone. Hoping to see what you see, hoping to see through your eyes, hoping you invite it in. It wishes you harm, and hopes you don't discover its secret. You turn around quick to catch it, but there's nothing there—at least nothing that can be seen in this dimension.

Only light can drive out darkness, but darkness feeds upon itself. Nighttime in the woods is a whole other venture. Demons dwell in shadows where they hide from the light. The trees stand guard with a stoic glare, they do not judge what goes here or there. As you pass them by so unaware, their shadows crawl where you would not dare. There is no driving out the darkness that roams The Valley; it has made The Valley its home.

Hazel told Skid that she embraced this feeling, that darkness, because she felt so alone in this world. She wandered about searching for whatever it was. Longing to find it and make it her friend.

Superstition has it that full moons are the times of odd behaviors, werewolves, vampires, demons, and goblins. But that is ill-informed. Full moons are when the moon is at its brightest, fending off the patient creatures of the night. It is on new moons when darkness thrives. Darkness that envelopes a body like a heavy wool blanket. When you lift your hand in front of your face it can't be seen. As you raise it, it feels like it's passing through thick, heavy fog. New moons are when the nights are as a dark as the depths of the salt mine. Where something ancient, evil, gloomy, lonely, powerful, and terrifying was dwelling.

At first it came to Hazel in her dreams, extending its will to her, till it found just the right way. The way was a little girl looking for a friend, just like her. Telling Hazel everything they had in common, all the things she wanted to hear. She could be her friend, if only she would come and dig her out of the salt mine. Then they could be together every day. She would never leave her.

On the nights of new moons Hazel was drawn in a trancelike state, willed to the salt mine by a dark, beguiling entity. She embraced the darkness of the salt mine. And rain or shine, sweltering summer, or freezing winter, it was always dark, damp, and cool down in its depths. She told Skid that she preferred the nights of the new moons for her excursions into the mine. Those were the nights that her friend would be there. She said it spoke to her in the voice of a girl her age. This chilled Skid to the bone, and he dared not tell anyone else about it.

On a very cold winter's night Hazel went on one of her new moon night wanderings. She was crossing the frozen river as she was being drawn to the mine. She slipped on the ice and fell face first onto it. She turned her head to one side so that her ear was flat on the surface of the ice. What she heard warmed her heart. She heard the ice singing its songs to her, cracking, popping, scratching, and screeching. It was like the sound of an ancient spirit awakening from deep under the ice. Under the water. Under the dirt. Trapped in the rocks. Singing to her. Calling to her. She heard her familiar friend who she would converse with in the salt mine. Her friend was calling her name, *"Hazel, Hazel, come down into the depths of the mine and dig with me. Come talk with me. Come dig me out."*

On that night Hazel dug in just the right place. Her friend appeared to her as the girl her age from her dreams. She was seduced into believing that they could leave the mine together—if only she made a deal. That's all it took. Hazel made a fatal mistake that night. An offer was made, and the terms accepted. Hazel invited The Witch in. Within Hazel was a vast area waiting to accept the love she so desperately desired, and that was the perfect place for The Witch to inhabit and move about.

Hazel carried a passenger now, and her body belonged to it. A war broke out inside of her. The battle began for control of her vessel. As the roaring

11

and crashing of the waves against a shore tear away at the structure of the land at their convergence, so the waves rolled inside of Hazel. Gnawing, and ripping apart the fabric of her mind. Whirling about, aiming to seize her very essence. Hazel was strong and she made a valiant effort. For many years she was able to keep it in check. But she could only do so much.

After that night Elsa and Skid noticed a turn in Hazel. Now during church, she would be in a trancelike state. Instead of singing along, she would rock back and forth in the pew. Glaring deeper and deeper into the valleys of the wood grain in the pew in front of her. Skid once asked her what she was looking at. With her eyes jittering and mouth foaming she said, "I roam through the valleys where I prowl like a lion. Deep in the valleys I rule." Skid became afraid of Hazel.

But she wasn't in charge. The Witch was in charge. Guiding her along through the wonderous valleys, shepherding her mind through the depths of The Valley. She would grin as the preacher's words from the pulpit caught her fancy.

Hazel used to object to her father killing an animal to feed the family. She considered them to be her pets—her friends. She no longer protested the killings. Skid noticed Hazel hiding behind a tree and peeking around it as he and his father butchered a couple of chickens. She was smiling.

The night wanderings became commonplace for them. Their favorite pastime was to wander around at night through the woods, the local cemeteries, into town, and onto other people's farms. And on new moons, into the dark depths of the salt mine.

When the moon was full, she would bark, howl, rant and rave, carrying on all night long. She became well known for showing up at all hours of the night on other people's farms foaming at the mouth and panting. She would be shooed away like an unwanted critter and off she would go mumbling and stumbling. It seemed whenever she had been around something came up missing. Mostly small amounts of money like spare change, but sometimes jewelry.

She always seemed to be in conversation with some person that no one else could see. Shuffling along, talking to herself back and forth. Though most everyone avoided her, she approached anyone that caught her eye. No matter how hard one tried to avoid her, if you had the bad luck to garner her observation, she was all over you like a duck on a June Bug. She had attained

12

the most annoying fashion of dealing with others, darting in and out of their lives. Akin to a nagging deer fly buzzing around your head on the hottest day of summer, that refuses to leave you alone, that you can't swat away no matter how hard you try. So was the makeup of the infamous Hazel Dill.

A headline from one of Peter Ertz's articles stated, "The Witch of Valley Center Confesses!" From that headline is how I, and many others, came to call the entity that entered and controlled Hazel *The Witch*.

Indeed, Hazel had completely lost her mind to The Witch—who was now captain of the ship.

To get Hazel prepared to commit heinous acts, The Witch stirred up excitement within her about attending funerals. It needed her to get used to death. To become numb to death. To enjoy death.

In those days most funerals were held in the family home. Elsa recalled that she was with Hazel at a funeral for their Aunt Edna. Edna Pine was their mother's sister. She was married to Jacob Pine. They lived over 20 miles away and had no children of their own. They kept to themselves, too, which meant most of the Marks children hardly even knew that these relatives of theirs existed.

Jacob had a family gathering in their home for loved ones to pay their respects to Edna. Hazel wailed and bawled over Aunt Edna. She went on and on how she just couldn't believe that she was gone. Their mother asked Hazel to quiet down, but Elsa said that she just kept at it.

Once they got back home Elsa said that Hazel acquired a keen interest in funerals. Whenever the Valley Center Visitor was printed she had to get one. She would fire through the Visitor to peruse the obituaries. She would sneak away from her duties on the farm to attend every funeral in Medina County. Even if she didn't know the deceased she would attend their funeral. She cried, wailed, and carried on at their funerals like they were her best friend. And then she would pocket a little something from their home for a keepsake. In later years she took pride in her ability to match every deceased person's name to the item she pilfered.

Her father didn't take kindly to her off-farm ventures. She returned to the farm after attending a funeral for someone that neither Hazel nor anyone in the family knew. She went into the kitchen to help Elsa and their mother after putting away a brand-new decorative plate. Her mother told her that her father wanted to see her out in the barn. She changed out of her halfway decent clothes and put on her everyday farm working clothes.

Skid was in the barn with their father milking cows. The older Marks children had one by one married off and moved away from The Valley at this time. Elsa had married Otto Sauer. They had five children of their own. They were going to take care of Elsa's parents and eventually take over the Marks' farm. Otto was out on the back forty with his two oldest boys baling hay.

Hazel went out to the barn. Skid said he saw a storm within Hazel. Her eyes no longer had that dull, vacuous look to them. Now there was a fire in them. An evil looking fire, he recalled years later. At the time he didn't think much of it. He just thought Hazel was growing up.

According to Skid, as soon as their father spotted Hazel coming he berated her. "Where in the hell have you been?"

Hazel burned with fury inside. She glared at their father and fired back, "None of your goddamn business."

Their father charged at Hazel. Hazel started giggling and ran away from him past the small crowd of cows. Skid said that she stopped and turned around. When she did, the cows went crazy. They started mooing like mad. Hazel slipped off to the side of the barn as they went into a stampede. There were only four cows. Skid didn't know how to explain it in any other way than a stampede. Skid saw his father go down in the middle of the frenzied cattle. He was trampled under their hooves.

Skid couldn't believe it. These always gentle cows freaked out and went on a stampede. He was afraid the cows would circle back and trample him. They went out about fifty yards, settled down and began grazing as if nothing happened. He ran to his father. He was a bloodied, muddied mess. He said his father tried to say something to him. But all that came out of his mouth was blood. Blood that The Witch wanted. Wanted Hazel to see.

Skid saw Hazel at the corner of the barn. He yelled to her to go get help while he stayed with his father in his dying moments. Hazel walked to the house and came out a few minutes later with their mother and sister.

There was nothing that could be done. Mr. Marks was gone. Skid tried to explain to them what had happened through choking tears. The family couldn't stand to look at their father in this way, all except Hazel, who just stared at his mangled corpse.

When Skid stood up to fall into his mother's arms he caught a glimpse at Hazel's cold eyes. For a brief moment he swore something moved in them. He couldn't speak anything of what he saw, the only sound coming out of his throat were wailing sobs as he buried his head in his mother's chest.

Elsa covered their father with a dry sheet from their clothesline, unable to think straight while his body lay there exposed. Immediately it splotched up with blood, looking like a Rorschach painting. As soon as Mr. Marks' body was covered by the sheet, Hazel was pulled out of her trance. Their mother was consoling a still sobbing Skid, so Elsa reached out to Hazel and asked, "What happened?"

Hazel looked away and said, "He got the cows all riled up and they ran him over."

The cows came walking back to the barn to be milked. Hazel walked over, sat on the milking stool, and milked a cow. She wouldn't have to travel far for the next funeral.

Chapter 4

Hazel Meets Her Mate

From Interviews of Elsa Sauer, Skid Marks, Old John Muller, Johnny Muller, Clyde Younger, Roy Frank, Luther Dill, and Dr. Morse

After their father died Hazel volunteered to slaughter any animal that would be used to feed the family. Skid said she did so with delight. After he witnessed her licking blood off the knife she used, he kept his distance from Hazel. He no longer wanted to be like her. She was different now. He was terrified of what she had become.

Elsa also saw a big change in Hazel after their father was gone. Around the house she acted like she was the ruler of the roost. Otto was able to keep her in line, somewhat. She was a great farmhand when she wanted to be, but she was becoming a real nuisance to have around the house.

Elsa said that Hazel would work out on the farm and then come into the kitchen giving orders. Bossing her and their mother around. Putting her dirty, filthy hands on the food without washing. Big arguments went on between Hazel and their mother. If their mother would say the sky is blue, Hazel would say it was gray. Hazel seemed to get a kick out of antagonizing their mother. As always, Elsa tried to be the peace maker.

Their mother was not about to take any orders from Hazel. There was back and forth bickering non-stop when they were both in the kitchen. Their mother would get so flustered with her. Telling her to just go out on the farm and help Otto and the boys. Hazel would spout off something and go back outside.

The one thing that Hazel was extremely good at was making and baking breads. She had to be scolded to wash up before digging into the dough. But once she got mixing her special herbs together in the flour, kneading it, and

16

baking it, the breads were delicious. Skid said that Hazel told him her friend from the mine taught her what herbs to pick and where to find them. The whole family raved over Hazel's breads. They would first look to Elsa in a silent inquiry. They needed the nod from her that Hazel's hands were clean, and the bread was okay to eat.

Her extended family knew of her breads, also. Hazel would wander to her Aunt Bertha and Uncle Henry Goehring's ranch. She liked to bake her breads with her aunt and help her cousins and uncle milk cows. They didn't particularly like Hazel being around. But after all, Hazel was family, so the Goehrings tolerated her.

She especially liked feeding and watering the animals. She liked to work the old rope and bucket well. It was the one thing that seemed to make her happy. The Goehrings couldn't understand why. The children all thought it was a pain to work that well. They preferred the further well for watering animals because it was closer to their watering troughs. For house water they used the well next to the house. That one was easy to use. It had a new pump with a handle. Once they put this well in they hardly ever used the rope and bucket well.

On one of her night wanderings to the Goehring's ranch Hazel found a patch of woods that she grew fond of. She would go to the center of that little patch and converse with her friend within her—The Witch. After The Witch had regarded the bloodied remains of Hazel's father, it wanted to see more. It was grooming Hazel to see more. To do more.

Hazel would slip to the front edge of the woods and peer out at the farmhouse. It was the farmhouse of Fred Dill. She would watch him as he worked on his farm. She set her sights on Fred. She asked The Witch to get her a man. That man.

Hazel wandered the woods more and more at night. During their night wanderings The Witch taught Hazel the right plants, leaves, and berries to pick. When The Witch first found brake fern Hazel's eyes lit up with fiery delight. It had grown on top of the old salt mine. Hazel stared at its beautiful dark green leaves. She picked it, smelled it, rubbed it on her cheeks. The Witch stirred with excitement inside her. Hazel brought the leaves to her mouth and tasted it. The Witch smiled.

She would hang the plants to dry in her favorite patch of woods. She hollowed out an old stump to put the dried plants in and grind them into

17

powder. The Witch taught her to make magic potions with the different flours, and how to bake them into her breads.

As Hazel grew older, Elsa and her mother became worried that they were going to be stuck with her forever. At the ripe old age of twenty four, she was considered a spinster. There was no hope of being rid of her. But the one thing that no one ever thought about was how well Hazel could cook. The family just took it for granted, all the women in the Marks family were good cooks.

An Annual Ice Breaker Social was held every spring in Valley Center. After a long, cold winter the young bucks would come out to sow their wild oats. The event was a meet and greet affair at the Town Hall. There would be dancing and flirting. All the young, single women would show off their cooking talents in hopes of catching a suitor.

Hazel had attended this many times over the years. This year her family encouraged her not to go. They didn't want to endure the ridicule, once again, of her presence at the event. There would be no one there that she could possibly meet anyway. For the past eight years she would bake her breads and take them to the event. No one would try to talk with her. She would grow angry and frustrated. She would growl and bark at passersby. No one dared to take a morsel of bread.

But this year The Witch had other plans for Hazel. Through cunning conversations with Elsa and her mother, Hazel got them to change their minds. The Witch had taught Hazel how to mix up a love potion that would hook a man. The man Hazel had been eyeing from her favorite patch of woods. The Witch set its sights on Fred Dill.

Fred was an upper forty-something-year-old bachelor. His small farm was a few miles away from her family's farm. He ran a successful business selling milk to the General Stores and various town folk. He was also well known for having a mouth so big that he could talk out of both sides of it at the same time. He was so full of hot air; it would be no surprise if he said that he floated up and met The Man in the Moon in person.

The Witch and Hazel wanted to live on that farm. They wanted to have that favorite patch of woods all to themselves. They conjured up some special recipe bread. A spell was about to be cast on Fred Dill to get him to marry her.

Fred had become well known around town for participating in some night wanderings of his own. He had been chased out of a few barns in his day due to his lascivious proclivities with other people's farm animals. It was an open secret that if you had a stabled pony on property, you'd have to keep an eye out for Ole Fred. If he wasn't at someone else's stable or his own farm, then you could almost surely find him wiling away in the pub.

The Salty Dog Saloon was the favorite of his haunts. It was always a great place to go to unwind and have a good time. You would open the door to the ring of a little bell that hung on the inside of it. All the heads would turn to see who was coming in.

Most days it smelled like stale beer, cigarette smoke, and cheap whiskey. There was a long bar to the right as you walked in. A seldom-played piano sat against the wall in the large dining area. For the poor saps that sat at the long bar, there was a mirror its entire length behind it where they could watch themselves getting all the drunker as long nights turned into long weeks, then into long years. Although, in an attempt to lift some spirits presumably, the owner had put up various stuffed animals above the mirror that over the years had soaked up all the second-hand residue from the chain-smokers.

On Friday nights the whole bar really came to life, though. They put on a great fish fry that acted as a beacon to the townsfolk. The saloon would hold that smell of the fish fry every weekend for a few days. Before reverting back to its usual stale beer aroma.

According to the guys at the saloon, Fred could be found there just about every single day of the year. He had a nickname that the guys at the saloon came up with, Red. How did brown-haired, pale-faced Fred become known as Red? It all happened years ago, when he told a group of guys at the saloon that he was going to sex-up a cow. If the fellas could produce five dollars, that would cover the entrance fee to let them watch. The guys thought that this was highbrow entertainment, so they ponied up, so-to-speak, the five dollars.

Ole Fred invited them over to his barn one evening and he placed a bale of hay behind a heifer, hopped up on the bale and announced to the guys that he was about to proceed. He dropped his drawers down to his ankles. His manhood had a unique and distinct quality to it. According to Old John Muller, who was in attendance that fateful night, "Fred's crank was red on the head like the dick of a dog."

19

Ole Fred lifted the heifer's tail, and right then, nature called. The heifer spewed forth a steaming stream of fecal matter down the front of ole Fred, filling his dropped trousers. The barn shook as it erupted with laughter. Ole Fred, he was a cussin'. Much to the relief of the heifer, the dirty deed went undone. That is except for the splattering of ole Fred and the filling of his trousers.

For the entertainment purposes, the guys let ole Fred keep the five dollars. The guys at the saloon called him Red after that. Old John called him Dog Dick, and Fred didn't seem to mind; Old John was his buddy. No one else dared call him that, though; heck, if you did, you might find your horse missing when you walked out of the saloon.

Suffice it to say, Fred was a hard sell to the bachelorettes around town. He regularly attended the Ice Breaker Social but never managed to make it to the Marks' table. He was either too drunk or had been shooed away by the fathers of some of the other attendees. On this particular year, Fred was drawn to Hazel's table. He became mesmerized by the arousing aroma of her amazing baked breads. It caught his fancy. He began chit-chatting with her. A slight smile broke through the chapped, leathery lips of Hazel's angry, broken-down face. She offered him a thick slice of one of her breads.

When she handed it to him, he noticed those big, husky hands and knew how useful she could be working on his farm. Fred always thought to himself that if he ever were to take a wife, she only had to meet two qualifications. Number one, she had to be a good cook, and two, she had to be a great farm hand. His mouth began to water before he could even take a bite. He devoured the first piece, and she handed him another. He went on and on about how amazing that bread tasted. He couldn't stop eating it. He asked Hazel who made those marvelous breads, her, or her mother. She barked at him, "If you don't think I made it you can piss-off."

His stomach made his brain overlook the nasty demeanor, ill temperament, and shoddy looks of gruff and grumpy Hazel Marks. Not that he was much of a catch himself. Fred Dill was twenty-two years her senior, mighty old to be taking on a first wife, but it's what The Witch willed. He had fallen for Hazel Marks.

After a brief courting period, Fred Dill married Hazel Marks, now Hazel Dill, and the happy couple moved into his farmhouse. And just like that, Hazel got her man and her family had rid themselves of Hazel. The honeymoon lasted all of one day. The big spender took Hazel to a rented room above Frank's General Store.

The next day he took Hazel back to his farm. Fred's dairy farm was the perfect place for her skillset as a farmhand. She especially liked milking the cows. She could hit a cat's mouth with a stream of milk from ten feet away and only spill but a few drips. There were other chores which Hazel outright refused to do, though. Chores Fred didn't want to trouble himself with anymore now that he had a wife. He wasn't going to let her pick and choose what to do like how she did on the other farms.

Fred hit Hazel once. In a fit of anger because he felt she wasn't obeying him like a proper wife, he smacked her in the back of the head. The Witch stirred up within Hazel. Her eyes burned dark orange like fire. She whirled around and beat the daylights out of Fred. Raining punches on him as he fell to the ground. Screaming and clawing at him. He told Old John that it was only his cries for mercy that made her stop. From the look in her eyes, he knew better than to raise a hand against her ever again. He was scared to death of Hazel.

She had gone to visit the Goehring's shortly after beating him, looking to cool off, most likely. When there, she had overheard her Aunt Bertha and one of her cousins giggling. The two of them were laughing about how there was a celebration at the Marks family farm the prior night about finally being rid of Hazel. She grunted, catching the attention of the two women who jumped at the sight of her. They could do nothing but watch in fear as Hazel twisted herself up, snarling at them, before seemingly coming to her senses, and scurrying off into the woods.

That little thicket in the woods. It was her own private retreat. Any time someone irked her she would flee deep into those woods deeper than anyone else dared to travel. The new moon treks to her place of solace in the mine were their favorite times. Where she would sit in the deep darkness all alone with her familiar friend. They would talk the night away, plotting and scheming. There was work to be done.

The town folk dreaded the thought for the first child to be born to Fred and Hazel Dill. The back-biting gossip of the town was to imagine what sort of progeny would be produced with the collision of chromosomes commencing in that union. To the tune of,

"That wicked hag Hazel must have old Fred spellbound."

"If the poor kid is anything like ole Fred, it'll have hooves."

"I bet it has horns."

"If it's anything like Hazel it will fly out on a broom."

"It's first word will be baa," Saloon talk like that.

The guys at the local saloon knew of Fred's habits. They figured that anything that walked, crawled, or flew low to the ground, bull-legged, no-legged, was right up ole Fred's alley. Hazel was a step up from what he was used to scraping his horn with. In less than a year along came a bouncing baby boy they named Fred, Jr.

No one knows exactly why, but Fred, Jr. didn't make it a week. It wasn't uncommon in those days that some children didn't make it. Dr. Morse said that he just wasn't strong enough. Some wondered if it was negligence by Fred and Hazel. Some wondered if Fred and Hazel just didn't know what to do with a newborn. But I know that her familiar friend required a sacrifice. The Witch demanded blood.

The Witch took young Fred, Jr. in Hazel's arms on the night of the first new moon after he was born. She snuck out of the house and to the center of their favorite patch of woods. There, Hazel pulled her baby tight against her chest, and squeezed the life out of the poor child. She hugged Fred, Jr. to death. She snuck back into the house and placed his lifeless body in the bassinet that Fred, Sr. had cobbled together for him.

Hazel was angry with The Witch for having her kill Fred, Jr. It had been nearly a decade since she first killed her father, and she fought hard to not kill again. The funeral gave her some comfort. Afterward she ran into the woods to confront The Witch. Once she had returned, she seemed entirely unaffected by the death of her firstborn. An understanding must have been reached by the two, and she never spoke of it again.

A string of young'uns soon cropped up, and the happy couple ended up with 4 more children that all survived, Luther, Ian, Vivian, and Elmer. Fred's workload had now more than quadrupled. The Witch made sure that he stayed busy doing the work that Hazel didn't like to take care of herself, which included looking after the children after they had weaned off of breast-feeding. She loved her children, but she wasn't a provider. In the first ten years of their oldest son's life, Fred looked as if he had aged twenty.

Once Luther, their oldest, got to be ten years of age, Fred delegated as many chores on the farm as he possibly could onto him. He stayed away from the farm as if he were allergic to it. When making deliveries, he would hang around until his presence was no longer welcome. Then he would sit in the saloon shootin' the shit and drinking. He was afraid to go home to Hazel. Rumors started circulating that he would get beaten at home, but out of respect nobody liked to talk about it.

No one could prove different, but everyone suspected that Hazel had something to do with the death of ole Fred. All the while Fred was keeping away from the farm on his milk deliveries and hanging out at the Salty Dog Saloon, The Witch was wishing him dead. A wish that it conveyed to Hazel to rid them of the old, worthless, drunken buzzard once and for all.

Fred had confided in his friend, Old John Muller, that he was afraid of Hazel. He made a big mistake by marrying her. He just wanted a cook and a farmhand. Instead, he wound up with this crazy lunatic that he's afraid of. She rarely sleeps. She wanders around in the woods at night. And during the day she's too much to be around. She's always barking orders and giving him hell. He wished himself dead.

He told Old John that he sometimes catches her glaring at him. With her face locked in a frightening grin. She seems to be in a trance. Her eyes would appear to be darting around. Like there was something inside of her. Like she was someone else. He would look closer to see her eyes. She would all of the sudden be back and snap at him, "What are you looking at?"

Old John noticed that Fred was no longer his usual, jovial, big-winded self as of late. Since marrying Hazel no one had caught him at their stables anymore, which was certainly appreciated, but there were more changes people noticed but didn't like to talk about. He walked slower. He talked slower. Most folk figured he was just getting older and slowing down. Perhaps the strangest development in Fred was his fear of the woods.

The Witch was guiding Hazel through the woods at night. She would collect the brake fern and other roots and leaves. The Witch taught her to make a special flour. Mix a little of this in here, a little of that in there. "Bake some bread for Fred," she would say. She talked to herself a lot. Her eyes would boil and glow as she kneaded the dough, always in conversation with The Witch.

Hazel would bake two loaves of bread at a time. One for the children and her, and one that she made just for Fred. His would have a little more special flour added to it with each new loaf she baked for him. Eventually, on one new moon, he had enough.

Fred Dill was found naked and dead on his bedroom floor by his eldest son, Luther. Luther said that his father had just finished eating some bread and had yelled out to the barn for his mother to meet him in the bedroom. Fred then went sauntering down the hall humming and laughing.

Luther heard the door to the bedroom close, and a few minutes later he heard a heavy thump. He bolted down the hall and opened the door. There was Fred, lying in a heap on the floor. He asked his father if he was okay, but he didn't answer. Luther ran out to the barn to find his mother. He said that she was milking a cow.

He told her that he feared that his father was dead on the bedroom floor, and he didn't know what to do. He said that Hazel slowly turned her head towards him, smiled, and squirted a stream of milk at him and hit him right in the mouth. She said, "Go into town and get Dr. Morse."

Dr. Morse was a good ole country doctor. He was good at patching up any wound, or a broken bone. He knew everyone and everyone knew him. He had delivered over one hundred and sixty-five babies for the families of Valley Center and the surrounding communities, including all of the Dill children.

When Luther returned with the doctor, they found Hazel sitting in Fred's favorite chair in the living room. She was rocking back and forth, humming Amazing Grace. Fred lay on the floor at her feet, cold, naked, purple, and dead. When she saw the doctor she asked, "Would you like a cup of coffee, Dr. Morse?"

The doctor gave her a puzzled look, declined the coffee, and said, "Luther, go in the kitchen and let me talk with your mother in private." Luther obliged. The doctor asked, "How did he get into the living room? Luther told me that Fred was unresponsive on the bedroom floor." He looked to Hazel for an answer.

"This is where he dropped. I tried to wake him by rubbing a slice of bread under his nose, but he just laid there," Hazel said, then cackled, "That's a first!" Then she cackled some more.

The doctor pressed his hand on Fred's chest to check for a heartbeat. And when he did, Fred's corpse produced a wretched, reverberating release of fermented ass-gas that had built up in his decaying intestines.

24

"Gesundheit!" Hazel blurted out while laughing to herself. She looked to the ceiling and said, "There must be rain movin' in, I hear thunder!" Then, a rancid stench that could knock a buzzard off a shit wagon wafted up. Hazel leaned down, took in a big sniff, and said, "Fred, your face has changed, but your breath still smells the same!" She cackled and rocked back and forth staring at the doctor, who was mortified at her behavior.

Dr. Morse looked into Hazel's eyes and before she looked away, he saw something. Something dark, lifeless, sinister, and profane. And then, it was gone, as if a curtain was drawn between them.

The doctor pronounced Fred Dill dead on the hot, muggy day of August 13th, 1923. Leaving behind his wife, and now forty-year-old widow, Hazel, and their four children. The official ruling was that he had died suddenly of natural causes. The doctor didn't mention that Fred was on the floor of the living room and not the bedroom in his official report. He did mention Hazel's attempt to revive her husband with a slice of bread, though. The rumor was that Hazel put some sort of aphrodisiac, magic potion, or whatever it was in the breads that she baked to snag Fred—and then to kill him.

Chapter 5

Moving On

From Interviews of Luther Dill, Elsa Sauer, Herman Hofstetter, John Johns, Clyde Younger, Johnny Muller, and Dr. Morse

Over the next couple of days, between Fred's death and his funeral, Luther noticed a difference in Hazel. He would see her wandering around the farm as if she were searching for something. She used to just mumble to herself. Now she was constantly yammering away with someone that wasn't there, at least something that no one else could see. He told friends that she seemed to be dancing with the devil.

Her mind was bruised and broken from all the abuse that she had endured. She had been beaten down by the world. Her own family despised her. Classmates ridiculed her. Life had driven Hazel into the salt mine. All the years of torment from The Witch inside of her were taking their toll. In some strange way her husband Fred had helped her to ward it off. But when he was taken out of the way, it didn't take long for Hazel to lose outright control. The gossip in town was that she had gone bat-shit crazy. That was an understatement.

The once lucrative milk business was in shambles. Hazel had no idea what to do with the milk other than to pour it into the tank and take some in every day to be used for the family. Hazel just kept adding the good milk to the rotten milk, till the tank overflowed, and still she kept adding in milk. The milk spoiled in the tank that Fred used to empty daily and take out for delivery. But Fred wasn't around anymore to empty the tank.

Luther tried to tell her that the milk needed to be cycled and sold. She scolded him to mind his own business. Luther said the ground around the bottom of the milk tank had the smell like a dead, bloated animal had exploded. Flies were everywhere. He couldn't tell his mother anything. Hazel wouldn't listen to him.

She didn't know any better. At least she brought in fresh milk for the family to use daily, and not the soured. She always used the same pail for every cow. When the pail was full, she would walk to the tank and empty it into it. The last pail would be taken into the house.

Herman Hofstetter owned the farm right next to the Dill farm. He had a hired hand by the name of John Johns. John had made the trip to the Hofstetter farm from Cleveland to buy hay with his father many times in his twenty-one years. He was traveling to Mansfield one day looking for work when he stopped by the Hofstetter farm to say hello and get a drink of water for himself and his horse. When Mr. Hofstetter asked him how his father was doing, he told him that his father had died. That was why he was heading to Mansfield for work, so he could send money home to his wife and mother. Mr. Hofstetter asked John if he would take a job on his farm.

He could live in the little shack on the farm. He would be able to deliver hay and sell it to the folks in Cleveland that he knew. It would be much closer to his wife, children, and mother than Mansfield. He could take money to them on his hay runs and visit with them for a spell. Better yet, he could probably even arrange for him to make his Cleveland deliveries on Saturdays. That way he could spend the rest of the weekend with his family and come back to the farm Sunday evening.

He accepted the job and had been working there for a few months.

John was a strapping young man. He was quick-witted, strong, tough, and a good worker. He pretty much kept to himself. If anyone asked, he was always willing to lend a hand.

Luther went over and had a talk with Mr. Hofstetter. He told him what a mess the milk business had become, and his mother wouldn't listen to him. He asked him if he could come over and have a talk with her, straighten things out.

Mr. Hofstetter sent John back to the Dill farm with Luther to have a look-see. John saw Hazel out in the field looking around and mumbling. As he and Luther approached her she asked, "What are you doing out this time of night?" Then she looked down at the ground and mumbled to herself.

John said, "Time of night. The day's yet young."

"I reckon if you stay out late enough, it gets early again," Hazel replied to the ground, drooling and grinning.

John chuckled. Hazel was a strange person. "Mr. Hofstetter sent me over to see if you all needed any help with the milk business."

Hazel was gruff, "Ain't no business of nobody's." She stared at Luther, then eyed John up and down. He noticed the caked white foam at the corners of her gaping mouth. He felt uneasy being near her. Her cherry red eyes jittered, "I'll let you have a look." She licked at the curdled foam at the sides of her lips, turned and led the way.

When they got to the barn Luther pointed to the tank of milk. Flies were buzzing with glee, gorging themselves on the rotten milk soaking into the ground. John saw the foamy, rotten milk on the ground. It resembled the foam on Hazel's mouth. John was overcome by the sight and the stench. He recalled what he had for breakfast as he heaved forth the ham and eggs that he had eaten.

John coughed as he said, "You know, Hazel, you have to cycle that milk, you can't just let it sit in there and rot." He stepped back and wiped his mouth before covering his nose with the handkerchief around his neck. Luther fetched a pail water.

Hazel fired back, "Fred would just let it sit in there and rot."

"He couldn't have, no one would pay for sour milk," John gagged as he backed away and gave her a questioning look.

"I wasn't talking about milk, you young whippersnapper, I was talking about his seed!" She cackled.

John was breathing heavy, wiping his mouth, and spitting. Luther held the bucket of water for John to rinse out his mouth and have a drink. "Thanks, Luther," he said as he turned his attention back to Hazel. "I can clean out the tank with Luther's help. That will get things back in order for you."

"Whatever trips your trigger," she said, lumbering over, sitting on the three-legged stool to milk a cow.

John and Luther emptied the tank and rinsed it out. Then Luther got pail after pail of water and doused the ground beneath the tank. Every now and again she would squirt a stream of milk John or Luther's way and hit them in the mouth. John thought she was a really odd duck.

John caught Hazel staring at him. There was something moving about in her eyes. He said it was as if she had two pupils in each eye and they were circling each other. When he looked closer, they each rolled back into one. The only thing that got through to John was it was time to hit the road Jack— or John, or whoever. So, he turned around and began to hightail it back to the Hofstetter farm. As he was hustling away he called out, "Bye Luther. Bye Hazel." He couldn't get off the Dill farm quick enough.

Hazel called out, "You'll have to come over some evening! I'll bake some breads!"

John kept high stepping it out of there as he raised a hand and waved. He could feel Hazel's glare burning a hole through the back of his skull.

Not many folks showed up for the funeral of Fred Dill. A few of the guys from the saloon, Dr. Morse, but mainly just family. John had accompanied the Hofstetters but was sure to keep his distance from Hazel. She wailed, and cried, and carried on, she was in her glory. She didn't want that day to end.

After he was interred at Hollow Hill Cemetery, there was a gathering at the Dill household. Even fewer people attended, just the Marks family. Hazel's sister Elsa had brought their mother, Sarah, with their horse and buggy. Otto and their children had rode on the hay wagon. Otto said his condolences and goodbyes. He said, "You know work on a farm. It never ends." He took the children and headed back to their farm.

Her father had been gone for many years. Hazel recalled his funeral and how wonderful it was. Otto, Elsa and their five children ran the farm now. It was their farm now. All her other siblings had moved away and were not in the area any longer. Sarah helped Elsa in the house cooking, cleaning, and taking care of her grandchildren.

Hazel looked to be in at least her sixties. She attained that from forty rough years of living a hard life. She had four young children to care for, a farm and all it entails to take care of, and a failed milk business that she had no clue how to run. She found out it was going to be a tougher row to hoe without Fred than it was with him.

She told her mother that she had noticed this young man named John Johns who worked on the Hofstetter's farm next door. She said, "I think I'll get that fella to marry me. I need someone to run the milk business, and that fella knows how. I'll bring him over for supper one evening so's you can meet him."

Her mother had seen him in town before and at the wake. She knew who he was. Anger overtook Sarah. She said, "You make my ass ache! You'll do no such thing; your husband isn't even cold in the ground! Why do you always have to ruin everything? You're twice that young man's age! And he's married, too! All you ever do is agitate me. You're a disgrace to this family!"

Hazel's eyes glowed burnt orange as she boiled inside. The Witch wanted to snatch her mother by the throat, claw her eyes out and choke the life out of her. Hazel thought of her father's bloody body lying in the mud. The thought soothed The Witch. Hazel relaxed.

Elsa tried to calm their mother down. She told their mother that Hazel was only kidding with her. That she always did stuff like that to get under her skin. Her mother said, "You'll have nothing to do with that young man. You'll not embarrass this family any further than you already have." Their mother was red-faced, tired, and angry.

Elsa took their mother by the arm and led her away from Hazel. She said, "Mother, please sit down. I'll make you a cup of tea. It will help to calm you."

Sarah sat in a chair and fanned herself. She reached out and grabbed Elsa's hand before she could go to the kitchen. She said, "Elsa, please take me home." She needed to get out of there. She needed to get away from Hazel. And home she was a taken.

Over the course of the following year, things looked up for Hazel for a short time. John reported to Mr. Hofstetter the state of the Dill farm. Herman made Hazel an offer to buy all but one of the milking cows. She would keep the one to milk for her family. She agreed and now had some money to keep things going for a spell.

Hazel used the sold cows as an excuse to get close to John. She would go over to the Hofstetters and talk to them. She said they were her friends. Her hope was to run into John and attempt to talk with him. He would talk to her because he was afraid of what she might do if he didn't. He wanted nothing to do with her beyond that. She had those crazy eyes that moved, and that foamy mouth. She was always wandering around babbling to herself. Luther told him that it seemed like she was talking with the devil.

Luther said that during this time his mother started leaving for days on end. He and his siblings were running the farm and doing okay for themselves. He preferred her not being around. She was attending every funeral within a twenty mile radius of Valley Center. It's not like there was a ton of funerals. But when there was one, she went to it. She would walk to the funerals. Her feet would be so swollen that she couldn't get her shoes off. She just loved funerals. All the tears. The weeping. The sadness. She loved seeing and being around sad people.

If she wasn't attending a funeral she was wandering the woods of The Valley. She still showed up at the Goehring ranch every now and again to help them with chores. And they appreciated the help. Even if it was from their weird cousin Hazel. But the other people whose properties that she showed up on didn't take kindly to it.

She would show up at all hours of the day. All wild-eyed. Talking to herself. She would be panting and foaming at the mouth like she had rabies. She was doing her best to get close to a man. Any man. If she didn't like what someone said she would bark like a dog at them. Not quite the best face to be putting forward to catch the fancy of a beau.

Word spread through The Valley like wildfire that Hazel was looking for a new husband. It wasn't just John, either. She was throwing herself at any man that would cross her path or catch her eye; young, old, in between, it didn't matter.

When the money ran out from selling the milking cows to the Hofstetters, things went downhill in a hurry. Hazel had heard all the gossip of the town from her mother. From the Goehrings. And from her sister. The Witch was making plans.

Chapter 6

The Witch Gets Fired Up

From Interviews of Johnny Muller, John Johns, Roy Frank, Emmitt and Ida Welks, Bill and Helga Braun, Walter Schmidt, Herman Hofstetter, and Sheriff Yoder

Hazel was searching near and far for a replacement for Fred so she could get some money rolling in. Her nocturnal wanderings started ranging further from the farm. Reports of a scant shadow scurrying out of people's houses circulated throughout The Valley. It was rumored that small amounts of money would be missing after the sightings. There was a sneaky suspicion that it was Hazel, but it could never be proven, and she was never caught in the act.

She was being driven by an evil force. A force that had no good intentions for any human being, including the one it was inhabiting. Hazel's foaming mouth might be doing all the talking, but The Witch was calling all the shots—to which Hazel would be held accountable.

When she would get around to trying to talk to people most of what she said didn't make sense. It came across as irrational. She would say things like, "I'll work for when I get back to my farm," or "I'll consider your opinion two dollars a day." It was as if she was combining two different thoughts together into her sentences. The Witch was steering her astray.

What did come across, that made any sense at all, was that she needed money. She would do the work of two people on the other farms if they would just give her a few dollars. She asked if they knew of any man that could replace her deceased husband. She would marry him, and he would come live at her place. He would have the run of the farm. She would cook for him and take care of him. She cast her nets far and wide trying her darndest to get any man. This caused a rift between Hazel and her mother, and the rest of the family, including the Goehrings.

A frequent farm that Hazel would appear on at all hours was the Hofstetter's farm next door. She wanted that John Johns. He couldn't stand it at first, he remembered those eyes that moved, and she was so nutty. But after a few times of seeing her, he felt she was harmless. Hazel reminded him of a chicken. How they go clucking about, scratching the ground, pecking away. He thought chickens were funny, and so was Hazel. So, whenever she wandered over, he had tried his best to be friendly to her. Even though she looked and smelled like a ratty old mule, and he thought she was disgusting, he would talk with her. He had told her over and over again that he was a married man, that she didn't need a man to run the farm, she could do it herself.

John knew Hazel, and he knew what everyone thought of her. For the most part his only interactions with other people were with the Hofstetter family and the other workers on the farm. He wasn't much of a drinker, so he rarely stopped in to the Salty Dog Saloon. The only times that he saw any other younger people his age was when he would deliver hay or stop in one of the general stores. On one such occasion, he ran into Luther.

John asked, "How have you been doing?"

Luther said, "I'm good."

"I heard some strange animal noises coming from the direction of your woods last night. Did you hear them?"

Luther said, "Yeah. Those weren't animals, that was my mom. She dances with the devil in our woods."

"Why do you say that?"

"She's always talking to someone that isn't there. And out in the woods it's scary. I've seen her in the woods. She's all alone, but she's talking with someone. It's got to be the devil. Who else could it be?"

The following day, John decided to get a look for himself. It was late in the evening, just before dark. That magical time of day just after the sun sets and the air turns pinkish. The time when lines are blurred, and shapes become confusing in the dark shadows. John hid behind a tree on the Hofstetter's side of the woods. Twilight fades fast in the woods. Peering through the trees he saw someone moving. He slipped a little closer behind some thick grapevines. It was Hazel carrying a chicken.

33

Hazel walked to the center of the woods and stopped. Holding the chicken by both legs in her outstretched arm, she reached to her side where a sheath was holding a knife with a long thin blade. With precision she pulled up the knife and whacked its head off with a quick slash. In the same precise move, she tucked the knife away. The same hand grabbed the chicken by the neck and squeezed the spraying blood into her gaping mouth and all over her face. The chicken flopped around in her grasp as she drank the blood with lust.

John's knees were knocking. He feared Hazel was going to discover him hiding in the shadows of the grapevines. He dared not move. Looking down he willed his knees to stop shaking. He thought Hazel was scary before. Now he knew she was stark raving mad. He didn't want to ever be in her presence again. Luther was right. She was dancing with the devil.

When the last drop of blood was drained from the chicken Hazel cried out, "*Yes,*" wiped off her mouth and licked her lips. She tucked the bird under her arm and walked towards her house. John waited till he saw her pass the barn, then slipped in silence back to his shack. He needed to get out of The Valley.

On most Saturdays he could get away. He would make his Cleveland hay deliveries. Then he would go back to his mother's home to be with his wife and family. They would go to church on Sunday and then spend all day together before he had to head back to his shack at the Hofstetters. He dreaded coming back now. It was getting too stressful for him and his family living this way. He needed to find a job near his home. He needed to get away from crazy Hazel. After seeing what she had done with that chicken, Hazel no longer reminded him of one. She more closely resembled a viper.

John made a wise decision, after the milk incident, to never again venture over to the Dill farm, till he went to see Hazel dance with the devil in the woods. Now he had seen enough. He knew Hazel had completely lost her mind. He didn't want Hazel coming around anymore, so he asked the Hofstetters to tell her to keep off of their farm.

The Witch didn't want to have another man around to interfere with its intentions anyway. It had to get rid of the last one, and all that did was feed The Witch's thirst for blood. They had plans to attend to. Another man would be an obstacle. By this time Hazel had lost the mental capacity to run anything. She barely had enough brains of her own left that her body could function.

The kids were taking care of the farm and themselves, and they were managing fairly well. There's just no way of helping someone that doesn't want to—or can't—help themselves.

Hazel showed up at Frank's General Store one day looking like she had just tangled with a grizzly bear. She went there to attain some flour and sugar. She was walking towards the ramp to the general store as Roy Frank, the owner/operator of Frank's General Store, looked on.

Hazel looked up to Roy and asked, "What the hell are you lookin' at?"

Roy grinned and said, "Nothing." He turned and walked back into his store.

Hazel walked up the ramp and ambled into Frank's General Store. She always had a way about her that made everyone who was in her proximity quite uncomfortable. Since Fred had died the level increased ten-fold. As she entered the general store everyone in there could feel the unease of Hazel's presence. The tiny dust streams that float in the sun streaks moved away from her. The air took on a heaviness. It seemed harder to breathe.

As she moved along she noticed some women looking her way and whispering to each other. Hazel recognized the two of them, Ida Welks and Helga Braun. She stared them down with an evil eye that chilled them to their bones.

Hazel didn't need to hear them; The Witch could feel what they were saying. The Witch was egging Hazel on. They were debating within her, *'I know what they are saying. I will tell you what they are saying.'* 'No, I want to hear for myself.' Hazel could barely hold The Witch back anymore. They were becoming one.

The two women looked away and moved to the back section of the store where the dry goods were stored. Hazel moved toward them undetected, smooth and low. She slithered along hissing like a snake stalking its prey. Creeping in slow and silent, she coiled up on the other side of the rack that held the flour, lying in wait. Hazel felt every word of their muffled gossip twisting in her demented mind.

Ida said, "She's probably in here because she can't get anything on credit anymore at The Valley General, the poor thing." They both chuckled. She continued, "I hear that she killed old Fred. Not that anyone would blame her, but still."

Helga replied, "I heard the same. Everyone knows she never sleeps. Why, I saw her the other evening out in the pasture walking towards the woods. She was blabbering out loud back and forth with herself, like she was talking to someone. It was so strange, it was like she was thinking out loud, you know? You know how you think to yourself? But out loud. Real loud, too. And she sounded like two people thinking out loud, back and forth, back and forth. It was very odd and unnerving."

"She's insane. Nutty as a fruitcake."

"She's always been that way. Her family tried all they could, but she's so difficult. I hear they almost disowned her because she was going after that young, married fella, that John Johns who works for the Hofstetters."

Hazel was seething. She felt every word burning inside her brain, blazing like molten coals in a furnace. Her mind was swirling like a boiling cauldron, her eyes glowing like jack-o-lanterns.

Hazel gave way to The Witch. They were now in concert with one another. The two were one. Hazel wanted them right then and there, but The Witch was thinking of a better way.

Ida said, "You don't say. I knew that she was up to no good when she showed up at our place one evening, all wild-eyed, foamy-mouthed, and rough looking. I told Emmitt that she was looking for a new husband. He laughed and laughed. Thought that was the funniest thing he ever heard."

"She's the nastiest creature that I have ever laid eyes on. Bill said that if she shows up on our place, he'll have a gun waitin' for her." Helga looked around to see if Hazel was near. "That would do us all a favor." They covered their gossiping mouths to stifle their chuckles.

Hazel calmed herself and slipped to the back of the store, slinking away unnoticed. She popped up along the back wall and walked towards the flour where the two backbiting women were standing. As she came near, the women were startled. Hazel gave them an anemic stare and said, "I wish I had time to mind other people's business." And mumbled under her breath, "Gossipmongers." She grabbed a twenty-pound sack of flour, ten pounds of sugar, and made her way to the counter where Roy Frank was waiting in angst.

She stood there holding the sack of flour and bag of sugar staring Roy down. Her bloodshot eyes burning red like the setting sun. She was looking deep into his soul. She could tell what he was thinking, she could see right

36

through him. Roy felt her probing through his mind. He did his best to mask how disgusted he felt in her presence. He then asked, "Do you need anything else?"

Hazel stood there staring. Roy was feeling uncomfortable. To cut through the tension he tried a little chit-chat. Roy was good at that. Being good at gabbing was great for business. He asked, "Did you clear up that rat problem on the farm?" Then he added, "Fred had told me that it was a big problem at one time. That poison that he bought must've taken care of 'em." Oh no. He was wishing he hadn't brought up Fred. He hoped she wouldn't start bawling and carrying on like she did at funerals.

Hazel's roiling eyes dug into Roy's. She gave him a slight grin and said, "Don't need no poison for rats. I can make my own potions. Got a black snake for rats. No more rat problem."

"That's good." He felt uneasy. He couldn't wait for her to leave the store.

Hazel turned towards Ida Welks and Helga Braun, her eyes glowing and burning. She said, "Some rats grow big. Some grow to be five feet tall, and others even bigger." Then she turned her attention back to Roy.

Roy asked Hazel, "Is there anything else I can get you?"

"No." She stood glaring at him.

Roy said, "The tally comes to two dollars and seventeen cents." He was hoping she would sign for it on credit. He was loathe to handle any money— if she had any—and catching whatever diseases she was bearing on board.

Hazel's burning eyes blazed at Roy. He was wishing to be home. In the back unloading flour, a task he despised. Fishing. Anywhere except for here, standing in front of Hazel. She said, "You'll have to put it on my bill."

Hazel finally set her goods down on the counter then signed for them. She picked her provisions back up and gave Roy an angry look. He said she looked like a mean dog that was going to start growling at him. She turned and walked out the door.

Roy said, "Thank you, Hazel." Finally. She'll be leaving. Roy followed her to the door and watched her lugging the load back toward the Dill homestead three miles away. He saw her pass by Walter Schmidt who was heading to the store. Then he went back into the store to wait on Ida and Helga.

Walter took notice of the burdensome load Hazel was hauling. He smiled and said to her in jest, "Gotta match, Hazelnut?"

37

Hazel barked back, "Yeah, your face and my ass." She cackled as she kept lumbering along.

He turned around and watched in awe as Hazel stopped and set her goods down. She hiked up her dress, plopped down on the dirt road, and commenced to alleviate her bladder of a massive quantity of urine that it had been saddled with. She sat in it, relieved, turned her head to Walter and asked, "What are you looking at?"

Walter said, "Nothing."

Hazel said, "C'mon in, the water's fine." She was cackling away as Walter turned away and ran to the general store. Hazel rollicked around for a minute before getting back up. She rolled her dress back down, picked up her goods and headed for home.

That night, Walter got home and found his wife at the stove in the kitchen cooking supper. He snuck in behind her and hugged her. He asked, "Whatcha cookin' good lookin'?"

She smiled and asked, "What's your nose tell ya?" as she turned around in his embrace.

"My nose tells me we're having venison stew." He had just butchered a deer the day before. And he took a peek over her shoulder to see what she was stirring before he answered.

"Your nose is correct." She pecked his cheek with a kiss. "Now wash up. It will be ready right quick." She turned back to the stove to stir the stew.

Walter said, "You'll never guess who I ran into outside of Frank's General Store today." He was busting at the seams to tell her.

She stirred the stew and said, "Let me see." She pondered for a moment. She guessed, "Roy Frank." She smiled and stirred.

"I knew you were going to say that. No, Hazel Dill."

"Oh, my. You steered clear from her, didn't you?"

"Kinda. She was hauling this heavy bag of flour. I knew she had a long ways to go, so I asked her if she had a match. You know, to kid around with her."

"Oh, my. You talked to her?" She put the stirring spoon down. "People say she's a witch. You shouldn't even look at her, let alone talk to her. I hear she's trying to land a new husband. I wouldn't want her to cast a spell on you and steal you away." She smiled at Walter.

"She's harmless. Ratty looking. Mean. Nasty. Belligerent. But harmless." He chuckled. "She squatted down and sat on the road and peed. Sat right in it. Splashed around like a duck." Then he laughed.

"Oh, my. How disgusting. I'm gonna be sick. Don't talk about it anymore." She turned and left the kitchen in a hurry. "Tell that to your friends at the saloon. Not to me."

Walter watched her leave. He grabbed the spoon and took a taste of the stew. Supper was gonna be good.

The Schmidt family went to bed late that evening. It was a long day, but a good one. They got a lot of work done that day. Walter got the pump working for the well at the barn. His wife got the house prepped and cleaned with the help of their two daughters. Walter and their two sons got stalls cleaned and the hay mow straightened away. They had a wonderful venison stew supper. He laid in bed thinking how blessed he was by having such a good wife, a good life. He smiled as he drifted off to sleep.

It is said that it's always darkest before the dawn. That is, unless there is an early light in the sky. Walter awoke to the sound of shuffling footsteps. He thought he caught a glimpse of a shadow dart out the door as he opened his eyes. Then he heard the sounds of crackling fire. He sprang out of bed and looked out the window. The barn was in flames. He got dressed and started yelling for everyone to get to the barn to fight the fire. They were able to get to the pump that had just been repaired and start a bucket brigade. It was too little, too late. The barn was going to be a total loss.

He looked back to the house and saw it burning. Some neighbors had shown up and helped to battle the blazes. They got to the pump at the house and were able to put the fire out. All in all, it wasn't as bad as it could have been. As the sun was rising they saw that the house would be saved with little damage. But they would have to build a new barn.

Two weeks later the Braun's barn burned down. And a week after that the Welks's barn burned down. All three fires from mysterious circumstances. All three families reported small amounts of money missing from their homes after the blazes were put out. The Braun family felt suspicious towards a neighbor who helped on the bucket brigade. The Welks family figured the money had just been misplaced. The Schmidt family suspected the slippery shadow that Walter had seen for the missing money, and the fires.

Hazel was running out of options. She was desperate and in need of money. They came up with a plan. Hazel would go to her mother's house to ask Otto if she could work on the old family farm for pay. She would use Elsa to sway him. Elsa was always the peacemaker between Hazel and other family members when they had their spats, most especially with their mother.

Hazel went to the old Marks farm and sat at the kitchen table with Otto, Elsa, and Mrs. Marks. They discussed how Hazel would do the same work on the farm that she did before she married Fred. Somehow she pulled it off. She was hired as a farmhand. Otto explained to her that the pay would be minimal. Hazel didn't mind. He told her she could start on Monday.

Otto went back out to work on the farm while the women talked about their children, the latest news, and life in general. Hazel told them about a funeral she had attended. She said, "Oh, how sad everyone was." Elsa and their mother hadn't heard of anyone passing that they knew.

Their mother asked, "Whose funeral were you at?"

Hazel said, "Martha Weidel."

Elsa looked to their mother in a puzzled manner. Their mother shook her head. She asked, "Who is Martha Weidel?"

Hazel said, "I don't know. I just wanted to pay my respects."

Their mother cut her short and said, "Respects, ha. You don't know what respect means. You don't just go to someone's funeral that you don't know. That's not respect."

Respect was the one thing that Hazel desired. She let The Witch know that she had always felt neglected and never felt respected. The Witch promised Hazel that she would be respected.

Elsa settled their mother down. She said, "Everyone should be so lucky to have people they didn't even know at their funeral." She gave her mother a 'be nice' glance with a tilt of her head. Then she looked to Hazel and said, "We have chores to get finished and supper to make." Elsa took Hazel by the arm and led her to the door. She said, "I know you'll be here Monday to work, but I want to invite you now. Bring the children and come join us for Easter dinner, next Sunday."

Hazel glowed inside. Everything was coming together as planned. She kept her gaze straight ahead. She didn't want Elsa to see the fire burning within her eyes. She said with glee, "I'll bring my special breads."

On the way home she chattered back and forth with The Witch in tremendous joy. "I'm going to get paid." "*They're going to pay alright. Heee-heee-heeee-heeeeee.*"

The next day Hazel wandered onto the Hofstetter's farm. She was seeking out John. She had a surprise planned for her mother. The Hofstetters were anxiously awaiting their chance to tell her to stay off their property. Herman and Lily saw Hazel wander on to their farm and approached her. Herman said, "Hazel, you can't be coming over here anymore. We are very busy, and you are disrupting things by keeping our men from doing their work."

Hazel said, "I just want to ask John a question." She had to do everything in her power to restrain The Witch from lashing out.

Herman said, "Okay, but make it quick. John has something to tell you anyway. He's in the hay mow." Herman said that it felt like watching a big scary snake slither away as she walked toward the barn.

Hazel found John in the hay mow. She could barely contain herself when she asked him to come to Easter dinner with her. She couldn't wait to see the look on her mother's face. What a delight it will be to see the look on all their faces when she shows up with her new man.

John felt a sense of terror by being near her. He wanted to be away from her. He said, "I'm going home to my mom's house after I deliver hay in Cleveland tomorrow. And after that I'll be staying there for good. Mr. Hofstetter is going with me to bring his wagon back. My family needs me there. I have a new job I'm gonna start on Monday that is close to my home. I won't be back no more." He was going to miss the Hofstetters. He was going to miss The Valley. He had thoughts of moving his family there one day. But he wasn't going to miss this insane person standing before him.

A burning fury of emotion was bubbling beneath the surface of Hazel. Her eyes became piercing daggers. She held it in check. She begged him, "Please don't go."

"There's no way I can stay here. I've got to be with my family. Besides, it's getting pretty crazy around here." John stepped back and away from her. He feared her response.

Hazel pivoted and left in a huff before she boiled over and attacked John. The Witch knew he would have been a burden to them. He would have had to have been taken out of the way at some point. This worked in a favorable way for The Witch. Hazel was burning inside for revenge. That put The Witch in good spirits.

Hazel's affection for John had spared them, but the Tuesday before Easter the Hofstetter's barn caught on fire. Hazel showed up and joined the bucket brigade who were doing their utmost to save the barn. When the fire was extinguished Herman chased her away. She snarled at him and ran off like an unwanted dog with its tail between its legs.

They were able to save a little better than half of the barn. It wasn't nearly as bad as the Schmidt's, Braun's, and Welks's barns. They lost everything when theirs caught fire. After the fire was out Herman and Lily's son George was tending to the animals. He noticed they were missing several chickens. They couldn't figure out how, but maybe the missing chickens were burned up in the fire. It was a head scratcher. One would think that chickens would flee a burning barn, not stay in it.

Chapter 7

Happy Easter

From Interviews of Luther Dill, Elsa Sauer, Otto Sauer, and Dr. Morse

Hazel had been working on the old Marks homestead for the past week. Things were going well, so far. She was going to get some much-needed money at last.

April 20th, 1924, Easter morning had arrived. Luther and the other Dill children woke up bright and early to the sounds of their mother working in the kitchen. They hurried out to take care of the chores on the farm.

Hazel and The Witch were preparing plenty of breads. They wanted to make sure that everyone at her mother's house got some bread. Hazel was humming and swaying.

Hazel and The Witch were bantering back and forth like crows in a murder calling out signals to one another. *"Put your arse into it."* Cackle. "I did." *"Not that arse, this arse."* Maniacal laughter. *"The arse that I taught you to make from the brake fern."* "Oh, ha-ha, yes. Not too much though. We just want to teach them a lesson." *"We really want to teach mother a lesson. What doesn't kill you makes you stronger."* "Everyone loves my breads." *"Let's make sure to make these breads extra special."* They were cackling and yammering away. They wanted to make sure that everything was just right. "But not the brown breads. The children will eat the brown breads." *"Okay. Not the brown breads. The rest of the breads will be like the special breads that old dead Fred liked. We'll make the brown breads normal."*

Hazel packed the special made breads in baskets, and the brown breads in bags. She yelled for the kids to get ready. Luther was handed the bags of breads. Hazel picked up the baskets of breads and said, grinning, "Follow me, we're going to your grandmother's house for Easter. Oh, how thankful she will be."

It was about three miles if you took the dirt roads to her mother's house from the Dill farm, but about two miles as the crow flies. Hazel would much rather take the paths through the woods. Ah, the woods. How Hazel loved the woods. She knew them better than anyone in The Valley. The woods were her real home. Where she felt free and unencumbered. There was a sense of unease in the woods of The Valley that everyone else could feel, but not Hazel. Hazel reveled in the woods.

The Dill family headed to the woods, walking on the well beaten path established by Hazel on her numerous nocturnal gallivants. Luther realized that they now had more chickens than just the four he remembered. He asked, "Mother, how did we get more chickens?" Hazel kept her eyes straight ahead and didn't answer. Again, "Mother—"

She stopped on a dime, turned around and said, "You children only eat the brown breads today." She stared at Luther with her eyes aglow.

He said, "But I like the other kinds of—" Hazel lunged at him.

She grabbed his face with a quick slap of her hand. She squeezed her hand tight on either side of his mouth. His lips puckered out. She pulled him up and close to her face, almost lifting him off the ground. She was burning holes through his mind with her glowering cherry red eyes. He saw what appeared to be tornadoes swirling in her eyes. Spittle flew as she said, "You'll eat only the brown breads." She pushed him back and released her grip. Her eyes spun back to their normal, bloodshot selves.

She turned around and led the children into the woods. Once they got to the center they veered onto the familiar path that led to the Marks homestead. Luther recalled how odd that journey was. Hazel was leading the way. He and the other children followed behind in a row, like little ducklings following their mother to a pond. He realized later that he didn't hear one bird or see a single animal on the entire route.

Whenever Luther had ventured beyond the Dill family woods on his own, he always saw a wide variety of creatures romping about. Rabbits scurrying along narrow trails. Squirrels gathering and burying nuts for the winter ahead. Birds flying, chirping, and singing. And even deer if he could manage remaining quiet enough. But not this time. This trip to his grandmother's house was unlike any trip he had ever been on into the woods. He couldn't hear any animals, let alone see them. Something about his mother caused a shift in the woods. He could feel it, too.

He said that the very air seemed to part from in front of his mother and come together behind them as they moved through the woods. Everything was still all around. No one said a word, not even his mother, which he found quite odd. She was always chattering away. He wanted to say something to one of his siblings, but he didn't dare to speak. He hardly even allowed himself to breathe, lest he exhale too loud and call his mother's attention back to him. Even as they walked he carefully plotted his footsteps to avoid twigs or anything else that may alert her to his presence. She moved as if the children weren't even there, and he almost preferred it that way. Like every creature in the woods—he was afraid of Hazel.

Luther couldn't wait to get there. He knew that Aunt Elsa and his grandma would have some good eats. He had been to Easter dinner there a few times before, they had the best ham that he had ever eaten. And he loved Grandma Marks's apple pie. He knew there would be some of that—that is—if he could beat his cousin Fritz to it.

About a year ago or so, he was over there helping bale hay and Fritz kept talking about this apple pie that their grandma had made. He mentioned it so many times that Luther's mouth was watering just thinking about it. When the hay was put up, Fritz said, "Let's get cleaned up and get some of that apple pie."

They went to the pump on the well and Fritz told him, "You pump first, and I'll wash up, then I'll pump for you." Fritz cleaned up really quick, then walked away and left Luther to pump water for himself to clean up. Luther rinsed off, got a quick drink, and headed for the house. He swore that he wasn't but two hot minutes behind Fritz.

When he got in the house, Fritz said, "I've got good news and I've got bad news."

Luther asked, "What's the bad news?"

Fritz said, "The pie's gone."

The life just about fell out of Luther. He was so dejected. He figured he may as well play along. He asked, "So, what's the good news?"

Fritz said, "It tasted great," and he laughed.

That no good dirty rotten so-and-so ate the whole pie. Luther had been looking so forward to eating just one slice of that pie. Not just any pie either, one of Grandma Marks's four-inch-thick, world-famous, Valley Center Fair blue ribbon winning apple pies. He was so disappointed. But so goes the world. What was he going to do about it? Fritz was twice his size. He used to look up to him. He used to think Fritz was fun and he wanted to be just like him, but not anymore. He hoped to be bigger than him one day. When he grows up, he's going to kick his ass, and he won't even tell him why.

The Dills got to the house. Elsa greeted them at the door. They went in and exchanged hellos with everyone. She took Hazel into the kitchen. They worked together with their mother getting things ready and talking. The children went off to play with their cousins.

The Witch was calculating and cunning. It had developed a keen sense of when to recede and let Hazel have the helm. Back and forth, back and forth they would go along. Hazel's consciousness was pushed to the side, but reemerged here and there. The Witch would boil up to the surface and Hazel would lash out. It would simmer down, and Hazel would simmer down, too. She had grown used to it and felt the combination worked well. It wasn't like she had a choice in the matter.

They got the tables set and the food ready. Everyone sat down to have their Easter feast. Luther said that it wasn't till later that he suspected there was something in the breads. When he looked back on his mother telling him and his siblings to only have the brown breads. At the time he was thinking about keeping quiet, the odd walk, and the extra chickens. And he was looking forward to having the ham. The last time it was so good.

Everyone ate. Luther even got some apple pie for dessert. He looked at Fritz as he was enjoying it. Fritz gave him a wink and smiled. That did nothing to get him back in Luther's good graces. He still didn't care much for Fritz anymore.

The women cleaned up and the children went back to playing. Elsa, their mother, and Hazel sat down at the kitchen table for coffee and pie. Hazel brought their mother a cup of coffee. She had sprinkled a little powder in it, unnoticed. They drank their coffee and chit-chatted. When they were finished their mother rubbed her tummy and said, "I'm going to go lay down, I'm not feeling well."

Hazel put on her sad, funeral face and said, "Oh, that's a shame." While inside The Witch was dancing with joy.

Elsa helped their mother to her room. When she returned she said, "I'm not feeling so good, myself." She rubbed her stomach and sat down at the table.

Hazel rubbed her stomach and said, "Yeah, me neither." As she kept up the sad funeral face.

Everyone in the house started complaining of stomach aches. Except for the Dill children.

Hazel said, "I think that ham wasn't right, we all got botulism, trichinosis or something from it." She got up from the table and went to check on her children.

Hazel came back into the kitchen and said to Elsa, "The children aren't feeling well, and neither am I. We're going to head home." She gathered up the children. She said, "I'll be back tomorrow to work on the farm, bright and early." They said their goodbyes and left for home.

On the way Luther said to his mother, "I ate some ham, and I don't feel sick."

Hazel spun around, snatched him by the face again and said, "Yes you do, we're all sick. Every single one of us, me, and all my children are sick." She released her grip and chuckled. Luther didn't know why that was funny, but his mother does and says some strange things all the time.

He remembered the walk through the woods on the way there. He wished they would take the roads on the way home, but they took the woods again. The walk home was quite similar to the walk to the Marks homestead; the dividing air, no birds singing, no animals running about. But on the way home, his mother didn't stop talking back and forth to herself the whole way. All the children were used to her doing this, but she didn't say anything on the way there, and wouldn't stop talking to herself on the way back.

That night Hazel made some special recipe chicken soup in a cast iron kettle for her mother, and Elsa's family. She toted the kettle through the woods and back to the Marks homestead when she went to work the next morning. When she arrived, she stopped at the house to see Elsa. She told her how she was up with the children all night, tending to them. She showed her the kettle of chicken soup. Hazel put on her sad funeral face and said, "I made this last evening after we got home. The children all felt better after they had some."

47

Elsa invited her in and said, "Let's put that in the kitchen" as she took the kettle from Hazel.

Hazel tried not to smile and asked how everyone was doing. Elsa said, "Otto, the children and I are all feeling better, but mother is still feeling ill." Hazel looked down to hide the spark of delight in her eyes. Then she put her best funeral face on for Elsa. She was disappointed that their mother was still alive. This morning she was going to teach her a real lesson for causing John to move away.

Hazel went into her mother's room to see her. Her mother gazed up to her and frowned. She said, "I'm still not feeling well, Hazel."

Hazel glared at her mother as she glided to the chair at the foot of her mother's bed and sat down. Her eyes were glowing like coals in a fire. The flame from the kerosene lamp danced in Hazel's eyes. Her tongue was licking her lips in concert with the flickering flame. Drool was leaking from the side of Hazel's mouth as she fantasized of fire.

She could barely contain herself. Outside she was tranquil, but inside there was a whirlwind swirling. The waves were roiling within her, she was about to boil over. She was jumping out of her skin. She wanted to strangle her mother, but held it back.

Easing up from the chair, Hazel moved closer to her mother. Shadows moved upon her face. Fixing her gaze into her mother's eyes, Hazel said, "It was the ham." She did her best to give a look of concern, she thought of attending her mother's funeral. That did it. She said, "I made some chicken soup for my children and after they ate it they all felt better. I brought the rest with me when I came here this morning." She was trying her best to hold a sullen look. Mesmerizing her mother, she continued, "We all had such a good time yesterday. Well, that is, till we all took ill from that ham. Let me get you some soup."

Her mother said, "Thanks, Hazel. I'll give it a try. Maybe it'll get me to feeling better, too."

"I'm sure it will." Hazel went into the kitchen and told Elsa that she was going to fetch her mother a bowl of her special chicken soup remedy. She took it to her room and spoon fed her mother, making sure that she got plenty. Her mother immediately slipped into a deep sleep.

Hazel went back out to the kitchen and told Elsa that their mother was doing much better, and she was sleeping. Elsa went in to check on their mother.

Elsa came back out and said, "Mother looks so peaceful. She appears to be smiling. Hopefully that chicken soup will do the trick."

Hazel thought of their mother's death. She said, "I hope so, too."

Elsa said, "Well, Otto and the boys are out in the barn. I've got things to take care of in here.

Hazel said, "I'll just put the kettle with the rest of the soup on the pot hanger in the fireplace. That way you can keep it warm, and everyone can have some for lunch." She grinned as she picked up the cast iron kettle and headed for the fireplace. The Sauer's dog, Champ, got tangled up in Hazel's feet. She fell face first into the hearth, spilling the remaining chicken soup into the fire.

Hazel leapt to her feet, grabbed the cast iron kettle, and looked inside. It was empty. Hazel cursed the dog, "You ruined it. Come here you mangy mutt. I'm going to kill you."

In a stern voice, Elsa said, "You'll do no such thing. It wasn't his fault that you're so clumsy. Besides that, the kettle didn't break. It'll be okay." She stood between Hazel and Champ.

Enraged, Hazel stormed out of the house, kettle in hand, and marched out to work on the farm.

Their mother, Sarah Marks, never woke up again. On April 21st, 1924, she was found dead in her bed by her daughter Elsa when she went in to check on her before lunch. Dr. Morse's official ruling was death by food poisoning.

Chapter 8

A Helping Hand

From Interviews of Elsa Sauer, Henry Goehring, Jr., Eleanor Goehring, Earl Goehring, Dr. Morse, and Luther Dill

Hazel barely slept before. She would nod off every now and again, and never get a good night's sleep. But now Hazel didn't sleep at all, and she was madder than a hatter. The kids were left to fend for themselves, and lucky for them they could. The Witch's lust for blood was in full blossom. It was about to become unquenchable. They wanted more.

They wanted to drive every horrid human six feet into the ground. The Witch was steaming along like a loaded freight train, going downhill, screaming along the tracks, and heading straight to Hell. The furious storm inside of Hazel was immense, and she embraced it. She let the storm guide her along the way. Whether it was through the woods at night, or the town during the day, evil was on the move. The Witch was seeing to it—Hazel was going to be respected.

At her mother's funeral Hazel wailed and bawled. She cried out, "If only she hadn't eaten the ham!" She cried aloud and that comforted her inside. She welcomed any sympathy that came her way. Her Aunt Bertha and Uncle Henry Goehring sat next to her to console her.

Hazel had already heard of Henry and Bertha's disapproval of her search for a husband, throwing herself at every Tom, Dick, and Harry that she saw. She also knew that they had sided with her mother on the whole John Johns episode. Her going after such a young man. She didn't have to listen in on the gossip of the town folk anymore. The Witch was perceiving every thought within every mind of every being that Hazel encountered. Her mother, Bertha, and Henry were the reason the man she wanted moved away. The

Goehrings were going to pay dearly for siding with her mother, just like she did.

Hazel wailed, "Oh, my dear mother!" As she tried to not let the Goehrings see the fire blazing in her eyes. She looked down and said, "Thank you for being here," as she wiped her dry eyes. Then she got up and moved through the crowd looking for sad people to mourn with.

Hazel wandered the woods in the light of the nearly full, waning moon that night. Luther recalled that he heard screaming, chattering, and laughter that kept him awake all night.

The trek to the Goehring ranch was half what it was to the Marks homestead. Unbeknownst to them, Hazel was on their ranch long before sunrise. Henry, Jr. first spotted her. She was toting water buckets to the barn. He walked to the barn and said, "Good morning, Hazel." Then asked, "How are you?"

"Fine as frog hair," she grunted as she toted two pails of water.

Henry, Jr. said, "I heard you were working on the old farm for Otto and Elsa."

Hazel said, "That, I am." She poured water into a trough for the horses.

Henry, Jr. was puzzled. He asked, "Then why are you here and not there?"

Hazel headed back toward the well and said, "I figured I'd work over here this morning."

"I think you had better go to Otto and Elsa's."

Hazel dropped the pails, gave him a mean look, and wandered off towards Otto and Elsa's farm. Henry, Jr. went to the house and called in to his father that Hazel was on their ranch.

Henry, Sr. came out of the house with his daughter Eleanor. They watched Hazel walking up the dirt road away from their ranch in the direction of the old Marks homestead. Henry, Sr. shook his head and said, "I'll never understand that Hazel."

Henry, Jr. added, "Old weird Hazel," and he went out to slop the hogs.

Not to be left out of the conversation. Eleanor chimed in, "She's so creepy." To which her father nodded in agreement.

Henry, Sr. said with a slight smile as he patted Eleanor on the head, "That she is, my dear. That she is." They kept looking on at Hazel until she disappeared into the woods. He took Eleanor by the arm and led her back into the house where they finished eating their breakfast.

Henry, Jr. fetched some water for the hogs. There were three wells on the Goehring ranch. One was out back of the barns, which was used to water the animals. Then there was the old rope and bucket well that Hazel always used. That one used to be the primary water source for the household. The front well was at the house, this one had a new, good pump with a handle on it. This well was now used exclusively for the household needs.

A few weeks later, on Friday night of May the 2nd, Hazel wandered onto the Goehring ranch. In the darkness of the night of the nearly new moon, she slid through the shadows. Quiet as could be she removed the handle off of the pump that was near the house. She was able to open the top pump chamber by hand. She poured a dry compound The Witch taught her to concoct in the plunger chamber and put it back together. She slipped away undetected into the night and tossed the pump handle into the swamp to the west of the ranch.

Hazel returned to the Goehring ranch on Saturday afternoon. She asked them if they needed help with anything. They said no, but out of pity for her having lost her mother, they invited her into the house.

Aunt Bertha, Eleanor and Hazel were talking in the kitchen when Eleanor said, "I'll make some coffee. I think we have just enough water to make a pot." She took off the lid for the water barrel and looked inside. She said, "It's going to be close. You know, it's the darndest thing. The handle for the new pump at the house well is missing. We have to go to the old rope and bucket well for water, till we get another pump handle."

Hazel got up and said, "I'll fetch some water for ya." Eleanor didn't mind at all. It was hard to draw water from that well, and she knew that Hazel was good at it. Eleanor remembered a few weeks ago seeing her dropping the bucket just right so that a full bucket could be drawn out. Dropping the bucket in, pulling it up by the rope, carrying and toting water buckets—Hazel was obsessed with making sure that everything had enough water.

Eleanor went in to the dining room and looked out the window, wondering what was keeping Hazel. There she was toting buckets of water to the barn. She smiled and shook her head thinking, 'That Hazel. She just can't get enough of working that well.' Eleanor went back to the kitchen to wait for Hazel.

Hazel came out of the barn and went back to the well. She had a little pouch of potion that she had ground up into powder from brake fern. She drew out a bucket of water to take to the house for coffee. Then she dropped the pouch into the well. Her eyes were glowing like fire, and she was grinning like a serpent. She had to calm herself before she went back into the house.

She got to the kitchen and set the pail of water on the kitchen counter. Eleanor said, "Thank you, Hazel. I had enough water to make coffee, and you didn't have to water the animals."

Hazel gave her a vacant stare. She shook her head as if she was uncluttering her thoughts. She said, "I just love animals." And kept staring at Eleanor.

Eleanor felt uneasy. She turned away and poured coffee into cups.

Hazel moved over next to her and said, "Here, let me help you." She reached for a couple of cups of coffee. Hazel held a pinch of potion between her thumb and forefinger in each hand. She stared deep into Eleanor's eyes.

Eleanor recalled that the irises in Hazel's eyes seemed to be moving. It made Eleanor feel uncomfortable. She looked close to see if she really saw them moving. To see what it was. She said when she looked into Hazel's eyes, she felt hypnotized for a second or two, and it was over. There was Hazel just looking at her with a blank, vacant stare.

It was in that brief moment that Hazel sprinkled powder in all but one of the cups of coffee. Hazel took that one for herself and she picked up another. She went to the kitchen table, handed a cup of coffee to her Aunt Bertha, and sat down next to her.

While they were having coffee Bertha invited Hazel to bring her children over for Sunday dinner the next evening. Hazel stared into dark depths of the coffee in her cup and said, "That will be just fine." She finished her coffee and headed home.

Eleanor felt relieved when Hazel left. Henry, Jr. walked in shaking his head as she left. He said, "We won't have to water the animals for days."

Eleanor remembered that they were low on water for the house. She was wishing that she would have told Hazel to bring more water to the house, so she didn't have to fight with the rope and bucket. She poured the pail that Hazel had fetched into the barrel. Then she went out to the well and toted water to fill all the wash basins in the house. And then more water to fill the pitchers that were used for drinking, and finally filled the barrel used for cooking, or to make coffee or tea at mealtime, all the way full. That night the whole family fell ill.

Luther recalled how his mother was dancing, singing, and laughing in the kitchen as she baked bread on Sunday morning. He had never seen his mother so happy, ever. He asked his mother, "What's the celebration about?"

He said she stopped short, turned to him, and snapped, "It's Aunt Bertha and Uncle Henry's anniversary, and we're going to celebrate it with them." She then commenced with her extraneous behavior.

Hazel got the kids together on Sunday evening. They headed down the well beaten path that led to the center of their woods. Luther always wondered why the path from the house led to the center of the woods and branched out from there.

As a matter of fact, the well-worn center circle was the exact dead-center of their woods. What Luther didn't notice was the ring of salt around the entire circumference of the center circle. The circle resembled a five-pointed star from the five well-trodden paths that led away from it. Further out, once off the property, there were other paths that branched off to even more trails.

Luther recalled that when he was little, his father had told him that the best squirrel hunting in The Valley was in the woods on the Dill farm. He said his dad told him that he used to see squirrels in their woods every single time that he went into them. Now, not a one. As he gave it a think, he couldn't recall ever seeing a single squirrel, or any other animal for that matter, in the woods on their farm in his whole life. There was no way that they were hunted out. Every year there were squirrels a plenty, but that was in the woods beyond the Dill's. It was as if something had scared them away, and kept them away. He had to go further out to see any animals at all.

Luther avoided the Dill woods now. He would walk around them no matter how much longer it took to get anywhere. Weird sounds came from those woods. He saw his mother dancing with the devil out in those woods. He hated those woods. He was afraid of those woods.

The Dill brood traipsed to the center circle and then took the path that led to the Goehrings. Luther kept his head down. He watched as each foot followed the other as he stepped. Heel, toe, gone. Heel, toe, gone. Hazel bantered back and forth with herself in a most spirited manner as the children followed her. When they got to the top of the hill that oversees the Goehring ranch Hazel stopped. She stood there staring down at the ranch. Whatever happiness The Witch was feeling that day had now subsided. A blazing whirlwind of fire was raging inside of Hazel. She was about to explode. The Witch was going to rain down destruction. Death was coming to dinner.

Say what you will about Hazel, she loved her children. She said, "You children are not to drink anything at all at Aunt Bertha and Uncle Henry's."

They descended the hill, walked through the field, crossed the dirt road and onto the Goehring ranch. Hazel knocked on the door. Her cousin Maria answered and said, "Oh, hi Hazel. I forgot that you were coming over for supper. We're not having supper this evening. Everyone is sick."

Hazel said, "Oh, that's such a shame. I brought along some breads and everything. I'll just put them in the kitchen and say hello to Aunt Bertha."

Maria let them into the foyer. Hazel said, "You children are to wait here. I'll be right back."

Hazel followed Maria into the house. As they walked through the kitchen she said, "Mother is lying down in the parlor, she's not feeling well."

Hazel grinned and thought, 'Well.' '*Yes, the Well.*' She set the breads on the kitchen table.

Maria led Hazel to where Bertha was lying down on the sofa. Bertha was holding her stomach and quietly groaning. She grimaced as she attempted to sit up. She laid back and said, "We seem to all have taken ill since supper last evening. Food poisoning or something."

Hazel gave her a pitiful, funeral pout and said, "You poor dear. Can I get you anything?" The Witch was spinning inside her with glee.

"No. I've just got to fight through this. Henry and the boys are out in the barn. They figured they would try and work through it." She stopped to take some quick, short breaths. She let out a little moan and continued, "Henry and Henry, Jr. are not doing well." She fought to catch her breath and let out a mild moan.

Hazel said, "It'll be okay. Don't talk. I'll make some of my special recipe chicken soup and bring it to you tomorrow." Her eyes were glowing. "That should do the trick."

"That is very thoughtful of you, Hazel. Thank you." She took a few short breaths and said, "Maria, could you please get me a cup of tea?"

Maria said, "Sure, momma." And she left for the kitchen.

Hazel said, "Well, I'm gonna be going. You get better now. I'll see you tomorrow." She leaned down and kissed her aunt on the forehead. Bertha moaned and waved a hand to her as she held her stomach with the other.

Hazel went into the kitchen and said to Maria, "I'll fetch you a fresh pail of water to make tea with and drop it off to you at the door."

Maria said, "Okay, thanks." She followed Hazel to the foyer.

Hazel got the children outside and told them to wait for her at the side of the house. While they had been waiting in the foyer, Luther had been thinking how nice it would be to live there in that big house. It had all these different levels in it, a well right by the back door—when it works. He also got to thinking how odd it was that his grandmother had gotten food poisoning and died. And now his Great Aunt Bertha was down with food poisoning. When he thinks back on these days he wouldn't blame the Goehrings if they never spoke to him ever again. If only he had warned them. But his thoughts were in a fog in those days. They were cluttered up by the influence of The Witch.

Hazel took a pail to the well and filled it with water. She reached into her pocket and added an extra pinch of potion to the pail. She walked back to the house and knocked on the door. Maria came to the door. Hazel handed her the pail and said, as she smiled to Maria, "Make sure you get a drink of that water, and have some bread. I made it especially for you."

"Thanks cousin Hazel," Maria said as she clutched her stomach.

It was all Hazel could do to keep her composure. She said, "You're so welcome," in the sincerest way she could muster. Then the Dills left for home.

Once there, giddy Hazel went about making her special recipe chicken soup. She fed some to her children before she mixed in the final ingredient that made it special. The next morning, Luther watched as Hazel lugged the heavy cast iron kettle down the well-worn path to the center of the woods. He snuck out behind her, careful to not be seen, and hid behind trees near the path, following along.

Luther looked over to the side of the center of the circle. He saw the hollowed-out tree stump. In it was a big, blunt stick. It looked like a mortar and pestle. He wondered why he had never noticed it before. It was the brain fog. He later found out that a mortar and pestle was exactly what it was. Hazel used it to grind up brake fern, roots, berries, and various other dried plants into powder.

Hazel got to the center spot and stopped abruptly. She stood motionless. A minute went by. She set the kettle down in the middle of the circle. Luther stood frozen in fear. Fearful that she had seen him spying on her. He trembled as he held his gaze downward. She had sensed his presence; he just knew it. Oh, what a mistake it was following her here. He hated these woods.

Then she began to spin. Slow at first, then picking up speed. He lucked out. She hadn't seen him. She spun round and round like a whirling dervish. Her bloody-red eyes rolled back in her head. Resounding cackles as if from a great multitude of voices erupted from the depths of Hazel as she spun. Deafening curses emitted from her foaming mouth; her spittle flew about her like rain.

Chills ran up Luther's spine as he was shaking in fear. His heart was pounding against his ribcage. It was going to explode. He knew at this moment what an innocent rabbit felt, running for its life as a vicious bobcat was bearing down upon it to lash it to pieces. His mother was going to pounce on him. She wasn't just dancing with the devil—she *was* the devil.

Hazel stopped on a dime, her head leaning back, her out-stretched arms reaching for the sky, standing like a statue. A dead silence clothed the woods. Time stood still. It felt as if it were an hour, but it was only for a moment.

The Witch burst out a guttural scream from Hazel, "*I Will Be Respected!*"

Luther's knees buckled. He grabbed the tree for support. His head ached. He could feel each beat of his heart throbbing in his temples.

He heard Hazel utter, "*Let's go.*"

He peered through squinted eyes and saw Hazel reach down and grab the handle of the kettle. She picked it up with a grunt and made her way down the path that led to the Goehring ranch. Luther stumbled back towards the house through the woods. He was barely able to lift his feet, dragging them along, his heart pounding in receding fear. He got to the edge of the woods and a calm came over him. He leaned against a tree. He was able to breath in a regular manner again. It was gone. That wasn't his mother, but whatever it was, it was gone. The fear subsided. He pushed off from the tree and staggered back to the house.

Hazel knocked on the Goehring's door. Earl, the youngest son, answered. Hazel insisted on coming in and playing nursemaid, but Earl told her that everyone was sick, and they didn't feel like having company. He thanked her for the soup. He took the kettle from Hazel, and she followed him into the kitchen. She noticed that the breads were gone. She smiled.

Earl poured the soup into a couple of their pots. He went to clean it out and Hazel said, "I'll get that." She took the kettle from Earl and went on her merry way.

Earl ladled some soup into a small bowl and slurped it down. His stomach began aching right away, but he figured it was from finally getting some victuals after not eating for a while.

He told the rest of the family that Hazel had dropped off the chicken soup and it was in the kitchen. Bertha, Henry, Sr., and Henry, Jr. were all in bed and couldn't get up. John was able to suffer through and made it into the kitchen and had himself a bowl of soup. Eleanor and Maria took big bowls of soup to their parents and brother Henry, Jr. They spoon fed them, took the dishes to the kitchen and then each had a small bowl of soup for themselves. All nine family members had eaten the breads, and some of the soup. And all nine members of the Goehring family were at death's door.

If not for the suspicion and persistent persuasion of young Earl, the whole family would have perished. He had an interior feeling that there was something about the water from that old rope and bucket well. Maybe a cat fell in the well and drowned, he didn't know for sure. But he had a feeling there was something in the water that was making the whole family sick.

Earl summoned up the strength to hitch up the wagon to a horse. He headed to town to get Dr. Morse and bring him back to the Goehring ranch.

He told Dr. Morse about his suspicions of the well water on the ride home. The good doctor agreed that it could be the source of the trouble. Earl told the doctor that he got the family to stop using that well last night. They were now drawing water from the back well by the barn. Dr. Morse said the well was something to look into. The way that underground aquifers can attain unwanted substances, and all. Drawing water from another well was a good idea.

When they got to the Goehring ranch, Dr. Morse saw how bad it really was. He found Henry, Sr. and Bertha both dead in bed. Henry had a mad, angry look on his face. Bertha looked peaceful. Dr. Morse was reminded that was how her sister, Sarah Marks, had looked. They held the same appearance. And Sarah had a stomach ailment, too, just like Bertha and Henry. That thought registered into Dr. Morse's head. He covered them so the children didn't have to see them this way.

Henry, Jr. was clinging to life by a thread, and all the other children were in various stages of this arcane illness.

The children would all survive. Henry, Jr. walked with a limp and used a cane for the rest of his life. Eleanor was partially paralyzed and bedridden, but after a month, she pulled out of it. John was in bad shape for quite a while, but eventually made a full recovery, along with the rest of his siblings. Earl replaced the pump for the well near the house and the family used that well once again.

Henry, Sr. and his devoted, loving wife Bertha were laid to rest the following week after a combined funeral. At the viewing, when Hazel heard the Goehring children weeping she wailed and bawled and wept along with them. "Oh, how I'm going to miss them," she cried. The children consoled each other and thanked Hazel for trying to help.

Dr. Morse watched Hazel carry on at the funeral. He remembered seeing something in her eyes when her husband Fred had died. He tried to get a glimpse of her eyes, but couldn't see anything. He had felt sorry for Hazel. In the past two years she had lost her husband, and her mother. Now she had lost her aunt and uncle. Instead of feeling sorry for her, he grew suspicious of her. Luther had his suspicions at this time, too. But he was deep in the brain fog from The Witch. They all were.

That was starting to change, though. The Witch, reveling in its killings, made the mistake of being inattentive to the spell it had cast over The Valley. Now, Dr. Morse was set to get a sample of that well water. The action which would ultimately lead to the demise of The Witch.

Chapter 9

Another Fire and An Investigation

From Interviews of Henry Goehring, Jr., Eleanor Goehring, Earl Goehring, Dr. Morse, Sheriff Yoder, Walter Schmidt, Roy Frank, Luther Dill, Otto & Elsa Sauer, Clyde Younger, Johnny Muller, and Richard Shroder

The next day, Dr. Morse went back to the Goehring ranch to check on the six children that were at home. Henry, Jr., Eleanor, and John were recovering in the hospital. He was also there to meet with the town constable, Clyde Younger. They were going to take some samples of water from the rope and bucket well to be tested.

Dr. Morse had checked the children, and they were all doing much better. He was standing outside breathing in the fresh air and enjoying the beautiful sunrise. He checked his pocket watch and expected to see Clyde any minute now. He looked over to the road and saw Hazel off in the distance walking toward the Goehring ranch.

When she started across the road Dr. Morse walked out to head her off at the pass. He asked her, "What brings you here, Hazel?" He was giving her a questioning look.

She said, "Oh, I just wanted to see if my cousins needed anything." She stared at Dr. Morse with devious, burning eyes. She had hoped to slip some more potion into water pitchers in the house.

Dr. Morse saw something in those eyes before. He remembered when Fred had passed away. It looked like something was moving inside of her eyes. Now he could see those eyes. He stared into them. It was there again. He could see her eyes moving. The Witch sensed this and hid within Hazel. It stopped. Her eyes returned to their usual vacant, bloodshot stare. Dr. Morse

60

said, "Your best place to be is on your own farm taking care of your own children, and minding your own business."

Hazel grumbled, "I just want to see them." She was fighting to keep the boil down to a simmer within her.

"You don't need to see anyone or anything. Clyde Younger will be here in a few minutes. Now, go on." He brushed his hand toward her to shoo her away.

Just then the sound of hooves clubbing the dirt road could be heard approaching. It was Clyde Younger with his horse and wagon. When Hazel saw the constable coming she figured she best be leaving. She turned and headed off in a huff.

Constable Clyde and Dr. Morse went to the well and drew some water from the old rope and bucket well. They poured samples into various mason jars the doctor had brought with him. They marked the jars and Clyde took the samples back to his second-floor office in the Town Hall. His office consisted of a chair and a desk on the west side of the room. It's main purpose was as a storage area, but it also held rarely used jail cells. There were two iron bar cells on the east side of the room. Off towards the front of the building were several piles of painted two by fours which were used for booths, glass cases for baked goods, and bunting for decorating the stage at the annual fair.

Clyde left the samples in a locked drawer in his desk and went back home. He would turn the samples over to Sheriff Luke Yoder when he came to town to pick them up.

Dr. Morse's office burned to the ground that night. Another fire from mysterious circumstances.

He was well liked in the community. There were common spats with differences of opinion—unpaid bills, and such. He wrote them off as doing his civic duty for the common good of the community. He was a good man. For all intents and purposes, he had no enemies. Arson was suspected.

An anonymous person reported that they had seen a hunched over figure scurrying away in the dark from the doctor's office and moments later flames were roaring out of the windows.

It started off as a cold, chilly day the next morning. Sheriff Yoder came to Valley Center driving his Model T. He was proud to have that vehicle for his use; paid for at county taxpayer's expense. He was there to pick up the samples of well water from Constable Clyde. He now had an arson to investigate first.

Sheriff Yoder had been working on piecing together any connections amongst the other mysterious fires that had occurred in and around The Valley. He saw some men gathered together across the street in front of the Salty Dog Saloon. He went over there to have a talk with a few of them.

He happened upon Walter Schmidt. He had talked with him when his barn had burned down, and his house caught fire. Sheriff Yoder said, "Howdy, Walter. You're looking a lot better than the last time I saw you." He really did, too. The last time he saw Walter, he was devastated and dirty after fighting the fires.

"Howdy, sheriff." Walter smiled as he replied in an upbeat tone. "We're almost rebuilt and back in business."

Sheriff Yoder said, "That's fantastic." He gave Walter a big smile.

"Neighbors are such good folk. It's such a blessing to have them. Couldn't get it done without them," Walter said as he gave his eyes a quick swipe.

The sheriff said, "There are some nice people around Valley Center. I could live here." He looked around and then went on, "We're thinking these fires around here are related. We're working on tying things together. We got a report that someone witnessed a suspect leaving the scene of the doctor's office fire last night." He pointed over his shoulder in the direction of the doctor's former office. "You didn't happen to see or hear anything about the fire that took down the doctor's office, did you?"

Walter motioned for him to walk over to the side so no one would hear him. In a quiet voice he said, "All I heard was, there was a dark, hunched over figure seen fleeing the scene right before the fire broke out."

Sheriff Yoder asked, "Who did you hear that from? Is that all you know about it?"

Walter looked around to make sure the coast was clear. He said, "It was me who saw her. I was leaving here for home." He pointed to the Salty Dog Saloon. "I saw the hunched over figure scurry away." He tilted his head to where he saw the figure. The sheriff looked over and back to Walter. "That got me to thinking of something that had slipped my mind. Something that happened before our fires."

"What was that?," the sheriff asked as he jotted something down in his notebook.

"I crossed paths with that old witch Hazel Dill outside of Frank's General Store. She was carrying this heavy sack of flour, so I asked her if she had a match. Just kidding around."

"What did she say?"

"She said, 'Your face and my ass.'"

Sheriff Yoder let out a quick chuckle. He regained his composure and said, "Sorry, but that's a good one."

"Yeah, I thought so too. I was just joking with her. I didn't think much of it before, but that very night after I asked her if she had a match was the night that our barn burned down, and our house caught on fire. And I remembered she was walking like that—Hazel was—all hunched over. I didn't pay much attention because she was lugging that load of flour. But the thing is, she walks like that all the time—all hunched over."

"Interesting." The sheriff kept jotting notes.

"On the night of the fires, when I woke up, I thought I saw a shadow move out of the house. Later we noticed the jar we keep spare change in was missing. Money, jar, and all. At first I thought I had dreamt seeing the shadow." He rubbed his cheek as he looked over his thoughts. "If I was a betting man, my bet would be on that old witch Hazel. She's no good. She's a pest; a nuisance."

Sheriff Yoder said, "Thanks for your information, Walter. I'm going to head up to Frank's General Store and talk with Roy to see if he has anything to add to this. Then I'm going to have a talk with this Hazel Dill."

"Good luck, sheriff."

"Thanks, Walter. It was nice seeing you." The sheriff gave him a nod and walked to his car.

"It's nice to be seen," Walter said with a smile.

With that, Sheriff Yoder traveled up the road to Frank's Corners to talk with Roy Frank. When the sheriff exited his car at Frank's General Store, he breathed out tiny puffs of condensation clouds that glistened in the low morning sun. He attempted to blow a couple of smoke rings and smiled. He preferred this time of year rather than the hot, humid summer. He went into the store and found Roy Frank in the back of the store. He was kneeling down and straightening up a shelf of dry goods. Sheriff Yoder blew into his hands to warm them. He approached Roy and said, "Hi there, Roy. It's cold enough to cut right through a man today." He rubbed his hands together.

Roy said, "Howdy, sheriff. Yeah, it's ass-bitin' cold out there." He got up real slow, stretching his leg as he rubbed it. He then said, "This god-forsaken weather really mucks up a man's knee."

"You don't say. Other than that, how are you doing?"

"I'm doing good, thanks. How can I help you, sheriff?" He straightened up with a groan.

"There was a fire last night that took down Dr. Morse's office."

"Yeah, I heard about that. I'm glad he's okay." He rubbed his knee.

"Yes. He got out alright. Wasn't anything he or anyone else could do to put it out. It went up in a hurry."

"That's a shame." He picked up his leg and bent it at the knee back and forth to stretch it out. "So, what brings you here?"

"Walter Schmidt mentioned that he ran into Hazel Dill outside of your store the day before his house caught fire and barn burned down."

Roy had to think a minute, still trying to work a kink out of his knee. He said, "The last time she was in here she signed on credit for the goods she purchased, I should say, that I purchased for her. She'll probably never pay me. I haven't seen her since."

"Would you say that Hazel walks hunched over?"

"That old hag—I call her old—she looks old anyway, has always been hunched over. She walks like an old mule pulling a plow."

"Thanks, Roy. I'm going to have a little chat with her. Can you tell me where she lives?"

"Go back through town and take a left on River Road. You'll go down about two miles and come to a sharp curve to the right, almost ninety degrees. It'll be the second farmhouse on the right after the curve. Sits up on the little hill."

"Thanks again, Roy. Take care of that knee." He turned and walked to the door.

"Don't let her get her hooks in you. I hear she's looking for a man." Roy chuckled. The sheriff smiled and gave Roy a wave. He left the general store and headed for the Dill homestead.

As Sheriff Yoder drove down the hill back into Valley Center proper, he thought, 'What a nice little town. The air is fresh. The people are friendly. Even the buildings seem inviting.' He drove past the Salty Dog Saloon and

64

out of town. Then he crossed the covered bridge and turned left on River Road. He looked back to the town and thought to himself, 'I could live here.'

As he rounded the sharp curve he looked up the road a ways to the second farmhouse. His gaze caught the home of the Dill family. It sat nestled between the trees on top of a small hill. He felt unnerved by its appearance. He couldn't quite put his finger on it, but as he drove up the driveway, it made him feel uneasy.

He didn't hear a sound on his approach to the door of the house. He breathed out hard to see if he could see his breath. No luck. The day had warmed up. He checked his watch. He thought, 'Heck, it's almost noon already.' The sheriff knocked on the door and waited. He knocked again. He heard the knob turning. The door opened with a clunk as it dropped a few inches from the frame that held it in place as it swung open.

A faint, dank, dusty odor drifted out; reminding the sheriff of a distinct smell from when he was a boy. It was the smell of old straw and dirty dog. It reminded him of the smell inside of the family dog's doghouse.

A young girl of about twelve years of age looked up at him. He looked past her into the home. Through the thick darkness he could see a platter of some sort of food on the table. That was good, at least.

The sheriff said, "I'm Sheriff Yoder. What's your name?"

The young girl said, "Vivian."

"Is your mother here, Vivian? I would like to talk with her."

"Mother's not home. She's never home much anymore. She works on our Aunt Elsa and Uncle Otto's farm. Or she's at a funeral. She isn't here."

"Is anybody else here that I can talk to?"

"Yes, my brothers are out on the farm working."

"Okay, thanks. I'm going to go out and see if I can talk to them."

"Luther's probably in the barn. He's the oldest. He might know where mother is."

"It was nice meeting you, Vivian." He turned his attention to the barn and walked towards it.

"Nice meeting you, too." She pulled the door closed hard to get it seated back in its place again.

The sheriff got to the barn. He saw a few chickens in the yard. He looked in the barn and saw some hogs, a cow, but no Hazel, just like Vivian said. He didn't hear the normal animal sounds that one usually hears on a farm,

65

though. The animals just moved around, not clucking, not oinking, not mooing. Not a sound from them. He was thinking how odd that was when an ear-piercing scream of a coyote came from the woods. Sheriff Yoder had heard many a coyote scream, but none ever made the hair on the back of his neck stand up—till then. He noticed that the animals stood still, frightened, for a moment, then got back to roaming around in their quiet way.

He heard a young man say, "There she goes again," from the back of the barn.

Sheriff Yoder said, "Hi. Luther? There goes what again?"

Luther said, "That howling. It makes the animals nervous. Who are you?"

The sheriff walked in the direction that he heard Luther's voice. He said, "I'm Sheriff Yoder. Have you seen your mother? Do you know where she is?"

"Oh, she's probably at Uncle Otto's working on his farm."

"Where's that farm at? Where are you at?"

"Oh, I'm milking the cow over here." He raised his hand so the sheriff would see it. "Yeah, we don't see her much anymore. She's working over there during the day and wandering around in the woods at night. Uncle Otto's is over on Hollow Hill Road. About a quarter mile past the cemetery on the opposite side of the road. You can get there in no time through the back woods." He pointed his hand in the direction of the woods. "I wouldn't go that way, though. It's creepy scary in those woods." He shook his head like a dog shaking off water.

The sheriff walked around the back of cow keeping a clear distance, so he didn't get kicked. He had seen people that had been killed from a cow kick. At last, he saw the young man whose voice he had been conversing with. There was Luther sitting on a three-legged stool, milking the cow. The sheriff said, "Creepy scary, huh. Why do say that?"

Luther stood and reached out to shake the sheriff's hand. He said, "You heard that howl. That ain't all."

Over Luther's shoulder the sheriff saw what looked like a cow pie in the shaded corner of the barn. He reached out to shake Luther's hand and he saw a pair of eyes looking up at him from the cow pie. He jumped back and blurted out, "What in tarnation is that?"

Luther glanced at the corner and said, "Oh. That's just mother's snake, it don't bother nobody."

"That's the darndest thing I ever saw." Sheriff Yoder said holding a hand to his chest, breathing heavy and looking on in awe.

"It's been around since I can remember. Mother keeps it around to eat rats. It'll follow her around."

"Hmm, you don't say?" The sheriff rubbed his chin in amazement as the snake slid away down the side of the barn and disappeared under the straw. "That's the biggest black snake I ever saw."

"Yeah, from eatin' all the rats."

That gave the sheriff the heebie-jeebies. He thought how odd that was for a minute as he shuffled around, uncomfortable as a worm on a hook. He asked Luther, "Don't you need your mother here to look after you kids?"

"Naw, we's alright, we don't need nothin'. Heck, I'm fourteen now, I'm pretty much a man. I've been running things around here for quite some time. We're better off without her around. She gets weirder and weirder with every day that goes by and death that comes along. And nowadays they've been comin' along in bunches. She goes to just about every funeral. I'm glad she stays away."

"Let's have a look at those woods. I'd like to see why you say they're creepy scary."

Luther had a look of concern on his face. He said, "I'll take you to the woods, but I ain't going in 'em. I don't go in 'em anymore." They walked down the well beaten path to the edge of the woods. Luther pointed as he said, "You can go in there if you want. This path leads to the center of the woods and then trails branch out from there. That's where mother goes to dance with the devil."

"Dance with the devil?" Sheriff Yoder gave Luther a questioning look. "Why do say that?"

"That's what she does. She goes in there and dances around and talks to someone that isn't there. I used to think that she just talked to herself all the time. But I really think that she's talking with the devil himself." Luther looked serious—and scared.

"I'm going to go in and take a look. Are you sure you won't come along? Maybe be my guide." He hoped Luther would come along. He was feeling a little scared himself.

Luther shook his head. He said, "I'll wait right here for ya." And he did.

The sheriff went down the path to the center of the woods. He felt an eerie presence near him—or was it following him. He turned around to see if something was there and saw Luther standing outside of the woods, waiting. He got to the center and saw the hollowed-out stump with the log in it. Beside it hung numerous dried plants and roots in a row. He looked inside the stump and saw some powder residue in it. He took out his handkerchief and carefully brushed some of the powder onto it with a stick. He folded it up and put it in his shirt pocket.

He walked out on one of the paths a little way. He looked around to see if Hazel was in the woods. He could feel that someone was in the woods with him. Again, he looked back to Luther. He could just barely see him through the leaves and tree branches, still standing there waiting. No birds were chirping or flying around. Not one animal moved. These woods were creepy. The sheriff began sweating like mad. He felt like he was going to vomit. He reached for his handkerchief to wipe his brow and stopped when he remembered the powder. It reminded him that he needed to pick up the samples of water from Clyde Younger. He hadn't done that yet. What if this powder was the same thing that was in the well water?

It seemed darker all of the sudden. The woods became creepy scary, just like Luther described them. He needed to get out of them. He walked with a quick pace back to Luther. Something was following him—he could feel it—breathing on his neck. He was breathing heavy. What was it? He saw Luther and popped out of the woods. The sheriff spun around to see what it was. Nothing was there.

He turned and with a quickened pace kept going past Luther towards the barn.

Luther walked up behind the sheriff and said, "That's why I don't go in there no more."

Sheriff Yoder leaned against the barn and looked at Luther. He saw a stout young man who looked much older than his fourteen years. He said, "You weren't kidding about those woods." He was feeling a little bit better.

Luther shook his head in agreement and said, "Yeah, I know."

The sheriff peered over Luther's shoulder and into the woods. Something was in there. Following him. He was sure of it. Calming himself, he turned back to Luther and said, "I'll be going over to your Uncle Otto's farm. I hope to find your mother there. It was nice meeting you." He reached out and shook Luther's hand.

Luther gave him a firm grip and shake. He said, "It was nice meeting you, too. What is it that you want to talk to mother about?" He gave a curious look to the sheriff.

"Oh, I just need to talk to her about a few things." He thought for a second and added, "Some people say she's been trespassing on their land, and I just want to tell her to stay away from their property. That's all." The sheriff didn't want to trouble him with what he really needed to talk with her about. "I'll be going now."

"Okay. She's been acting very strange. Stranger than usual. I've got work to get done." He gave the sheriff a quick wave and went back into the barn.

Sheriff Yoder walked to his car and thought to himself, 'Strange, I'll say. And stranger than usual. I've got to meet this woman.' He got in his car and drove to Otto and Elsa's farm.

He had no luck finding her there, so he drove back to town. He was going to meet with Clyde Younger and pick up the well water samples. On the way he remembered that he had the sample of powder in his handkerchief. He took it out of his shirt pocket and placed it on the seat beside him.

He and Clyde had known each other for a number of years. They both served in the Army during the first World War, and now they were both in law enforcement; Clyde to a lesser degree, but they had a lot in common.

He parked at the Town Hall and checked the jail. No one was there. He figured that he'd just walk over to Clyde's house since it was right around the corner. As he walked up through the yard, he saw Clyde burning some trash in a fifty-five-gallon drum that he used as a burn barrel. He was stirring the contents and staring at the flames. He seemed both mesmerized and delighted at the same time at the sight of the fire. Sheriff Yoder said, "Howdy, Clyde. How you been?"

Startled, Clyde said, "Hiya. I didn't see you walking up. You about scared the daylights out of me."

"Sorry about that, old friend." Sheriff Yoder grinned at Clyde with sincerity. "The way you're staring at that fire makes me wonder if you're the arsonist."

"Ha-ha, no." Clyde hocked up a loogie and chewed it like a piece of gum while staring at the fire. "You might want to talk with Hazel Dill about those fires."

"Yeah, that's what I'm here for, and to collect the well water samples. Have you seen her?"

Clyde searched his thoughts for a moment, while chewing and extracting every last bit of flavor out of the loogie. He then turned and spit it with tremendous force at the burn barrel, where it splattered and stuck, sizzling away. Clyde said, "No. I haven't seen her, but I bet she's the one. I've been trying to find her, too. People around here think she's the one startin' 'em. And they're on edge to put an end to the fires."

"I need to question her and get some answers. I haven't had any luck finding her. I tried her house, her sister and brother-in-law's house. I can't locate her."

"I tried those places myself." He gave the fire one last look and walked towards the Town Hall. "I haven't seen her in a while. My gut tells me she's hiding in the woods around The Valley somewhere. Let's go get those samples."

"After what I felt over on the Dill farm my gut tells me the same."

They walked over to the Town Hall. Clyde said, "You can wait down here. No sense going up the stairs and right back down." He went up and retrieved the samples. The sheriff could hear ruckus laughter coming from the saloon on the other side of the fire station. Clyde came back down and handed him the samples.

"Thanks, Clyde." He opened the trunk of the Model T and placed the samples in it. He closed the lid and walked back to Clyde. "What's the celebration?" He nodded towards the saloon.

"Workday's done, I guess." Clyde grinned and shook his head.

"Thanks, Clyde. I'm going to go in there and ask around. See if anyone has seen Hazel."

"You betcha. Good luck." Clyde gave him a wave and went back to his home.

It sounded like they were having a good time in there. He opened the door of the Salty Dog Saloon. The little bell jingled its alarm that a new customer had arrived. The clamor fell to a near silence as the patrons turned and saw

70

who had entered. Johnny Muller, one of the Salty Dog's best customers called out, "Look what the cat drug in." The place erupted with laughter.

Sheriff Yoder said, "Good day, gentlemen. I'm not here to break up your fun, I would just like to ask some questions about Mrs. Hazel Dill, if any of you fellas knows her."

Johnny said, "Know her, hell, who wished they didn't know her." More jubilant laughter followed. The sheriff walked over to where Johnny was sitting.

"Can I sit with you and ask you a few questions?," addressing Johnny.

"As long as you don't tell my wife that you saw me here, she doesn't think that I drink," Johnny replied nice and loud for the whole saloon to hear. Laughter rang out in the saloon.

Johnny looked over to his friend, Richard Schroder, another good Salty Dog customer, and said, "Slide over a stool and let Sheriff Yoder cop a squat between us."

Sheriff Yoder asked, "How well do you know Hazel Dill?"

Johnny said, "Well enough to keep a great distance between me and her. I see her passing over our property at all hours of the day. If she sees me 'a comin', she scurries off. Ya' see, I always carry a shotgun on me on the farm. You never know when you might spook something up and have a chance to shoot you some dinner."

"Does she always seem to be hunched over when she walks?"

"It ain't just when she walks. Hell, that old witch was born hunched over. Why would you want to know that?"

"We suspect that she may be involved in the mysterious fires that have been occurring around Valley Center. A hunched over figure was seen leaving the latest fire."

"We been figurin' it's her who's been doin' 'em." He then turned and said to the whole saloon, "Everyone been figurin' that she killed ole Fred, too."

A few guys started baaing like sheep, "Fre-e-e-e-e-d, Fre-e-e-e-e-d." To a rumbling round of rafter-rattling laughter.

He turned back to the sheriff, "She wanders all over The Valley at night. I've seen her dart across the road ahead of me when I'm coming home late at night from a delivery, all hunch-backed and all. She looks like a big raccoon scurrying along. I bet it's her that's been doin' 'em. I bet she had something to do with her own mother's death, and her aunt and uncle, too. I can't prove nothin', but I bet she did."

"Why would you think that?"

"She's a vindictive old witch. Her mother had a fallin' out with her. Didn't like the fact that her daughter was chasing after a married man half her age. She's been seen on every farm in The Valley." Then he spoke loud, "Trying to land a husband to replace ole Fre-e-e-e-e-d."

To another round of, "Fre-e-e-e-e-d, Fre-e-e-e-e-d!" And more laughter.

Johnny continued, "An old hag like that acting all a fool. Her aunt and uncle had sided with her mother on that, they and our good buddy Henry, Jr., too. My bet is the whole family got bit by her. It had to be her that done it. I know it was her that killed 'em."

Sheriff Yoder thought for a moment. The well water samples, powder residue from that bowl in her woods. Fires at the Schmidt's, Welks's, Braun's, and Hofstetter's. And then Dr. Morse's office. Then his thoughts came out loud, "So, that makes one think of a motive."

Richard said, "Damn straight. She had motive alright. She cast a spell on 'em and conjured up a potion to get revenge on 'em."

Sheriff Yoder asked, "What do you mean?"

Richard said, "That John Johns fella that worked for the Hofstetters, the farm next door to the Dills. The young guy that Johnny was talkin' about. Married. Got kids. From Cleveland. We seen him quite a few times around town. He, and her son, Luther, told us they seen her doing some weird stuff out in the woods. Spinning around, shouting out strange things in strange voices. Scary stuff. Said she drank a chicken's blood and danced with the devil. Said she was a witch. I say she's a witch."

Johnny said, "I say she's a bitch, but we all say she's a witch. That one's for sure."

Sheriff Yoder asked, "So, you all think she's a witch?"

Johnny said, "Just ask ole dead Fre-e-e-e-e-d, he'll tell you."

Another echo of, "Fre-e-e-e-e-d, Fre-e-e-e-e-d," and a few chuckles.

Johnny said, "Ole Fre-e-e-e-e-d told us that she used to put something in the breads that she made for him. He said that it made him all horny for her. It would take a sick man to go for a roll in the hay with Hazel, and ole Red was a sick man. He tried to plow a cow once. Yeah, I know exactly. My

72

dad told me, he was there, he saw it. Ole Dog Dick Fre-e-e-e-e-d didn't need any enticement. Every animal in The Valley breathed a sigh of relief when he died." A few chuckles could be heard. "I know she was putting potions in ole Fre-e-e-e-e-d's food. I think she also done some witchery to the Goehrings, and her mother, too."

Sheriff Yoder said, "Thanks for your time, it was very insightful. You gentlemen have a nice day." He got up and headed for the door.

Johnny said, "Any time sheriff. How about buying us a beer before you go."

The sheriff laid down a dollar on the bar. He said, "Get these gentlemen a drink."

Johnny said, "Thanks, sheriff. But remember. If you run into my wife, don't tell her that you saw me in here." They all laughed it up and got back to the business of enjoying the end of their workday.

The sheriff left the saloon and saw Dr. Morse over by his burned down office perusing through the charred remains. He walked over to him and said, "There's been rumblings about town that maybe Hazel Dill had something to do with this and all the other fires, too. On top of that, as you may by now suspect, she might have put some kind of poison in the Goehring family's well."

Dr. Morse said, "It's a definite fact that the Goehrings died of stomach inflammation. So did Hazel's mother. It could have been from food poisoning, like botulism or something. But then again, it could have been from some kind of poison. And I mean *poison*, poison. Like some sort of cyanide, or arsenic, or something." The doctor shuffled back and forth a bit, ruffled up his hair, scratched his scruffy beard, then continued, "I'll be setting up shop in the back of the general store, till I can rebuild." He gave a look and waved a hand toward the Valley Center General Store across the street next to the saloon.

Sheriff Yoder asked, "Do you think there's a possibility that Hazel Dill poisoned her own family members?"

Dr. Morse said, "It wouldn't surprise me one bit that she's the arsonist, and it would surprise me even less that she poisoned these folks."

Sheriff Yoder said, "We need to determine if she did poison them."

Dr. Morse said, "Then we'll have to exhume one or both of the Goehrings and do an autopsy."

Sheriff Yoder remembered that he had forgotten to ask Roy Frank if there was anyone else that he could think of that interacted with Hazel in the store the last time she was in there. "I'll be getting back with you on that, doctor."

With that he hustled back to his Model T and drove back to Frank's Corners to talk with Roy again.

Sheriff Yoder walked into the general store. In the front corner he saw a tiny mouse looking up at him. This cute little mouse was sitting there flicking its nose, and looking like it was smiling at him. He thought, 'What a neat pet this little guy would make.' Then he and cringed at the thought of that black snake at the Dill farm. That little mouse was lucky to not have that thing around.

Roy said, "Back so soon? What happened, she propose to you?" He chuckled. "And she got you to come back here and pay her bill for her! What a nice guy you are!" They both chuckled.

Sheriff Yoder said, "Yeah, part of the dowry." Roy snorted. "There's a little mouse right here, just sitting there smiling at me."

Roy said, "Thanks, I'll put some traps down and catch that little rascal." Sheriff Yoder wished he didn't say anything about that mouse. It's such a cute little guy.

Sheriff Yoder asked, "Was there anyone else that you can remember that talked with Hazel Dill in the store, other than yourself, of course, the last time she was in here? Maybe someone that got Hazel riled up?"

Roy put his hand on his hip, leaned his head back and looked up into his brain like he was going through a rolodex. He stood there with a grimace on his face as if deep thought hurt him.

Sheriff Yoder said, "I know you're thinking, I smell wood burning," to which Roy grinned.

Roy said, "You know what, there were two women in here, standing right over there when she was checking out. And she turned towards them. Then she said something really strange about rats."

The sheriff asked, "Rats? What did she say about rats?" He squirmed at the thought of that black snake.

Roy said, "I thought it was odd what she said. I said something to the effect of, 'You had a big rat problem at one time.' She turned to Helga Braun and Ida Welks, that's who they were, and said, 'Some rats are over five feet tall.'

I remember that now. She seemed to be ticked off at those two for some reason."

Sheriff Yoder said, "Isn't that something." He pondered on that for a moment, then added, "The Dills have a black snake in the barn that takes care of rats." He thought to himself that the Braun's and the Welks's barns both burned down after the Schmidt's barn burned down. Things were starting to pile up on Hazel Dill.

Roy wasn't paying close attention to the sheriff, but he heard him say rats. He said, "She told me she didn't need poison for rats anymore, she can make her own poison."

The sheriff was in deep thought. All of the sudden he said in a startled voice, "Holy Moses smell the roses. She makes her own poison. The poison can't be for rats because it would kill her snake." He had to get those samples tested immediately.

Roy said, "It was quite a while ago, now, but I knew they had a big rat problem at one time. Her, and her husband Fred had told me. They purchased arsenic from me to take care of them."

The sheriff said, "Do you know that a pea sized bit of arsenic is fatal to a person?"

Roy said, "I did not know that." He thought for a moment and added, "It was potion she said, not poison. She made her own potion." He had an eureka moment. "She didn't need poison for rats because she had a black snake for them. She could make her own potions. That's what she said." Roy smiled; he was so proud of himself that he remembered that.

The sheriff said, "It could be one in the same. I came to Valley Center today hoping to catch a break on the case of these mysterious fires; and now a big-ole can o' worms just busted wide-open. I'm going to meet with Judge Giles and get a warrant. See if I can bring in a suspect."

Roy said, "Best of luck, Sheriff. Go get her."

Sheriff Yoder said, "Thanks, Roy. And thanks for your help. Be seeing you soon."

Roy said, "Not if I see you first." They chuckled. Sheriff Yoder headed out the door and to the judge's house in Medina to meet with him.

Chapter 10

A Witch Hunt

From Interviews of Sheriff Yoder, Clyde Younger, Old John Muller, Johnny Muller, Art Gunther, Richard Schroder, Ed Ungrich, Harry Ungrich, James Hadcock, and Dr. Morse

Judge Giles was a man to be feared if you were on the wrong side of the law. His ways were by the book, and he was a fair man. His whole life revolved around the law. He spent his days traveling to the different towns of the county to try cases. In the evenings he liked to read law cases from his massive law library that he kept in his home. In his free time, he liked to walk around his hometown of Medina. That's when he could think his best and deepest—about law.

Sheriff Yoder arrived at his house and found the judge to be home. He had been in his study when the sheriff arrived. Judge Giles opened the door and said, "Good evening, Luke. What brings you over here on this fine evening?"

The sheriff began to explain the reason for his visit when the judge invited him in for a cup of coffee.

Sheriff Yoder told him the whole story of the turn of events in the arson investigation, that leads him to believe that the Goehrings were murdered. He took water samples from the Goehring's well and powder from the Dill farm to the police lab for testing. The judge nodded as the sheriff told him of his fact-finding mission. When he was finished, he asked the judge to write out a warrant for the arrest of Hazel Dill.

Judge Giles was deep in thought. He took a sip of coffee, cleared his throat, and said, "We have a witness that saw a dark, hunched-over figure leaving the scene of the latest fire. We have overwhelming suspicion to believe in the culpability of a prime suspect in said fire. We have circumstantial evidence

76

that the suspect is involved in all the other mysterious fires in and around Valley Center. On top of that, there is speculation that the suspect in question may have committed a murder, and/or murders. We first and foremost need to have positive empirical evidence in order to prosecute the suspect. The suspect must be brought in for questioning. Questions of responsibility for the arsons, and murders, may be directed to the suspect at that particular time. I will issue two warrants. The first, for the arrest of Hazel Dill. The second, for the exhumation of one of the Goehrings to have an autopsy performed."

"Thank you, judge." The sheriff was overcome with relief. He knew Judge Giles would do the right thing. He was under a lot of pressure to solve the mystery of the fires. He needed to get some sleep. Tomorrow was going to be an even longer day than this one.

Judge Giles filled out the warrants and handed them to Sheriff Yoder. With a stern look and a slight gleam in his eyes he said, "Good luck, Luke. I'll see you in court on this one."

The sheriff took the warrants from the judge in nervous excitement. He shook the judge's hand and said, "See you there." He left for his home. On the way he thought of how he was going to nab Hazel Dill.

The next day Sheriff Yoder headed back to Valley Center to meet with the his old friend Clyde Younger. Clyde was not only the town constable, but also the curator of the town's cemeteries. Hollow Hill Cemetery is the biggest one. It sits on a hill on Hollow Hill Road, overlooking The Valley. This is where the Goehrings were buried.

The sheriff pulled into Clyde's driveway, got out of his car, and walked up to the door. As he did, Clyde opened it with an expectant look, waiting to hear what news he had from Judge Giles. Sheriff Yoder cleared his throat and started, "I need to get right to the point of why I'm here. I'd like you to get some help to exhume one of the Goehrings from their grave. We need to check and see if they were poisoned. I have a warrant here from Judge Giles to do so, and I would like to get this done—yesterday."

Clyde saw the serious look on the sheriff's face. Clyde had a solemn look on his. He said, "Let me get my grave digging clothes on and I'll be right out." He left the door open and went to change his clothes.

The sheriff wandered over next to his Model T. He was enjoying the singing of some songbirds when Clyde came out of the house. The sheriff opened his door and said, as he climbed in the car, "I'll follow you."

Clyde said, "Let me get my horse hitched up to my wagon. The township doesn't give me any fancy perks like you get." He smiled at the sheriff.

The sheriff hopped out of his car and said, "I'll help you."

Clyde shot him a grin and said, "Do you remember how?" They chuckled. As they hitched up the horse, Clyde said, "I know just the fellas for this job. Follow me over to the saloon."

Clyde knew where he could recruit a couple of young men to help with the digging. His house was only a block away from the Salty Dog Saloon, and that's where he knew he could find his help. Ed and Harry Ungrich, jacks of all trades and masters of none. These two brothers were seen almost every day sitting on one of the benches out in front of the saloon. They would wait for someone to stop by and recruit them to take care of any odd job that needed to be done. Everybody in The Valley knew where to find help if they needed it.

Clyde drove up on his wagon and stopped in front of the saloon. He asked the brothers, "Would you young men like to make some easy money? Get back some of the taxes that you pay to the county?"

In unison, the brothers said, "Yeah."

"Come with me. We're going to the cemetery and dig one of the Goehrings up out of their grave."

Harry hopped into Clyde's wagon and asked, "Dig one up? What do you mean?"

"Sheriff Yoder has a warrant to exhume and examine one of them to see if they were poisoned." Clyde gave a quick point behind the wagon to the sheriff, who gave the two men an acknowledging salute.

Ed said, "Oh yeah. We've all been wondering about that. So, is it true? That old witch killed 'em?" The brothers looked at each other like giddy kids at Christmas.

"They're not sure about that. They want to have their innards examined."

Harry said, "Well, let's go." They climbed onboard Clyde's wagon.

On the ride to the cemetery, Clyde said, "Digging will be easy, fellas. They were planted not long ago." The brothers were grinning. They were glancing back at the sheriff and talking about how exciting it was to be doing this. To be part of the investigation.

Clyde stopped the wagon as close as he could get to the fresh graves of the Goehrings. He and the Ungrich brothers grabbed shovels and walked to the graves. As they were approaching the gravesite Clyde asked the sheriff, "Do you have a preference as to which one?"

Sheriff Yoder said, "It don't make no difference. Henry, I reckon." He was looking at the headstone.

So, they commenced to digging up Henry Goehring, Sr. When they got down about three and a half feet, Clyde said, "Go easy now boys, we don't want to bust the vault lid." The Goehrings were lucky enough to be able to afford concrete vaults.

They started scratching away the dirt with their shovels instead of plunging them into the soft dirt. The distinct sound of steel scraping stone rose out of the ground. Clyde said, "We're there."

At the same time, a harrowing howl of a coyote bellowed from the valley below. Sheriff Yoder said, "I heard that same coyote scream just like that, yesterday, over at the Dill farm."

Harry said, "That ain't no coyote. That's that witch Hazel. I heard her howling like that before."

The hair on everyone's arms was standing up. Sheriff Yoder headed in the direction from where the sound came, with his gun drawn. He was thinking, 'If Harry knew that was Hazel, that must have been her in the woods yesterday.'

He peered through the fir trees, down into the valley. He just knew that it had to be a coyote. No human could make a sound like that. But in the back of his mind, he knew Harry was right. That was Hazel. And if Hazel was a real witch, she had a pretty good idea what they were doing here. She had been watching him yesterday. He knew there was something in the woods with him. It was her—he could feel her.

He perused the tall grass of the field and saw a dark shape in the distance standing as still as a frozen pond. It was too tall to be a coyote. It was probably just a bush, or some brush. He squinted and stared at it to see if it would move.

It didn't.

He raised his gun, aiming low on purpose, and pulled the trigger. When he did, he blinked. When his eyes returned to where the figure was, it was gone. Another screaming howl wailed from further out in the valley below.

Harry called out, "Did ya get 'er, sheriff? Do us all a favor if'n ya did."

The sheriff said, "No, I didn't get it."

Clyde asked, "What was it?"

"Don't know, but it's gone now." The sheriff came walking back to the gravesite. He kept looking back to where he had seen the figure standing.

The crew finished pulling the coffin out of the burial vault and loaded it onto Clyde's wagon. They climbed aboard the wagon and went back to Valley Center to turn their cargo over to Dr. Morse for his examination. They unloaded the coffin from the wagon and carried it into the back of the general store. They helped Dr. Morse pry it open. He rubbed his chin and said, "Ah, poor Bertha, I hate to have to do this to you."

Sheriff Yoder said, "Bertha. I thought you fellas were digging up Henry."

Clyde said, "I must have planted them on the wrong sides. We'll have to move Henry over before we put Bertha back." Clyde left to put his horse and wagon away.

The sheriff wondered how many headstones in the cemetery had the names on the wrong sides because of that, but didn't say anything. He asked, "How long before you have a sample, doc?"

Dr. Morse said, "Oh, less than an hour and I should have a couple of samples for you to take to your lab."

Sheriff Yoder said, "That sounds good. I'll wait out front. I did have some other business to attend to, but this is of utmost importance."

Dr. Morse proceeded with the unenvious task of probing around Bertha Goehring's innards while Sheriff Yoder waited outside. Clyde came walking back from his house and met the sheriff on the sidewalk in front of the general store.

Clyde saw Old John Muller pulling up with his wagon in front of the saloon. He said, "There's trouble."

Old John is Johnny Muller's father. He was friends with Hazel's father, Johannes Marks. He lost out by ten votes to be town constable to Clyde, although he never held that against him. They were on good terms. Old John said, "Trouble with a capital T," then chuckled. Clyde and Sheriff Yoder chuckled, too. The sheriff knew Old John from years back. Old John wondered what was going on that the sheriff and town constable were together. He climbed down from his wagon and came over to where they were standing and asked, "What skullduggery is going on here?"

Sheriff Yoder said, "We're waiting on Dr. Morse for some samples to be tested."

80

"Tested? To see if his place burned down from arson?"

"You're close."

"Have you talked to Hazel Dill?" Like everyone else, it seemed, Old John held his suspicions of her.

"I attempted to yesterday, but she wasn't home. She wasn't at her sister's. She wasn't anywhere. I'm hoping to find her today."

"I know where to find her," Old John said with confidence.

"You know where she is? Tell me."

"It ain't gonna be that easy. Art Gunther owns the property of the old salt mine. He sees Hazel going into the mine from time to time. Tonight's going to be a new moon. He, my son, Johnny, and I have seen her go in the mine on many a new moon. That's where she'll be."

"Let's go get her." The sheriff was anxious to bring her in.

"Art knows that mine better than anybody. Let's meet over at his place and talk to him about getting her out of the mine."

"Where's he live?"

"West River Road. Go out of town north about a mile. After you go through Gunther's Flats, you go up a big hill and then down the other side, his house is on the right." He was pointing in a northward direction. "You can see the area of the old mine in the distance from his place."

"I'll do that. But I'll check her place first, just to be thorough. Clyde, would you be my guide?"

Clyde said, "You betcha." They hopped in the sheriffs Model T to go on the hunt for Hazel.

"See ya in a bit." Old John knew they wouldn't find her. He knew where she was at. He waved to the sheriff and Clyde and walked into the Salty Dog Saloon.

Dr. Morse came out from around the back of the general store with two sealed sample bottles in his hands. He watched the sheriff begin to pull away in his car. He thought to himself that the other business he had to attend to needed attending. He yelled out, "Sheriff, I've got your samples for you." The sheriff stopped and turned around. He saw Dr. Morse holding up two sample vials.

The sheriff backed up and reached out. Dr. Morse handed him the vials. He said, "Thanks, doc. I almost forgot."

"I think you did forget." Dr. Morse gave him a wink and a wave of his hand, then went back in to finish up with Bertha.

As they drove off in the Model T the sheriff told Clyde that they would drop the samples off at the lab first. They would check the south of The Valley on the way, and go to the Sauer's and Dill's when they came back. If they came up empty, they would go to Art Gunther's.

Old John sat next to the Ungrich brothers who had recently returned from their excursion at the cemetery. They were spilling it around what they had been up to that morning. They told Old John that they heard Hazel howling at the exact moment they scraped the lid of the burial vault. And that the sheriff thought it was a coyote. They both let out a nervous laugh—it was no coyote.

That howl had been heard many times before around The Valley. Old John told the Ungrich brothers to put down their drinks and come with him. They needed to be sober for their next job. They left the saloon and got on Old John's wagon. They were going to Art Gunther's house.

They all met on Art Gunther's farm. Johnny, Old John's son, had gotten Richard Shroder and James Hadcock to come with him. The sun was going down and they were just waiting for the Sheriff and Clyde to arrive. The guys stood around talking. They needed to put an end to the destructive fires. An end to the evil, menacing grip that the witch Hazel held over The Valley. They knew she was the arsonist, if you really thought about it, the mysterious fires were never a mystery at all. Sheriff Yoder and Constable Clyde came pulling in about ten minutes after Johnny.

Old John asked, "Any luck, sheriff?"

Sheriff Yoder got out of his car. He said, "Nothing. Same as yesterday. No one's seen her." He was disappointed. Disappointed because he knew exactly where Hazel was hiding.

"Not to worry. We'll get her," Old John assured him. Out of all the men in that room, Old John was perhaps the only one brave enough to take charge in capturing Hazel. If it weren't for him, Hazel may have continued her trail of torment or fled from The Valley altogether.

A plan was hatched with Old John acting as the de facto leader, a responsibility Sheriff Yoder was all too happy to hand off to someone else. The best place for her to hide would be the old salt mine, which is where they would look first. Old John would lead the way to the mine's entrance while

Johnny was put in charge of tying up Hazel when they got ahold of her. Clyde and Sheriff Yoder would be waiting to officially arrest Hazel, and the unenviable task of actually entering the mine was left up to one of the five remaining men.

Once the plan was laid out, Sheriff Yoder made sure to say, "Now fellas, I appreciate your help and all. Clyde here tells me that you know the mine and The Valley very well. This isn't a lynching party; we're just bringing Hazel in for questioning." He looked at each one of them. "Understand?" They all nodded.

Old John had his wagon ready to go. In it were seven sturdy sticks, each with a rag that had been soaked in coal oil and wrapped around one end of them to be used as torches. They would need them to see down in the dark mine. There were a couple of pitchforks and hay hooks that were always in the wagon. They were used when he and Johnny delivered hay. Old John threw in a rope with a lasso and some bailing twine in case it was needed to bind Hazel's hands.

They gathered up some courage, hopped into Old John's wagon, and made their way to the mine. Sheriff Yoder and Constable Clyde followed close behind in the sheriff's Model T. The guys in the wagon could feel the end of the Hazel's reign of terror was near. They were going on a hunt for The Witch of The Valley.

The wagon was full of conflicting emotions. They could feel the lumps in their throats as they got closer and closer to where they would enter the woods. In silence, they all followed Old John carrying various equipment with them. The mine wasn't far from them, well within one hundred feet of the edge of the woods, but they all figured they should be prepared.

Once they reached the mine's entrance, Old John turned to the men and said, "Any volunteers?" Everyone just looked down. He may have been brave, but Old John was much older than the other men. The mine's landscape would be too much for his bad knees. It was time for someone else in their posse to step up.

Art Gunther was a man that knew the area well. His great grandfather first owned the land where the abandoned salt mine sat. He also knew Hazel well; he went to school with her. And he knew the salt mine better than anyone in The Valley, except for Hazel. Art was big, and Art was tough. He said, "I'll go in if someone will come with me."

James said, "I'll go. This oughta be big fun." It didn't take much for him to be entertained. Truth be told, he was scared to death. He figured that the guys would think he was tough and brave, just like Art, if he went in the mine with him. James later claimed this night to be the wildest experience of his life.

They lit the torches and gathered around the mine entrance. It was about a six-foot wide by ten-foot-long hole in the ground. There was a rock-hard floor path that led gradually down to a depth of about thirty feet in the main shaft. After you levelled off at the bottom of the main shaft, a tunnel went northwest about two hundred feet. There were two different tunnels that branched off from the main one. The furthest one out from the entrance branched off to the west. The westward tunnel ran out roughly another two hundred feet.

The other tunnel was the deepest of the tunnels, it was the first one that you came to off the main tunnel. It branched off to the north. This northward tunnel ran along the river in a gradual descent of another thirty more feet to the bottom. That branch also went further out, about three hundred feet.

The salt was more plentiful and easier to obtain in the deeper branch. That's where everyone that still mined near the end of the salt mining days chose to dig. In those days the miners started throwing the rocks down the main tunnel past the deepest branch instead of carrying them out and throwing them in the river. The rest of the old mine was sealed off by the rocks and debris from the deep branch.

The deepest, darkest place in the mine is where Hazel loved to go. That's where she met her friend. Where she loved to go to on the nights of the new moon. To talk with the little girl that was her only friend. The friend that was buried in the rocks. The one she dug out. The one that she now carries inside of her.

Art said, "Wish us luck." Then he and James moved into the main entrance of the mine. With Art leading the way, and lit torches in hand, they descended into the mine. Even with their torches, they could only see through the darkness of the mine no further than fifteen feet, perhaps twenty if they squinted.

Art had been down in the salt mine hundreds of times. He saw Hazel there many times with her father and brother, hauling rocks out, digging, extracting sinew for salt, just like all the other miners. He could make his way through the mine blindfolded.

Old, loose, rotted wooden beams struggled to hold the integrity of the tunnels. Art and James carefully maneuvered past them with their torches to avoid disturbing them. The still air smelled of dirt, rock, and a slight hint of salt. Long forgotten memories came rushing back to Art. He never liked digging in the deepest tunnel, even though it was easier work. He would rather work harder in the other tunnels than to deal with the strange sounds he heard coming from the deepest part of the mine.

Whenever he would leave the mine, he would stop at the deep branch entrance and stand still as a stone. Breathing deep and slow through his mouth so he could calm himself and hear as best as he could. He would put his ear to the side of the tunnel wall and listen. He swore that he could hear a voice. It was whispering. It was the voice of a young girl. Saying the same words over, and over again. But he couldn't quite make out what she was saying.

He could never tell for sure, but what she appeared to be saying was, "*Come dig me out.*" It would send chills up his spine. And he would run up the main tunnel and dash out of the only entrance. He would think about those words, "*Come dig me out.*" It couldn't be, but if not, what was it saying? He couldn't make sense of it. He wasn't about to go dig anything out. It was scary down in that tunnel. Then one day—It stopped, and he never heard it again.

Art had forgotten about that, till he and James arrived at the deep branch entrance. He looked to James and whispered, "You ready?" James nodded his head. Art continued, "We're going to have to go down to the deepest part of the mine, that's where I would go if I wanted hide." The Witch was even more familiar with that place than Art—and The Witch was there.

As they trekked slowly in silence down the northward tunnel, James began to feel drips of water tapping him on his head and back. They cautiously advanced over loose rocks and wood. James quivered with each strike of a water droplet. He imagined tripping over a support beam, causing the mine to cave in on them—trapping them. Then the drips of water would turn into torrents, rushing through the rocks and drowning them. And the witch Hazel will escape out a secret tunnel.

James was shaking. He didn't want Art to see that. Tap—a drip on his head—tap—another. It was driving him insane. He tried not to panic, but peering down that deep, dark tunnel gave him an unearthly feeling that he couldn't shake.

85

They got about halfway down the deep shaft of the mine when Art put his hand up for James to stop. He whispered, "Do you hear that?"

James offered back in a whisper, "Yeah, it sounds like Hazel." He stood motionless as he tried to tame his breaths through an open mouth to get a better listen. He was hoping he wasn't really hearing what he was hearing. Art nodded in agreement. He noticed beads of sweat glistening on James's forehead in the dimly lit tunnel. "But who is she talking to?" His eyes were pleading to Art for a plausible explanation. Art put his finger up to his lips as a 'shhh, don't talk' sign. They stood there and listened.

They heard The Witch and Hazel bantering back and forth with one another. There was barking—there was laughter—there was insanity.

"You got me to do it. You made me do it."

"*You wanted to do it.*"

"I know, but still."

The Witch barked like a dog baying at the moon and laughed, "*you loved it. Why wouldn't you?*"

"I don't know."

"*Yes, you do know. They had it coming. Too bad the others didn't get theirs.*"

"Yeah, too bad."

"*Maybe soon.*"

"Maybe not soon enough."

"*That's the spirit. There's more work to be done.*"

"More funerals to attend."

"*Oh, so sad,*" The Witch cackled.

"I can't take it anymore. You make me want to die," Hazel sobbed.

"*You are mine. You can handle it. You've handled it this long. Sit still and relax. I got this. I scratch your itch. Now you scratch mine. I want all to die. All will die.*"

"I just wanted respect."

"*You got it. I want blood. You need to give me more. Do what you're told. You came to dig me out. You let me in.*"

Art thought to himself out loud, "'You came to dig me out,' that's it. The voice I heard was saying, 'Come dig me out.'"

The Witch snapped, "*You hear that?,*" in a stifled manner. The blabbering ceased. There was a cold, dead stillness.

Art would never admit it, but he was scared to death. James stood behind him, knees knocking, frozen in fear. They both had goosebumps on their entire bodies, the hair on their arms was standing straight up, their hearts pounding in dreadful anticipation.

Art leaned toward James and whispered, "Let's get out of here."

As they turned to flee the mine, a blood-curdling, shrieking howl reverberated from only a few feet beyond the torch lit sides of the tunnel. The extreme clamor in the tight space tore into their ears and made their heads throb in pain. Art pushed against James, who slipped and went down on the tunnel floor.

Art ran right over him and left him behind to fend for himself. That couldn't have been Hazel, he thought, as he sprinted towards the main shaft. He could feel The Witch breathing down his neck as he made his way out of the mine. Whatever that was, he knew it would catch him and tear him to pieces.

He saw the entrance ahead. He felt like he was moving slower than his old steam tractor. His mind was telling him he would die in the mine. He saw a torch light on the outside of the main entrance. He could make out Old John's face as he ascended closer and closer to freedom. The Witch was gaining, it had him. As he approached the entrance, Art let out a yelp as James bumped him and went streaking by. They re-entered the world above.

Art said, "She's right behind me, get her!"

James was bent over gasping for air as the other guys stood waiting, ready to rope her. Nothing.

Johnny looked at James, who had soiled himself, then back to Art. He said, "What were you guys thinkin', James pissin' and shittin' hisself was the perfect bait to lure her in?" Everybody thought that was funny, except for James. He went down to the river to clean himself up a bit.

Art was struggling to breath. He said, "I swear she was right behind me, clawing at me! You should have heard the weird stuff she was saying down there."

As Art was gasping, trying to catch his breath, Sheriff Yoder ran up and put a hand on his shoulder and asked, "So, was that Hazel down there?"

Art said, "I think so." As he panted. "It sure sounded like her." It also sounded like there was someone—or something—down there with her, but Art didn't mention that.

"We heard her howl," Old John added.

Art said, "You should have heard it down there. I can't believe I didn't shit myself, too."

Old John said, "I heard it well enough out here. I've heard her howl before. I've also heard her blabbering some strange stuff to herself, too. I know exactly." He pushed his torch into the entrance and peered into the mine and saw nothing but the emptiness in the main tunnel. He asked, "Who's going to go down there and get her out?" Not a peep.

Art had caught his breath. He said, "I've got a better idea. There's a fresh air vent that not many people know about. It's about a hundred yards over yonder." He lifted his arm and pointed. "It's right above the deepest part of the mine."

Right where The Witch was in conference. The air shaft had four posts around it and iron bars over it so no one would fall into the mine by accident. "We'll build us a fire nearby, pull the iron bars out, and push the fire into the air shaft down into the mine. We'll smoke her out. Like smoking a fox out of a den."

They all agreed that this was a grand idea.

The sheriff said, "Old John, Johnny, Clyde, and I will keep an eye on the mine entrance."

James came walking up from the river and said, "I'll stay here with you guys."

Johnny said, "No, stinky, you go with them guys."

James slinked away in shame to catch up with Art and Rich who were preparing to start a fire with sticks, branches, and brush that was near the fresh air vent. All the while, Ed and Harry gathered more sticks and brush for the fire.

James walked up and asked, "What do you need me to do, Art?"

Art said, "Go with those guys and collect more fuel for the fire."

They brought more sticks and brush to the fire. Art told them to take it over to the air shaft, be careful not to fall in, and toss it down into the mine. Art and Rich used the pitchforks that they took with them from out of the wagon and began pushing the fire towards the air shaft and down into it.

The brush and sticks that were thrown down in the mine started burning. A huge grunting, groaning sound echoed up from the belly of the mine. The ground moved like there had been an earthquake.

Smoke started palpitating out of the mine entrance like a dragon's breath. This huge smoke ring puffed out that drifted up into the air. They could hear that witch Hazel coughing, gasping, and cursing.

She called out, "I'm gonna wrap your balls around a tree!"

Instead of paying attention to the task at hand, they were enthralled with the smoke ring. Watching as it floated up and away. All of the sudden Hazel came running out of the mine like a bat out of hell. Johnny said later that she came flying out of there like a witch riding a broomstick. It happened so fast that they couldn't grab her. They weren't ready for anything like that. She fled towards the river, tripped over a rock, and went down face first onto the turf.

When she hit the ground she tumbled onto the path that goes along the river. They thought that was it, they had her. She was wallowing around and cursing away. As the posse walked towards her, she jumped up and took off running up the path.

Old John yelled for Johnny and his gang to go after her as he took his wagon and headed up West River Road. Sheriff Yoder and Constable Clyde got in the sheriff's Model T and headed over the bridge on Hollow Hill Road, then up River Road. They were chasing after the old witch. Johnny and his gang could see her up ahead, about a hundred feet away, and they were gaining on her.

Every so often a ball of light popped up from the ground and bounced beside Hazel on either side of her. They would appear—boom—then bounce along and fade away. It was like they were lighting the way for her, leading her.

Old John could be seen over to the right on West River Road keeping pace with Hazel. The river was to the left. Sheriff Yoder and Constable Clyde were keeping pace with her on the other side of the river on River Road. She was penned in and had no place to go but right where they wanted her to go, right into town—where the jail is.

They figured to just keep pace with her and make sure she didn't leave the path. They knew she wouldn't go in the river; she would be caught like a catfish. They figured she would wear herself out, then they would just walk right up and escort her into town.

James was bringing up the rear. He had lost his torch on his escape from the tunnel, so he was following along last. He tripped over something and went down. He slid on his backside down the bank and ended up with his feet splashing into the river.

Ed said, "Scrape out your shorts and warsh your ass while you're in there."

The posse kept pace with Hazel. A single, sideways lightning bolt flashed from the direction of the mine. It ripped through the sky a few feet above their heads and struck the ground behind Hazel. The ground shook behind them as the mine collapsed.

There hasn't been anyone in the mine since that night. You can't go in; it's all covered over now. Out of the dust cloud where the lightning bolt hit, this big, thick, sheet of fog came floating up and hovered over the river alongside Hazel. It was grey as a ghost. It might have been a ghost. It looked at times to contort into some sort of animal. No one could tell what it was. The old witch Hazel paid it no mind and just kept mumblin' and stumblin' her way up the path—and the fog followed her.

At the point where River Road could no longer be seen from the river, the fog moved across the path and broke away from Hazel. It looked like a giant hand as it floated just above the ground and moved towards West River Road. It was going after Old John. The vigilantes broke off the path and followed the fog. Johnny yelled out to warn his dad. Old John saw the sheet of fog and took off fast. The fog floated along and up West River Road behind him, then disappeared from their sight. Old John had gotten away. The vigilantes headed back to the path to pursue the witch.

They were unaware that she had doubled backed on them. Hazel was lying in wait in the brush by the path. They got almost to the path and were looking up to see where she was at.

Hazel jumped up out of the brush shrieking, "Leave us alone! We're gonna rip your balls off!" She had blood in her eyes, and she was foaming at the mouth. She yelled, "Why are you following us?"

Johnny said, "To put you in jail where you belong, Hazelnut." He threw the lasso around her. Rich grabbed the rope, and they took her to the ground. Then they hog tied her and stood there for a minute to catch their breath.

Hazel said, "You'll have to carry me, I ain't gettin' up and I ain't walkin'." She kept yelling and cursing at them.

Harry asked, "What are we gonna do now? We don't have the wagon."

Art said, "Oh, damn. We'll have to tie her to a log and carry her."

She was tied to a small, sturdy log. Ed and Harry hoisted her up. Hazel said, "Let your balls dangle close enough to my mouth if ya got any. I'll grit my teeth all I could. You can holler, scream. I'll bite 'em off! Rip 'em off, and spit 'em in your face!"

Ed was afraid she could reach him, so he scooted to the side to keep away from her mouth, and they dropped her. She hit the path with a thud, let out a loud grunt, and yelled, "You no good dirty little pricks! If we ever get ahold of you, we'll rip your balls off, shove 'em down your throats, and claw your eyes out!"

There was no way they were going to listen to her claptrap all the way to the Town Hall. Johnny said, "James, give me your soiled shorts, I'm gonna gag her with 'em." They looked around, and didn't see him anywhere, James was gone. Johnny said, "He must'a had enough excitement for one night."

So, against Johnny's better judgment, he took his dust scarf off and gagged her with that. Ed and Harry took the first shift, while Rich, Art and Johnny led the way and looked out for that sheet of fog, ghost thing in case it returned. To the best of their knowledge, the strange fog was gone. They were afraid it would come oozing back at them and try to free Hazel, but they never saw it again.

The vigilantes took turns lugging Hazel up the path and into Valley Center. When they crested the river bank, where the river bends and the path ends, there sat Old John in his wagon. Sheriff Yoder and Constable Clyde were right behind him, waiting for them to bring in Hazel.

Old John said, "I see you fellas got ahold of her."

Art said, "Sure did." He and Johnny set her down.

Sheriff Yoder said, "Easy now fellas, let's load her up and take her to the jail." Four of them lifted her up and put her in the wagon.

Old John said that the thick fog he saw was like nothing he had seen before. It seemed to be aware and alive. It came floating towards him on West River Road. He admitted later that it scared him, and his horse. He ran the horse as fast as it would go for a ways, looked back, and didn't see the fog anymore. He figured from there, he would go into town to meet up with Sheriff Yoder and Constable Clyde. They came to wait at the river where the path ends by the little bridge on Maple Street. Old John was confident that they would have the old witch.

The posse rode to the Town Hall and carried Hazel up the stairs to the second-floor jail. They set her down on the cot in the cell that Constable Clyde pointed to and untied her. She just laid there, didn't say a peep. Then she rolled to the side, sat up and started rocking back and forth, back, and forth, staring at the wall. Johnny let her keep his dust scarf. He wasn't ever going to wear it again.

Chapter 11

When It Rains, It Pours

From Interviews of Clyde Younger, Anna Younger, Sheriff Yoder, Luther Dill, and Guys from the Saloon

Hazel had ceased fighting back by the time they met Old John. She had quit mumbling to herself, too. It was odd, she wasn't talking to herself anymore. She wasn't talking at all. She seemed to have embraced her fate. What was really going on was The Witch had receded into hiding, buried within Hazel. What was left of Hazel's damaged and demented mind was left in charge.

The jail cell door clanked closed. Constable Clyde locked the door and hung up the key. The prime suspect in the death of Henry and Bertha Goehring, and all the mysterious fires, was in custody in the Valley Center Jail. Where she would be housed and fed at the town taxpayers' expense. She had it better now than she ever did in her entire life.

Clyde glanced over and saw what looked like a tear on Hazel's cheek. He walked over to the cell and said, "It's too late for tears now. Is there anything that you would like to talk about? Get off your chest?" She just looked forward and rocked back and forth on her cot. "You're lucky that son of yours knows how to take care of himself and your other children." He thought maybe hearing about her children would get her to talk. Nothing. Just rocking back and forth while the tear evaporated.

Sheriff Yoder stayed out of sight, but was listening with great interest. He walked up and said, "Nice try, Clyde." He looked to Hazel, "I met your son, Luther. And your daughter, Vivian. Nice kids." No response. "It's been a long day, Clyde. Let's go home and get some well-deserved rest. I'll be back bright and early tomorrow morning."

"That sounds good to me."

"Good night, Clyde."

"Nite, Luke." They walked out of the jail. Clyde locked the door to the second floor of the Town Hall behind them. He followed Sheriff Yoder down the stairs and watched as he got into his Model T and drove away towards the covered bridge on the east side of town. On Tuesday, June the 3rd of 1924, that was how the sheriff met the elusive, Hazel Dill. On the ride home he wondered how long it had been since she had cried.

The sheriff arrived early in the morning, just like he promised. He met Clyde at the second-floor jail above the Town Hall. Clyde was going to be spending all of his days for the near future minding a prisoner, who was sitting on her cot, rocking back and forth, staring at the wall. Sheriff Yoder said, "Good morning, Hazel."

Hazel said, "Good for nothin,'" staring straight ahead, rocking back and forth.

"Do you know why you're here?"

"I hope the food's good." She stared straight ahead rocking back and forth on the cot.

"But do you know why you're in jail, why you're being held in custody?"

"It ain't gonna rain today." She looked up as if she was testing the sky.

"You're in jail because you are accused of poisoning your Aunt Bertha and killing her."

"Poor Aunt Bertha, what a shame she had to die." She rocked back and forth.

"Did you kill her, Hazel? I hear your aunt was full to the brim with poison," the sheriff lied, hoping for a reaction. Tests hadn't been confirmed, yet.

"I know what you're full of. We didn't kill nobody." She turned ever so slightly towards the sheriff. Her eyes boiled up for a second and then simmered back down.

Sheriff Yoder thought for a moment and asked, "We?" Hazel just rocked back and forth, staring straight ahead at the wall, grinning. The sheriff said, "I can make it easier for you, if you just tell me what happened. How you did it. Why you did it."

"I told you; we didn't do nothin'," staring straight ahead rocking back and forth.

"We know that you and your husband Fred purchased poison for a rat problem, we have his signature on the bill from Frank's General Store when you purchased it," the sheriff pressed.

"Poor Fred. He's gone now." She stared at the wall. "We had that stuff a long time ago to kill rats. It's all gone. Don't need it no more anyway. We are innocent. We had nothing to do with the deaths." She seemed to be recollecting as she rocked back and forth.

"How about fire. Do you like fire? Did you light some barns on fire?" He leaned to the side so he could see her eyes. His eyes glued to hers to see if there was a reaction. There was none. Hazel rocked back and forth. "Did you light a fire in Dr. Morse's office?"

"No fires. We lit no fires." She stared straight ahead rocking.

"The Welks', the Braun's, the Schmidt's barns all burned down. Any of those names ring a bell?"

"Bells are for ringing; songs are for singing. I got a song for ya'." She rocked forward and spit on the floor.

How about the Hofstetter's barn? They said that you were there." He was hopeful that would put a burr in her bonnet. Nothing. She just rocked back and forth.

Sheriff Yoder couldn't get a confession. What the court wanted—what the court needed—was a confession. He was getting nowhere with Hazel. He was going to turn his attention to interviewing townspeople for the time being. He would come back and try again another time.

County Prosecutor, Paul Whitman, was bringing people in for interviews to build the case against her in court. The prosecution had plenty of witnesses. All the Goehring children would be in court to testify against her. Everyone they ran across that knew her was willing to say what a nasty, wicked person she was and testify against her. Even her son Luther was going to testify against her.

For many days Sheriff Yoder returned to talk with Hazel, to no avail. She wouldn't talk with him other than to repeat her claims of innocence; that the poison for killing rats was gone a long time ago. She didn't light any fires. But she did talk to Constable Clyde's wife, Anna, who was bringing her meals to her.

Anna began slow and easy to gain her trust. She had known of Hazel for years, though she hadn't ever talked with her. She had heard plenty of stories of confrontations with old nutty Hazel, but she never had a problem with her. Now she figured was as good a time as any to really get to know her, since they would be seeing a lot of each other. And maybe she could get her to talk.

Anna was a good cook. She always entered a peach pie in the Valley Center Fair pie baking contest. Hazel remembered that her mother also entered her world-famous apple pie. Anna would talk with her about the pies at the fair, farms, children, the weather, usual chit-chat. All the while, Hazel would rock back and forth on her cot, staring at the wall. Sometimes she would say a few words, but mostly just rocked, stared, and listened.

Hazel devoured the food that Anna would bring her and seemed interested in the recipes of the dishes. She mentioned that when she got home, she would make some of them for her children. Anna gave her a sheet of paper with of few of Hazel's favorites on it. She dropped it on the floor. Anna tried to get Hazel to confess, but all she got out of her was, "We're innocent, the poison for rats was gone long ago. We didn't light no fires." The same song and dance that she always spewed.

Anna said to Clyde, "The Hazel I heard about must be a different person. That one was mean. Nasty. Ruthless. Evil. The one that's in the jail is not the monster that committed those crimes."

The next day, the headline in the Valley Center Visitor stated: Valley Center Woman Arrested on Suspicion of Murder. The story was written by Reporter Peter Ertz. He was assigned to cover the case. The story covered the basics of an investigation of arson leading to the arrest for murder by poisoning. It mentioned how two of the family members had died, the other family members were ill, and a few were hospitalized. It was possible that they were all poisoned.

That day, the county prosecutor paid Peter Ertz a visit. He told him to back off on the accusations, till facts come out in the trial. He explained to him that nothing is to be said in the paper about the murders, other than there being an ongoing investigation into them. She had been brought in on suspicion of arson. Peter Ertz agreed to lay off for the time being, but he was itching to get the story out. The public was demanding it. He couldn't wait for the trial to begin.

Days rolled by. Every evening town folk gathered on the sidewalk in front of the Salty Dog Saloon to talk about the local happenings. As of late, the crowd that gathered spilled over to the front of the fire station next door. And some evenings, to the front of the Town Hall.

Hazel was the talk of the town. She was in the jail cell on the second floor of the Town Hall, less than a hundred feet away. Peter Ertz mingled through the crowd with notebook and pencil in hand. He struck up conversations that led to him asking if they had anything they'd like to say about the goings on in The Valley. Some folk shied away from talking, but others beamed at the thought of their names being in a Visitor story.

George Hurtzel said, "This one time me and Gerald Jager were standing right about here." He looked around to get his bearings straight. "Fred and Hazel had just got married. We saw them walking out of the general store." He pointed to the store next door. "Fred reached to grab Hazel's arm and help her up on their wagon. She pulled her arm away and backhanded him across the face. We could see fire in her eyes. She barked at him, 'Get away from me. I don't need your help.' Her mouth was all foamy, spit was flying. Fred cowered away from her and walked around the wagon. She glared at him the whole way with those angry eyes. It looked like he was scared of her. We were scared of her."

Charles Dellis said, "Henry, Jr. is crippled up. He may never get back to how he was, as of old. I heard John and Eleanor aren't good, either. But the others are coming out of it and doin' fairly well." People who heard him smiled. Charles continued, "They probably should have dug up Henry, her mother, and ole Fred, too, and had their innards examined. She poisoned them all, is my bet." He thought for a few seconds while looking into his thoughts. He added, "Family. All members of her own family." Some folks nodded in silent acquiescence.

Joseph Kraus relayed to Peter, "I chased away some kids that were hanging around at the Town Hall late the other night. When I came up the alley to go to the saloon I overheard them daring each other to go up the stairs to the second floor and try to talk to Hazel." He pointed to where his vantage point was. He continued, "I stayed in the shadows so they wouldn't see me. One of them went up the stairs. I hollered, 'She's gonna get ya.' That kid came flying down the stairs, scared out of his wits." He chuckled as he pointed at the stairs on the side of the Town Hall. "I told them to leave the old witch alone and go home. They left."

97

His gaze went up the stairs. The smile left his face. In a quiet voice he thought out loud, "I looked up to the top of the stairs and saw a thick, grey, sheet of fog float up to the door." Old John was standing near to him. His eyebrows curled up. He gave a slight nod of agreement as if he'd been there and seen it himself.

Joe shook his head as he caught himself speaking. Then he continued, "I could hear Hazel talking." His hands raised and made a sign like an explosion. "And poof, the sheet of fog was gone." He was staring up and away like he was seeing it right then. He went on, "I don't know if my eyes were playing tricks on me or what. I was about to leave, and I heard Hazel cackling loud with laughter. It was like she knew I was there." Joe's countenance turned grey like the fog that he saw. "As I hustled away I heard her say, '*Come up and see us some time, brave man.*' She cackled away. And it sounded like multiple people cackling." He stared into the distance.

Behind him, Peter heard the clamor of stomping feet. He turned around to see a group of about half a dozen young men marching into town. They were chanting something that he couldn't quite make out. It got louder as they drew closer. Then he heard what it was they were chanting, "Kill the witch. Kill the witch." And they were fired up.

Clyde Younger saw them coming. He moved to the side of the Town Hall in front of the stairs to the second-floor jail. He spoke up, "You fellas settle back now. She's got to have her day in court, first," as he looked over the crowd out to the young men on the road.

One of the young men, Don Braun, yelled out towards the second floor above Clyde where Hazel sat, rocking on her cot, "We're gonna get you, you old witch! You burned down my father's barn!"

The young men chanted, "Kill the witch! Kill the witch!"

Clyde couldn't afford these actions to stir up the crowd. He was fearful they would form a lynch mob. He said, "This is why we have courts. Let the court do its job. Let it play out."

Don said, "She's not only a barn burner, she's a murderer!"

The young men chanted, "Kill the witch! Kill the witch!"

Old John Muller moved through the crowd to stand next to Clyde. He spoke up, "You young men are full of piss and vinegar. I appreciate that. What do you fellas think you're really gonna do here?" Quite a few town folk moved in front of Old John and Clyde and faced the young men. Old John waited on the young men for an answer. The young men stood there with their fists clenched and their mouths closed. Old John went on, "That's what I thought."

Clyde Younger spoke up, "Young men, gentlemen, these things take time." He was hoping they had calmed themselves down. "Your time and energy are best served back on your farms with your families. She'll pay for what she has done. Now you fellas go on home."

The young men mumbled amongst themselves and dispersed. Much to the relief of Constable Clyde.

Even though Hazel was locked up over and above them in the jail, it was little relief. There was an unsettling sensation in the air amongst them. It felt as if she was right there, hovering over them, listening to their conversations. What they felt was the presence of The Witch. It was still there; still residing within Hazel.

That night, it started to rain, and rain—and rain. It rained for days. No lightning. No thunder. No heavy downpours. Just a steady rain. As it rained, every raindrop that tapped on the roof of the Town Hall started to tap onto Hazel's head. Tapping into her mind. Tap, tap, tap. Raindrop after raindrop. All day—and all night. The Witch could feel the reverberation of individual drops as they hit. Tapping Hazel's brain like a clapper strikes a bell. After days of listening to the raindrops beating their way into her brain, the bond holding Hazel and The Witch together began to break down. The Witch subsists within Hazel on its lust for blood and Hazel's desire for revenge. However, Hazel no longer desired to exist.

The Witch stood up and grabbed the bars of the jail cell and began blathering, *"Not the rain. Not again. The rain drives us insane."* Hazel was panting. *"Locked in a prison. How did this happen?"* Her eyes were boiling with fire.

She pulled at the bars trying to stretch them apart. *"He promised. Yahweh promised. No more floods. The constant tap, tap, tapping on our heads. Tapping our brains. Driving us insane. Pitter patter, hear it splatter, pounding down, the incessant clatter. Every drop building up. It'll knock us down. Drive us into the ground. It's going to cover us again. Bury us in a muddy, watery grave. It's going to drown us all again. We must get higher. Get out of the rain. Out of the reach of the rising water. Save us from the flood."*

Hazel scooted backwards and up the jail cell, clinging to the bars. She screamed, *"We've got to get out of here! Let us go!"* But she was in there—all alone.

Clyde came in the next morning and found Hazel clinging to the roof of the jail cell. Foam was drooling out of her mouth into a puddle on the floor. Her teeth were clattering, and she was chattering a bunch of nonsense that couldn't be understood. It seemed like words, but in a foreign tongue.

Clyde said, "Hazel, get down from there."

She just kept on spitting out her psychobabble. Clyde grabbed a broom and poked her with the handle of it. She latched onto it with her teeth, ripped it from his hands and tossed it aside. He hustled to the back of the general store to get Dr. Morse.

Dr. Morse received the news of her state. He grabbed his doctor bag and went up to the jail. There was Hazel, out of her god-forsaken mind and hanging like a bat in a belfry. He asked Clyde, "How long has she been like this?"

Clyde said, "Most the night, I suppose. I came in about a half hour ago and tried to get her to come down, but I couldn't. That's why I came to get you."

Dr. Morse looked up to Hazel and said, "Hazel. Get down from there." She just clung to the bars, drooling. "Clyde, please get a chair so I can stand on it." He walked over to, and under Hazel. Clyde slid a chair over to where Hazel was clinging. The doctor hopped up on it, reached through the bars and tried to pry her down. She held fast.

He got down from the chair and said, "I'm going to administer a sedative." He got his doctor bag, opened it, and pulled out a bottle of phenobarbital pills. He mumbled to himself, "This is going to be a little tricky." He crushed two pills and poured the powder into a separate little bottle. He got a little bit of water from Clyde and added it in. He gave the bottle a good shake. He filled a syringe with the liquid, tapped the plunger and little squirt shot out. He got back up on the chair, jabbed the needle into Hazel's hiney, and pushed the plunger. He looked up at Hazel and there was no change. He got down from the chair, rubbed his chin, and said, "I swore that would have done the trick."

Clyde asked, "What's that, doctor?"

"That sedative. I figured that would have calmed her down and put her to sleep. I'll have to try a little more." He filled the syringe about halfway and again got up on the chair. He gave her round number two. He looked up at her and could see that something was happening. Her eyes rolled back in their sockets; she lost her grip on the bars of the cell and plopped down on the cot. Hazel had fallen into a deep sleep. The doctor put the syringe away and grabbed his stethoscope to check Hazel's heart and breathing. He reached through the bars of the cell, probed around for a few seconds, and said, "Just what the doctor ordered."

Clyde said, "Thanks, doctor."

"By thunder, you should get a little peace and quiet around here for a bit. She should be asleep for quite a while." Dr. Morse packed up his bag and left.

And Hazel dreamed…She drifted away, floating above an expansive valley. She was riding a giant lion up in the sky. She saw people in the valley looking up to her from below. They were smiling and waving. The lion drifted down to be among the people. Hazel showed the people that the lion was kind and loving. The people loved the lion. The lion loved them. Everyone was Hazel's friend. Peace and harmony prevailed. The sun was always shining. Every living creature held a youthful appearance. There was food in abundance in the valley. Every bite of every fruit of every tree provided a magnificent taste of euphoria. Each morsel was divine. Water that was sweet as honey flowed from bountiful fountains. No thirst or hunger. A body was always fulfilled.

The people lived freely, and everything was provided to them. The lion pranced through the valley, but grew bored with the people. It demanded the people of the valley to obey it—then to worship it. The people resisted and their love for the lion faded. They now hated the lion. The lion began to prowl through the valley on a mission to seek out and destroy the people. To devour them.

Everyone hated Hazel for bringing the lion to them. She was attacked and beaten with sticks and stones. The ferocious lion let out a great roar and protected Hazel. The lion wreaked havoc throughout the valley and caused the people to become corrupted. To save themselves they worshipped the lion instead of the Creator. Corruption became absolute. The ever-present light dimmed. Clouds formed in the sky and the light was extinguished. Then it started to rain.

No one had felt rain before. At first it was refreshing as the rain fell on their faces. Day after day it rained. The rain became burdensome. People built

101

shelters to hide from the rain. Animals hid in caves and then drowned. Slow and steady the rain persisted. Pools formed and began to flow like rivers. Rivers turned into lakes. It rained for what seemed like a year straight. Hazel couldn't go out to worship the lion anymore. The lion watched as the rain built up. The cry of the people rose up as they cursed at the sky. The people clawed at the water and gasped as they drowned. Their bodies got stuck in the muck beneath the rolling waves. The muck held them tight. The rain covered them and left them in their muddy graves.

Hazel sunk deep into the muck in her dream. She could hear the water sloshing above. She was stuck in the mud, underneath the lion, among the rocks, beneath the waves—in a prison. Darkness enveloped the water-covered earth. Hazel rocked back and forth in her prison in the rocks. The body of the lion decayed around Hazel. Its rib bones formed the bars of a jail cell. She was trapped in the underground jail on the northern end of the vast valley. The salt in the remains of the great lion's body clung between the bones of her jail cell. Back and forth she rocked in her prison, back and forth.

All the while she was locked in her salt-laden prison of bones. Every being was trapped in its own separate prison where they fell after death. Enmeshed with the decayed remains of the body in which they once lived. Their only communication was to hear each other moan through crevices beneath the ground. Water sloshed above. Prisoners groaned below. The earth kept turning. Hazel kept rocking back and forth in her prison. Eons passed. Bone turned to stone.

The waters receded and land reappeared. Some remained buried deep under oceans. Hazel remained buried under dry ground. Only a few people survived. They began multiplying and filling the earth. Hazel rocked back and forth in her prison. Eventually she heard people above her walking about. She would groan on occasion to try and get someone's attention. If only she had another chance she could make things right. She needed someone to come and dig her out. Time rolled on. She rocked back and forth, back, and forth. Her concentration emanated to the people above to come and get some salt. 'Come dig me out.'

Some men answered her beckoned call and began digging in the ground. A young girl would come into the mine to dig with her father and brother. Hazel began concentrating on this young girl. Her thoughts connected to hers. Calling her to dig her out, 'Come dig me out.' The lion pushed Hazel aside.

The lion appeared to the young girl in her dreams. *"I'm a young girl, too. I'll be your friend. Come talk with me. Come dig me out."* The young girl came to dig her out. The lion saw the young girls face. The young girl was Hazel. Hazel was the lion. She tried to warn the young girl that she was no young girl herself. She had become a maniacal monster. She told her young self to run away. But the young girl desired a friend. The monster is no one's friend. Hazel hollered, "Don't let it in! Don't let it in!" The young girl welcomed the lion. The lion leaped out of the rocky prison and into the young girl's body. Hazel and the lion were one. "Don't let it in!"

Peter Ertz met with Constable Clyde Younger at the jail. He had high hopes to interview Hazel for a story in the Visitor. Constable Clyde told him that she was still sleeping off Dr. Morse's sedatives, but he could sit and wait for a spell to see if she would wake up. He told him that his wife Anna would be there at any moment with some food for Hazel. Just as they sat down, Anna came through the door. She walked over and put the food down on the desk.

Anna said, "I see that sleeping beauty is still sleeping."

Clyde and Peter chuckled. Clyde said, "Hello, my darling, you remember Peter Ertz, the reporter for the Visitor." He looked from Anna to Peter.

Peter said, "Nice to see you again, ma'am."

Anna said, "It's nice seeing you."

The three of them sat down at the desk chit-chatting. They were discussing local happenings, Hazel's bizarre behavior and the many days of rain they were experiencing. Then they heard Hazel say, "Don't let it in." She moaned. Then she groaned. She shot up off of the cot and clang to the bars of the cell. She noticed Clyde, Anna, and Peter, then sat back down on her cot. She began rocking back and forth while staring straight ahead at the wall.

Peter stood up, walked over to her, and said, "Hello, Hazel, my name is Peter Ertz. I'm a reporter for the Valley Center Visitor. I would like to hear your side of the story."

Hazel said, "We've got no story to tell," as she sat on her cot rocking back and forth.

"I heard that you like fires." No response from Hazel. She just rocked back and forth and stared at the wall. "Do you like fires?" No reply from Hazel. "You said, 'Don't let it in' when you first woke up. Don't let what in?" Again, nothing from her. She just rocked back and forth.

Hazel was listening to the rain hitting the roof. The raindrops were talking to her. Digging into her mind. The Witch was telling her to block it out. '*Don't listen to them.*' She heard the raindrops saying to her, "God sends the rain. He has sent us. Listen, Hazel, hear the rain. God wants you to tell him what you did. Hear the rain. Hear it speak. It says, tell him what you did— tell him what you did." She sat staring at the wall rocking back and forth, back, and forth.

The Witch fought back. '*The raindrops say nothing. They know nothing. No one knows what we did. Don't tell them anything.*'

Peter had given up. He walked back over to grab his raincoat and slipped it on. He said his goodbyes to Constable Clyde and Anna then made his way to the door. He stopped as he grabbed the doorknob. He turned back and said, "Oh well."

Hazel heard the rain speaking to her, "Pitter patter water splatter. The water in the well will start to swell. It will cover you unless you tell."

Hazel shrieked aloud in a frantic, "The well. The well!"

The Witch argued back, '*No, don't tell them.*'

Hazel went on, "The well. The well. We put a potion in the well."

The Witch screamed within Hazel, '*Nooooo! Don't tell! Don't say anything about the well!*'

Peter ripped out his pencil and pad and began writing as he moved towards Hazel, sitting in her cell. He stood there soaking in her every word as she continued spewing forth her discussion with herself.

"We put potions in the breads, potions in the chicken soup. Potions here. Potions there. Potions everywhere." "*Why do you say that.*" "Why not, it's true." "*We want them all dead. We want you dead. We want all to die.*" A splinter took place between The Witch and Hazel. Then came the confession of Hazel Dill.

"Oh, I did it, I did it, oh God, yes I did it. The devil told me to do it. I love funerals. I love having sad people around." She admitted that she had first put poison in the breads that she fed her husband. Then she made more of her special breads and took them to her mother's house on Easter Sunday. It wasn't the poison that Fred had purchased a long time ago. That was used for rats, and it was long gone. She learned how to make her own potions from brake fern and other plants that she found around The Valley. She then spiked her mother's chicken soup with it. She intended to kill her sister, brother in-

104

law and their five children, but the family dog tripped her, and she spilled the rest of the soup. After her mother's death, she threw a potion into the Goehring's well. She put potion in their coffee. And potion in breads that she left on their table. Then she put some in the chicken soup that she took to them the next day. While she was there, she drew some water from the well for the Goehring household. She laced the water bucket with more potion.

She mentioned a dream she had of a lion that tricked her. It was kind at first, but turned wicked. In her dream, she introduced the lion to the people of The Valley, and they all hated her for bringing the lion to them. Everybody in that god-forsaken town made fun of her. She put up with their ridicule her whole life. Well, not anymore. She showed them. She earned their respect.

Peter, Constable Clyde, and Anna listened in amazement. There were three witnesses to Hazel's confession, and Peter wrote down her every word. He kept up with the whole story in the fastest pace that he had ever written in his life. He didn't miss a beat. He looked up and saw Hazel sitting on her cot, rocking back and forth, staring at the wall. He glanced over to Clyde and Anna and said, "Somebody lit a match under her, she was on fire."

"Fire. I love fire. I love to watch the flames lick the sky," Hazel said with her face all aglow. She looked up with a gleam in her eyes. "I lit them all; the Schmidt's, the Welks', the Braun's, the Hostetter's, Dr. Morse's. I wish I could've burned down the whole miserable town."

Peter jotted that down. He gave a look of surprise towards the Youngers and asked, "Is there anything else you'd like to say? I heard you mention that you like funerals."

"I love funerals. It's such a comfort to be around sad people. There weren't enough funerals, so I made more." Peter said her eyes were glowing like dark orange flames within rolling black smoke. The fire was collapsing in on itself and descending into Hazel.

Peter blinked and the fire was gone. He looked into her eyes to see what that was. A cold, blank stare was returned to him. "Your eyes. What was that? Hazel, what was that?" No more talking, just staring and rocking. He said, "Very good. This is gold."

He left the jail and headed straight to his office, down and across the street, to hammer out his story for the next day. On the way—it stopped raining. The headline in The Valley Center Visitor the next day read: The Witch of Valley Center Confesses! The story went on about Hazel concocting potions to put in her special breads, chicken soup, and in the well. The story also mentioned her admitting to lighting fires, and her passion for funerals.

A mental competency test was ordered for Hazel to be tested to see if she was sane. If found to be sane, she would stand trial. The prosecution was awaiting tests of the well water samples, powder residue, and autopsy report to come in. The talk about town was that there could be no way in the world that Hazel would be declared sane and competent to stand trial. She would be sent to a mental institution and get away with her evil deeds. There was no way the town folk were going to let that happen. They decided to take things into their own hands.

Chapter 12

The Crowd Grows Restless

From Interviews of Clyde Younger, Johnny Muller, Karl Seidel, Roger Graf, and Otto Sauer

The Witch had sunk into the depths of Hazel to hide. It had given up all hope of being free from custody ever again to wreak havoc on the people of The Valley from within Hazel. It was figuring out the next move to make. The Witch didn't know if it would be forced to join Hazel with her remains when she died, or if it would be sent back to its old prison in its original remains. At least it would have some company if it were with Hazel's. The Witch lay in wait conjuring up a scheme, hoping that maybe—just maybe—it could escape from Hazel and be freed from either prison. It lay dormant holding out hope for the latter. Hazel was on her own. The Witch had hung her out to dry. There she sat, rocking back and forth. They were like two bitter enemies who were once best friends. Facing away from each other. Neither one wanting to be near the other. Hazel was willing to do whatever it took to be rid of The Witch. Hazel was prepared to die.

Could you imagine being in Hazel's shoes? Not that you would do what she had done, but to be put on trial for anything in a community where everyone knew you. Where everyone held a predetermined opinion that you were guilty. How could a jury of peers be chosen for Hazel? She had no peers. No one was like her. No one liked her. The verdict was already in, and she was found lacking. Lacking in mental capacity—lacking in morals—lacking in common decency—lacking in common sense—and most of all—lacking in innocence. When all the evidence and all the fingers in the whole community are pointing at you, what kind of defense could be raised for you? Everyone in The Valley knew of her misdeeds, and they had had enough of her devious machinations. It was long past due to be rid of this menace to society—The Witch of The Valley.

The town was abuzz with excited anticipation outside of the Town Hall of Valley Center. Hazel's attorney, Roger Graf, was upstairs in the jail talking with her. The townspeople were shuffling about outside in the streets. They were talking and gossiping about the latest news on the case that everyone had read about in the Visitor. The story went on about Prosecutor Whitman preparing the case of Valley Center versus Hazel Dill, with a list of witnesses that were lined up against her, Hazel's confession, and a mention of potions that she had conjured up. Emotions were running high out on the street.

Roger Graf was appointed by the court to defend Hazel. He was a young up and coming attorney who hoped to use her case to make a name for himself. He sat with Hazel in her cell as Constable Clyde waited at his desk, reading the Visitor. Roger told her that the prosecution had three witnesses to her confession that were going to testify against her in court. She sat on her cot rocking back and forth staring at the wall. She said, "Never did no such thing." As she stared straight ahead and continued to rock back and forth.

The defense was waiting for the results of the samples from the toxicology lab to come in, along with the finding from the mental competency tests. From what Roger Graf had seen, he would plead insanity on Hazel's behalf. She sat on the cot rocking back and forth.

He broke the news to Hazel that her sister Elsa had a mental breakdown. She was set to be the only witness in Hazel's defense. She and Otto had visited the cemetery where her mother, aunt, and uncle were buried. Elsa collapsed on her mother's grave. When she came around, she could not be consoled. She had come to the realization of the diabolical deeds that Hazel had done. Elsa was taken to a psychiatric hospital. Hazel stared straight ahead, unmoved by the news.

Roger told Hazel that their only hope was for her to be found insane. Then she would be sentenced to a mental reformatory for treatment. Again, he got no response from her. The sun was going down and he wanted to get home to get some rest. He left the jail and went home.

Clyde sat with Hazel in the jail on the evening of Thursday, June 12th in 1924. The crowd of revenge-minded town folk had moved to the back lot of the Town Hall below. The sun had set. People started lighting torches around the perimeter of the outer area in the back. The crowd wanted blood. An eye for an eye, a tooth for a tooth, a life for a life. Every person in The Valley was culpable in the event. There were those who did the dirty deed; those who cheered it on; and those who did nothing to stop it.

Someone in the crowd yelled, "What if all of our wells were poisoned?"

"She was on all of our properties," called out another.

Chants erupted, "Kill the witch! Kill the witch!"

"She can't get away with this."

"Kill the witch! Kill the witch!"

A secret court was in session in the back room of the Town Hall. It resembled a Star Chamber proceeding. They remained in there for hours. The easy decision—to get rid of Hazel—was made early on in the proceedings. The secret session was called by the superstitious leaders of the vigilantes in the posse that arrested Hazel.

The term, "Star Chamber," received its name from the room in which it met in Westminster Palace—a room in which stars were painted on the ceiling. The Star Chamber was originally established to ensure the fair enforcement of laws against socially and politically prominent people deemed so powerful that ordinary courts might hesitate to convict them of their crimes. However, it became synonymous with social and political oppression through the arbitrary use and abuse of the power it wielded. The first depicted use that I could find of the term was in the year 1398.

For centuries, The Star Chamber has symbolized disregard of basic individual rights. It had become synonymous with misuse and abuse of power. The term refers, in a derogatory manner, to any secret or closed meeting held by a judicial or executive body, or to a court proceeding that seems grossly unfair, or that is used to persecute an individual.

I bring this up because I don't know what to call the secret session that was wielded against Hazel; Star Chamber, Kangaroo Court, Vigilante Justice, whatever name you want to call it, it was a sham. Four prominent members of the Valley Center Town Council took it upon themselves to delve out their perceived justice. No trial, no due process rights. They decided what was right for the people of Valley Center.

Two of the four members were Old John Muller, and Art Gunther. Their family burial plots are side by side at Hollow Hill Cemetery. They were afraid of Hazel escaping her grave, and coming back to terrorize The Valley. They let their superstitions get the best of them when they came up with a plan to rid themselves of The Witch. They dispersed from the meeting and blended in with the crowd.

Old John moved to the center of the crowd in the back of the Town Hall. He called out, "Ladies and gentlemen. Justice will be served. You can rest assured that the worry of further mysterious fires is over. No more wells will be poisoned. We have the witch locked up. Her trial will be soon, very soon. It's been a long day. Let's put these torches out and go home to get some rest." Art Gunther, and the rest of the vigilantes that brought Hazel in, moved through the crowd nodding their heads in agreement, corralling the crowd away from the back lot.

Clyde looked on in amazement from the window of the second floor jail as the crowd begrudgingly dispersed. He locked the door, came down the stairs and passed the back lot on his way home for the night. Johnny Muller and the Ungrich brothers were snuffing out the torches one by one.

When Clyde arrived at home he was greeted at the door by Anna. She said, "I'm so glad you're home. I was afraid something was going to happen to you with that angry mob." She hugged Clyde.

"Yep. I thought so, too. It's good to be home." He hugged her tight and smiled.

They went to the living room and looked out the window at the back of the Town Hall. Anna said, "All is quiet, now." She closed the curtain.

Clyde said, "But for how long, no one knows." They sat together on the sofa.

Anna said, "I fear for the very soul of Valley Center." Clyde put his hand on her knee. He felt the same thing. "Hazel told me about this crazy dream she had when I took her supper to her. Remember her saying, 'Don't let it in' when she woke up?," she asked.

"Yeah. Not now, dear. You can tell me all about it in the morning. Right now, let's pray together for the people of the town, then go the bed and get some sleep." And they did just that.

At around three o'clock in the morning of Friday, June 13th, the Ungrich brothers sneaked upstairs to the second-floor jail. They unlocked the door with a key.

Ed grabbed the key to the jail cell from Clyde's desk. He met his brother Harry at Hazel's cell where she sat on the cot rocking back and forth. Ed

110

unlocked the cell door. They both rushed in and took hold of her and tied her hands behind her back. Hazel sat on the cot rocking back and forth as if nothing had happened.

There is an extended lifting beam above the stone lintel of the back door of the second floor jail. It juts out to the north above and over the door. It has a hook bolted into it that was used to attach a pulley onto it. A rope was pulled through the pulley and used to hoist things up to the second floor, like the jail cells for instance. Harry grabbed the rope for pulling up supplies. He tied a noose at its end. Then he secured the other end of the rope to the nearest bar of the jail cell. He cracked open the second-floor door to make sure the coast was clear.

He went back inside and into the cell with Ed. They stood on each side of Hazel and lifted her by the elbows. She stood as if by command. They walked her to the upper door and pushed the door open all the way. Harry put the noose around Hazel's neck and pulled it taught. She didn't even blink. Ed asked her, "Any last words, witch?"

Hazel just stood in the doorway, silent. The Witch laid buried deep within her. They pushed her forward. Her body fell, listing ever so slightly to one side for about six feet, and then—Crack. Her fall ended abruptly as the rope pulled tight and her neck snapped. Out of Hazel a voice called out, *Revenge shall be mine!*" A gurgling sound could be heard emanating from Hazel as she swung back and forth, her feet dangling two feet off the ground. Her body twitched as she fought for air. The gurgling ceased. A strong gust of wind blew over the vigilantes' heads that made their hair stand on end. Her body dangled, motionless, swinging gently back and forth, back, and forth. The wind blew back towards the building as the vigilantes left her and skedaddled.

Early in the morning Clyde Younger left his home for his daily routine of guarding a prisoner. As he approached the back of the Town Hall he saw Hazel hanging motionless, two feet off the ground, from a rope. Her contorted face, etched in his memory forever, held an evil grimace. Dried blood was on her cheeks where it had oozed out of her bulged eyes and ran down her face like tears. He went to the back of the general store and got Dr. Morse.

Dr. Morse pronounced that Hazel Dill—The Witch of The Valley—was dead. He sent word to the town undertaker, Karl Seidel, of Seidel and Sons Funeral Home, to come and get Hazel.

Karl Seidel and his sons came into town with their horse drawn hearse. They met Dr. Morse and Constable Clyde at the back of the Town Hall. Karl said, "Morning, Clyde. Morning, Dr. Morse. Clyde, how about you going up there and cutting the rope while we hold onto her." His sons set a coffin on the ground next to Hazel.

Clyde said, "Good morning, Karl. I'll head up."

Dr. Morse said, "Good morning fellas. Pretty bad way to start the day." He shook his head as he stared at Hazel hanging there.

"I've seen worse," Karl stated matter-of-factly. The doctor looked at him puzzled, but didn't dare to ask.

The Seidel's got in position on either side of Hazel. Clyde looked down from the upstairs door. Karl called up, "We'll hold onto her, and you cut the rope." They grabbed ahold of Hazel. Clyde snatched the rope and cut it. The rope coiled like a snake as it fell to the ground. The Seidels laid Hazel in the coffin. Clyde closed the upstairs door and came downstairs. Karl Seidel and his sons removed the noose that was around Hazel's neck and tucked her in the coffin. Then one of his sons picked up the rope, wound it up all neat and tidy, and set it on the ground beside the coffin.

Karl and his sons placed the lid on the coffin, picked it up and slid it onto the floor of the hearse. His sons hopped on and got in their seats. Karl said, "We'll take her to the funeral home and see what the family wants to do from there. Probably just have a graveside service is my bet."

Clyde said, "I'll have her grave ready for you later today."

"Thanks. I'll see you there." Karl climbed aboard the hearse. He called out, "Yaw," as he snapped the lines, and the two-horse team began to move.

Dr. Morse and Clyde walked back to the corner following the hearse and watched as the wagon left to the east out of town. It disappeared into the shadows of the covered bridge. Then it reappeared on the other side growing smaller and smaller as the Seidels took Hazel up the hill.

Dr. Morse followed after the hearse and went back to his makeshift office in the back of the general store. Clyde turned and walked home. As he passed the back of the Town Hall he gave a glance to the empty space behind the Town Hall where not long before Hazel had been hanging. He felt that he had failed in his duty as constable. He wondered how he didn't hear this happen. Feeling ashamed and empty, he wished things were done in a proper manner.

112

The sequence of events were vigorously debated by the vigilantes. People protect themselves from the unknown—the supernatural if you will. To admit that there exists a supernatural realm would mean to admit we are not alone—that there are other dimensions—there is a Creator—and everyone will be held accountable for all deeds done in their lives.

To keep things in their own little worlds all neat and tidy, everything must have an explanation. This is reality and there is nothing else. Anyone who believes in that supernatural stuff is either a nutcase, or a witch—just like Hazel—who was both. A few of the vigilantes did believe in the supernatural.

They all agreed that Hazel was standing in the upstairs doorway with the noose around her neck. Then Hazel was asked if she had any final words to say.

The prevailing opinion was that Hazel called out, '*Revenge shall be mine*' before Ed and Harry pushed her out the door. The second most popular opinion was that she said nothing when asked, but her final words came out as she fell. Old John Muller, Johnny Muller, and Art Gunther held the opinion of what really took place. They knew what they saw and heard. The real sequence was, Hazel remained silent, she was pushed out the door, she fell, listed slightly to one side, her neck snapped as she stopped suddenly, and then a voice called out from her, '*Revenge shall be mine.*' Then a sudden burst of wind rushed out over them, that they all physically felt, that caused their hair to move.

The next day Karl Seidel and his sons delivered Hazel to her gravesite, next to her husband Fred, in Hollow Hill Cemetery. Just as he had predicted, Hazel's family requested a graveside service. Truth be told, they wanted nothing to do with any service for her. The only people in attendance were the Seidels, Clyde Younger, and Pastor Thomas, the preacher of Valley Center Christian Church.

The Seidel's removed the black drape that covered the coffin. They dragged the coffin off the wagon and carried it over next to the grave that Clyde had dug. The coffin was put down on top of two straps they had laid there.

Karl and one of his sons grabbed the straps on one side and his other two sons grabbed the straps on the other side. The four of them lifted the coffin, stepped towards the grave, and just like clockwork they lowered the coffin into the ground. Karl and his son let go of the straps on their side and the other two sons pulled the straps out.

The preacher said a few words over the earthly remains of Hazel Dill.

Karl reached down and grabbed a handful of dirt. He said, "I always throw in the first handful." He tossed the dirt onto the coffin, "Ashes to ashes, dust to dust." He and his sons got on the family hearse and left the cemetery.

The preacher went home.

Clyde buried Hazel.

The group of vigilantes that were members of the posse that brought Hazel in, were going to make extra certain that The Witch of The Valley would be laid to rest for good.

The Gunther family has quite a unique marker for their burial plots at Hollow Hill Cemetery. The marker is a one-ton black granite marble ball that sits on a pedestal. Most family plots have an obelisk or an animal as a marker, the Gunther family wanted something different. One of the coats of arms for the Germanic Gunther family had two circles that looked like the letter O on a black backdrop. Art Gunther's dad, Heinrich, came up with this idea that if you were looking down from heaven the O would look like a little black marble.

Art commissioned Cleveland Marble Works to get the family marker made. When Clyde left the cemetery after burying Hazel, Art, the Ungrich brothers, and Richard Shroder went to work on laying the foundation for the pedestal of the marker. What they did was dig a four-foot square hole—ten feet—straight down. Then they covered the hole with planks.

That night, the vigilantes went to work to finish their plan. Old John and Johnny took Old John's wagon to the cemetery. They parked the wagon at Hazel's grave where they met the Ungrich brothers, who were there waiting. Johnny hopped off the wagon and went to the back of it. He reached under the hay and felt around. The two shovels clanged together as Johnny retrieved them from their hiding spot. The team worked fast taking turns shoveling down to Hazel's coffin.

Harry and Ed climbed down into the grave and pried off the lid from the coffin. They hoisted up Hazel to Old John and Johnny and they slid her on the ground next to the grave. Harry tapped the lid back on and crawled out of the grave. Old John and Johnny carried Hazel to the wagon and slid her onto it, while the Ungrich brothers speedily shoveled dirt onto the empty coffin, burying it. They all cleaned up the site to get it as close as possible to the way they found it. Then they all four climbed on the wagon and went over to the Gunther family plot.

While Hazel was being dug up out of her grave, Art, Richard, and James were busy getting things ready at the Gunther family plot. They had pulled the planks off of the hole that was dug earlier that day. A homemade coffin had been fashioned out of some old crates by Richard and James. It was sitting on the ground on one side of the hole waiting for its occupant. On the other side of the hole were jugs of water, and a tub with dry cement, sand, and stone in it that they had mixed to pour the base of the Gunther family marker.

They heard the rest of the vigilantes pulling up on Old John's wagon. Old John looked over and said, "It looks like you fellas are ready for us." He got off the wagon and walked over to the hole. Looking down and inspecting it, he said, "That'll do. Johnny and Art, bring the witch over here."

Johnny and Art slid Hazel off the wagon and brought her over to the coffin. Ed and Harry helped them lower her in it. Richard and James placed the lid on the coffin and nailed it shut. Four of them tipped her up on end. Old John said, "Now wrap this rope around the coffin and we'll lower her down nice and slow, till we feel a little slack." They lowered her down, headfirst, into the hole. They couldn't see in the hole, but they knew the foot of the coffin had to be about four feet beneath ground level.

Old John said, "Art, you hold the rope up to keep it centered. Johnny, you hold a stick down on that side and I'll get one on this side. Rich, you shovel dirt in on this side." He pointed to the north. "James, you shovel in dirt on that side." He pointed to the south. "Ed and Harry, you fellas shovel in the dirt on the other sides. We'll hold it steady. Let's make short work of this."

They shoveled in the dirt. After about twenty shovel fulls each, Old John said, "Hold on fellas." He pulled out his stick. Johnny pulled out his stick. "That's got it. Johnny, cut the rope." Johnny reached down as far as he could, cut the rope, and Art pulled it out. The dirt was shoveled in till the hole was filled to about three feet below the surface. Ed and Harry got busy pouring water in the tub and mixing up the cement. Richard and James tamped down the dirt, added more dirt and tamped it down, to make a solid base.

A square form was placed on top of the hole and the concrete mixture was shoveled into it. The base for the pedestal was poured for the Gunther family marker. They stacked bricks around the foundation and set the planks down on them, covering it up. They gathered up their tools and left the cemetery.

The leaders of the superstitious vigilantes, Old John Muller and Art Gunther, felt the need for this endeavor. Valley Center will be protected from the witch ever escaping the grave and coming back to haunt and harass the citizenry ever again. The new one-ton Gunther family marker will keep the witch secured beneath it in the ground.

Unbeknownst to them, their entire plan focused on the wrong entity. They bound the empty vessel that The Witch had used, while the real Witch of The Valley was on the loose and seeking revenge.

Chapter 13

A New Day Dawns

From Interviews of Clyde Younger, Johnny Muller, Jake Muller, Ben Younger, Judge Giles, and Dr. Morse

The worst thing that could have been done was to hold Hazel's execution in Valley Center, thus releasing The Witch from the corpse of Hazel Dill. She should have had her day in court. Then she would have been shipped off to the Mansfield Reformatory for Women to either be locked up in the insane asylum, sit on death row and await execution, or serve out a life sentence. At least then the Witch may have taken up a home down there, where its reach would be far less significant.

Though The Witch holds locality, it had freed itself from its underground prison through the possession of Hazel. Beneath the ground, The Witch was inhibited by the earth and rocks from reaching out very far. When The Witch left Hazel it entered into the Valley Center Town Hall. And now, unconstrained by the rocky ground, or Hazel's body, it could reach out further.

The sun came up the next morning in Valley Center like any other day. No one wanted to talk about the happenings of the previous day. Conversations were short and sweet. Eye contact with others was minimal, at best. Sheriff Yoder made a brief investigation and quickly closed the case. No one would point the finger at anyone else. No one was ever held accountable for what the community had done to Hazel Dill.

It was time to move on, get back to normal. Everyone just wanted to forget about what had happened. The whole thing was swept under the rug, but whatever gets swept under a rug is still there. The town folk may have been wanting to forget everything, but The Witch wasn't about to let them. It rained that entire day.

I have always loved to watch the rain, especially thunderstorms at night, when lightning flashes would turn darkness into daylight for a hurried moment. When I was a boy, we had a front porch that was a great place to watch storms from. There was a wooden bench swing that hung by chains from hooks in the porch ceiling. Our dog, Sam, would love to swing on it. He didn't need anyone to be on it to enjoy it with him; he would get a running start and leap up on it, sit down and swing away, till it coasted to a stop. Then he would jump down, run back, and do it again. You could see the back of the Town Hall when you were sitting on the swing. And it was a great place to watch the rain and lightning from when it stormed.

This one nasty storm came rolling in. I went out on the porch with Sam to watch it. It started out like a normal late summer evening thunderstorm, but turned ugly in a hurry. Pulsating wind was pushing sheets of rain sideways. Puffs of cool misty rain were hitting us on the porch swing. A lightning flash and immediate BOOM of thunder rocked Valley Center.

Sam jumped off the swing, my mom opened the front door to let him in and told me to get in the house. I didn't want to, but I reluctantly followed Sam into the house. And boy was I glad I did. A few minutes later the wind turned violent. I was looking out the front window onto the porch, and saw the swing being thrashed and twisted. The sideways rain was drenching the entire porch. Massive gusts of wind pushed through layers of sideways rain, accompanied by continuous lightning strikes with massive blasts of thunder, as it swept across The Valley. It persisted like that for over an hour before calming down.

I looked out my upstairs bedroom window before I went to bed and watched the storm moving away. I went to sleep feeling safe from the storm. Another storm raged while I was sleeping. Back then, the house could've fallen all around me, and it wouldn't wake me up. After I had children of my own, if I hear a flea fart from afar it wakes me up in an instant.

I opened my eyes and saw the morning sun was lighting my room. I got out of bed, looked out my window and saw the shining sun. I looked down and there was my favorite climbing tree laying on the ground. It had gotten struck by lightning and blown down by the strong winds while I slept.

I hit the john, brushed my teeth, got dressed and went outside. I went over to my tree, crawled under the branches to the main trunk and sat down on it. I can smell the wet maple leaves and bark of the tree right now, just thinking about it. There was a gentle breeze blowing that fluttered the leaves. They looked to still be alive. I looked up through the leaves and saw the golden light of the sun streaking down through them. Birds were chirping, it was so peaceful. I was thinking that twenty-four hours ago I was in this same spot in the tree, but up in the air about twenty feet behind me. What a difference a day makes.

My dad and some other men from town were going around with chainsaws and cutting up the downed trees. There were quite a few of them, as I recall. They got to our house and made quick work of my favorite tree. My dad had me drag the small branches to the back of our lot where I tossed them on the burn pile. Then he had me haul the cut pieces and stack them behind the shed. I grabbed a rake and cleaned up the sawdust, leaves and twigs and put them on the burn pile. And just like that, it was as if nothing had happened, the town was back to normal, except for the missing trees.

There was no normal for a very long time in Valley Center after what had happened with Hazel. Like the day after the storm when I was a boy, the town folk got busy putting the world back on its axis after the storm named Hazel had blown through.

A huge, collective sigh of relief was expelled throughout The Valley. The town folk had rid themselves of a witch, or so they thought. They didn't realize that the person they rid themselves of was not The Witch. And for a brief time after, just like in Salem, people were paranoid that there could be other witches among them.

There were a few suspected cases, but no one else was ever formally accused of witchcraft. Mainly jealous spats where someone was trying to even a score, or they just didn't like someone because they were different. The same kind of thing that still happens today.

The 4th of July celebration came and went. The people of Valley Center had now considered The Witch incident to be a thing of the past. As time rolled on it was clear that the arsonist was Hazel. The mysterious fires came to a sudden end after her apprehension. But other mystifying occurrences persisted.

Have you ever had a strange thought enter your mind and you wonder, *'Where did that come from? I wasn't thinking about that. I don't think things like that.'* It's like the cartoon with an angel on one shoulder and the devil on the other. The devil whispers for you to do something wrong, and the angel whispers for you to do what's right.

A lot of people around The Valley started getting evil thoughts that popped into their heads out of the blue. The Witch was busy at work coaxing people to hurt themselves and others. Some people reported to have seen the apparition of Hazel Dill appear before them in their rooms. Others said a young girl would appear to them in their dreams. One woman said, "She said things like, *'Come into the woods and set things in motion, come into the woods and we'll make a potion.'*"

Another woman claimed of the apparition of Hazel, "She was wanting me to kill for her. She said, *'We will meet in the woods under cover of darkness. We will make little dolls in our enemies' likeness. We poke and we prod, and we thrash them around. Tear them apart and drive them into the ground.'*"

The only thing The Witch was concerned with was death and destruction. It lusted for blood, and feasted on fear.

There were several reports of earthquakes from different town folk in and around The Valley. My grandfather claimed that one of the earthquakes moved the big rock he had at the corner of his property on Maple Street. He kept the rock there to keep wagons and trucks from cutting ruts in his yard as they navigated the corner when making the turn. He claimed that after one of the quakes the rock had slid up the street, almost to the Town Hall.

Maple Street starts at Center Street where the Town Hall is located on the corner. It runs past our old house at the corner of School Street and continues down to a dead end. In those days it used to keep going to the river, which it ran alongside of for about another quarter of a mile. Then it would fork into West River Road where they intersected on the bottom of the hill that opens up to Gunther's Flats to the north. The path that ran along the river that the vigilantes chased down Hazel on was below the old Maple Street. The river bends around to the east at the little bereft bridge. The path along the river came up and ran alongside Maple Street into Valley Center proper at the bend. That's where Sheriff Yoder first saw Hazel Dill when Johnny and the rest of the posse brought her in.

It had rained pretty good for quite a few days, and now the sun was shining. As my grandpa would say, "You've got to make hay when the sun shines." Old John and Johnny had been delivering hay all day. They both had barns with hay mows on their respective farms, and Johnny was using his own wagon now. He followed Old John on their deliveries who still used his old wagon, the one they brought Hazel in on. It made hauling hay a whole lot more efficient with the two wagons than how they used to do deliveries with just one.

After a long day, they decided to stop at the Salty Dog Saloon to knock back the dust. Johnny got to bragging about how him and Old John had caught The Witch. He told his usual story with all the highlights about smoking her out and chasing her down. Guys were buying them round after round of beers. They finally had their fill and left the saloon. They climbed on their wagons and headed for their homes.

Old John went out first and Johnny followed behind. They turned down Maple Street and went straight through towards the river to connect with West River Road. When they got alongside the river Johnny slowed down and was reflecting on how just a short time ago they were coming the other way, up and over the bank from the path below. He watched as Old John crossed the little bridge and started around the curve along the river as he made his way toward Gunther's Flats.

As Johnny started for the bridge, the ground began to shake. His horse reared up on its hind legs and pawed its hooves at the air. The horse landed back down and began snorting and digging its hooves into the rumbling ground. The side of the hill had broken loose at the top, near West River Road. Johnny looked on as the hill came slipping down in slow motion, taking trees, rocks, Maple Street, Old John, his wagon, and his horse with it—into the river.

Johnny called out to his dad.

No response.

He got off his wagon and ran to the bridge. From about twenty feet past the bridge and beyond, all of Maple Street was no more. The whole side of the hill was now in Rocky River—and Old John was under it. Johnny climbed down the riverbank and onto the path where it abruptly ended. He waded into the river, through it, and to the other side. He yelled for Old John, but he was nowhere to be seen. The river started to reroute itself around the fallen debris.

Johnny ran to his wagon and hightailed it back to the saloon. He busted through the door and called out for everyone to come help him dig out Old John. The saloon cleared and the guys headed to the little bridge on Maple Street.

It took two days for the men of the town to clear the side of the hill off of Old John. He, his horse, and his wagon were stuck in the muck of the former hill in the river bottom. Old John's mouth, nose, and lungs were packed with mud.

Old John Muller was laid to rest in Hollow Hill Cemetery on July 13th, 1924. His headstone is at the north cardinal point of a square of headstones that surround the Gunther family marker; beneath which the superstitious vigilantes placed the body of Hazel Dill.

Art Gunther walked up to Johnny at Old John's funeral. He placed his hand on his shoulder and said, "Even though I'm closer to his age than yours, Old John was like a father to me, Johnny. I'll always be grateful for him and all he has done for me."

Johnny said, "Thanks, Art. It means a lot to me. He really liked you; you know. Heck, you're like a big brother to me. I don't know what I'm going to do without him." He held his head down. If he were to look Art in the eyes he would cry. And he wasn't about to let anybody see him cry.

Art said, "I've got my wheat field to cut down. We're going to have a threshing party at my place, day after tomorrow. Why don't you come over and help us thresh the wheat and bale up the straw? I'll give you a wagon load. It'll be good for ya, take your mind off things."

Johnny said, "Sounds good. I'll be over, day after tomorrow."

Art said, "Great. See you then." Art left and went back to his farm.

He had an old Case fifty horsepower steam tractor that his dad handed down to him. It was a brute. The Gunthers had been threshing barley, oats, and wheat by hand with all the other farmers of Valley Center since he was still wet behind the ears. Once Art's dad bought that tractor, it made all the difference in the world. The flywheel would churn and make a whirring sound that could be heard for miles around. You feed it wood, coal, and water, and in turn, it gives you massive force. It would go chugging and steaming away, clanking along.

He and his dad used to put chains around large stumps and that tractor would pull them out like they were clinging to warm butter. No stump could stump it. They plowed their fields with it and some neighbors' fields, too. There was nothing like that powerful steam tractor. He had already used his tractor to help thresh for all but two of the farms that had wheat in The Valley. He figured with the rest of this day, and the next, he could finish up threshing the wheat on those remaining farms. He would at long last be ready for a threshing party on his own farm the following day.

On the day that Johnny was going to be at the farm for the threshing party, Art had trouble sleeping. He got out of bed early that morning and went out to get things ready before everyone arrived. It was still dark out, but he could get that tractor ready blindfolded. He oiled up the machine, filled it with water to the proper level, tossed some wood and coal into the furnace box, and lit it up. He let the temperature build up till it was making steam.

His plan was to have everything in place by the time folks started arriving. The only thing left to do was move the tractor out of the barn, drive it to the threshing machine and hook it up. He was stoking the fire and watching the sun rise. The boiler began steaming. Art hopped on the tractor and pulled the chain on the steam whistle. The melodic tune wailed away. It was going to be a wonderful day.

He put the tractor in gear, and it lunged forward. He wasn't paying close attention, maybe he was looking at the sunrise instead of where he was going. As it lunged forward the tractor struck a main support post for the barn. The collision caused the water in the boiler to slosh forward, then back, exposing some of the firetubes to the intense heat within the boiler. Some tubes in the boiler failed. There was a catastrophic explosion as the water surrounding the firetubes flashed to steam.

Water expands one thousand seven hundred times its size when it turns to steam. The steam had nowhere to go but out, blowing through the steel walls of the boiler. The explosion was heard five miles away. Bits of the tractor shot everywhere. The top of the boiler tore open and shot shrapnel through the roof of the barn. Art was thrown twenty feet where his body smacked against the side of the barn. He stuck to it like a wet blanket and slid down the wall to the barn floor. His wife and son came running out and found him lying in a pool of his own blood.

His wife said that Art mumbled something about a ditch as he died. There was a little dip in the barn floor next to the tractor, but that could have been from the explosion.

I say that he mumbled something about The Witch before he died.

Arthur Gunther was laid to rest in his families plot at Hollow Hill Cemetery on July 16th, 1924. His headstone is at the south cardinal point of the square that surrounds the family marker.

Later that summer, in August, came the Valley Center Fair. Every year a parade is held to kick off the event. Farmers dress up their tractors like farm animals. Town folk decorate hay wagons as floats that are pulled by tractors. Young men and women ride horses. The fire department was showing off the brand-spanking-new 1924 LaFrance Model 12 fire engine the township had purchased. And proudly leading the parade was Sheriff Yoder in his Model T. Riding along with him was Judge Giles.

They were smiling and waving at the happy crowd, tossing candy to children. The parade ended behind the Town Hall where the participants parked. Sheriff Yoder and Judge Giles walked around the building and up the stairs to the stage that is always set up at the front of the Town Hall. The crowd clapped and cheered as the sheriff took to the microphone.

"Ladies and gentlemen, boys and girls, welcome to the fourth annual Valley Center Fair." The crowd cheered, the town band played The Star Spangled Banner, and the flag was raised.

Judge Giles spoke, "It is with great honor that my colleague and I were invited to participate in this fine event." He nodded and waved to the crowd.

He and the sheriff handed out ribbons of blue, red, and white to the participants of the parade. Then, with blindfolds on, they judged the pies. This was always quite the contest with the local ladies. Local bragging rights for the next year were at stake. Most of the women were humble and accepted the blue ribbon with grace. And they all secretly hoped that the winner wouldn't be Agnes Murry, the bombastic braggart. She would rub that ribbon in their faces at every chance she could get if she won it.

Luckily for the ladies the judge and sheriff picked Henrietta Stout's cherry pie as the winner. She was about the nicest person in The Valley. The judge and sheriff thanked the crowd and received another big cheer as they left the stage. They mingled with the crowd for a while, then got back in the Model T and headed home to Medina.

Taking a right on River Road after traveling through the covered bridge, the sheriff said, "You know, judge, I could live in that town." He smiled.

"I can picture that, Luke. It is a nice little town. However, there's something off about it, though. I can't quite work it out. It's quirky. Anyway, I prefer a bigger town. I like living right where I'm at in Medina." The judge looked forward to getting home to his law library for some reading.

As you leave town on River Road you climb a small hill. After about a mile the road veers to the right to a bridge that crosses Rocky River. The sheriff maneuvered the Model T around the curve towards the bridge. He glanced to the judge and said, "I think I'm going to live in Valley Center." The judge was looking at him, smiling.

As the sheriff's gaze turned back to the road, a thick patch of fog rose up from under the bridge. The judge said that he saw out of the corner of his eye what appeared to be a white wolf, but it had to be just the fog. Sheriff Yoder swerved to the right to miss it, then yanked the wheel to the left. Something in the front end must have broken because the car didn't move back to the left. The sheriff called out, "Hang on," as he turned the wheel, but the car went straight. They missed the bridge and plunged nose first off of the cliff and forty feet straight down to the river.

The Model T came to an abrupt stop as it stuffed between two big rocks. The force of the impact sent Judge Giles flying out of the passenger door, across the river, and onto the west bank. Both of his femurs and both of his hips were broken. He couldn't move, but he was conscious, and alive.

He looked back to the Model T where he saw the sheriff's head poking through the smashed windshield. His arms and legs were wedged between the seat and the driver's door. He had been held securely in place by the steering wheel jammed into his thighs. The sheriff was talking. Judge Giles saw his mouth moving, but he couldn't hear him. The ringing in his ears vanquished all other sounds. He tried to read his lips.

As he lay there, the judge noticed the fog grow thicker as it wrapped around the bridge and settled over the river near the Model T. A large amount of blood was smeared on the sheriff's neck. His carotid artery had been slashed. With each beat of the sheriff's heart a stream of blood sprayed up like a fountain, then fell back like rain to the river where it blended in with the water of Rocky River. The judge passed out while the sheriff continued to bleed out until there just wasn't any more blood to lose. The fog clung to the surface of the current and flowed along with it towards Valley Center.

Sheriff Yoder didn't get to live out his dream of living in The Valley. However, on Friday, August 22nd, 1924, every ounce of his blood flowed through it.

Judge Giles had a long road to recovery. He did walk again, but he never went back to the town of Valley Center for the rest of his life.

Chapter 14

Patience is Learned

From Interviews of Clyde Younger, Johnny Muller, Jake Muller, Ben Younger, Bob Filmore, Mary Filmore, Karl Seidel, and The Construction Bosses

It is my intention to track how The Witch moved, and went after those that wronged Hazel. One thing that The Witch learned from all its years of imprisonment was patience. It learned from the best. Yahweh had been longsuffering towards it during its entire existence. He is still waiting on The Witch to ask for forgiveness. That was long ago a lost cause, yet the olive branch is still held out. The Witch felt it now had all the time in the world to be patient and let opportunities come to it, as it lay in wait in the Town Hall.

Dr. Morse moved his practice into a quaint little house on Maple Street right next door to the Filmore Grist Mill. His new office was across the street and to the north of Clyde and Anna Younger's home. Bob and Mary Filmore owned and operated the grist mill. People came from miles around to have their grains ground to flour by the Filmores.

A channel was dug from the river to form Mill Race Creek which was utilized to power the grinding station of the mill. The creek was dammed to form a small holding pond that was behind the mill. The dam, and a plate in the feeder chamber, would hold the water in the pond. When the mill wasn't in use, water from the pond would trickle over the waterfall of the dam. In order to run the mill, the plate in the feeder chamber would be removed. Then water would flow with force to turn the waterwheel that powered the grinding station within the grist mill. From the mill, the creek ran its lazy way back to Rocky River.

A short time after Dr. Morse had moved in, he asked Clyde if he had heard a baby crying early in the mornings. Clyde had told him that he hadn't heard it. The doctor mentioned that every morning since he moved into his new digs he had been awakened by the sound of a crying baby. But when he got out of bed he didn't hear it anymore.

One of Dr. Morse's favorite things to do in his spare time was to walk around the little pond and along Mill Race Creek to the river and back. He loved to watch the water flow, and the waterwheel turning. One early evening he was watching the waterwheel turn and he thought he heard the baby crying again. He moved away from the waterwheel a few feet, stood still, and listened. Yes, it was a baby crying. He heard it. It sounded like it was coming from inside the mill.

He walked around to the front of the mill, put his ear to the door and listened. He heard the cries coming from inside of the mill. He opened the door and went inside. All the inner wheels and gears were creaking and churning. The stone for grinding barley, corn, wheat, and oats into flour was spinning. Flour dust floated about the room. The building seemed to be alive. He didn't see anyone, yet he heard the faint cry of a baby over the din.

He called out, "Bob?" No answer. "Bob, Mary? Is anybody here?" Nothing, except the creaking and churning of the mill, and the baby crying. It sounded like it was coming from upstairs.

He had never been up there before, but there was a crying baby, and he was going to find it. As he climbed the stairs he wondered why no one was answering him. He called out again. No answer. He neared the upstairs section of the mill, and he heard the baby crying over the creaking wooden gears and wheels that turned the grinding stone. It was coming from behind the big gear, the gear that is attached to the axel of the waterwheel.

He could hear the cries coming from the corner. He called out, "Bob, Mary?" No response. "Is there someone over there that needs help?" Nothing.

The baby was wailing. He thought he could also hear a young woman weeping. "Are you injured? Is your baby okay?" The only answer was the baby bawling, the young woman weeping, and the mill groaning.

Dr. Morse made his way over to the outer edge of the building. He couldn't see too well in the dim lit upper workings of the mill. The light color of the flour dust helped him to see, somewhat. He moved toward the main driving wheel. He could hear the baby crying behind it. He peered through the spokes of the wheel trying to catch sight of the baby. He couldn't quite see the floor in the corner behind it. That must be where the baby was at. He moved to get a better look. His foot slipped on the coating of flour dust on the surface of the upper floor. His leg slid into the spindles of the main wheel.

The spindles grabbed ahold of his leg and spun his whole body with merciless force as they turned up and around and down. Dr. Morse ripped out a brief scream that went silent in an instant as his bones crunched and splintered when he went through the workings of the gears of the mill. His blood sprayed out of his body and pooled on the floors. What was left of the doctor clung to the spindles and gears of the mill. Pink bread dough was formed as flour dust settled on the wet remains of Dr. Morse as they lay on the floor, and spun round and round on the wooden wheels of the gristmill.

Bob and Mary Filmore returned home the next day to find the grist mill operating. They lived in the house on the opposite side of the mill from Dr. Morse's new office, but had been at their daughter's home in Lodi for the past few days helping her and her husband with their first child. The baby was born the day before Dr. Morse stopped by to check on the crying baby he heard.

Mary said, "Bob, you left the mill running." She pointed to the waterwheel turning.

Bob gave it a questioning glare and said, "I most certainly did not. I shut down all the gears inside and locked them in place, then put the gate back in the chute for the waterwheel myself before we left."

He walked over to investigate the waterwheel. The plate for the chute was gone—not just out—it was missing. It wasn't hanging on the hook where he always kept it when the mill was in use. He said, "That's strange. I wonder where it is, what could have happened to it?" He looked around in the pond, the outlet channel, and on the ground.

Mary asked, "What's strange?," as she walked to the waterwheel.

Bob said, "The plate, it's gone." Then he went inside the mill to shut it down. Bob went upstairs to pull the levers to stop the gears and lock them down. He saw what was left of Dr. Morse all dried out and spinning around on the main wheel. Flies were feeding on patches of dark flour that were scattered about the gear section and on the floor of the mill. The sight caused his stomach to wrench bile into his throat. He gagged. He coughed. He puked.

He shut the mill down, for what turned out to be the last time. After word got around as to what took place with Dr. Morse, no one brought their grains to the Filmore Grist Mill anymore. The guys at the saloon would tell newcomers to ask for Doc Morse Flour at the general stores. You'll get the finest flour in The Valley.

There was a huge funeral held for Dr. Morse. Karl Seidel and his sons were called to the gristmill to gather his remains. Karl claimed that the flies feeding on the clumps of flour weighed more than what was left of Dr. Morse. They could have used a shoe box to bury him in, but they plucked and scraped off his few remains into a normal sized coffin. On August 1st, 1936, what little that was left of Dr. Morse was laid to rest in Hollow Hill Cemetery on the top of the little hill along the fir trees.

Starting in 1936 and through the summer of 1940 a new addition to Valley Center Elementary School was being added. During the construction of the new addition to the school, classes were held in the Town Hall. In the fall of 1940 the work was done, and classes were once again held in Valley Center Elementary School.

The Ungrich brothers worked as laborers for the construction company that was building the addition. Ed and Harry were in the basement boiler room as concrete was being poured to finish the floors. Two chutes were constructed, one on each side of the new section of the school. Kleiber Cement Trucks backed up to the chutes and poured load after load into the basement.

Ed kept yelling up that they were having a hard time down there. He said the concrete that had been poured was pulling them down, it felt like they were working in quicksand. He and Harry had to keep pulling each other out. The boss yelled down for them to keep going, they were just about done and would be out of there in no time. Ed yelled back up that it seemed like no matter how much concrete they put down in the boiler room, the level stayed the same.

One of the drivers was backing up to the chute by the boiler room. The brake pedal went to the floor when the driver tried to stop the truck. The back of the truck struck the side of the school. The ground shook from the impact. A crack ran up the outside of the building all the way up to the chimney. On the top of the chimney there sat a massive stone cover to keep rain and snow from entering. The sides of the chimney collapsed inward and dropped down through its interior, followed close behind by the massive stone rain shield. A huge splash could be heard over the noise of the cement truck. It was followed by a gurgling sound.

The boss yelled down for Ed. No answer came. He yelled for Harry. No answer. He ran around to the construction entrance and went down to the boiler room. All he saw was finished cement work right at spec level. The huge stone cap and all the bricks and debris that fell with it were all gone—as were the Ungrich brothers.

You can't hold back the progress of man. Since August 18th, 1940, Ed and Harry Ungrich lie buried under the boiler room of Valley Center Elementary School; sealed in concrete under a massive, nameless headstone.

A bell tower once sat on top of the Town Hall. In 1940 the roof needed to be replaced. The roof leaked in numerous places when it rained. One of the worst areas was around the bell tower. Strange noises could be heard coming from the upstairs of the Town Hall. Those who heard them figured the sounds to be the bell tower sinking and creaking as the old building settled.

They eked by with pails and patches into the mid 1940's. It got to the point where they feared that it would cave in, possibly destroying the entire building. They knew the time had come to spend some of the taxpayers' money and get the roof replaced.

The Town Council decided that when the roof replacement was being done, it would be a good time to get rid of the bell tower that was a pain to maintain and wasn't used anymore. A unanimous vote was taken to donate the bell tower to the Valley Center Christian Church down the road.

Richard Schroder worked for the company that the Town Council hired to move the bell tower. The first plan was to remove it piece by piece and reassemble it on top of the church. A change of plan occurred when the company acquired a new crane truck. The new plan was to use the crane to pluck the bell tower off, set it on a trailer, move it to the church, and put it up all in one piece. Easy peasey. While they were at it they would also lift out the old jail cells and scrap them out. The cells hadn't been used for years. There was a county jail now that handled all the malcontents.

The day came when the work was to begin. It was Friday, August 13th, 1948. Richard Schroder was up on the roof at the bell tower. He and two other workers were pulling up the old flashing around the base of the tower. Two other workers were removing molding down below them on the second floor;

working from scaffolding that was constructed around the bottom of the bell tower, at the ceiling level. The boom lift was going to be used to keep tension on the bell tower so they could begin unhooking it from the structure. The workers on the roof had to attach four cable lifting straps around the bell tower and hook them to the lifting hook of the crane.

Richard climbed a ladder that straddled the peak and was leaning against the roof of the bell tower on the back side of it. Another worker handed up to him a large shackle to connect the loops of the straps that would in turn latch onto the lifting hook of the crane. He wrestled around with the loops of the cables for about fifteen minutes and couldn't get them assembled properly. The other guys told him to come down and take a break while they think it over.

Richard suggested that they get another ladder on the front side of the bell tower. It was too hard for one person to hold the cables and run the shackle through the loops. He'll go up one ladder and somebody else will go up the other. Two men working together holding the cables and clasping the shackle should make the task a lot easier. The crew agreed, got another ladder, and leaned it against the tower on the front side.

Richard climbed up the front ladder and another worker climbed up the back ladder. The two of them fought with the cables, pulling, and yanking, while the other two workers adjusted the straps around the bell tower. After about twenty minutes they got the shackle on and centered. One of the workers on the roof was giving the boom operator directions on moving the crane. The boom truck operator wheeled the crane around and brought the lifting hook over the bell tower. Richard and the other worker were holding the shackle in one hand and reaching up for the lifting hook with the other as it was being dropped to the center of the bell tower.

A big gust of wind came out of nowhere, causing Richard and the other worker to hold on tight to the bell tower. The wind caused the cable to coast back and forth, back, and forth above them. The wind had calmed but the cable kept swinging. Richard was watching it swing, mesmerized by the motion of the drifting cable within the backdrop of a beautiful blue sky. He remembered seeing Hazel drifting back and forth just like that at the back of this very building. It seemed like such a long time ago now, in another lifetime.

He let go of the bell tower and reached up to the swinging cable with his free hand hoping to tap the headache ball and slow the swing. The lifting hook caught under his glove at the wrist and pulled him backwards. He let go of the shackle and grabbed the lifting hook with his other hand. When the hook reached the apex of its swing it jerked Richard's grip loose from it. The momentum of the swinging cable caused Richard to be flung from the lifting hook and spin halfway around on his descent to the ground. He landed headfirst on the sidewalk below. He hit with a loud—THUNK—as his head cracked like a muskmelon. Richard let out a loud, "Oomph," as he hit. His eyeballs popped out. Blood spatter sprayed all over the sidewalk. Bits of brain matter were oozing out of his ears, nose, and eye sockets.

The rest of the job went along without incident. The bell tower now safely sits atop the Valley Center Christian Church. Richard Schroder was buried in one of the smaller cemeteries in The Valley.

Chapter 15

The Wandering Witch

From Interviews of Jake Muller, Johnny Muller, Clyde Younger, Ben Younger, Slim, The Fire Chief, and The Truck Driver

It was 1948. Looking back on that time, the people of The Valley thought they had it made. World War ll was over, businesses were booming, cars were common, roads were improved, there was indoor plumbing, and drinks were flowing. Things were looking good all around, not just in Valley Center. Some things in The Valley never change—until they do.

Ever since Hazel, the town folk knew that evil had walked among them. There had been plenty of mysterious happenings; accidents, injuries, and deaths. Sometimes the wind wasn't right, there was something in the air, something that you could almost feel. Something that no one could put their finger on, something no one liked to talk about.

A witch has familiars to help them with their dastardly deeds. The main purpose of a familiar is to serve the witch. A familiar provides protection for a witch as they come into their new powers. Hazel was no witch, but her familiar friend sure was. For one thing, it taught her how to mix potions and deliver them to her victims. Hazel was the familiar to The Witch of The Valley, not the other way around. She provided cover for it. Hazel had no intention of being a witch. She was just looking for a friend, a companion. There would never be another like her.

Many years had rolled by as The Witch lashed out, looking to destroy the equilibrium and inner peace of every mortal soul that lives in The Valley. In order to better achieve this goal, The Witch had to get out of the Town Hall and into the Valley Center Elementary School. The school is built on top of the long-buried remains of an ancient ziggurat, built long ago before the great flood and buried with The Witch. From the Town Hall, The Witch could feel the immense power that could be drawn from the ziggurat. But in order to attain that power, The Witch had to be situated on top of it.

The Witch wasn't looking forward to inhabit a human body once again. This was only out of necessity—from the burning desire to get to the school. It had far more power when free from a host, but its reach was incredibly limited. I believe that's why it took so long for it to exact revenge on the members of the posse that arrested Hazel. If the Witch was able to possess a new host and free itself near the school, then not only would its power grow, but its reach as well. The time had arrived to hunt for a new Hazel.

The Witch needed to take command of another vessel to use and destroy on its journey to the school. It started seeking out candidates to possess and control, all while plotting the deaths of the posse that arrested Hazel. The Witch in its true form is terrifying to behold. So, it would appear to potential victims in their dreams by masking its actual self. Tempting aspirants to invite it in through subtle hints of their own desires.

Sometimes it showed up under the aspect of a young girl, or an old wise woman. Sometimes under that of a coyote, or of a bobcat, or of a bear. Throwing out bait, hoping for a fish to bite. Trying to work its way in through a common interest. Trouble was, no one would invite it in. It took the Witch millennia to find Hazel, but that was when it was limited underground. Now that it could reach within the town's limits, the process was much faster, taking only a few decades. One night it happened upon someone to suit its needs just fine. It came to Lottie Rowland in one of her dreams. In Lottie's case, The Witch came to her as a horse.

Lottie lived at the southern tip of The Valley. She always wanted a horse. When she was a little girl she pretended to be a horse, whinnying, snorting, and trotting about as she played. She asked for a horse on every Birthday, and each Christmas, to no avail. Her family could never afford to give her a horse of her own. She had frequent dreams of horses. And when Lottie was sixteen, she did get a horse.

The name of the horse that came to Lottie every night in her dreams was Wander. The horse was shiny, black, beautiful, and majestic. Its flowing mane hung over one eye. Her long perfect tail would flick as she trotted.

Lottie would ride Wander through The Valley in her dreams. It's powerful hooves ripping up the turf as they as they sailed along. Everyone waved and smiled as they passed them by. At times Wander would lift off the ground and fly into the sky. Wander talked to Lottie on their rides. "*Find me and invite me in. I will be all yours, all the time. All you have to do is find me—and let me in.*" Lottie searched high and low for Wander, but only found her in her dreams.

Lottie was sent to pick up some supplies for her family at the Valley Center General Store. When she came out of the general store she saw this big, black, beautiful horse standing in front of the Town Hall. The horse gazed at Lottie out of the one eye that wasn't covered by her silky mane. The horse snorted and smiled at Lottie. It was the horse from her dreams. It was Wander.

Lottie heard the whinny of Wander whisper to her. She felt the horse reach into her mind, as she drifted closer to be near to it. Thoughts were projected into Lottie's mind as she stood mesmerized at Wander's side, '*We could run and play all day long.*' '*You can have me all to yourself.*' '*All you have to do is to invite me in.*' Lottie did so without a second thought. The Witch had found a new home.

The ebb and flow of The Witch allowed Lottie to function, but it was too much for her to handle long term. She fought hard to control Wander, but the horse ran wild within her. Hazel was able to handle The Witch for many years because she wanted a friend, and revenge, so they worked well together. Lottie only wanted a horse—not have this wild monster running rampant inside of her. It didn't take long for her to snap.

She started doing all sorts of crazy things. With her hair combed over one eye, and a stick in her mouth like a bit, she would skip and trot around her yard pretending to be a horse. She would talk to the rider while foaming at the mouth and acting all crazy. There was a barbed wire fence on the property line to keep the cows from wandering off the farm next door. She would try to jump over the barbed wire fence and get all tangled up in it. Her father had to cut her out of the fence so many times that he put up a wood fence to keep her out of it.

She had a job in a cheese factory near the family's home that was supplied with milk from the surrounding farms. Word got back to the owner that Lottie used to plop her face right in the tanks of milk and drink like a horse. She was fired from the cheese factory.

Her father was at his wits' end with her. Instead of doing her chores, all she wanted to do was run around and pretend to be a horse. He would berate her and give her certain tasks to perform. She would snort and stomp her feet in the ground like hooves, throw her head around and neigh. She would trot off and pretend to take care of the assigned task, till her father was out of sight. Then it was back to playing horsey.

Somehow she managed to last two years with The Witch. The last straw for her parents was when Lottie was told to get the stove ready to cook supper. She piled wood under the kitchen table and lit it on fire. Her mother and siblings doused the flames. Lottie just stood there staring and licking her lips. Her one brother had third degree burns on his arms from fighting the fire. She told her parents that she couldn't watch the fire as well when it was in the stove. Out in the open she could see the flames so much better. Her father kicked her out of the house.

Lottie wandered into Valley Center proper looking for work and a place to stay. She had taken up to living in barns, unbeknownst to the owners of them. The Salty Dog Saloon was owned and operated by a man that everyone called Slim, and his wife, Mae. Slim also had a farm at the Dead End of Maple Street. The rest of the street is now a pasture, but the little bridge still sits at the back of the property where Grandpa Johnny Muller last saw his dad, Old John, alive.

Slim saw Lottie leaning on a fence and talking to the horses on his way to the farm to do chores. He stopped and asked her what she was doing. She struck up a conversation about horses. Slim was so intrigued by her knowledge of horses. He told her she could talk with the horses all she wanted. Little did he know, but Lottie was already living on the farm and had quite a few nice little hiding places so she could trespass undetected.

James Hadcock lived in the old rundown house behind my grandfather's house on Maple Street, right across the street from the back lot of the Town Hall. Lottie would see him on the porch of his home on her trots around town. She set her sights on him in hopes of finding a home in which to live.

Lottie walked into the Salty Dog Saloon one morning. She talked with Slim about his horses, and when his guard was down she asked him if she could work as a barmaid for him. He told her he would discuss it with his wife and get back to her. Lottie left out of the saloon and trotted down the sidewalk. Slim talked with Mae about having some help on their busy nights of Fish Fry Friday, and Steak Fry Saturday. Mae said that she could use another pair of hands on those nights—and all day on Saturday. When Slim went to the farm to feed and water the animals, there was Lottie talking to a horse. He told her that she could start working in the saloon on Friday afternoon.

A lot of town folk thought that James and his business partner, Jeffrey Bottum, were brothers. One thing for sure, they were frequent patrons of the Salty Dog Saloon. On Lottie's first shift as a barmaid, they were her first customers. They came in the back way and sat at the little bar in the back of the saloon.

Lottie started flirting with James right away. She had high hopes of moving in with him. She flung her hair as she approached them. Her hair fell back in place, covering one eye. Looking at James with her uncovered eye she asked, "What'll ya have, handsome?" She smiled at him.

"Depends. What are you offering?" He grinned at Lottie.

Jeff said, "Nothing that she's got."

Lottie glared back at Jeff. He saw fire burning in her one bloodshot eye that was exposed. It looked like a cauldron about to boil over. She snorted and said, "Nothing that I've got. What's that supposed to mean?"

He said, "Nothing," and saw the cauldron simmer down. But that one eye kept glowering at him.

She looked back to James, "So, what'll it be?"

He didn't even look at Lottie. He was smiling at Jeff. "Just give us a couple draft beers and then leave us alone."

Lottie snorted and shook her head from side to side as a bit of spittle flew. She wiped away some slobber that was hanging off side of her mouth as she drew the drafts. Lottie felt slighted by James. She returned and said, "Choke on 'em," as she slammed the mugs down on the bar. Then she hurried away in a huff.

James and Jeff talked and laughed. Lottie perceived they were making fun of her. She stood by the draft dispenser staring at them from her one eye. They finished their beers and left.

Before sunrise the next morning the town was awakened by the fire siren. James Hadcock's house was in full flame. Even though the fire department was just around the corner, the house was gone in minutes. Some sort of accelerant was used. The fire department could only spray water on the trees, the house to the south, and my grandfather's house to the north to contain the fire and keep it from spreading.

138

Jeffery Bottum had sounded the alarm. The fire chief questioned him after the fire.

Jeff said, "I was awakened by the smell of smoke. I jumped out of bed and ran to the kitchen hoping to get some water and put out whatever was burning, but the room was in flames. I ran back to get James and the door was wedged. I couldn't open it. The smoke was choking me, so I had to get out of the house. I ran to the fire station, broke the glass for the alarm and pressed the button to sound the siren." He dropped his head into his hands and sobbed. "I couldn't save him."

On the morning of June 6th, 1950, James Hadcock's charred remains were found in the basement of his old house. His body locked in the fetal position, and with what looked like a permanent grin on his face.

A week after James was buried, Jeffery Bottum went to Hollow Hill Cemetery. He stood on top of James Hadcock's grave. After placing the butt of a Browning 12-gauge shotgun on the ground, tucking the barrel under his chin and removing a shoe; he used his big toe to blow his brains out. Jeff Bottum was discovered by a couple who were visiting the cemetery. He was lying on his back in the blood-soaked dirt on top of the grave. His eyes, brain, and the top of his head were pulverized into a mist and clung onto the surrounding grass like morning dew.

Lottie wasn't working at the Salty Dog for very long before she wore out her welcome. Her accomplice had also worn out its welcome within her. The Witch had desperately wanted to embed itself in the school, but Lottie fought it as best she could. She got fired from the Salty Dog Saloon and kicked off of Slim's farm. First, he caught her stealing from customers by taking their money off of the bar when they weren't paying attention. Some of them had even been generous tippers. Then, he caught her sleeping in his barn surrounded by empty beer bottles that she had polished off from his stash that he kept in a refrigerator at the farm. She had a strange way of showing appreciation.

She also had a strange way of keeping warm at night when she wasn't in a barn. Lottie would lay down on the road. A road retains heat from the sun for many hours, just like the black marble ball of the Gunther family's marker. The Witch taught her that. On the late foggy evening of June 13th, 1950, Lottie laid down right on Center Street for a rest, not far from the school. As she closed her eyes to sleep, the fog had enveloped her completely.

Not long after, a semi-tractor trailer was barreling down the road. Lottie rolled up onto her elbow but wasn't fast enough to take notice of what was about to happen.

The driver of the rig that ran her over said, "The fog was thick as thieves. I could see good for about ten feet ahead of the truck. I thought it was a big burlap sack in the road. At the last second, I saw her eyes—they got as big as saucers. Then I ran her over. This big gust of wind blew the thick fog that way." He pointed towards the school. "Then some of it trickled back, but not the thick stuff. The thick stuff kept creeping away. It was strange." He looked off into the fog in the direction of the school.

Lottie was freed of The Witch.

The Witch leaped into a new abode. It took up residence in the Valley Center Elementary School. The school was an ideal spot for The Witch. It sits on the exact dead-center of The Valley. From there The Witch could expand its reach to get its devious deeds done by connecting to the demonic power of the ancient ziggurat that lies beneath. The Witch stretched forth its tenacles from its new home. Emanating its will throughout the entirety of The Valley, not just the town of Valley Center. Extending its evil thoughts to influence everyone within its reach. Issuing desires of destruction into the minds and the dreams of every living being for many miles around. And best of all, there are a great number of young souls to torment within the walls of the school for nine months out of the year. The Witch was going to be respected.

The old school may appear stoic, empty, and cold, but so did Hazel. And just like Hazel, the school offered the most hospitable environment for The Witch to infest. No more cold prison to sit in. No more unstable human vessel to try and navigate.

A bunch of strange slips, trips, and falls began happening in the school and on the playground. They were written off as clumsy pre-adolescent kids stumbling and bumbling incidents. Broken bones, chipped teeth, bloody noses, fights, all the usual kid activities.

It wasn't relegated to just the school. A lot of weird and bizarre things were going on all over The Valley in those days. There were many near misses, minor injuries, car crashes, farm accidents, deaths, and much more that was taking place. The Witch wasn't responsible for all of them—just most of them.

Chapter 16

School Days

Things in The Valley were progressing. Old businesses and dilapidated buildings were torn down and replaced by new ones. The town was growing and prospering. At long last, a time of peace—for a change. Right about then is when my buddies and me came along.

We thought we owned the town when we were kids. The whole town of Valley Center was our own personal playground. In the summertime we played outside all day long. Whether it was riding our banana bikes around town, jumping over and off of stuff, playing baseball, football, wiffle ball, mumbley peg, pole vaulting across the creek; you name it, we did it.

All the neighborhood kids played outside. After supper we would go back outside and play till the streetlights came on. Then, in the summertime, we would go back outside with the neighbor kids to play hide and seek. When school was on, we would hang out in our homes, do homework, and watch TV with our families. It was as carefree as could be and there was nothing to fear.

During the school year all of us town kids walked to school. After school we had to wait for all the buses to leave before we could walk home. I would rush home and hurry through my homework, then watch Speed Racer and Ultra Man, then go out and play with my buddies. Whenever my buddy Mike Muller needed a haircut, he would walk to the barber shop and his mom would pick him up at our house when he was done. I knew which kids were bus riders who were also going to the barber shop for haircuts after school. So, to cut them off at the pass, we would take a short cut through the tunnel that was across the street from the school to beat them to the barber shop.

That gave us more time to run around town before his mom came to pick him up.

The school is at the northwest corner of the intersection of West River Road and School Street. The tunnel entrance was on the southwest corner of the intersection. The tunnel was put in by the owner of Valley Center Builder's Supply that sits above it. The tunnel goes under West River Road and extends to the south where it ends after going under Center Street. The south end is across the street and just west of the Town Hall. From there, the creek continues south before cutting over east and emptying into Rocky River.

I learned from the Parson brothers, Skip and Jack, on how to navigate through the tunnel from side to side without getting a soaker or falling down. Skip was about seven years older than me, and Jack was four or five years older. They treated me like their kid brother. And they taught me to be competitive, just like them. Everything we did was a game—a challenge. Who could do what better and faster.

I remember the first thing they taught me to do was how to balance. They could both walk the entire length of the little handrails along the sidewalks to the school entrance. One of them would be on the left rail and the other on the right rail. They would race each other from one end to the other; even up and down both flights of steps. It was impressive. I couldn't do that at the time. I could barely walk without tripping over my own two feet. They taught me how to watch, observe, and learn; I grew into an aficionado of observing and learning.

You had to step real fast, one, two, three, jump, one, two, three, jump to run through the tunnel. Faster and faster, I would go. Bring your right foot across the creek first when going left and your left foot across first when going back to the right. One, two, three, jump, one, two, three, jump. It was a great formula that worked well.

When it was the dry season in summer that was no problem, but when school was on it was a bit tricky because the water was higher. You had to have just the right momentum going from the curvature of the tunnel as gravity brought you towards the water to jump over it to the other side and do the same thing going back. I practiced in the tunnel a lot and I got very good at running through it.

I would always go first. I didn't need someone ahead of me to slow me down. If you didn't do it just right, you would get a soaker. And if you got a soaker, you would catch hell from your mom if she found out. Worse yet, if you slipped on the slimy tunnel floor and fell in the water, you really got soaked. There was no hiding that, you really caught hell when you got home.

My good buddies Mike Muller, Matt Warner, and I were together all the time. Mike, Matt, and Mike. We came to be known as the M&M Brothers. Everybody called us that. It was one thing after another with us. In school when one of us got called to the office for some infraction of the rules, all three of us would head there.

The loudspeakers in the classrooms were blown out from the constant throat clearing and bombastic blasts of, "Testing, testing, this is your principal speaking," being sent through them. No kidding, we all know who you are, we all know your voice. All that was heard was staticky names being barked out as he held the microphone right up against his mouth instead of a few inches away like a normal person.

One would be overcome by a brief sense of doom if you heard your name called out to report to the office. Everyone 'oohed' and 'ahhed' and stared at you as you got up from your desk to do the office death march. Mike Muller, Matt Warner, and Mike Younger sounded the same to us over those speakers. We would meet in the hall on the way and question each other to figure out which one of us was the real Wanted Man. It was always a relief when it wasn't you. It was guaranteed that one of our siblings would rat us out to our parents that we got called to the office. The punishment at home was way worse than what you got at school.

None of us M&M Brothers really cared about school. We got decent grades without even trying. We weren't challenged in school. We needed to be challenged. Challenges would come later—especially for Muller and I.

Mike Muller's grandfather was Johnny Muller. He and my grandfather, Clyde Younger, were the only ones remaining from the posse that arrested that witch Hazel. Between the colorful stories of Grandpa Johnny and my grandfather's more straight-to-the-facts story, I got the full picture of The Witch—or so I thought at the time.

We would go to school and tell all the kids that our grandpas had arrested a nasty old witch when they were young. They told us all sorts of stories about her from their firsthand experiences. She was an evil, menacing old hag. We

143

came up with some good stories of our own. We would tell the girls that when they are home, and all alone, to go into the bathroom, stare deep into the mirror and say, Hazel Dill, one hundred times—and she will suddenly appear in the mirror. A bunch of girls told us that they did it and they saw her. That tickled our funny bones. The news spread like wildfire. Everyone was trying to do it. I did it once—and saw her. I ran out of the house. I was scared to death. I never told anyone that it happened—and I never tried that again.

My grandpa was also the caretaker of Hollow Hill Cemetery. He, my uncles, and my dad would mow the grass, dig the graves, and put in concrete footers for the headstones. I was there a lot when I was growing up. I was too young to help dig when I first started going there with my dad; and they didn't trust that I wouldn't plow into headstones with a mower, so I just ran around the cemetery and played.

People talked about the Gunther family marker being scary. It was dubbed, the Witch's Ball. If they wanted to see some scary headstones, all they had to do was walk towards the peak of the hill. There are two scary headstones there that are profound. The first one reads, 'Died of an axe.' I asked my grandpa about it when I just started reading. He told me it was a woman's grave and that her husband had killed her. I later learned that they lived near the old salt mine. Her husband came home and found her in bed with another man. He grabbed an axe and chased after the guy, but the guy got away. So, he went back to the house and took the axe to his wife.

The other headstone is the most profound headstone. It stands tall at the highest point in the cemetery. It is an old, dark, stone obelisk that keeps watch over The Valley. People think it's a family marker, but it's not. It's the headstone for four Civil War veterans. Captain Raymond Klein is buried at the north face. Major Cecil Minor is buried at the west face. Herbert Shoemaker is buried at the south face. Unknown is buried at the east face— the face with the haunting poem.

The inscription on it reads,

Memento Mori

See and behold as you pass by,

As you are now so once was I.

As I am now so you must be,

Prepare for death and follow me.

The first time that I read it—and understood it—chills ran up my spine.

When I first could read I thought that Memento Mori was the name of the deceased person that was buried there. I asked my grandpa to tell me all about that person. He said, "Memento Mori is not the name of a person, it's some sort of saying in Latin, the name of the poem. You'll have to look it up."

I looked up the saying. It means, 'bear in mind that you will die.'

From then on, when I played at the cemetery, I stayed away from the big, dark obelisk that had the death poem on it. That one was the scariest headstone to me. But that big, round, black marble headstone that had the name of Gunther on it was fascinating. I was drawn to it. I liked to touch it and feel how warm it was from absorbing the sunlight. I asked my grandpa about it, and he told me to talk with Johnny Muller because he knew the Gunther family very well.

I asked Grandpa Johnny about the Gunthers and why they had that round black marble headstone. I wanted to know all about the person who had that headstone made for them. He told me that it wasn't a headstone at all, it was a family marker for the Gunther family. The Gunthers have individual headstones for each member of the family that are buried all around the big black marble ball.

Matt, Muller, and I made up our own story about the Gunther family marker. We told everyone in school and around town that the matriarch of the Gunther family was a witch. The Witch's Ball is her headstone. You talk about running with it. Everybody ran with that story. It is known far and wide these days. There are YouTube videos, stupid, untrue stories about a kid drowning in the shitter at the cemetery—you name it—we heard them all. Our story about the Witch's Ball was stupid and untrue, too, but many people believed it—and still do.

We first heard about the school being haunted from our friend's older brother and his friends. They told us about the Ungrich brothers being buried under the boiler room in the school, thinking they could scare us—yeah, right. One of their stories was that when you walked past the boiler room you could hear a trowel scraping across the floor. That was the Ungrich brothers down there, still working on finishing the concrete floor. Another one was on the nights of a full moon you could see Ed and Harry through the windows, wandering around in the school, trying to find their way out.

Even though we heard a bunch of stories about the school being haunted by the Ungrich brothers, what we feared most was—The Witch. We M&M Brothers secretly talked about how we felt The Witch was watching us from the shadows, toying with us. She was still around, still doing her evil deeds. We knew that she had somehow escaped the grave. We never caught a glimpse of her, but we could feel the presence of The Witch.

During recess one day, this kid was running across the playground when a softball rolled towards him. I saw the whole thing, it happened so fast, but in slow motion. I was watching him running towards me, and I saw the ball curve right into his path. He didn't see the ball coming his way and he stepped right on it. His foot rolled out from under him, and his face hit down hard on the ground. He got up and his mouth was bleeding. I heard a girl laughing. I looked all around and saw no one laughing, or even smiling. I was convinced that it was The Witch who was laughing.

That was my first clue as to the true nature of The Witch. It couldn't have been the Ungrich brothers because they are stuck in the school and can't get out. This happened outside on the playground.

The next clue was when our M&M Brother Matt Warner was mowing the lawn in the springtime at his parents' house. The grass got all clogged up underneath the mower deck. He swore his concentration was taken away by The Witch. His dad had told him a thousand times to turn the mower off to pull clogged-up grass out. He heard The Witch speak to him in his head. Telling him to reach his hand in through the opening while it was running. He said it felt like he was in a fog. He couldn't help himself. He saw the wet grass bunched up and didn't even think about shutting off the mower. It was like something took him by the hand and pulled it into the spinning blade. His hand got all tore up. He almost lost two fingers. In all, it took forty-two stitches to close up the wounds. He told Muller and I that he heard a little girl giggling, but there was no one around. That had to be The Witch.

Then, in fourth grade, Muller sealed the deal. On the playground at recess, this older boy and I were standing up on the swings, a big no-no, seeing who could go higher. The older boy called out to Muller, "Hey Mike, look how high we are going."

Muller asked, "What?" In a fog, he turned and heard a voice in his head say, *'Go to him.'* He walked right into the path of the swing. The seat of the older boy's swing caught Muller right under his nose. Blood sprayed out as he flew backward and hit the ground. We jumped off the swings and ran to him. The first of seven broken noses he has endured in his life moved his nose over and under his left eye. A teacher came running over screaming. Someone brought out a towel and held it on his bloody face. We got him up and helped him to the office. His parents were called, and they took him to the hospital. He told Matt and I later about the thought that was placed in his mind.

In the summer before fifth grade, I went to a friend's house who lived near the railroad track. We heard a train coming down the line, so we stopped what we were doing and walked to the tracks to watch and wave as the train goes by. The neighbor girl was grooming her horse out in their front yard. As the train approached the horse broke away from her and trotted toward the tracks. The engine struck the horse right across the face. It looked like a prize fighter being clobbered by a hard left hook. The horse spun around, hit the ground, rolled over, got up, and again ran headfirst into the passing train. This time it got gobbled up under the wheels of the tons of rolling steel.

I knew it was The Witch, enticing that poor horse into the train, right in front of the young girl that loved it. The neighbor girl was screaming and crying. I'll never forget the look on the face of the conductor, smiling and waving to us from the caboose as it passed. He had no idea what had just happened.

We spread many stories around about the school being haunted by the Ungrich brothers. We were just kids playing. We didn't know what was haunting The Valley, but we knew there was something more powerful, evil, and menacing than ghosts. It took a lot of growing up and many years to attain the knowledge to figure out what it was, so in the meantime, we called it— The Witch. Every bad thing that happened was attributed to it by us.

A couple of teachers were prime suspects of being a witch. They did some evil things to their students. You send your kids to school in hopes to get them a good education. You think they are safe and protected. You would be wrong. You've only got one chance when you're raising your children. Keep involved in your children's education. Don't just let the system take them. Most teachers have the students' best interest in mind, but not all of them do.

Valley Center Elementary School had three bad apples that I know of firsthand. They all three lived in The Valley. Back then I wasn't sure if it wanted to possess them or was just harassing them, but I knew they were heavily influenced by The Witch.

147

The first one that I encountered was Mrs. Sink in first grade. I lucked out and didn't have her for my teacher, but my buddy Mike Muller had her. He told me how she used to whack him with a thick doll rod on the knuckles, the buttocks, the arms, legs, face, nothing was off limits for her.

My classroom was in the room next door to hers. My teacher had left the room and told us all to stay in our seats. I walked out into the hall to see where she was going. That old bag Sink was lying in wait. She latched on to my neck with a Vulcan nerve pinch. She had her teeth clenched tight as she said, "You were told to stay in your seat." The old bitty stared me down with her dark, evil eyes and dragged me all the way to the office like that.

So, it wasn't just my buddy she tormented. She spread the wealth around pretty good. We had heard of her before we got into first grade. Her reputation preceded her. She was a real prize of a teacher, and we couldn't wait to get away from the old battle axe. However, there were two more that sunk even lower than Sink. Miss Wesson in fifth grade, and Mr. Barlow in sixth grade. Back-to-back years of pure hell.

Miss Wesson was a dried-up, grumpy, humorless old bat, with a real peach of a personality. She had been tormented by The Witch for years. You didn't even want to make eye contact with her. She would start barking at me the moment she saw me. Even before I had her as a teacher she came after me. "Younger! Stop talking so loud. Younger, don't run in the hallway."

Younger this and Younger that. I don't know what it was with her, but she had it in for me. Probably because I was always smiling. She never smiled. She was mean. She always had a look on her face like she had just bitten into a lemon.

Nowadays her behavior would be frowned upon. She would be disciplined and threatened with imprisonment. But back then it was condoned. It may have even been a job requirement, I don't know. It wasn't just me, though, she went after anyone that smiled. I think that's what it was, she didn't like seeing anyone being happy. I don't think that she liked herself at all. She was miserable, so everyone else should be, too. And I was as happy-go-lucky as could be.

In her class, God forbid if you were talking out of turn or laughing. She would make you stand at the front of class holding your hands out in a Jesus pose. It seemed to be for hours, but was probably ten minutes. If you were a favorite target, like me, she would place books in your hands. If you dropped a book, you got swatted.

By the way she swatted, there's not a doubt that she could have been a professional tennis player. She had this favorite paddle she used that was made out of ash wood. It had holes drilled in it for less resistance and more velocity. Little round welts would crop up wherever they landed. Sometimes she would get so wound up and swing so wild that you'd get hit on the hamstrings with the side of the paddle instead of the flat part on your ass. I thought for a time that she was actually possessed by The Witch—she wasn't—she just relished the attention The Witch gave her.

We had gym class on Tuesdays. She was a drill sergeant in gym. We had to do calisthenics to start every class. We hated that. We would rather play dodgeball and blast each other in the face to see who was king of the class. I don't remember ever winning dodgeball and I don't know why; I was pretty good at it.

After this one gym class we were about to head out of the gym and I called out, "See you next Tuesday, Miss Wesson." A couple of kids cracked up laughing.

Miss Wesson came charging at me like a bull. She punched me in the chest with her left hand and grabbed ahold of my t-shirt. She punched me across the face, then back hand punched me the other way. Punched me across the face again, and back hand punched me the other way. She stood there holding me by my t-shirt. There was complete silence as the other kids looked on in astonishment.

She asked, "Would you like to repeat what you just said?"

I asked, "Will it get me the same response?" I heard a couple of my buddies crack up.

She slapped me across the face real hard and glared at me with a cold, diabolical stare. I looked into her eyes. I could see burning hatred within her. I never felt like punching a woman ever in my life, but this one time I sure did. And she could tell that I wanted to hit her back.

She pushed me away and screamed, "Get out of here, all of you!" The other kids started running out of the gym. I kept looking at her eyes as I backed away from her. I was looking to see if her eyes moved. Grandpa Johnny had told us that Hazel's eyes would move around. All I saw was a cold, hard stare.

If she threw down on me ever again, I was throwing back. She never did. That's when I knew she was only influenced and not possessed by The Witch. If she had been possessed she would have beat me to a pulp—or worse.

I remember telling my mom about that in hopes that she would do something about it. She thought it was funny. She laughed and said, "Oh, that Miss Wesson. I think she needs a husband."

I had more fun that summer than any summer that I can remember. I knew I had to enjoy it because when it was over, I was going to have Mr. Barlow as a teacher in sixth grade. He made sure of it.

When we were in fifth grade a bunch of us yahoos—I think there were seven of us in all—were coming in from recess. We started chasing each other around in the school. Us M&M Brothers got ahead of the others. We yelled out to them that they couldn't catch us.

There are two stairwells in the school. The one at the main entrance has two long stretches, one from the entrance to the second floor, and the other from the second floor balcony landing to the third floor. The west entrance stairwell starts from higher up because of the little hill that the school is situated on. The west entrance stairwell has four small flights of stairs. One down to the basement, one up to the second floor, one up from the second floor to a landing that wraps back and around the outer wall, then up to the third floor with the last one.

We ran up the small flight of stairs to the second floor, ran across the hall to the other side, ran down a different small set of stairs that lead to the stage in the gym, jumped off the stage and ran across the gym, jumped up and grabbed the railing for the balcony, pulled ourselves up, ran out on the second floor and down the big flight of stairs at the main entrance. Then we ran back toward the gym. When we got to the basement we figured it to be a good idea to hide from the other guys down in the boiler room.

We ran down the steps to the boiler room, rounded the corner and there was the janitor sitting in a chair and smoking a pipe. Mr. Barlow was sitting in another chair smoking a cigarette. Miss Carson was sitting on Barlow's lap, smoking a cigarette. Miss Carson was one of the other sixth grade teachers. She was the teacher that all of us boys wanted to have for sixth grade. We thought she was smokin' hot, but didn't know that she was really smokin', till then.

They all three looked at us, shocked. We looked at them, shocked. We all smiled at each other; it was odd, Mr. Barlow was smiling when he asked, "What in the Sam hell are you boys doing down here?"

Just then the other four guys that were chasing us came running down the stairs. Mr. Barlow's smile left his face in a hurry. He pushed Miss Carson off from his lap. She doused her cigarette and left the boiler room.

Mr. Barlow said, "I know you Muller, and Warner, and Younger. The rest of you give me your names. You boys are all going to be in my class in sixth grade." And when that summer was over, we all were in Mr. Barlow's sixth grade class.

Mr. Barlow was the biggest bully I ever met in my life. We had heard stories about him long ago, as far back as kindergarten. He lived out his life like he was his students' big brother or something. He was demented. He made sure that all us boys took a shower after gym class. He would chase us around when we were naked, hitting us on the behinds with his whistle lanyard. When you jumped and turned, he would stare at your junk with delight. He was twisted.

When his students pushed back and resisted him, he came down hard on them. It was obvious to us that he wasn't a witch, only women can be witches. Mr. Barlow was being guided by The Witch, who was pulling the strings.

He took great joy in embarrassing you in front of the class. His goal was to make every student cry in front of their peers. He succeeded in making most of the kids in class cry. He tried his best to make Muller, Matt, and I cry. We were the M&M Brothers, and M&M Brothers don't cry. We made a pact that if you cried in front of the class you would have to write on the chalkboard: 'I'm a Wuss.' That was all I had to think about to keep me from ever crying. I knew if I wrote that on the chalkboard all the kids would laugh at me. Then, Mr. Barlow would swat me with the black paddle for writing that on his chalkboard.

The black paddle was reserved for the most brutal of swats. We had heard about the black paddle since we first heard of him. A former student had made it for him, after he had him for sixth grade, of course. He was the star athlete in high school when he made the paddle in shop class. It was rumored around town that he was Mr. Barlow's lover. All seven of us that went running into the boiler room got the black paddle taken to us at least once. I got it twice, myself.

151

When school first started we had to take tests to see where we placed in reading, math, and science. We would change classes for those subjects, and gym class. Mr. Barlow taught the top third of the students of those three classes. He taught all the sixth grade boys for gym class. Had I known ahead of time, I would have not tried my best on the tests. I placed in the top third on the reading and science tests, then came the math tests. I had screwed around so much that previous summer that I had forgotten how to divide. I bombed the math test.

Mr. Barlow sat at his desk and graded our tests. He looked up and stared me down. He got up and came walking to me as I sat at my desk. Nice and loud he asked, "What's wrong with you, boy?," as he stood there glaring down at me with his hands on his hips.

I said, "Nothing," looking up to him puzzled.

"Stand up." I stood. "You got something against me, tubby?" I heard some sighs and muffled chuckles.

"No."

"No, what?" He poked me hard in the chest with his middle finger.

"No sir." He poked me again.

"You don't like being in my class, do you boy?" He poked me in the chest with his middle finger. The bully singled me out to be the first kid he would make cry in front of the whole class.

"No sir, I—"

"No? No? Why not?," he questioned me as he poked my chest harder.

"I mean, yes, I don't mind—" Every time I spoke he poked me harder.

"You don't mind." Poking me again. He looked like his was going to burn up. I wished he did. I held my ground.

"I forgot how to divide over the summer."

"You." Poke. "Forgot." Poke. "How." Poke. "To divide." He stopped poking and turned around to address the class. "This dummy forgot how to divide." He smiled as he looked around for approval of making me look like a fool. He got a few mild chuckles from the class in response. "Get up to the board." He waved me to the chalkboard.

There I stood in front of the class with this grinning lunatic staring at me. He made me write down problem after problem on the chalkboard and work them out. He barked out commands like a drill sergeant, but in a sarcastic tone. After about ten times of erasing, and writing, and working out a problem, I regained my division skills. He told me to sit down.

I was never able to leave my desk like my other friends. I had Mr. Barlow for every class—all day long—every day—for the whole school year.

Muller got caught throwing a paper airplane out the window. He didn't even get busted by Mr. Barlow directly. The old janitor was out on the lawn and noticed what window the plane came sailing out of. About ten minutes after Muller launched the plane, the janitor came walking into class with it and handed it to Mr. Barlow. He pointed to the window that he saw it come out of—and it was on.

Mr. Barlow knew right away it was Muller. He marched over to the kid sitting in front of him and berated him into tears. The poor kid pleaded with Mr. Barlow to believe him. He cried, "It wasn't me," as he covered his face with his hands, weeping.

Mr. Barlow set his sights on the kid behind Muller. "Why did you throw this out the window?" He held the paper airplane in his face.

He was scared to death. He blurted out, "It was Mike, not me," as he pointed at Muller.

"What in Sam hell do you think you are doing?" He circled around in front of Muller.

"Nothing." Muller was petrified.

"Nothing, what?" Mr. Barlow blasted him in the chest and pulled him up out of his chair.

"Nothing, Mr. Barlow, sir," in a Yogi Bear voice. I almost cracked up laughing. Muller and Mr. Barlow stared each other down.

"Out in the hall." Mr. Barlow pushed Muller toward the hallway. You could hear a pin drop in the classroom. We heard the locker open. We knew which one. At least everyone who had gotten swats knew which one. The one with the collection of paddles in it. We heard Mr. Barlow say, "Pick one, boy." That was followed by, "Grab your ankles." And then the massive, "WHACK!"

Muller came walking back in the classroom all red-faced. Mr. Barlow came back in smiling. That's how Muller got his black paddle swat.

Mr. Barlow called Matt Warner, "Leather Ass." He got that name because he got a lot of swats. And when he got swatted he would just walk back in and sit down like nothing happened. It drove Barlow nuts that Matt could take his hardest hits.

Matt would forget to do his homework. Not do his homework. Lose his homework. Whenever the dog ate Matt's homework, he got swatted by Mr. Barlow. Lucky for him he didn't have Mr. Barlow for every class, all day long, like I did. He got to leave for math, reading, and science. He was smart when he took the tests.

Matt had one of the messiest desks in class. Every kid would try their best to not let Mr. Barlow see inside of their desk. Matt would only open the lid on his desk if Mr. Barlow wasn't looking. Mr. Barlow would walk up alongside of his desk and ask him to get a certain book out while he stood there watching. Matt would crack the lid and reach his hand in and feel around. Mr. Barlow would say, "I bet I can find it."

His way of finding something was to tip your desk upside down and kick its contents all over the classroom. Then he'd kick the garbage can over at your desk while you gathered your stuff back up. He'd stand over you as you sorted through your things. Telling you what to throw away, and how to arrange what was kept. Matt's desk would stay somewhat okay for about a week before reverting back to its natural, messy condition.

Mr. Barlow's stated goal was to get you to keep a neat and tidy desk. His real goal was to embarrass you in front of the class and make you cry. It didn't work with Matt. Mr. Barlow wasn't going to make him cry. It didn't work with any of the M&M Brothers. We were toughened up from living in The Valley. He didn't make any of us M&M Brothers cry.

We couldn't wait for summer to come after that year of torture. When it finally rolled around, we felt so relieved. Not just to get away from Mr. Barlow, but to get away from that school in general. There was something about that place. It wasn't just haunted by the Ungrich brothers. Something more was there. Junior high will be out of The Valley, and away from that place. We couldn't wait for the next adventure.

Chapter 17

Oh Well

That summer went by in the blink of an eye. Then school started. The junior high and high school are magnet schools for three communities. The schools are situated on a campus about five miles away from Valley Center proper. There were no reports of those schools being haunted.

Junior high sucked at first, but then we got to meet all these new kids from the other communities. Matt, Muller, and I spread our stories around with our new friends. They didn't have any good stories about their elementary schools being haunted. All their stories were dull and tiresome. For instance, an old-time janitor that everybody knew died of natural causes and came back to haunt the school. Stupid stuff like that. There were a few stories of creepy cemeteries, but they don't really count. Most cemeteries are creepy. None of them had any good headstones like, 'Died of an axe', or 'Memento Mori', or best of all, a Witch's Ball.

Their stories were boring because their schools were boring. The elementary schools they attended didn't have two brothers buried under the boiler room. And their communities never had a witch running rampant amongst them.

Having these new friends to share stories with made school bearable. We made it bearable because we made it fun. We were all in the same boat—we knew it—we dealt with it. And the time in junior high school went by like the speed of light.

It was the summer before we started high school. Right off the bat, Matt told us that his family would be moving away. He was gone from Valley Center a week later. Good thing we weren't known as the musketeers, the two musketeers just doesn't have the right ring to it. But the M&M Brothers can live on with only two of us.

When I look back at this time, this is when I came to the realization that the entity that we call The Witch lacked mobility. At first I thought that certain places were favorite haunts of The Witch and others weren't. I wasn't sure where it was centered, just yet. Then I figured it just changed up its tactics. But then, I started to see how its influence grew less and less the further you got away from not only Valley Center proper, and the school in particular.

The way The Witch wielded its power was by projecting its will through telepathy. By using the power of suggestion into a person's mind to entice them to do things they normally wouldn't do. Coming to them in their dreams. Like Miss Wesson, for instance. In normal times, if The Witch wasn't influencing her, I think she would have been a great teacher and a good person. That goes for Mrs. Sink, too. Mr. Barlow, not so much, he was rotten to the core.

The Witch was also patient. Singling out certain people to harass. Grandpa Johnny was key to me figuring out that The Witch wasn't a ghost, but a demon that operated from the spiritual realm. It wasn't till after I graduated that I realized he wasn't talking about Hazel. He had told us there was something about blood that drew The Witch to it. Whether it loved to see it, smell it, taste it, whatever it was, it lusted after blood. He also told us that he and my grandfather were the only two left of the posse that hadn't been done in by The Witch.

There was this old abandoned well that sat next to the path that leads to the back forty of Johnny Muller's farm. He used to love to sit out in the woods, back beyond the well. He would drive his tractor out to the back woods. He told us how calming and relaxing it was for him. Out in the peaceful woods he would listen to the birds, watch the animals run around, breathe in the fresh air, and take in all of nature's wonders. It was a joy to him.

For some reason that we could never figure out, he stopped at the well on one of his trips to the woods. The only thing that makes sense to us is that The Witch was drawing him to it. Maybe he heard a baby crying down in the well. Maybe a puppy yelping. Whatever the reason, we'll never know.

Muller and I were playing catch in his front yard waiting for Grandpa Johnny to show up for supper. Muller's dad, Jake Muller, got to wondering where Grandpa Johnny was at. He was supposed to be there at six, and he was late. Johnny Muller was never late for supper. Jake drove over to Grandpa Johnny's farm and saw his tractor out in the field. He knew that it had to be close to the abandoned well.

He drove out to the tractor in his pickup truck and found the tractor just sitting there. Jake looked at the fuel gauge and noticed that it was empty. He thought it was odd that his dad wouldn't have had plenty of fuel in the tractor before driving out there. He looked over towards the fuel tank by the barn to see if Johnny was there. Something told him to have a look in the well. He walked over to it and could hear Grandpa Johnny groaning from the depths.

Muller and I heard Jake's truck screeching around the corner. He came flying in the driveway, jumped out and yelled for us to get the extension ladder and grab a rope.

Muller asked, "What's going on?"

Jake said, "Your grandpa fell in the old well."

Our stomachs sank. We hurried to the garage and grabbed the ladder and a rope. Jake ran to the door of the house and called to his wife, "Honey, call the rescue squad and tell them to go to dad's farm. They'll see us out in the field." He ran back to the truck and said, "You boys hold on to that ladder and hang on, we're gonna be burnin' up the road."

We hopped in the back of the pickup truck with the ladder and held onto it and the truck bed for dear life. We raced around the corner and sped up the road to Grandpa Johnny's farm. On the way Muller and I had tears welling up in our eyes. The look on his dad's face told us everything we needed to know. It was not looking good for Grandpa Johnny. Muller's dad was a trained EMT, that was what he did for a living. This fact did nothing for bringing any of us any sense of calm.

We about sailed away with the ladder a few times on the way trying to hold onto it. And then we damn-near flipped out of the bed of the pickup when he turned onto the path in the field. We bounced along the path and could see the empty tractor next to the well. The truck came to a sliding halt as we braced ourselves against the rear window. We were beat up by that ride, but that didn't matter. We knew we weren't near as bad off as Grandpa Johnny had to be.

Jake jumped out with rags and a flashlight in his hands, and yelled for us to bring the ladder. We set it down next to the well. Jake put his feet on the bottom of the ladder and told us to walk it up to him. We stood the ladder up and the three of us picked it up and moved it, so it was hovering over the well. Jake said, "We've got to be careful now. We're going to lower it down one rung at a time." We heard Grandpa Johnny groan from below.

Jake held one side of the ladder with one hand and the flashlight in the other. He said, "Okay, lower it down."

We lowered it down, nice and steady. We had to make a few adjustments on the way down to get around roots, boards, and other stuff that had fallen in the well. At last, we hit bottom.

Jake climbed onto the ladder and started making his way down to Grandpa Johnny. He told us to lower the rope to him when he got to the bottom.

We heard Jake say, "Damn, dad." We knew it was bad. He called up to us to drop the rope down to him.

Muller lowered the rope. Jake said, "He's wedged in here and bleeding like a stuck pig. Mike, get some more rags out of the truck and bring them down here and help me." I ran to the truck and got some rags.

I climbed on the ladder and started my way down into the well. Muller looked at me and said, "I'm glad you moved. I didn't know which one of us he was talking to, and I can't go down there."

I said, "I know. I don't want to either, but your dad and Grandpa Johnny need us." I descended into the well.

With each step of the rung, I caught a new sensation. The ladder would creak. Grandpa Johnny would groan. The smell would change. The air changed from dusty to dank. The air in the well had the smell of a freshly plowed field in the spring along with the smell of damp wood—that was soaked with blood.

Jake grabbed the rags from me and fast as lightning he wrapped up Grandpa Johnny in a couple of places. He said, "There, that outta do for now." It took a minute for my eyes to adjust to the dimness of the well bottom. My foot slipped on one of the blood-soaked rungs of the ladder near the bottom. I clasped the sides of the ladder and caught myself. I looked at Grandpa Johnny and saw that it was going to be very difficult to pull him out of where he was wedged without doing further damage. On top of being wedged between old boards that had fallen in, he was impaled on a steel fence post that was sticking up out of the floor of the well. There was no water in base of the well, only Grandpa Johnny's blood that was forming a pool.

The rescue squad showed up. Captain Schafer called down to Jake. Jake told him that I was down there with him and there wasn't room for anyone else. Captain Schafer told me to come out so that he could go down. I climbed out and Captain Schafer went in. He called up to have the reciprocating saw lowered down to them. Someone from the rescue squad pulled the rope up, tied the saw to it, and lowered it down to them.

Muller asked, "How it was down there?"

I said, "Grandpa Johnny is in a bad way. He's been impaled by a fence post." Muller turned grey as a ghost. We were both feeling sick.

We heard the saw running a few different times. Then Captain Schafer said to pull up the rope nice and gentle-like, remove the saw and lower the rope back down. One of the rescue personnel pulled up the rope real slow and removed the saw. Then lowered the rope back down to Captain Schafer.

Captain Schafer said, "Pull the rope till its tight and then help us pull Mr. Muller up and out of here." The rescue squad guys pulled the rope to help lift Grandpa Johnny. Captain Schafer and Jake came up the ladder with Grandpa Johnny. At long last they pulled him out of the well.

That sight seared into my mind forever. The fence post had pierced him all the way through the upper left leg, and was stuck in his throat. We heard a few gurgles and saw bubbling blood coming out of his neck, mouth, and nose. He had lost a lot of blood. They laid him on the gurney and put him in the back of the rescue squad. Captain Schafer climbed in.

Jake looked at us and said, "You boys be really careful now and get the truck home." He climbed in the back of the ambulance and rode along as they took Grandpa Johnny to the hospital.

We watched the rescue squad drive away. We looked at each other, stunned. We were only two weeks into summer vacation. Our good friend and fellow M&M Brother had moved away, and now this.

As we walked back to retrieve the ladder and head back to Muller's place, we heard what sounded like muffled cackling coming up and out of the well. We approached the well nice and quiet. It sounded like a horse was slurping water down in there. The slurping stopped and then we heard very faint giggling. We both heard it—we swore we did—the same thing. We both described it to each other later the exact same way.

We heard muffled cackling, then slurping, then faint giggling.

We were afraid to look down into the well. Afraid of what we might see. Afraid of The Witch of The Valley.

We touched the ladder and didn't hear anything down in the well. Then we pulled the ladder up and out of the well. We were half afraid that something was going to be clinging to the bottom of the ladder, but nothing was there. Just the dripping blood that I had slipped on in my descent. Muller got a look at that and gasped.

I said, "Don't look at it." I wiped as much blood off as I could and tossed the rags in the well. We put the ladder in the back of Jake's pickup truck. Muller got behind the wheel while I tied it down with the rope. I got in the truck, and we headed back to his house.

We were only fourteen, but we both knew how to drive. We had driven many times before, albeit mostly off road. We both had minibikes, then dirt bikes. We both drove riding lawn mowers, tractors, and our dad's pickup trucks. As Muller was driving, I got to thinking about all the fun times we had with Grandpa Johnny. All his great stories and the way he would tell them. I said, "You know, Grandpa Johnny was a good dude. He made me feel like he was my grandpa, too."

Muller said, "Don't talk like he's gone."

I said, "Let's be real. He was the last living member of the vigilantes that brought that witch Hazel in. You saw what condition he was in when they pulled him out of the well. The Witch of The Valley was down in that well today."

He said, "I know that for a fact." He slammed on the brakes and stopped the truck in the middle of the road. He had tears in his eyes, his face was twitching, and his voice was breaking. He looked me square in the eyes and said, "Swear to me that you and I will get The Witch someday."

I nodded, but it felt wrong. We needed something more definitive than mere words. "Let's make it a blood brother oath," I said as I pulled out my knife. I never went anywhere or did anything without having a lighter and a knife on me.

Muller just sat there in the driver's seat looking at me expectantly. I took my knife and brought it to my hand. I meant to cut a slice in my right hand in the meat of my thumb, but I missed and cut my wrist. I looked down at it. It wasn't so bad.

160

I handed my knife to Muller. He said, "You're serious."

I said, "You're damn straight. Let's get that bitch."

He smiled and took my knife and put a slice in his left hand. I turned my hand upside down. We slapped our hands together gripping each other's wrists in an Indian wrestling hold and shook on it. In his dad's truck, in the middle of the road, we swore a blood brother oath to one another that one day we would get even with The Witch of The Valley.

We got back to Muller's house and put the rope and ladder away in the garage. Then we cleaned our wounds in the slop sink and put gauze on them from the First Aid Kit. We didn't dare let anyone know of our blood oath. Muller went in and asked his mom if there was any news. She told him, "Not yet."

He came back out and handed me an RC Cola. We held the cold bottles of pop on our blood brother cuts to soothe them. Hiding our cuts, the best that we could, we sat in the garage drinking our pop and waited for Jake to return.

Somebody from the fire department dropped Jake off. He walked into the garage. The look on his face and in his eyes told us the news.

"Just so you fellas know, his last words were, 'Mike & Mike,'" Jake told us. He struggled to talk more, but that was it.

For a few minutes the three of us just sat there in silence with each other, only letting out a muffled sob now and then. Eventually, Jake managed to muster enough courage to say, "He really loved you both and thought highly of you."

The M&M Brothers both cried.

Sometimes when you're growing up, things change so little from day to day. And then out of the blue, sudden big changes occur. What a difference one year can make. The incident at the well drove an unforeseen wedge between Muller and me.

I had lived right in downtown Valley Center for my whole life up to that point in time. Later that summer we moved a mile away, still in The Valley, but not Valley Center proper, as I like to call the town. Things were never the same after that. I didn't go into town very much. It was time to move on to high school anyway. I reckon we grew up quite a bit in that one year.

When time comes for a change you either move with it or against it. Change is going to take place whether you like it or not. Tragedies have a way about them of bringing about change. There is never sameness after a tragedy. It can make a relationship stronger and bring you closer together, or it will create a chasm and drive you apart. The latter is what took place with Muller and I after what happened with Grandpa Johnny.

Every time I saw Muller, I pictured Grandpa Johnny hanging on that rope with the fence post piercing him like a hog on a spit; with the gurgling, bubbling blood coming out of his neck, mouth, and nose. I'm convinced that Muller saw the same thing when he saw me.

As usual, summer vacation flew by. We were in high school before we knew it, and the next thing we knew we were graduating. That time seemed even shorter than the time in junior high. Crazy how time flies.

A math teacher, Mr. Cramer, once told us that the reason time seems to go by faster as we age is because when we are three years old, one year is one third of our age. When we are ten, one year is one tenth of our age. Fifty is one fiftieth, and so on. He knew what he was talking about. I see it, and I have lived it.

Chapter 18

Back in School

I got a sports scholarship to play football and baseball for a small college in northern Michigan in a little town called Midland. This summer vacation was going to be the shortest ever. I was going to jam in as much fun as possible before I went to school later in July to get ready for the upcoming football season.

I was making the rounds of the graduation parties being held for our classmates. At one of the earlier parties, I ran into Muller. He looked to be about half in the bag. Our eyes met, we both smiled, and he came walking up to me and said, "Hey, Younger man," and he gave me a big hug. He had called me 'Younger man' since we were little kids because his birthday is two weeks before mine.

"It's been a long time, old buddy." I gave him a quick hug, pushed him back by the shoulders, and looked him in the eye. "Can you believe that we're out of school? Graduated? Already?"

"No, I can't." His eyes were smiling as he held a devious grin.

"What?" I knew he was up to something.

"Speaking of being out of school. We should break into the old elementary school and go up to Barlow's room. I'll shit on his desk, and you write, 'Mr. Barlow sucks donkey dicks' on the chalkboard." I busted up laughing. He said, "I'm serious. Let's do it."

"Oh, really?" The sound of that intrigued me for some reason. But there was no way I was going to do that and risk getting caught. I had a lot to look forward to with college and my scholarship.

"Yeah. Could you imagine the look on his face?" He looked at me grinning and sipped his beer.

163

"Can you imagine the looks on the kids' feces—I mean faces?" He spit his beer out and started choking. He recovered. I continued, "Damn, it's been a long time ole pal. How have you been? I mean, really, how are you really doing?"

"Good. I'm doing good," but his eyes said otherwise. "The elementary school lets out in another week, you know. Let's do it. Let's go into the school." He pointed towards a group of older guys that were at the party. He said, "You know Bonson." I saw Bensen, but didn't see Bonson in the group of guys he pointed to. "He's the afternoon janitor at the school and he's in there right now as we speak."

"Yeah, I know him. I named him." Benny Jensen and Bobby Johnson were two of the older boys that we grew up with in town. They were once known as the BJ twins. They were a few years older than us. They were the ones who told us about the school being haunted by the Ungrich brothers.

They were always seen together, and people had trouble telling them apart. I had no problem telling them apart. Bobby is my good friend Brian Johnson's older brother. Bensen was always over at their house when we were growing up. I had known the both of them since I was a little kid. I called Johnson 'Bonson' because he always wore an AC/DC shirt and their lead singer's name was Bon Scott—it was a no-brainer. Everyone began calling him that, and then started calling Jensen, Bensen.

Muller went on, "I heard him talking one day that he leaves the side door of the school unlocked while he's working. He said the old part of the school scares him."

"What's he think, the Ungrich brothers are haunting the place?," I asked sarcastically.

"Probably. He's such a wuss. Anyway, I heard that he starts on the third floor and works his way down, turning the lights off as he goes. Then he leaves out the side door and locks it behind him. We can hang around outside. When we see the third floor lights are on, we can sneak into the gym and hide. We'll hear the door close behind him when he leaves, and we'll have free run of the school." Muller had it all planned out.

I didn't want to get busted breaking into the school, but I didn't want to disappoint him. The two of us had grown so far apart after all this time, and I felt to blame for that. Grandpa Johnny is the reason we no longer spoke, but that was *his* grandfather. The more I thought about it in that moment, the more I realized I should have been there for Muller these past four years. We used to be brothers and now he was almost like a stranger to me. I figured it was time to try and make up for lost time. "Yeah, that sounds good," I said. "When are we going?"

He said, "Right now. Let's go." And away we went.

I never thought I would ever go back into the Valley Center Elementary School in my life, but I had agreed to do just that. We left the party and I drove us into town. I parked my car behind the Town Hall.

We walked to the corner at my grandfather's house and turned toward the school. Muller pulled out a pint that he had stashed away. He handed the bottle to me.

I said, "You've had your fill already. We don't need to be drinking that stuff, do something sloppy in there and get caught." I handed the bottle back to him. I had a future to worry about.

"It's bad luck to break the seal on another man's bottle anyway." He twisted the cap off and downed a big slug of whiskey. Then he handed it back to me.

I took a swig. I said, "That's all I'm taking. One for the show." I handed the bottle to him. "Now put it away." I felt like I sounded like my father. I probably did sound like him. But I wasn't going to encourage his behavior.

He snatched the bottle and said, "No. It's one for the money, and two for the show." He downed another slug. "Three to get ready." He downed another. "And four to go." He downed the rest of the bottle and threw it into my grandfather's back yard.

I grabbed Muller by the arm to stop him from walking. I yelled in a hushed tone, "What the hell, Muller? Go pick that up so my grandpa doesn't have to."

He said, "At least you've got a grandpa. Mine's dead."

I felt bad for Muller. I didn't know what to say. His eyes were red and tearing up. He was probably thinking about those lost years of ours just like me. And I was leaving for college while he would stay back in town and waste away. I started to feel terrible for thinking of him the way I was.

I said, "I'll go get it. I don't want him to hit it with his lawn mower." I retrieved the bottle and came walking back to where Muller was standing on the sidewalk. He looked a little better. I smiled at him and said, "Barlow's desk ain't gonna shit on itself."

Muller smiled back to me and said, "Let's do this."

The moon was nearing its fullness. It had just risen behind us as we walked to the school. I tossed the empty pint into the creek by the tunnel as we passed it. The third-floor lights came on as we approached the school. We went around to the side door, and it was unlocked, just like Muller said.

Muller said, "Wait a minute. Let's pray." He bowed his head, clasped his hands together and acted serious. "Yay though I walk through the valley of the shadow of death, I shall fear no evil." He looked up. "For I am the meanest son-of-a-bitch in Valley Center." We chuckled and slipped into the school.

We went up the little flight of stairs to the second floor. Then we snuck across and down the back stairs onto the stage in the gym. We hid behind the backdrop curtain on the stage. We whispered quietly, reminiscing how we used to run around playing tag, escaping a pursuing teacher up and down those stairs. We snickered. This was fun. I needed this. We both did.

We waited on Bonson to finish up his janitorial duties. We heard him hustling around the rooms of the second floor. I was worried that Muller would be loud and talkative, but he remained as quiet as a church mouse. Then we heard Bonson running across the hall, down the steps and out the door. The door closed behind him.

We came around and out from the backdrop curtain. Muller ran to the edge of the stage and jumped off onto the gym floor. He said, "Remember when we would run across the gym and jump up and grab the balcony railing? Just like this." He ran and jump-kicked off the side wall of the gym and grabbed the rail, pulled himself up and looked down at me from the balcony. I was shaking my head and grinning.

"Yeah, I remember." I walked to the stairs that we came down from the second floor. "I'll meet you in the hallway."

Muller went out the door from the balcony onto the second floor landing at the front of the school. That stairwell was monstrous. From the first floor up to the second wasn't so bad. But from the balcony landing on up to the third floor was a fearful climb. If you were to fall over the railing, you would either break your back on the handrail along the platform leading to the balcony, or splat on the concrete floor at the main entrance. Or both.

I stepped away from the stairs into the hallway and looked to the right. It was Miss Wesson's room. I stood there staring into our old fifth grade class.

It felt strange looking in there. In a flash I remembered how rotten our teachers used to be. How it was as if there was something influencing them.

Muller walked up behind me and asked, "You want to pinch a loaf on her desk and then I'll get Barlow's?"

"No, I was just thinking how The Witch has been influencing Miss Wesson since we can remember."

His grin faded. "Yeah, there ain't a witch, so let's get going." Muller walked toward the back stairwell.

"The hell there ain't. You know damn well there is. Remember what happened with Grandpa Johnny?"

Muller turned around quick and said, "Yeah, I do remember that. We were kids. And I'm not so sure what happened in that well. And besides that, he was my grandpa, not yours." He was glowering at me with a mean look on his face.

I could see in his eyes that he said that to hurt me. I shot back, "You know full well that I always called him Grandpa Johnny. And he always treated me just like he treated you." I was pissed and about to leave. He stood there breathing heavy, but didn't say a word. I went on, "It was The Witch. I'm telling you. Let's have a talk with my grandpa. He knows a lot more about it than I do."

He rolled his eyes and huffed at me. "There ain't a witch. That's just superstition. Let's just go up to Barlow's room." He turned and headed for the stairs.

He had gotten under my skin, and I should have left. But instead, I followed him up the stairs to the third floor. The wind was blowing outside making the branches of the trees sway. Shadows were crawling around the steps and walls of the stairwell from the little bit of light from the nearing full moon that seeped into the school.

Reaching the third floor a loud creak and pop let loose out of the old building from over by Mr. Barlow's room. I whispered, "What the hell was that?"

Muller said with confidence, "It's not the Ungrich brothers, scaredy cat. It's just the building settling."

I turned towards Mr. Barlow's room. Muller grabbed me by the arm and asked, "You ever been in this room?," as he pointed to the little room around the corner behind us.

167

I said, "Yeah, that's the little library where they had speech therapy. It's the room with the ladder alongside the chimney that goes up into the attic." I knew that because I had seen the janitor walking across the roof to raise the flag on the flag pole.

Muller said, "I want to go in there." We walked into the room. Muller pointed up the ladder and asked, "You ever been up there?"

I said, "No."

Muller said, ""There's windows up there. Let's go up there. I bet we can see the whole town from up there." Against my better judgment, we went up there.

I went first, as usual. There was a trap door that I pushed open and then kept climbing into the attic. I looked down and told Muller to come on up. I looked around for a light switch or a light string hanging down and saw no such thing.

Muller got up to the attic. I said, "We have to be careful walking around on the trusses up here, so we don't drop through the ceiling."

He said, "No shit, Sherlock," as he was looking around, "I see there ain't lights up here either."

We got out our lighters and lit them so we could better see what was up there. He saw a box over on the side of the attic and walked over to it. It was a time capsule. Muller said, "Hey look, it says open in the year 2000. You want to open it and see what's in there?"

I must have looked like I'd seen one of the Ungrich brothers' ghosts. I said, "Hell no, that's bad luck. Just leave that alone."

Muller gazed at the steps going up to the roof as he said, "Let's go up there. I bet we can see the whole town from up there."

"Naw, that's what you said about up here. Let's just get out of here." I was feeling uneasy.

He climbed up the steps and pushed against the trap door to the roof. He knew full well I didn't want to go up there, so he pretended it wouldn't open. He said, "It won't open. It feels like someone is sitting on it." He grinned.

I know I had a look of terror on my face. I said, "Let's get out of here." He laughed as he came down the steps and asked, "Why, you scared?"

"Yeah, this place gives me the creeps." I made my way back to the trap door and the ladder by the chimney.

He said, "Wait. I'm going down first." He nudged his way between me and the ladder and gave me a look of disgust. "You look pale. Are you sick, or something? Scared?" He made a face and lurched towards me. "Boo!" He cackled after I jumped, then he took his good old time going down the ladder.

I looked down to watch him descend. As soon as his top hand on the ladder was below the opening in the attic floor, I heard a noise. It sounded like an air compressor. That's the best way I can describe it. It went, "*Shh, Shh, Shhhhh,*" in succession, with each sound louder in progression. The last sound stopped what felt like an inch from the back of my head. I lifted my head up and turned to see whatever it was that had made the sound. I could feel someone—or something—staring at me. It was burning a hole in the back of my head. It couldn't be, it had to be just my imagination.

A voice spoke within me sounding like my own inner voice, but they weren't my thoughts. *'Scared, Younger?'* *'You can swim.'* *'Dive out of here.'* I almost listened to it and dove out of there through the open hatch, but I was able to stop myself.

Suddenly, I felt something touch the side of my head above my ear. I raised my hand over my head to feel for what touched me, thinking it may have been something dangling from the ceiling, like a light string. As I raised my hand to pass it over my head, I remembered that there were no light strings anywhere. My hand passed over my head and there was nothing there, not even a hanging spider, but I could still feel the sensation of something lightly pressing against the back of my head.

Now I'm thinking the feeling on my head is more like that of a hand. It was too strong of a touch to be something small, and the longer it lingered the more I could feel as though there were individual fingers pressing against me. Another foreign thought came to me, *'Let me in, and I'll protect you.'*

I turned to see what it could be, and the pressure on my head increased into a strong force to prevent me from turning around to see it. My eyes widened as I realized there really *was* something up there with me. I darted down the ladder. The trap door slammed down above me, just missing hitting me in the head.

Muller was still on the ladder, taking his gleeful time descending. He looked up at me racing down the ladder and I stepped on his hands. My foot slipped off his hand, causing me to lose my grip and I fell to the floor taking Muller down with me.

He barked, "What the hell are you doing?"

"There was something up there. Something touched me!" I rolled off of him and stood up.

"Ah, bullshit! You're so full of shit." He got up slowly and massaged the hand I stepped on.

He was looking at me wanting to have an explanation of why I came flying down the ladder. I said, "Muller, it's The Witch."

Just then, we started hearing all sorts of creaking and cracking in the school. We thought we could hear faint laughter—just like we heard that day in the well—but I didn't dare mention that to him. Then we heard a huge creak and pop.

I grabbed him by the shoulder. "I'm telling you, Muller, it's The Witch. That thing made a sound like this, '*Shh, Shh, Shhhhh,*' and then put this idea in my mind to dive out of there. And to let it in. Then it touched me. It's The Witch."

"There ain't no witch." Muller chuckled uncomfortably. I could see in his eyes that he believed me, but he didn't want to.

I was about to panic. I said, "Let's get the hell out of here." I had to get out of the school.

Just then the bell started ringing in the old schoolhouse next door—the school that Hazel had attended. I bolted across the third floor away from the little library. Away from the clanging bell. Away from the easy flights of stairs. Although it would have been easier to exit the building going that way, I wasn't going to exit the school right next to the old schoolhouse.

Muller was hot on my trail. We made tracks for the precarious stairwell. It was going to be a much more dire descent to exit by these stairs. Especially when you're running and skipping four steps at a time. I could feel the presence of The Witch. Muller could lie to himself all he wanted, but we both knew it. The Witch was real. She was real and she wanted to kill us. And the last place in the world that I wanted to die was in that god-forsaken school.

The Witch was prying into mind, '*Make it quick, jump over the railing.*' I put that thought away and a new one popped in, '*Leap through the window.*' I approached the landing at the bottom of the top flight of stairs. The thought of bashing through the second-floor window wouldn't leave me. I was going to end up all sliced up with shards of glass sticking in me, my twisted pile of flesh bleeding out on the sidewalk below. I would be found the next day lying in a pool of my own blood at the main entrance.

As my foot touched the landing at the second floor, Muller ran into me, and I blasted against the wall. If not for that, I may have crashed through the window. We streaked past the balcony and rounded the corner to the last flight of stairs. I was right on Muller's tail. I had never seen him run so fast. I usually outran him, but on that sprint, he stayed just ahead of me. We fired down the stairs. Muller blasted against the crash bar of the front door to the school. The door flung open, and we were outside. I raced past him down the little hills and stopped under a streetlight, near the tunnel entrance I had ran across hundreds of times when I was a kid. The bell stopped ringing.

Muller came walking up laughing. He said, "I never knew you to be a sissy before."

"Piss off." I had enough of his soused lip. "I'm telling you, that was the same entity that killed Grandpa Johnny—The Witch—that we swore a blood brother oath to get even with."

"I don't ever want to hear you say his name again," he fired a stern finger at me, as if he were scolding a kid. "He's not your grandpa." His eyes were full of anger.

"Grandpa. Johnny." I just had to say it. Muller lunged at me and took a wild swing. I stepped aside and he landed on his face on the ground. He rolled over and shot up off the ground. I wasn't ready for him. He punched me square in the jaw. I fell back then danced to the side. An anger filled thought entered my mind, *'Bust him up. I want to see his blood.'* I readied my fist, but as I did, I could see a scar on my wrist. The scar from our blood brother oath. I perished the thought from my mind. "Let's not fight," I said, "I don't want to fight with you."

He huffed, looked down, opened his fist and saw the remnant of our oath on his hand, too. "Okay, we won't fight," he relented. "But you're not my blood brother. You're not my blood. And you're not my brother. And you're most definitely not my Grandpa Johnny's blood." He turned away.

I said, "We need to talk to my grandpa. He knows about this."

"I don't need to hear anything from your grandpa. I heard everything I need to know from mine."

I tried to not let what he said get to me. "Look, man—" I didn't know what to say. The words escaped me. "Just—let me give you a ride home. We *have* to talk about this."

"I'd rather walk," he spat, "And besides that, your grandpa was in that posse, and he's still around. If that Witch is real, we know who it'll be after next."

What he said stuck in my mind. I also knew that Muller understood that we had just encountered—The Witch.

At my graduation party later that Summer, the first person to arrive that wasn't a family member was an old friend of my dad's, Peter Ertz. What a character he was. He always had a smile and some funny story to tell. He pulled into the driveway in his mom's old, light blue Chrysler Valiant. He held the top of the door to pull himself up as he exited the car.

I stepped out of the garage and said, "Hi, Pete. I always liked that car."

He walked towards me smiling. He said, "Yeah, me too." He turned back to take a look at it. "They don't make 'em like that anymore." He came over to me and shook my hand.

"You don't look so good, Pete. Is everything okay with you?," I asked with concern from his pale complexion and the bags under his eyes.

He replied, "Yeah, I'm doing alright. I was up half the night from the noise of some scurrying critters running around in the attic. I thought the bastards were going to fall right through the ceiling and land on me in my bed." He grinned. "How about you come over and take a look around? Get rid of 'em for me. I'll pay you."

"Sure. I can come over tomorrow." I cringed inside at the thought of the attic in the school. The Witch actually touching the back of my head.

People steadily came pouring in. Pete made his rounds talking and laughing. Muller actually showed up. We didn't talk much beyond saying hi. I was busy trying to make sure I thanked everyone for coming and for their much-needed gifts of cash that I would be putting towards college. I could tell something was bothering Muller, but I didn't get a chance to talk with him about it. He left without even saying goodbye.

The next morning, I borrowed my dad's truck and drove to Pete's house. I ambled up to the front door and knocked on it. Pete answered the door. He looked about the same as he did the day before at my grad party. He said, "Morning, trooper. You're right on time, as usual."

172

I said, "I'm going to take a walk around the house to look around. Maybe see where the critters are getting in."

"I'm going to have some coffee. You want some?"

"No thanks. I had a cup before I came over. Another cup of coffee and I'll be wound up like an eight-day clock."

When I got to the back of the house I noticed a roof vent peeled up. I went around to the garage and saw Pete sitting in a chair enjoying his coffee. I said, "I think I found where the critters are getting in. I'm going to have to go up in the attic and look around." He nodded me in the direction of his attic, and I pulled down the collapsible ladder leading up to it in the corner of his garage.

"You might need this." Pete said as he tossed me a flashlight.

I caught it from the air. "Yes, thanks." I went up to investigate.

I could feel the temperature increase with each rung of the ladder as my face got closer to the attic space. I poked my head up and shined the flashlight around. I could see dust particles and fiberglass floating in the hot, stagnant air. Over by the peeled-up roof vent I could see a pile of acorns. Squirrels.

I banged on the trusses and made some noise to make sure the critters were out of the attic. I didn't see or hear anything up there. I went back to the much cooler garage space and asked Pete for a hammer and some roofing nails to fix the vent. I carried a ladder around back and Pete followed me with the hammer and nails. When I got on the roof and saw the vent, I noticed it would need to have some screen inside of it to keep out the squirrels. We went back to the garage, and I cut a piece of screen from a roll that Pete found. I went back up on the roof and secured the roof vent.

I took Pete's flashlight and a small cardboard box and headed back into the attic where the squirrel had been gathering the nuts. As I was picking them up I wished I had done this first. It was getting hotter by the minute. It was early June, but it was a warm one that day. I straightened up the insulation and headed back to the ladder. On the other side of the attic, above the garage, I saw a trunk. I went over and opened it up. I shined the flashlight inside. It was full of old Valley Center Visitor newspapers and stacks of notebooks. The headline of the paper on top stated: *The Witch of Valley Center Confesses!* My mind wandered back to all the old stories that my grandfather used to tell me about The Witch.

"Hey Pete," I called out with excitement.

"Yeah, you need something?"

"There's an old trunk up here. Can I bring it down?"

"Sure."

I latched onto it and dragged it back to the ladder. I handed down the box of acorns to Pete. Then I slid the trunk down the stairs with me as I descended them. I closed the collapsible ladder back into the garage ceiling.

Pete whistled, "I haven't laid eyes on that in quite some time." He seemed as excited as me. "Bring that thing over here." He walked over and sat back down. I hurried over and set the trunk down next to Pete. He opened it up like it was holding the holy grail.

"Can I go through that paper?" I pointed to the top paper, about the confession of the witch.

"Of course," He handed it to me. "Oh yeah, I remember putting this up there years ago." He started going through the trunk while I sat down and read the story.

I finished reading it and handed the paper back to him. My voice cracked with excitement when I said, "I'm really interested in the story about the witch. Can you tell me all about it?" This was going to be great; hearing and reading the stories from the reporter who wrote them.

"Sure, I'd love to." And he did just that. He pulled out paper after paper, notebook after notebook and talked. He went through the whole story from Hazel being a little girl through to her demise. Then I told him all about my grandfather's stories, and Grandpa Johnny's stories.

I was on information overload. We talked well into the afternoon. He said, "You can take this and read everything for yourself." I looked at him in amazement. He continued, "I don't need it anymore. Tell you what, you can just keep the whole thing. Papers, notes, trunk, and all. I picked through the good stuff, anyway."

I grinned from ear to ear. "Thanks, Pete. You have no idea what this means to me."

I must have been glowing because Pete said, "By the look about you, I think I have a pretty good idea."

I took the trunk back to my parents' house and carried it down into the basement and set it down on the old puzzle table. Then I spent the next few days going through the trunk and separating all the newspapers and notebooks into two piles. One pile for The Witch, and one pile for anything unrelated.

For the rest of the summer break, I worked on trying to compile the complete story of The Witch. Because of what Muller had said, I also closely observed my grandfather's behavior. He took extra careful precautions in his every move because he, too, was well aware that he was the only one left from the posse that captured Hazel.

If he was on foot, he would never cross the street unless there was no traffic—whatsoever—even if a car was a few thousand feet away he would wait to cross the street. He looked both ways at least three times before he would pull out into traffic when driving. Even waiting at intersections when he got a green light for a few moments before driving through, just in case one of the other drivers got it in their head to run the red. Whatever he did he was constantly looking over his shoulder.

I was with my grandfather at the Valley Center 4th of July Parade. What a grand time the parade always is. Every fire truck would be in it. Kids would decorate their bikes and ride them through town. The members of the Town Council would ride in antique cars and wave to the crowd with smiling faces. Hay wagons turned into floats being pulled by tractors. People on horses, the Valley Center Marching Band, and, leading the parade, the veterans of the many wars that our country has fought.

Seeing the veterans march always brings up an emotional response from within me. I think about the sacrifices these men made when they were young; the carnage, death, destruction, and violence they endured. A terrible thing to go through only to come back home and act as though they hadn't seen the things they did.

My grandfather, also a veteran, was to be honored in that year's parade with a plaque for sixty years of service as a member of the Valley Center Fire Department. He was so excited. He got to ride on the leading fire truck, everyone's favorite, the old Number 12, 1924 LaFrance.

The parade would start at the Valley Center Christian Church at the east side of town. As the band approached the edge of town they would play: *It's a Grand Old Flag*. The crowd would wave and cheer. The Town Council members would throw candy to the kids. The parade would march down Center Street to West River Road and end up at the park behind the elementary school. It was such a joyous occasion every year.

Slim, whose real name was Simon Svoboda, was riding his prized horse, Lone Star. That horse was a beast, and Slim was the only one who could handle him. Lone Star was a tall, handsome Appaloosa with a white star on his forehead. He strutted and pranced as he walked. Slim was proud as a peacock riding Lone Star in his fancy riding outfit.

I took my spot on the front steps of The Town Hall as the veterans led the way. They were followed by the band, then the floats, the kids on their bikes, the antique cars, the horses, and the fire trucks. As Slim and Lone Star arrived at the front of the Salty Dog Saloon that he owned, Slim tried to get Lone Star to stand on his hind legs. I saw him practice this many times at his farm. Lone Star would hop along on his hind legs for a few strides, while pawing the air with his front legs, with Slim sitting high and proud in the saddle waving his riding crop.

Lone Star got up on his hind legs, but didn't hop. As they approached the Town Hall I saw a yellow jacket circling around the chest of the mighty Appaloosa. I say the horse got stung, others said they saw Slim hit Lone Star across the face with his riding crop. I didn't see that. What everyone saw was Lone Star go up on his hind legs again, turn around towards the LaFrance fire engine behind him, hop twice, and then lurch way up in the air and flip over on his back, slamming down hard on top of Slim on the pavement of Center Street.

Lone Star rolled off of Slim and reared up in the air, then came down hard on Slim's head with both powerful front hooves. When I think about it, I can still hear the SMACK sound of Slim's head crushing. Lone Star continued to pounce on poor Slim's body. I didn't know what to do, but I knew I had to do something. I ran out to Slim and as Lone Star was about to rear up again, I grabbed the reins and pulled as hard as I could.

Lone Star pulled back and dragged me with him. His hair had flopped over one of his eyes. The other eye was staring at me with an evil glare. I swear, for a moment, it looked like his eye was dancing. My heart skipped a beat, and I called out, "Lone Star, stop!" I thought I would be lying next to Slim in about two seconds, but Lone Star pulled up and out of my grip. Then he turned and bolted down Maple Street, back to Slim's farm.

Just behind where Slim and Lone Star were in the parade was the LaFrance fire engine stopped in the street. My grandfather wasn't on it. I spun around trying to find him and saw that he was standing on the raised sidewalk in the doorway of the Salty Dog Saloon, grimly looking down at Slim. He had preemptively gotten off of the fire engine and raced away before Lone Star could reach him. Call it luck, or premonition, but I think he could feel something was amiss and got out of Dodge. His face was ridden with guilt as he looked at Slim. He realized that Slim had taken his place. The Witch intended for it to be him on the ground.

My eyes followed my grandfather's gaze, and I looked down to see Slim. His head was lying to the right side with his left eye hanging out of his skull and dangling by the optic nerve. His right eye was gazing at the trail of blood slowly winding its way through the small crevices of the asphalt, towards the storm drain on the side of the street. The blood stream matched the shape of Rocky River that I had seen on maps of Valley Center.

I leaned down to try and comfort Slim. Paramedics rushed in and told me to move away. All I could do was stand there and watch. I didn't see his chest moving at all. His rib cage was crushed, rib bones were poking through his leather vest. Both of his legs looked like they had extra joints in them. Slim looked like a scarecrow, but instead of straw for stuffing, his mashed up, bloody body filled his clothes.

I looked to the sidewalk where my grandfather was standing, but he was gone. I stepped back from the scene and in the corner of my eye I saw a familiar face. I turned, and my eyes met Muller's, who had witnessed the carnage from across the street. He looked down and slipped away into the crowd. I moved to the side of Center Street and stood where thirty years prior Richard Shroder had met his fate.

After Slim was taken away by the rescue squad, I wandered down Maple Street to Slim's farm. When I got there, I saw Lone Star. Saddle on, reins hanging to the ground, and grazing lazily in the pasture like nothing had happened.

Chapter 19

It was Time for a Change

Leaving for college was bittersweet. I was overjoyed to be getting away from The Valley—away from The School—away from The Witch. I was looking forward to my next stage of life. But I was also looking back at my childhood. You can take the young man out of Valley Center, but you can't take Valley Center out of the young man.

I was afraid for my grandpa. I didn't want him to end up like Slim or Grandpa Johnny.

I hated what had happened between Muller and I. We had to do something about The Witch. I knew that's what it was, and we swore an oath to get even with that thing. But how? How could we do anything about it? It's got to be some sort of a spirit, and my former blood brother no longer believes it exists. Maybe he just didn't know how to fight it, either, or he was scared. Maybe there really was just nothing we could do.

I got to college and tried to push all of those thoughts out of my head, keeping my mind busy practicing football hard and studying the playbook even harder. I set a personal goal to be a starter on the football team as a freshman. Two-a-day practices were much harder in college than they were in high school, but they were much more organized. I made a few friends on the team and couldn't wait for school to start and the season to begin. Practices were gravy once the season started.

What I began to notice about being away from The Valley the most was the lifting of the fog. I was starting to think more clearly now. At home there was this brain fog that kept me from figuring things out. I used to think that only the gullible could be hypnotized. But everyone living in The Valley seemed to be hypnotized, lulled into not paying attention—in a hypnotic state. I was free from that in college. It was there in northern Michigan where I put the puzzle pieces together.

I tried to concentrate on football, but in the back of mind The Witch was always there. I had brought all of Peter Ertz's witch notes with me to college, and no matter how hard I tried, I kept finding myself pouring back over them. I spent all of my free time piecing together, what I thought at the time, was the full story of The Witch.

I had to keep my mind occupied, I couldn't wait for classes to start. It was increasingly more and more difficult to not spend sleepless nights drawing connections here and there. Practice could only keep me so preoccupied, and even during practice I was powerless to stop myself from picturing what The Witch had done to people like Slim and Grandpa Johnny. At night, I even started seeing flashes of other victims during my sleep. As if I were living out the gory details firsthand. I couldn't tell if it was some kind of curse or just my mind playing tricks on me after extensively reading about how each member of that posse was killed.

Eventually school started up, and I had a Theology class that I figured would be a breeze. When I was in high school, I had read the Bible from beginning to end. I had always wanted to do that ever since I was a kid. After I did, I began studying it, similarly to how I now poured over the story of Hazel Dill, I had spent my free time in high school pouring over the Bible. I became a firm believer in the saving grace of a Holy God through our Lord and savior, Jesus Christ.

I sat near the front of the class on the first day of Theology, and I noticed this beautiful young woman that came into the room with another good-looking gal. The young woman that caught my eye looked right at me and her eyes lit up. She turned to her friend and whispered something to her with a smile. Her friend looked at me and smiled, too. They headed my way, but there were no open seats next to me, so they drifted to the back row and took a seat.

Class started and any excitement I previously had immediately left me. The professor had made it clear that this was not like the kind of course you would find at a Bible college. Instead, he was only interested in deconstructing religious texts. He had tenure and used it to allow him to criticize every religion we would cover throughout the course and chastise those who actually believed it.

179

I challenged him. I had to. It simply just wasn't right. He could critically analyze the texts, but to say it was entirely unreasonable to be religious was an insult. The rest of class was spent in heated debate, with many of the students sitting around me butting in and siding with the professor. I couldn't believe it.

After class, I got caught up in a debate with these guys sitting by me. I meant to catch up with the young women and introduce myself, but I didn't make it. When I got to class the next day, I sat where they had been sitting the day before.

When they came in, they didn't notice me up there and walked to the place I had been sitting the day before and sat down. The gal that had caught my eye turned around and glanced up to where they had sat the day before. I smiled, waved, and shrugged my shoulders. She waved to me with a smile.

This time, I avoided causing any sort of a stir during class. I was determined to catch up with those girls after class. Thankfully, the professor ignored my presence during his first lecture on Zoroastrianism. As soon as class finished, I bolted to the door and caught up to the two girls. They both were wearing these flowing, multi-colored, multi-layered, shear, gown-like sundresses. They seemed to glide along as they walked.

When I finally caught up to them, I tipped my imaginary hat, nodded, and said, "Ladies." I gave them a slight bow. When I looked up I saw the girl's green eyes that I had my sights on glowing with joy. I was nervous. I said, "My name is Mike Center from Valley Center." I smiled.

She said, "My name is Doreen." She looked to her friend. "This is Olivia."

Olivia looked from me to Doreen and said, "This guy's really Centered." They both chuckled.

"I mean—my name is Mike Younger and I'm from Valley Center. It's in northern Ohio. South of Cleveland about twenty miles." I couldn't believe I screwed up like that, my face must've turned beet red. I thought they'd probably never talk to me again.

Doreen dismissed my embarrassing introduction with a laugh and asked, "What brings you up here to go to school?"

"I got a scholarship to play football and baseball. And get edu-ma-cated, of course." She smiled. I had made some new friends.

"I see. Where are you living at?" She was genuinely interested in me. I could tell.

"A small apartment above an older couple's garage on the edge of town." We walked along and talked. I noticed how the sundresses that Doreen and Olivia both wore bounced about them as they ambled along.

"How about you gals, where do you live?"

"We share an apartment not far from here with my sister, Trudy. She's working on getting her master's degree."

"In what?," I asked with interest.

"Spirituality." She stared straight ahead and looked into the distance.

"Wow. How cool is that?" I was eager to meet this Trudy chick and pick her brain about the spiritual realm. "Where are you gals from?"

Olivia chimed in, "We're from a small town called Leslie. It's about one hundred miles south of here."

We sat next to each other every day after that. I would speak up and question the professor, Mr. Stevenson. I usually kept my personal beliefs to myself. For one thing, I didn't like to be ridiculed about them. And for another, they're personal. But I didn't care up there because Professor Stevenson didn't like me, so I returned the favor. He also didn't like to be questioned, so I questioned him. There was no debating and discussion to be bandied about. It was the professor's way or the highway. He would make verbal attacks against my stances and gather up his little group of suck-ups to join in with him. That all led to me earning the nickname, Preacher Boy.

Professor Stevenson was teaching on Genesis 6:2, That the sons of God saw the daughters of men that they were fair; and they took them wives of all which they chose. In his version, the sons of God are the sons of Seth, who is Adam and Eve's third son.

I piped up, "But professor, the original Hebrew words for sons of God are, *Bene ha Elohim*. Which means, sons of the Elohim. Therefore, they cannot be the sons of Seth. I believe this is speaking of fallen angels, not of Seth. In the book of Jude—"

I was rudely interrupted by the professor, "You believe? I don't think you have a clue as to what you believe. All you ever do is irritate me. If I say the earth is round, you will say it's flat."

"You're wrong. I'm just trying to have an intelligent conversation of what I interpret."

"Intelligent conversation, huh? That's what you call your inane spewing." He looked around to his little gang of sucks and got a laugh out of them.

"The book of Jude mentions the angels who sinned and kept not their first estate. And the book of Enoch talks about the fallen angels—"

"Enoch. The Book of Enoch is not considered inspired scripture, Preacher Boy." Another look around for the approving laughter of ridicule at my expense. "Shows how much you know."

"I know it's not inspired scripture, but it is mentioned in the Bible. I just feel it should be discussed."

"You disgust me. That's the 'disgust' in this class." He stared me down. "No more discussion on this topic. Understand, Preacher Boy?"

"Yeah, I get where you're coming from." I stared back at him. "Theology is not a product like you push. It is a process. One is led by the Holy Spirit to interpret scripture."

"In this class you will interpret scripture as I see it, Preacher Boy."

"Just as I said. You teach what to think and don't promote *how* to think."

"I think we aren't going to waste any more time on your silly arguments." I let him get off on his little power trip. I knew I had to find a circle of friends to talk with outside of his class. This guy was all about himself.

He would always belittle me, call me Preacher Boy to get a few laughs, criticize me and my way of thinking. I got to the point where I knew it wasn't worth it to try and have any discussion on any topic in that class. So, I was done. I shut down and didn't even try to debate with anyone in the class anymore. I still piped up once in a while just to irritate the professor. It was mainly just for something to do, because I was bored, or if I wanted to get him fired up; let him know that I still stood up for my right to hold my opinions. College sucked just like all the lower schools.

Doreen and Olivia were the only ones in class that I cared to talk with anyway. They were sincere friends. I had another class with Doreen, Psychology, where we sat next to each other, too. It was great getting to know her.

One day, she invited me over to their apartment. It was in the newer part of town. When I walked through the door, the smell of fresh fruit and burning candles greeted me. I saw a dreamcatcher hanging in the corner, surrounded by neat pictures of forests, waterfalls and other wonders of nature hanging on the walls. It made me feel comfortable. It made me feel at home.

I met Doreen's sister, Trudy. She reminded me of every mom I had ever known. She was all business. A few grey hairs stood out in her long dark hair.

She also wore a flowing sundress and glided along as she walked, just like Doreen and Olivia.

Trudy said, "So, I hear that you try to debate with the know-it-all professor, Mr. Stevenson. And he calls you Preacher Boy?" She smiled as she reached her hand out to me. The gals giggled.

"Yeah, I'm a glutton for punishment, and a slow learner. I don't like being ridiculed by that pompous ass." I shook her hand. "He doesn't like me for some reason. The feeling is mutual. I like to chime in just to get under his skin nowadays." I smiled.

"In the Wiccan faith his kind is known as a self-centered imbecile." She smiled as her comforting eyes gazed into mine. "I had my Theology class with him, also."

Thoughts raced through my mind. Wiccans? Things started to piece together for me about the girls. The candles, their appearances, these pictures on the wall. They couldn't be, though. Wiccans are witches, aren't they? The Witch that I know is a monster. I recalled all the stories I heard of Hazel and Lottie. Nothing about them was even close to resembling these girls.

My insides were aching. I had to know. Nervously, I asked, "So, Trudy... are you a witch?" I couldn't believe that question even came out of my mouth.

"You could say that I suppose." She held a calm confidence about her.

I saw that I had a clear shot to the door in case I might have to flee the scene. I was worried that I was about to die in there. If the door was locked I was going to blast right straight through it. I looked to Doreen. She was smiling. And to Olivia. She was smiling, too. I asked, "Is it a Satanic, Satan-worshiping deal?"

Trudy said, "Heavens no. Nothing of the sort."

That was a relief, but I was still sweating it. They weren't hemming me in, I still had a clear shot to the door. Yet, they were just lounging about the apartment calmly. None of them looked like they even considered hurting me, but I was on guard. I asked, "What is it that you do believe in?" I looked to all three of the gals for their responses.

Trudy started off, "First of all, we are *Wiccans*, not witches. Most of Wicca is considered occultic. But what we practice is a more nature-centered religion. We are not connected to any order of Wicca. At first we just called ourselves Wiccans because it was fun. But now we are getting into our own sect of Wicca."

Olivia chimed in, "Yeah, like, there are all these different sects—or orders—of Wicca. There are the Gardnerian, Alexandrian, Dianic, and others. There is an order for everyone. Everyone is welcome," she said with a glowing smile.

My mind eased a bit. I said, "I had searched for the truth in every religion. The universe just doesn't make sense to me without God. After much study, reflection and self-examination, I concluded the one cannot save himself. God becoming one of us, to show us the way to live and to die for our sins, is the only thing that makes sense to me. I thought I had searched every religion, but I haven't. I'm going to have to investigate this Wicca one." I was being sincere. I was curious about their beliefs.

I had this urge to tell them about the witch that I know about, The Witch of The Valley. But I needed to get to know them better. I had to be confident in what I say, and in how I present it to them. I had to get the whole story sorted out in my mind. If it *was* possible to hurt The Witch, then maybe they could help me.

Trudy giggled, pulling me back out of my thoughts, "That professor named you right. You really are a Preacher Boy." We all chuckled. And the nickname stuck to me.

For hours we talked, the three of us, in their apartment. I eased up more and more as our conversations went on.

Doreen said, "We believe that nature and the earth are sacred manifestations. We believe in preserving nature and getting along with our fellow man."

"Wow, how awesome. You see, love is the key. My mom instilled this in me from my beginning. She taught me that I am no better than anyone else. To pray for everyone and treat others like you would like to be treated. Like Jesus said, '*Do unto others as you would have them do unto you.*'"

"Preach," Olivia said as she put her hands in the air, smiled and danced. We all chuckled. "Everyone has their own individual spiritual path to follow, Preacher Boy."

Trudy said, "Everyone has the divine within, and everyone has a life-force—a soul—if you will. Our order has the same principles that your mother taught you. The Golden Rule."

"I like it. We are supposed to love our neighbor as ourselves. That is a hard thing to do. Love is the key." I truly liked these women. "It's so cool to me that Native American Indians and Wiccans have common core beliefs. My bloodline is of the Potawatomi tribe of Native Americans. I always pretended to be Chief Babek Shati when my buddy Mike Muller and I would play at the river." I felt such a true connection to these gals.

From that day forward we became great friends. I became very interested in their beliefs. We had many discussions. I grew close to them, especially to Doreen. The conversations with them all led to life-long friendships.

Doreen and I started dating. I saw a lot of her, Trudy, and Olivia. I had more fun discussing and debating with them than I did in any class that I had in college. We got around to exchanging ideas on our beliefs in the afterlife. Trudy brought up demons and how occult practices can lead to detrimental effects on a mortal soul.

I said, "There are spirits and there is The Great Spirit, The Holy Spirit. The Holy Spirit helps you. Helps you keep your focus where it belongs. The other spirits want to lead you astray. You don't call on these spirits to cast spells on others, do you?"

Trudy answered, "We do not channel or conjure spirits. That is not allowed."

I looked to Trudy and said in jest, "You should focus on Jesus instead of hocus pocus." She smiled. I was beginning to feel comfortable enough to rib her like that.

Doreen said, "Our order of Wicca just may have Jesus as the focus." I chuckled. Doreen, Olivia, and Trudy smiled.

Trudy said, "Seriously. As serious as we can be." She had a serious look about her. Nah, they couldn't be serious. They were such jokesters.

Another time we talked about how there are objective moral truths just as there are mathematical and scientific truths. Without God as the source of moral standards, there is no moral truth; there are only moral opinions. And because there are moral truths, good and evil are the same for all people. We are all divinely created in the image of God. Therefore, we are all the same. We are on equal footing with one another. There are no races, there is only one race—the human race.

I had a dilemma on my hands. It was difficult for me to build trust. I did trust Doreen, but how was I going to tell her about The Witch that I knew about? I had to tell her the story of the real Witch. I didn't want to offend her, though. And it wasn't just her, but Trudy, and Olivia. How was I going to tell them without having them laugh at me, or hate me? When I told our bullshit stories to the kids in school, I laughed at them. But when I was serious about The Witch, they laughed at me. That's why I usually don't talk about it. People laughed at me and looked at me like I'm nuts. So, I pretty much kept it to myself. I only brought it up with good friends, people I trust to not make fun of me, like Matt, and Muller. I didn't want to risk having these real modern-day witches make fun of me or put our relationships in danger. But from what I saw, these modern witches are normal, everyday people just trying to get by in this crazy world.

My entire existence became about learning the history of The Witch. The Wiccans only exacerbated it. I couldn't stop thinking about it. I couldn't sleep without dreaming about it. I couldn't concentrate in football practices or games. My studies were put aside. I was obsessed with trying to figure out how to get The Witch, like Muller and I had promised each other.

It wasn't until one sleepless night that it clicked for me. I was reading through Peter Ertz's notes on Hazel's confession. While I was reading her confession, I felt myself falling. Like when you're sleeping and suddenly have the sensation of falling that scares you awake, but instead the inverse, I fell into sleep. I felt myself drop and I was there, in the jail cell with Hazel.

I was deep in sleep and had a dream. And in this dream, I saw it all. The things that Hazel had seen in her dream. I walked out of the cell and through the extensive valley of the old world where the ancient people worshipped powerful beings, and I saw The Witch—in its true form.

A humongous creature that seemed to be over one hundred feet tall. Standing on giant paws with razor sharp claws that would retract or snap out like switchblades. There were two faces on its giant head, one on the front and one on the back. Each face had four eyes. It could see all around itself while pompously prancing around and terrorizing the people. Two great wings could carry it into the sky. Big mouths with sharp teeth and dripping drool blathered constantly back and forth to each other. It was able to hide its true nature from the people. By projecting thoughts to them, it masqueraded as a lion. Flying over the inhabitants of the valley, looking down on them and smiling. The lion landed on the platform on top of a stone structure, it forced everyone to bow down to it or suffer death. I was awestruck.

I tried to get the people to not bow down. No one would listen to me. No one could see me. I looked back to the temple and no longer saw the lion; I saw the beast that is The Witch. And the beast saw me. It stared at me, digging into my mind. Trying to make me bow down. Then both drooling mouths started laughing, and laughing, a deep thunderous laugh. I turned to run away. I was running, but not moving. I could feel claws swiping at me. The world turned dark. Still, The Witch laughed. Then it started to rain.

I awoke, somnambulant directions had led me to the front yard of the Wiccans' apartment. It was a cold, rainy night in late Autumn, and the crisp windchill crept up my spine. Shivering, I got up and stumbled to their door and buzzed in.

Doreen answered, her voice staticky through the intercom. I couldn't even make out what she said because my teeth were chattering. "It's me," I said.

The door mechanism clicked, and I pushed my way in. I was freezing. My hands were shaking like an alcoholic going through DTs. I had to get warm.

Down the hall, Doreen opened her door. "Mike?," she called, probably wondering what I was doing out at this hour. She saw how much I was shivering. "Mike." She ran up to me in a hurry and wrapped the blanket she had wrapped around herself around me. "You're freezing. What were you doing out here?"

I didn't answer. She led me into her apartment and sat me on her couch. Once I was in the apartment a wave of warmth enveloped me. I sniffled, blew into my hands, rubbed them together and warmed myself up. Before I knew it, I was feeling normal once again.

Once I became comfortable enough, Doreen questioned me again. I just knew that now was the time. I could finally tell her about The Witch. But, before I did, I made her promise not to tell anyone. It may sound foolish, but I didn't want to be teased about it. First, I threw out a little tidbit. I said that it couldn't have been real. Matt, Muller, and I were just kids. She listened and nodded.

When I was done talking, she told me that her and Trudy had an experience with an entity, as she called it, a few summers ago. Her neighbor had been harassed by it for years. A priest came to the house and Trudy joined him. They did some sort of cleansing in the house, and it went away.

How awesome was this? All of the intersecting beliefs of these Wiccan gals that I met that coincide with mine. Me taking the scholarship to come to this particular school. Having the Theology class that led me to meet these women. Everything was coming together. I had to pinch myself to make sure this was all real. One thing I knew for sure, The Witch was real, and something had to be done about it.

It was the week after Thanksgiving. Christmas break was right around the corner. Doreen and I had been out on a date when she convinced me to tell Trudy and Olivia about The Witch. We got back to their apartment late at night. Doreen got the gals to join us in the living room. She lit a candle on the coffee table, and we sat down around it. Doreen said, "Preacher Boy has something he wants to tell you."

I went through the whole thing, looking from Trudy, to Olivia, to Doreen. The gals listened and nodded in silence. I told them how there was a woman named Hazel in my hometown that killed her father, husband, mom, aunt, and uncle. She was rumored to be a witch. I told them of the stories from my Grandpa Clyde and Grandpa Johnny. How they brought her in and after she was dead, all the members of the posse started dying in strange ways. I mentioned how Muller and I scared girls in elementary school with the chanting into the mirror business. They didn't find it as funny as I did, since they said such a ritual actually *did* put one in contact with other spirits.

I told them the story about the Witch's Ball that went around like wildfire. What happened to the Ungrich brothers, and that the school was being haunted by them. Muller and I knew that Hazel had been possessed by an entity that we call The Witch. The entity was still around. I had even felt it when Muller and I went back to the school. I figured that it must have been there.

I finished up, "When we were kids, Muller and I swore a blood brother oath to get The Witch. And now, I don't know what to do. I need help. Somehow, we've got to get rid of it." There. The weight was finally off my shoulders.

Trudy was staring at me. The soft light of the candle flame flickered in her eyes. She said, "It is very dangerous for you that it touched you. Did it try to entice you to invite it in?"

I would be lying if I said the question didn't chill me to the bone. "Yes."

"Whenever you go back home, stay away from the school." She had a stern and concerned look on her face.

"I will. I won't go near that place. I hate that school." I must have looked tense, Doreen started rubbing my back.

Doreen said, "It's going to be okay." She smiled. I believed her.

Trudy said, "One of these days, we are going to have to see this town of yours."

"Sounds good. So, when could we do this? How soon?"

They all glanced at one another in uncomfortable silence. "This sounds like a powerful spirit, Mike," Trudy said. "The spiritual world ebbs and flows like a tide, and it follows the seasons. This 'tide' is the strongest in these colder months. Expelling this entity from our realm now would be practically impossible."

I couldn't believe what I was hearing. "That's it? We just have to wait?"

"I am sorry, Mike," Trudy said.

"The Witch is still out there, and it's still after people. After my grandfather! And I have to just bide my time?"

Doreen sighed. "It wasn't as if you were going to do anything about it *before* we told you that we could help you."

That was it. I had heard enough. Without saying another word, I stormed out of there. Doreen reached for me, but I pulled my arm away before she could grasp it. "I'll see you in the Summer," I said with venom. It was the last time I spoke to any of them that semester.

Football season ended and it was time for Christmas break. It was time to go back to The Valley. I was hopeful that I could meet up with Muller and patch things up. Then, maybe when I got back to college, I could try and patch things up with the Wiccans. I hated how I had left things. They were only trying to help, after all.

Mostly, I was concerned for my grandfather. I wasn't sure if The Witch had been messing with me in college or what. If it was, then it knew I was coming for it, and it would do anything to finish the job and stop me before I could do something about it.

189

Chapter 20

Back and Forth in College

On the first morning at home on Christmas break I emerged from my old room and got a cup of coffee. I sat down at the kitchen table to drink it. The local paper, the Medina County Gazette, was sitting there. I picked it up and perused the stories. An article on the front page caught my eye: Judge Giles Retirement Celebration.

In the article, I read that there was going to be a party held for the judge in the cafeteria of the old Medina High School on the square. The party was to be held this afternoon, and it was open to the public.

I recalled all of the notes I had read from Peter Ertz's trunk. Judge Giles' name was all over them. And he was a close companion of my grandfather. It lined up almost too perfectly. The Witch may strike and kill my grandfather right in front of Judge Giles.

I borrowed my dad's truck and sped to the old High School. Once there, I burst through the front doors and followed the signs to the cafeteria. Being the well-known and well-respected man that he was, I expected there to be a lot of people at his celebration. Unless I got there late and missed the crowd, he wasn't as popular as I thought. There were about twenty to thirty people mulling around. I saw the judge sitting at a table. I walked over and sat next to him.

I said, "Congratulations, Judge Giles." I reached out my hand to shake his and looked around the room. I couldn't see my grandfather anywhere.

He smiled and said, "Thank you, young man." He clasped my hand with a firm grip and gave it pump.

"My name is Mike Younger. I was wondering if I could talk with you about something that happened in Valley Center a long time ago."

His smile faded. He said, "Valley Center. That's a place that never seems to leave my mind." He was looking at me, but I could tell his mind was a million miles away. He asked, "You're from Valley Center?"

I grinned, "Yes. The place where men are men and sheep are scared."

My attempt at humor went over like a lead balloon. The judge didn't return a grin to me. He said, "I'll tell you, *that* is a scary place. There's something amiss about Valley Center." He thought for a moment, then asked, "Are you related to Clyde Younger?"

"Yes. He's my grandfather." I could feel a lump welling up within my throat.

"He stopped by earlier. He's a good man. I've known him for many years."

"Yes, he is. I've known him all my life." The judge chuckled. It eased me to know that my grandpa came and went. I should have just stopped at his house in Valley Center. Thankfully, I didn't see any signs of anything dire happening on the way into Medina, so I figured he made it home safe.

Judge Giles sat there looking at me expectantly. Now that my mind was clear, I thought back on The Witch. I realized that the judge may even have records of Hazel's case, or at least more knowledge of it. Although, something told me he wouldn't be so chatty about it. "My grandpa told me that you have an extensive law library. I'd really like to see it. I have an avid interest in law myself."

He reached into his pocket and pulled out a little note pad. As he was writing, he said, "Why don't you stop over at my house tomorrow around noon?" He tore the sheet out of his pad and handed it to me.

I looked at his address and said, "That will be great. I'll see you then. It was an honor meeting you, Your Honor." Judge Giles chortled.

We shook hands. He said, "It was nice meeting you, Younger One."

We smiled at each other. I congratulated him again and left for home. Before stopping at my parents' house, I visited my grandfather and made sure he was okay. It felt so strange, as if he were some child that needed looking after. I didn't stay long, we merely acknowledged one another. He looked just as he did when I last saw him at the parade. I left him alone and returned home, anxiously awaiting meeting with Judge Giles the following day.

I arrived at his house the next day right on time. I walked up a small ramp and knocked on the door. Judge Giles answered the door and let me in. I hadn't realized at the party because he was sitting the whole time I was there, but he used two canes to get around. His face grimaced as he did his best to hide the pain that his slow, steady gait relayed to him.

He welcomed me into his home and offered me a cup of freshly poured coffee. I had to accept and took a sip. He watched and smiled before shuffling off into another room, nodding for me to follow him.

A faint scent of Lemon Pledge mixed with the smell of fine wood and old hardcover books came to me. It reminded me of the shelf of encyclopedias at my grandma's house. It was his law library, and what a library it was. Books all around in solid oak shelves from waist high to as far up as I could reach to the ceiling. There was a large window facing south that let in perfect light for reading.

I ran my hand along the solid shelving as we made our way to some comfortable chairs. I said, "I love this room."

The judge said, "It's my favorite place to be." He took a sip of his coffee and placed the cup on the desk in the center of the room. He looked up to the ceiling. "Medina's fire chief, Dean Berringer, has a small Cessna airplane. A few months ago, he took me up in it and gave me a tour of Medina County from the sky. It was his retirement gift to me. To let me see all of the towns and villages that I had presided over cases in from above." He took another sip of coffee as he sank into the chair behind his desk. "Memories came flooding back to me. What a unique perspective it gave me." He smiled.

His smile fell away. He leaned forward in his chair and looked me in the eye. "When we flew over Valley Center I started to feel queasy. Waves of sideways gravity started pulling at me, dragging me down to the floor of the plane. My face smacked against the window. I was about to vomit…Then it went away. Dean asked me if I was okay. I was. I felt fine—after we got away from being over that town." He took another sip of coffee, set it down, and leaned back in his chair.

He stared off into the distance. He said, "I didn't want to go to that god-forsaken place when Luke and I went to the fair that day. But he insisted. He said he wanted to live there one day. He was always talking about it, and thinking about it." His stare went even further into the distance. "Well, that day never came. It looked like he was saying, 'Help me,' but I couldn't hear him… And I couldn't move." A tear ran down the judge's cheek.

This wasn't what I wanted to talk about, but there we were. I just wanted to hear his take on what happened with Hazel, not with The Witch of The

Valley. "I'm really sorry those things happened to you and Mr. Yoder," I said. "Can you please tell me everything that you know about Hazel Dill and what happened with her?"

Judge Giles took a long minute to reflect on my question. I thought it was going to be a fruitless effort. Then he snapped out of his thousand yard stare and proceeded to tell me his version of what took place in The Valley. We took a little break. We went to the kitchen and the judge got us another cup of coffee. I enjoyed his company. His detailed story went on for over an hour. He was such an articulate speaker. I left with a deep understanding of what had transpired at that time.

I thanked him for his time, returned both of our coffee cups to his sink for him, and then I left. I could still see him sitting in his library as I drove away, listlessly staring out the window.

The next morning, I was awakened by the house shaking. There was a rare earthquake from the New Madrid fault that rumbled through the region. I thought nothing of it as I had witnessed a few of these before. Two days later, I read in the Gazette that Judge Giles had died. He was crushed by a large bookshelf in his law library and suffocated to death. His body was discovered under some shelving and a pile of books that had tumbled on top of him.

I was in that law library. I don't know how that could have happened. Those shelves were secured to the walls and floor—the shelves *were* the walls. There was a picture in the paper of the floor where the judge had been found. He had clawed a big V into the floor with his fingernails trying to free himself from under the mound of books and debris.

After that, I felt the need to find Muller and make amends. I had searched for him in every possible place I could think of, to no avail. It seemed as though he had disappeared off the face of the earth. I was worried that The Witch may have got him. I ran into his dad, Jake. He told me that he had moved away, but didn't say where he was going, but that he'd be back some day. I had hoped he left to try and figure out how to fight The Witch, but last I knew he didn't even believe in it. I could only hope that he was okay.

Before I knew it, my winter break was over, and it was time to go back to college. The whole ride there I was bothered by the fact that Judge Giles had lived a full life, free from The Witch, until I showed up. I shouldn't have went to see him. The cause wasn't from the earthquake from New Madrid fault. It was my fault. After thinking on it all the way back to college, I knew The

193

Witch was messing with my mind. It was only a matter of time before it got to my grandpa, then it would be coming after me.

From all of my studies before college, in college, and all the information from Peter Ertz. The deep discussions I had with the Wiccans, what I came away with from Judge Giles, and then what had happened to him—I couldn't stop thinking about The Witch. Day after day, night after night, I scoured all the information I had gathered. Categorizing the events as I knew them. Running everything through my mind over and over again. My nightmares worsened.

I was away from the influence of The Witch, and out of the brain fog, but my brain wouldn't let me rest. My own mind was driving me crazy. I lost all interest in my classes. I was barely keeping my grades up, doing just enough to keep my scholarship. I was different now. The young man that went away to college was no more. The dreamer, the happy-go-lucky, fly along by the seat of your pants, fun-loving soul—was long gone.

I reconnected with Doreen and apologized for how I had ended things. She didn't forgive me at first but relented that she had missed me. We started talking again and I told her about what happened when I went back home for break. She eventually forgave me for my outburst, realizing that it would be only natural for me to act in such a way with how gruesomely people involved with The Witch were being picked off. Knowing that I could be next.

Doreen also perceived that I was losing myself. She tried her best to help me, and she did. Our talks and the talks with Trudy and Olivia helped me a lot, once they had all forgiven me. If it weren't for them, I think I would have driven myself insane. Thankfully, I didn't have to worry about my Theology class anymore, but I was still slipping.

The only class I had that I held the least bit of interest in was a pre-law class. We were studying contract law. When we got to studying the legality of offer and acceptance, that grabbed my attention. I mentioned this to the Wiccans.

Trudy said, "That is what an evil entity does to work its way in. It cannot possess someone without a contract with them. An offer is made, and the terms are accepted. Then the entity has the 'legal' right to enter. That is what it attempted to get you to do when it approached you in the school." That gave me chills.

My hope was that playing baseball would take my mind off of The Witch. But when the season started—for the first time in my life—I couldn't care less. Playing up north wasn't so much fun; it was always cold and rainy up there. I hated playing baseball in the cold weather. When batting, if you didn't hit the ball just right, your hands would sting. It felt like you were holding a hornet's nest. I never understood why baseball isn't played in the fall when the weather is warm and dry, rather than in the spring when it's cold, rainy, and wet. I had other things on my mind, but I still played ball anyway.

Before I knew it, Spring Break had arrived. Trudy felt the urgency of what was going on within me. She wanted to see Valley Center, but most especially, the school. Just to see if there was anything we could do now, rather than waiting for the Summer.

My team had a baseball tournament coming up the following week, during Spring Break when Trudy wanted to see Valley Center. I told the coach that I needed to take care of something at home. He gave me leave but warned that I had to make the bus at 5:00 a.m. sharp the following Monday morning. If I didn't show up, I was off the team. I had never quit anything in my life, and I wasn't about to start now.

I talked my parents into letting the gals stay at our house for a few days, while omitting the fact that they were Wiccans. Friday morning, we packed into Trudy's olive green 1972 Mercury Montego and headed for Ohio.

When we arrived in The Valley, but before we went to my parents' house, we stopped at the old elementary school. We got out of the car and walked to the playground. Doreen sat on a swing, and I pushed her. Trudy and Olivia walked over to the side of the big, vacant-looking, brick school building. I saw Trudy pointing to the upper windows as she was talking to Olivia. They both stopped walking and looked back in our direction. Trudy waved for us to join them.

As we approached them, Trudy raised her hand and pointed to the side entrance of the school. She said, "Look how the topography comes up to the building."

I never had paid much attention to this before. I knew there was a small hill that wrapped around the side of the school that we were on, but as I looked at it, I could see that it seemed to be connected to the hill by roots. In a strange way, it appeared to have grown out of the ground.

We walked between the little schoolhouse that Hazel attended and the elementary school. At the front of the school, Trudy said, "Ah, I see." She pointed over to the other side of the school. There were two small hills that led away from the building down to the corner of West River Road and School Street.

I didn't see much of anything. "What do you see?"

Trudy said, "Come over here." We walked around the building again. At the side of the school, on top of the second little hill, she continued, "We are going to form a sacred circle."

We sat down with our legs crossed and facing each other. The ground was damp, but it looked like I was the only one who had reservations about getting dirty. I sat on the wet grass and mimicked the spacing the other girls had. Trudy was to the north, Doreen was to the west, Olivia was to the east, and I was to the south. We reached out to each other and joined hands. Trudy said, "Close your eyes."

I was feeling weird about this whole thing. I didn't mind sitting in this circle and holding hands, but closing my eyes was the last thing I wanted to do. Thoughts of The Witch touching me in the attic came to mind. I pictured Muller and I racing down the stairs, fleeing the scene. Doreen squeezed my hand and smiled. She said, "You'll be okay, Preacher Boy. You're protected."

Olivia leaned forward with a reassuring smile, "Trudy's got this. Just keep your eyes closed."

I closed my eyes. Trudy started speaking in some alien tongue that I couldn't understand. Then they all three began chanting. A jolt of intense energy shot through us. It went around and around within us in the circle. We were vibrating as it was pulsating round and round and rushed through our bodies. We were a whirlwind, spinning like a tornado. It felt like were floating above the ground. The Wiccans kept chanting. Then—BOOM—it stopped.

Trudy said, "We must get away from here."

I opened my eyes and felt dizzy, as if we really were spinning, but all of us were in the exact same spot we were before we had closed our eyes. Haphazardly, I stood up and followed the Wiccans back to Trudy's car. We all stared at the school as we got in the car. My world stopped spinning once I sat down. The school glared back at us with its cold, empty gaze. I felt that it was laughing at me.

196

Trudy asked, "Where is the Town Hall?"

I said, "Take a left at the stop sign and then a right at the next street you come to." Trudy drove us to Maple Street. I asked, "What is it? What did you see or feel back there?"

"I will tell you when we get to the Town Hall."

"That's it right there." I pointed to the back of the building. Trudy pulled into the parking lot behind the Town Hall.

We got out of the car. Trudy said, "The school sits above an ancient ziggurat that was built a long time ago. At first, animal sacrifices were held there to appease the gods. The sacrifices graduated to humans. The entity that occupies the school draws tremendous energy up from the ziggurat and is able to protract its evil intentions by telepathic means for quite a distance."

I recalled my dream. Seeing a massive stone temple. It must have been the ziggurat. If that extended its reach, maybe it really *was* messing with me in college. "How far of a reach are we talking, here?" I asked.

"Many miles. I cannot say exactly. The mental fog that you spoke of is very strong here. If we were to drive away maybe I could get a better idea of how far it can reach."

We drove to my parents' house. Introductions were made and the Wiccans got settled in, then we went for a drive. My parents' house is about a mile from the school. We drove a mile and stopped. Trudy said, "I can still feel it here, but it is not as strong." We drove another mile and stopped. Trudy got out of the car. "I still feel the energy moving through the ground. However, it is weaker here."

We drove to the Valley Center Township line and parked by the side of the road. We hopped out of the car. Trudy said, "I can barely feel it here, but I do feel its presence."

It couldn't reach the college. That was a relief. I thought out loud, "So, about four miles? Hmm. No wonder things felt different in middle school and high school."

"What do you mean?," asked Doreen.

"Oh, I was just thinking that after leaving the elementary school the fog kind of lifted a bit. At least in school."

Trudy said, "Oh yes. Being beyond the point of influence would to that. But you were going home every day and back into The Witch's swamp."

"But what about the judge?," I asked. "How could The Witch reach the judge? He lives five miles away from where we are right now. That's nine miles from the school."

"Who is to say it wasn't the earthquake that shook the area?" I gave her a look of doubt. She went on, "There is the possibility that The Witch was able to project its will through underground fissures during the earthquake. If so, then it could have stretched forth that far. There is no doubt that The Witch is becoming more powerful as time goes by."

"So, how can we get rid of that thing?"

Trudy thought for a moment. "It will not be easy. I am going to have to meet with Bishop Charles."

"Bishop Charles, who's that?"

"The one that did the exorcism at our neighbors' house. He is very good."

"I thought he was a priest?"

"He was at that time. He got a promotion."

The Wiccans and I went back to my parents' house. My dad was working, so they didn't get to see much of him. My mom loved them, though. We hung out and played Trivial Pursuit until heading off to bed. It was strange not being able to talk about what we were doing with my mom, but it felt like we were protecting her, in a way.

The next day, we walked along the river and hung out for a while. Trudy said, "We should leave. You have the baseball tournament to get to and I am starting to feel the mental fog. It is time to go."

We went back to the house and said our thank you's and goodbye's. Before we left town, I wanted to show the Wiccans the Salty Dog Saloon. As we approached the saloon I saw Muller sitting on the steps in front of the Town Hall. I told Olivia to park across the street on the side of the road. I hopped out and gave Muller a wave and an awkward smile. He smiled back. I walked across the street up to Muller and held out my right hand upside down to his left hand, in the same manner we made the blood brother oath. He grabbed my right hand with his right hand, turning them both over and shook it in a normal manner. He said, "Younger man, it's been a while."

I said, "It sure has. How ya been, ole buddy?" The Wiccans had followed me across the street in their flowing sundresses looking like a bloom of flowers. I forgot my formalities because of the shock of seeing Muller.

Muller said, "Great," but his face said different. "Who are these lovely ladies?"

"Oh, yeah, sorry. Trudy, Doreen, and Olivia, this is Mike Muller."

Muller meant to say, 'Nice to meet you', but what came out of his trap was, "Nice," as he smiled and ogled at the gals like a panting dog.

"Down, boy, this one's spoken for," I said as I put my arm around Doreen. Muller looked from her to me smiling. I asked, "What have you been up to, Muller? I looked for you at Christmas break and your dad told me you moved away."

He said, "I just came back home yesterday. Patched things up with my parents."

The gals and I sat on the steps next to Muller. I asked, "What happened?"

"Oh boy, where to start." Then he proceeded to tell us of his latest adventure. "I went to this frat party a little before Christmas at Kent State. I was planning on staying overnight with Jones." He was a friend of ours from high school. Muller continued, "He goes to school there and lives in College Towers. The party was on the other side of town. I was kissing this chick at the party, and her boyfriend didn't appreciate it. He lived there in the frat house. He got his roommates together and they threw me out of the party. Jones was my ride and he had left with another gal.

"Now, in my defense, it was colder than a witch's tit out that night. I saw a pizza delivery guy stop and go up to a house to deliver a pizza. I figured that since he left his car running, I would sit in it and get warm. He came back to his car and yelled at me to get out of his car. I asked him to give me a ride to College Towers. We had words. I said some to him like, 'Fuck you, and eat me' and he didn't like that. He lunged at me across the front seat of his car.

"And if he hadn't hit me in the nose and made it bleed, there would have been a different outcome. It wasn't even his fault. I think he was only going to grab my arms to try and pull me out of his car. I reached out and bumped his hand as he was coming at me, and his hand went up and hit my nose. You know how my nose bleeds easy. And just as sure as Bob's your uncle, I got a bloody nose and a taste of my own blood. And you know what happens then, I go nuts. I beat the living dog shit out of that poor bastard. Then I drove off in his car and went ball-hootin' around the corner. I lost it on the ice and slid down into a ditch." I laughed.

199

Muller went on, "When the campus cops arrived, I was still sitting in the car, listening to the radio, and keeping warm. I got charged with assaulting the pizza delivery guy and stealing his hunk of shit car. At least the radio and heater worked. There was a brief hearing. I apologized to the pizza guy and agreed to pay for any damage to his car. He, in turn, dropped the charges. And that was that. Boy did I make my parents proud."

I was smiling, nodding, and shaking my head throughout his story. I said, "I bet you did. And I bet your mom is making her world famous twelve hour spaghetti sauce as we speak."

He smiled and said, "You know it."

I said, "Gals, his mom makes the best spaghetti sauce on the planet." I stood up and said, "C'mon Muller, let's go in the Salty Dog and bowl a few games."

Muller said, "Nah. I'm not going in there. I quit drinking."

"Really. Well, that's good. You needed to do that." I sat back down and asked, "What are going to do now?"

"I'm going to start working for my dad at Muller's Construction. One of our contracts is digging graves and putting in headstone foundations at the cemeteries. The fun stuff your grandpa, dad, and uncles used to do."

"Yeah, my grandpa still mows the grass at the cemeteries." I thought of how we used to scare the girls in school. I said, "Ooooh, the Witch's Ball," in my best witch voice I could muster.

He gave me a look like he was scared. Then he smiled and said, "Yeah, The Witch's Ball." He moved his hands like he was rubbing it.

"That'll be good, working with your dad. So, where did you go when you left The Valley?"

He continued, "I had seen better days; I'll tell you that. After making friends with the pizza delivery guy, I knew I had to do something. Something about my drinking, something about my life. So, I went to Cleveland to talk with a priest."

"You don't say."

"His name is Father Patrick. I actually thought of becoming a priest. Father Patrick secured me a room in the Diocese. In exchange for room and board I helped around the grounds doing maintenance work. During our discussions I brought up exorcism. You see, I also knew that something had to be done about The Witch."

"So, you're a believer again? Last I knew you didn't think The Witch was real."

"I came back around. Father Patrick does exorcisms. And from what I have read and heard about them; I think I can exorcise The Witch from the school. It can't be that difficult."

Trudy said, "You do not know what you are dealing with."

Muller looked from me to Trudy and asked, "What do you know?"

Trudy said, "Do yourself a favor and stay away from the school."

Muller shot me a look and asked, "What do you know about the school?"

Trudy said, "We stopped at the school on our way here. You know the little hills that the school sits on?" Muller nodded. "There is an ancient ziggurat beneath the school. It was once used for human sacrifice. The entity that you call The Witch pulls great energy from it."

"What's a zig-or-rat?" Muller asked.

Trudy answered, "It is a step-pyramid structure with a temple on the top that the ancients used to get close to their gods."

"Really? I've never heard of them before."

Trudy continued, "Yes. They don't teach these things in school. Some of these structures were used to summon spirits; both good and evil. I had no idea just how evil and powerful The Witch was—till we visited the school."

Muller asked, "And how do you know this?"

I said, "Think of Star Trek and Mr. Spock doing the mind-meld. When we first got into town, we stopped at the school. Trudy led us to a spot beside the school and we sat in a sacred circle. These gals were able to connect to the earth; to read what is in, under, and around the school, and the schoolgrounds. In the sacred circle, I could feel the deep wickedness of The Witch. Remember the thoughts that were entering our minds when we ran out of the school?" Muller looked pale. He wouldn't acknowledge what I said, but I knew that he knew what I was talking about. "The Witch is pure evil that wishes us all harm."

Muller thought for second. Then he asked, "How could you feel it? And why didn't it go after you?"

I said, "These ladies are Wiccans. We were protected in a sacred circle. I was protected by them." I pointed to the gals. "They know what they're doing."

Muller shot back, "Wiccans! That's how they connect with The Witch. They are one in the same."

Trudy said, "We are not witches like you are thinking."

"How do you know what I'm thinking?" Muller's eyes were darting back and forth between us. He looked into Trudy's eyes. He said, "The way this chick's looking at me is freaking me out."

I interjected, "Look, Muller, you know I would never steer you wrong. You and I both know that witches are rumored to be possessed by a demon, or demons. The spiritual entity that you and I call, The Witch, is not possessing a person. It has infested the school. And there are thousands of demons within The Witch. Trudy works with a bishop, Bishop Charles, on expelling these entities."

Muller soaked that in for moment. He said, "I didn't think of that. Not in a million years would I have figured that Wiccans and The Church would work together." He thought for another moment and said, "Also, from what Father Patrick had told me the only exorcisms he knew of were done to extract demons from a person, not a building."

Trudy said, "Exactly, it is not that simple and easy. I will meet with Bishop Charles, and we will come back together to take care of this."

Muller said, "It can't be that powerful." He looked from Trudy to me.

I said, "But it is. Remember what it did to Slim." I turned and pointed to the middle of Center Street, "Right there. And what it did to Grandpa Johnny."

Muller stood up and said, "I told you to never call him that."

I stood up and said, "That was over two miles out of town."

Muller stared me down. We were in a Mexican standoff. Neither one of us were going to back down. Doreen stood and moved between us. With her back to me, she said, "I love this guy, Muller. And I know that he loves me. He loves you, too. Arguing is fruitless. If we work together we can get this done."

I reached my right hand, upside down, out and around Doreen. Muller clasped my wrist with his left hand in our blood brother grip. We shook and sat back down.

Muller said, "It's the brain fog coming on. I know that when I got out of The Valley the brain fog lifted. You know what I mean; lost words, forgotten phrases, jumping to conclusions, getting angry at friends." He gave me a look with forgiveness in his eyes. "You know how it is."

I said, "Yes. Everyone walks around this place in a funk. It's like everyone is mesmerized. There's something off. You and I both know what's causing it. It's The Witch. And The Witch's reach is far beyond the school."

Olivia said, "We all feel the fog. That's why we're leaving town today." Doreen and Trudy were looking on and nodding their heads.

I said, "We'll work together on this when we come back. Maybe we can get together with Father Patrick and get him to help us, too."

Muller said, "We'll see."

I said, "One things for sure, we can't do it without them." I pointed to the gals. "It's not like we can go in there and physically fight it. The Witch must be dealt with on the spiritual level. Trudy and Bishop Charles know how to do that."

Olivia said, "Yeah, we're hitting the road, heading back to college."

Muller looked at Olivia and then back to me. He joked, "Is there a funeral you have to get to?"

I laughed off his remark and said, "I just wanted stop down here and show the gals the Salty Dog before we left. There it is." I pointed to the saloon and smiled. "And as fate would have it, we ran into you."

Trudy piped up, "We should go now. Muller, do yourself a favor, please stay away from the school." She stared into Muller's eyes. She could read something from him. I knew Muller well. I saw doubt in his eyes. He was doubting how powerful The Witch truly was.

We said goodbye to Muller and left The Valley. The gals and I got back to our college lives. I made it to the baseball tournament and the rest of the season went along well. I hit the books in my law class hoping to keep my mind occupied on something other than The Witch. Muller always had to learn things the hard way. He was about to learn for himself just how powerful The Witch was.

Chapter 21

Muller Gets Schooled

From interviews of Mike Muller, Bobby Johnson, Brian Johnson, and Benny Jensen

All I could do in college was bide my time until we could finally confront The Witch. Muller, on the other hand, needed solid proof of his own. He wasn't sure The Witch was 'all that', like his good friend Younger was convinced it was. Was he right, or was he wrong? Muller used to question if The Witch was real? Before that he questioned if it were Hazel, and Hazel alone? He tried hard at one time to convince himself that it was. He kept telling himself that The Witch of The Valley was buried next to her husband in Hollow Hill Cemetery, and it was her ghost that was haunting The Valley. He knew better now, but now he questioned how powerful could The Witch be?

After talking with the Wiccans and I, the vision of Grandpa Johnny being extracted from the well wouldn't leave him. The giggling, gurgling sounds from the depths of the well echoed in his head. He brushed off the fact that it happened two miles away. He was seeking vengeance for his loss.

Muller recalled the carefree kid he used to be that thought he knew everything. Running around the town with me and all of our buddies. He drove to the old elementary school, sat in his truck and stared at the vacant building. He laughed at himself for having his childish beliefs. The blood brother oath, the ridiculous fantasies he once had about the far-reaching effects of The Witch. Fantasies that every bad thing that happened was attributed to it. His old friend Younger still believes it can wield its wickedness throughout The Valley.

Gone was the cocky, confident kid that owned this town with his old friend. Now that he had grown up and become a man, he felt the loss of his grandfather more than ever. He knew everything when he was young. He learned it all from Grandpa Johnny. Now, he no longer felt he knew anything at all. He wished that we never would have gone into the school. That was a dumb idea.

Muller's eyes were riveted on the windows in the attic of the school. The windows of the school stared back at him with their cold, dark eyes. He wondered what it felt like being touched by The Witch. Was The Witch all that powerful like Younger and his Wiccan friends say it is? Younger wouldn't lie to me. And he doesn't scare easily, but he was scared when he came flying down that ladder. Why would The Witch mess with Younger and not me? It went after *my* grandpa, not his. The Witch can't be as powerful as they claim. If it was, why did it let us leave unscathed? I have to go back in there and see for myself. I've got to kick its ass out of there.

More thoughts started coming to him as he gazed at the school. Thoughts that weren't his, *'There's nothing to fear in there.' 'Younger knows that.' 'He was playing a joke on you.' 'He's making you look like a fool.' 'He's laughing at you.' 'Come back up here and see for yourself.' 'Then you can tease him.' 'Laugh at him.' 'Make fun of him.'* Muller drove home.

On his drive home, he recalled the times he and I used to play over at his house when we were kids. The first time I came over to his house that he could remember was when we were both four years old. His dad had this fiberglass tube laying on its side on the little hill in his backyard. We crawled down in it and pretended it was a spaceship. He had drawn these controls on the sides with crayon and everything. He chuckled. What a great adventure that was.

When we got older, we would venture over to Rocky River and play. We found the remains of one of the little log cabins that was near the old salt mine. Grandpa Johnny had told us about the Native American Potawatomi Indians first living on that land, and how Art Gunther's great-grandfather bought it from them. We would run around there, up and down the path along the river playing cowboys and Indians. Muller was the cowboy, and I was the Indian.

We would shoot each other with our Daisy BB guns. If you got hit you would play dead, dying in award-winning Hollywood fashion. Never giving it a second thought that we could shoot each other's eyes out. We stumbled upon the old salt mine entrance. We tried digging into it, but there was no way. We found the old fresh air shaft. We got rocks out of the river and would drop them down the shaft, listening for them to hit bottom. It was a lot of fun. Muller got home and went to bed.

When I was a kid I asked my grandpa about the time of the Native American Indians. He had heard from his grandfather, who had heard from his father before him, of a local Potawatomi chief that he knew. His name was Chief Babek Shati from the turtle clan. He mentioned how Potawatomi means *Keepers of the Sacred Fire,* but they call themselves Neshnabek, which means *The True People.* He also told me that my great-great-great grandmother was Chief Shati's daughter. I felt an alliance with the Potawatomi.

The tribe connects to their community, to nature, to their ancestors, and to the supernatural world. They unite with their ancestors through Matchimadzhen, *the Great Chain of Being.* I would think of Chief Babek Shati and my affiliation to him and this land. I would pretend I was him when we played by the river.

The inner battle of waiting on the Wiccans and getting retribution for what The Witch did to Grandpa Johnny brought Muller to his knees. He couldn't stop thinking about it. There had to be something done in the school. He became obsessed with going back in there. And he knew just the guy get the job done. Muller was going to play him to get in the school and do an exorcism on the building once he got inside.

He stopped down at the Salty Dog Saloon on a Saturday afternoon. He drank some pop and shot the shit with Eddy the owner and a few of the regulars. Then in walked Bonson. He sat on the barstool next to Muller. Their eyes met in the mirror behind the bar. Bonson was smiling. Muller asked him, "What do you suppose is in the school?"

Bonson's smile faded, and his face froze. He stared back at Muller in the mirror, dead in the eyes. Muller could tell that he had seen and heard some real shit in the school. His lips quivered and his voice cracked as he said, "You tell me, you're the one who says somethings in there."

Muller said, "Naw. I just said that stuff to scare everybody. Besides, Younger's the one who said that. I don't think there's anything in there."

206

Bonson continued, "I'm not sure about that. I hate going into the old section of the school. That's where I used to hear weird things coming from. Locker doors slamming, strange noises, weird breezes that swept by me even though all the windows were closed. I heard chairs sliding on the floor above when I was mopping second floor classrooms.

"At first I figured it was old man Humphry, the day janitor, messing with me when I was green, and he was showing me the ropes. But I heard some scary stuff in there when no one else was in the building. I turn all the lights on, on each floor as I go in the old part of the school. I start at the top and run through as fast as I can go. I turn the lights off and run down the stairs to the second floor and do the same thing. I finish and get out of there in a hurry. I feel so much better in the new section. But I still heard stuff coming from the old part when I was in the new part." He was shaking a little as he lit a cigarette.

Everyone had heard Bonson's stories about the school. Muller just wanted to see his facial expressions as he told it again. The rumor was that Bonson made all of that stuff up to make himself look brave. He was older than us and everyone thought of him as a wuss. His brother Brian was the brave one. Brian was our age, and he wasn't afraid of anything. I saw him grab an angry raccoon right by the scruff of its neck with his bare hand. It was digging in the garbage can in his garage. He snatched it up, carried it out back and tossed it in the river. We watched it swim to the other side.

Muller could tell by the look in his eyes and the conviction in his trembling voice that Bonson had felt the workings of The Witch. He stared into the mirror and thought to himself, 'Say Hazel Dill one hundred times.' He said, "I tell everyone that it's the ghosts of the Ungrich brothers that haunts the school. That's what you and Bensen told us when we were kids. Do you think it's them?"

Bonson said, "Could be. They really are buried under the boiler room floor."

"I don't believe the school's haunted. Take me in the school. I want to see for myself."

"Really? Bensen said he wants to go in there, too. He doesn't believe it, either." Bonson seemed warm to the idea. Probably because he wouldn't be alone in the school.

"Yeah, let's us three go."

"I haven't really heard anything out of the ordinary in a long time. It was mainly when I first started. Tell you what, let's scare the shit out of Bensen. I'll get Brian to go with us. We'll go up to the third floor. We'll have Brian sneak off on our way up there and run around the second floor slamming locker doors. Bensen will shit his pants and run out of the school like his ass is on fire." He chuckled at his devious plan.

Muller asked, "When can we do this?"

"Tonight. Meet us at our house this evening. When it gets dark, we'll cross the river and sneak into the school."

"Sounds good."

Saturday evening May 10th, 1980, Muller went to the Johnsons' house. He had a crucifix tucked into his blue jeans under his shirt and a small bottle of holy water in his pocket. Bensen was already there when he arrived. They hung out and played pool for a few hours. Then Bonson said, "We should do some ghost bustin' at the school."

Bensen's face lit up. "Really? Let's go." Muller and Brian looked at each other and smiled. Muller almost told Brian his real plan, to do an exorcism, but he kept it to himself.

Bonson grabbed his keys and off they went to the back of the property towards the river. The moon was lit by just a sliver of light as it was sinking in the west. Bonson was delighted by that because stealth was a priority. The darker the better. He would lose his job if anyone found out that he was sneaking people into the school. They crossed the river and headed into town.

The guys stood around on the playground to make sure the coast was clear. Bonson waved them over to the side door of the cafeteria in the new section of the school. He unlocked the door nice and easy, opened it and let them in. Taking a quick look around, he quietly closed and locked the door behind him.

Bensen asked, "Where's the scariest place in the school?"

Bonson answered, "For me it's the third floor, but the whole old section is scary. The boiler room, the basement under the stage in the gym. You name it, the whole place is scary over there."

"Let's go up to the third floor." Bensen was smiling.

Bonson looked at Muller and his brother Brian grinning. "Okay, if you insist." He and Bensen led the way.

They all rounded the stairs up to the second floor. Bensen, either in trying to be brave or just out of pure excitement, was right on Bonson's heels, so he didn't see Brian slink off down the hall on the second floor. Muller continued up the stairs right behind Bensen and Bonson as they crossed the landing and headed up to the third floor.

Just then, they could hear the sound of slamming lockers on the floor below them. For only a moment did Bensen seem scared. He had turned around to ask the others what that sound was, and immediately took notice of Brian's absence.

Brian came jogging up the stairs as quietly as he could, but it was too late. Bensen shot Brian an angry look and said, "That was you. That wasn't funny." Muller and Bonson tried their best not to let on that they thought it was funny.

"No, it wasn't. I just stopped in the john to take a squirt." Brian was grinning.

Bensen said, "Yeah, right. Let's go." Brave Bensen led the way up the last flight of stairs and across the third floor. The four of them crept along, feeling a sudden eeriness around them.

Three big, loud, locker slams rang out from the second floor beneath them. Bensen turned to Bonson and Muller and asked, "Who else have you got in here?" He was mad, he just wanted to hunt ghosts, not get messed with incessantly.

Bonson said, "Nobody. Really. We planned on messing with you by having Brian sneak off and slam a couple locker doors, but honest man, I don't know what that was." Bonson was scared. Muller looked at Bonson and Brian. Even Brian looked scared. It was no longer funny.

Muller said that they felt trapped. They wanted to get the hell out of there, but they didn't want to go down to the second floor. It was too high up to jump out a window. A chill came over them as they moved to the center of the third floor by the water fountain to figure out what to do.

A loud air compressor sound echoed above them, "*Shh, Shh, Shhhhh!*" The first sound was from directly overhead, the second was louder, and the third was the loudest, even as it moved away from them—towards the little library. Muller's entire body was covered in goose bumps.

Bensen whispered, "We've got to get out of here."

The building let out a loud crack, and pop as it settled. A screeching sound of claws dragging along a chalkboard bellowed from the classroom on the other side of the little library. Muller pulled out the crucifix from under his shirt and held it towards the noise. Before he could speak a huge gush of wind blew at them. The crucifix was ripped from Muller's grip, slicing his fingers. It zipped over their heads and stuck in the wall like a dart, high above the big stairwell at the front of the school. Next door, the bell started clanging in the little schoolhouse.

Bensen led the way as they ran for the south stairwell at the front of the school. The long stairwell that Muller and I ran down a year before. The sound of the clamoring claws grew louder and closer behind them. The thought, '*Jump, it will be quicker,*' entered Muller's mind as he ran. Thankfully, he recalled similar thoughts from his previous visit, and instead crashed himself into Brian and Bonson at the top of the stairs. They all three slammed into some lockers, and just like last time, this action saved them from putting themselves in danger.

Bensen wasn't so lucky. Nobody could stop him as he jumped over the railing. Muller could only watch as Bensen's body disappeared as it fell. Then he heard an agonizing scream come from Bensen as he hit the railing on the second floor. His back crunched on it, causing a ding to echo throughout the school.

As Muller ran down the stairwell he looked down to see Bensen fall to the railing of the lower staircase. His body bent over backwards as he struck the steel newel post hard at the bottom; then flopped onto the concrete floor at the front door main entrance.

Brian, Muller, and Bonson raced down the steps to where Bensen lay in agony, their minds clear of any outside influence. Once they reached the bottom they looked on at Bensen, moaning and groaning—battered and broken. They didn't dare move him. Muller reached in his pocket and pulled out the holy water. He poured it over his cut fingers and then sprinkled some on Bensen. A cackling sound eased its way down to them from above. They looked at each other and bolted out the front door; leaving Bensen behind. As they fled the school, the bell stopped ringing.

They ran to the pay phone and made an anonymous call that someone was laying on the floor inside the school at the front entrance. Then they ran out of town and hid out at the Johnsons' house.

The rescue squad gathered up Bensen and took him to the hospital. His back had been broken in two places. He had four broken ribs, two of them were compound fractures, and two of them were broken in two places, one of which punctured a lung. He also had a broken jaw and a broken nose.

When the sheriff interviewed Bensen he spilled the beans on the other guys. He was pissed off that they left him in the school all alone with that thing—whatever it was—that dug into his mind. The official story they told was that they were screwing around in the school and Bensen sat on the railing to slide down the long flight of stairs. He lost his balance and flipped over backwards.

When I talked with him much later, after that Summer, Bensen told me that all he ever thought about was getting well so he could get even with those guys.

He said, "When we were in the school these evil thoughts ran through my head. The first thought that came to me was up on the third floor when we were running to the stairs to get out of there, '*Jump, it will be quicker,*'" the same thought that Muller had. "But as I was lying there all alone these other thoughts kept creeping into my mind. '*Your friends hate you.*' '*Nobody likes you.*' '*You are worthless.*' '*Do the world a favor and off yourself.*' '*Get even with them.*' '*Burn their houses down.*' '*Kill them.*'" Tears were rolling down his cheeks. "I was scared to death of my thoughts. And I hated the guys for leaving me in the school like that."

I told him they weren't his thoughts. The thoughts came from whatever it was that they were running from. It took a long time for Bensen not to hate Muller and the Johnson brothers. Eventually, he forgave them, and they've all been friends ever since.

Bonson got fired. Jake Muller, Muller's dad, used his pull as a Town Councilman and kept the guys from doing jail time. He went to bat for the guys in court. They got off with probation and doing community service.

Chapter 22

Lesson Learned

Baseball season was over along with my first year of college. My dad came with his pickup truck to move my stuff out of my apartment. On the ride home he told me the real story about what happened with Muller, the Johnson brothers, and Bensen. Muller confided in his dad, Jake, and Jake told my dad. I wasn't ready to tell him yet what I had found out about The Witch. I was hoping that Muller and I could handle things.

It was the Thursday before Memorial Day weekend. My grandpa always called it Decoration Day, the holiday's original name. He was a veteran of WW 1—the war to end all wars—yeah, right. He had been gussying up the cemeteries for the fallen soldiers ever since he came back from the war in 1918.

I went with him on Friday morning to help him mow the cemetery grounds. Other times that I had helped him mowing the grass, I would rush through to get it done as fast as possible. I had better things to do. But for Decoration Day everything had to be just right, so I took my time. We would mow the grounds real neat, and then Saturday we would come back and decorate every veteran's grave with a small flag.

Hollow Hill Cemetery is the biggest cemetery in Valley Center. There are a few smaller ones that we took care of first. My grandpa said, "By saving Hollow Hill for last, the grass won't have as much time to grow for Monday's parade." He shot me a grin. A rare sight, as he almost never smiled.

We unloaded the mowers from his truck and began cutting the grass. There's a small hill that separates the old section in the back from the newer section towards Hollow Hill Road. My grandpa used to mow that hill with a riding lawn mower when he was younger—no pun intended. I had done it too, but my dad told me not to do that anymore. To instead use a push mower and a rope. It was a bitch to do, but my uncle had rolled a riding lawn mower on the hill the year before, nearly crushing himself under it as it rolled. He only narrowly escaped by jumping off the mower at the last possible moment. After that happened, my dad made me promise to never do that myself and to especially never allow my grandfather to do that.

I figured I would start at that hill and get it over with. I pushed the mower to the bottom of the hill, started it up, pushed it up, then back down, over and over across the bottom half of the hill. I didn't want to try and push it up too high, slip, and then be butchered up by the blade, so I only went up about six feet. After I finished the bottom half, I shut the mower off and pushed it around to the top.

I walked past the Witch's Ball and gave it a glance. I thought of all the people that think it's a headstone and smiled. Then my attention shifted to the big, dark obelisk near the top of the hill that I was mowing. The Memento Mori headstone with the haunting 'Prepare for death' poem.

As I approached the obelisk, I looked around to see where my grandpa was at. He was finishing up along the other side and circling around to make his way to where I would be at the top of the hill. I tied the rope around the lower bar of the mower, pulled the cord and brought it to life. I lowered the mower down to where I had already cut to from the bottom and pulled the mower back up. I got about halfway done with the hill and heard my grandpa coming my way on the rider.

My arms were burning, so I took a quick break. I shook my arms to get the blood going and watched my grandpa. He was mowing along the edge of the fir trees on top of the hill. Instead of waiting for me to finish the hill and trim it first, he kept going into each tree then backing out. Mowing the tree line, slow and deliberate. He was being so careful not to hit a headstone. I lowered the mower another time and had just gotten it pulled back up, I glanced over to my grandpa. I saw the Memento Mori headstone out of the corner of my eye. My grandpa turned as he came around the last tree by Dr. Morse's headstone on the top of the hill, and the front right wheel came off of the mower.

The right front of the mower dipped down; the blades dug into the turf at the crest of the hill, shooting out a plume of dirt and grass. The mower turned up on its side. I saw my grandpa throw his right leg over the steering wheel

213

as he planted his left foot on the ground. His left hand had come off of the steering wheel. I jumped towards the mower and tripped over the rope, but was able to snatch his arm by the wrist with my left hand.

The mower went tumbling over, following after the discarded wheel. Grandpa's right foot came down below his left on the side of the hill. My forward momentum took me with him as we fell over the hill. We bit the turf and slid face first toward the spinning blades of the mower that had come to rest on its side at the bottom of the hill.

I dug the fingers of my right hand into the ground and swung my left leg around in front of my grandpa's face. Smoke was chugging out of the mower as the engine stalled, seizing the blades. My foot slammed into the deck between the blades, and we stopped against the mower. My grandpa stared at the blades that were inches away from his face. I saw a tear trickle out of his eye. I said, "Are you okay?"

His face trembled as he spoke. He asked, "Are you?"

I said, "Yes," as I got to my feet and helped him up. He dusted himself off and walked away through the little valley and around the fir trees. I figured he went to get a drink of water from the well.

I could hear the push mower still running at the top of the hill. I climbed up the hill and shut it off. I saw my grandpa over by the Witch's Ball. He was looking at Grandpa Johnny's headstone. I walked over to him. I said, "Muller sure misses him, and so do I."

All he said was, "Yep," as he walked back around the tree line to the wrecked mower. I took the short way back to the push mower and down the hill to the meet him there. He saw how close my leg, or his head had come to being chopped up by the blades of the mower. When he got to the mower, I asked, "Are you sure you're okay?"

He looked deep into the undercarriage of the overturned mower. He said, "Somehow, that old witch got back at everybody that was in the posse that brought her in. I'm the last of the bunch." His eyes moved up and he looked over at Hazel's grave. "She almost got me today." He started walking to his truck. He shook his head and said, "What a way that would have been to go. I'm going to grab the other mower. I'll be right back."

I pushed the mower back over onto its three remaining wheels. The wheel that came off had rolled about thirty feet away. I walked over and grabbed it. As I came back towards the mower, I couldn't help but notice the Memento

Mori obelisk standing tall on top of the hill as it looks over this little valley below. I admired the way it assumes its position as sentinel over the dead, and warns the living of what's to come.

I dropped the wheel next to the mower and went up the hill to the push mower. As I finished up trimming the cemetery I couldn't stop thinking about The Witch and the close call that was just avoided. How lucky it was that the mower stalled, and the blades weren't spinning.

Thoughts started popping into my head. *'Almost.'* *'He'll get his, yet.'* *'You'll get yours, too.'* *'You're all going to die.'* Chills ran up my spine. I was thinking something was going to jump out from behind a headstone and attack me. I kept looking all around as I mowed. This stupid loud mower. Anybody—or anything—could sneak up on me. I shook off the fear.

My grandpa came back followed by his neighbor who was driving his flatbed truck. His neighbor and I half-assed the wheel on and we pushed the damaged mower onto his truck. His neighbor hauled it away and the mowing got finished without further incident.

All day Saturday my grandpa and I put flags up on veterans' graves. There were a few town folk that joined us. Everyone gave homage to my grandpa about how nice the cemeteries looked. That made him both proud and happy.

I was happy that he was still here. Once again, we saved Hollow Hill Cemetery for last. I got to Fred Dill's grave and placed a flag on it. I saw Hazel's name staring up at me from her headstone. I gave it quick a thought to piss on it, but there were too many people around.

My gaze went off to the little hill where the only sign of what had happened the day before was the shaved off turf on the crest of the hill. The divots from the rolling mower had been replaced and repaired. I was mesmerized by the dark, stolid obelisk standing there. In a brain fog, I began moving towards it. Thoughts entered my mind, *'Memento Mori.'* *'As you are now, so once was I.'*

I heard a baby crying. I looked to where I heard it coming from. There's a farm on the other side of Hollow Hill Road, and there was a young woman fighting to open the door of the barn that's near the road. *'Go to her.'* *'She needs your help.'* *'Help her or her baby will die.'*

Out of the corner of my eye I saw movement near the obelisk. A union soldier floated down the hill and towards the young woman across the road, pointing to the barn. *'Memento Mori.'* *'Come with me.'* *'She needs our help.'*

215

I looked back at the young woman. She was crying as she struggled against the locked barn door. I heard the baby crying. I drifted after the soldier who was crossing the road. *'Prepare for death and follow me.'*

"Mike, bring me some flags." My grandpa's voice startled me out of the trancelike state I was in. I turned and saw my grandpa at the back of the new section. "I ran out. I need a few more." Just then a speeding van went flying down Hollow Hill Road. Across the road at the barn, there was no soldier, no young woman, and no crying baby.

We finished up decorating the graves at the cemeteries and headed home. On the ride I thought of the blood brother oath that Muller and I had made. I thought about my Wiccan friends. I missed Doreen. I needed to call her. I needed to meet with all three of the Wiccan gals. We have to come up with a way to expel The Witch from the school. But how? When we got home I called Doreen.

Her voice sounded so different on the phone. At first I wondered if it was actually her. I told her that I missed her. I missed our conversations into the wee hours of the morning. Then I got to the point. "We need you gals here as soon as possible. Something has to be done about The Witch."

"What happened?"

"It came after my grandpa when we were mowing the cemetery lawn at Hollow Hill. Then I got thoughts from The Witch directly. Telling me that it was going to get my grandpa, and it was going to get me. Then today it enticed me to walk out on the road. If it weren't for my grandpa running out of flags and calling for me, I would have walked right into the path of a van that went whizzing by." There was silence on the other end. "Are you there?"

"Yes. I didn't want you to hear me cry."

"It's okay, Doreen. We're okay. But we need help. We need Trudy and Bishop Charles's expertise."

"I know." She sounded strong. "Trudy's not here. I'll get ahold of her right away and she'll call Bishop Charles. We'll be there."

"Thank you. You have no idea how much this means to me."

"I think I have an idea..." she trailed off, then held the phone close to her lips, "I love you, Preacher Boy. Don't let anything happen to you."

"I love you, too. I won't let that thing get me." Nor my grandpa, I hoped.

216

I called Muller as soon as I got off the phone with her. I said, "I think I found a way to get rid of The Witch." I was excited. I told him all about my conversation with Doreen and a possible exorcism of the school.

Muller answered, "I know I can't do it, but we've got to do something. I've been discussing it with Father Patrick. He's been talking with someone about it, and I know that he will help."

I said, "Sounds good."

Muller said, "You and your dad come over and we'll talk about setting something up."

"When?"

"Right now. My dad's out in the garage. I'll tell him you guys are coming over."

"We'll be along." I told my dad what was going on, we hopped in his truck and headed over to the Jake Muller residence.

As my dad and I got out of his truck, a puff of smoke wafted to us out of their garage. The distinct smell of one of Jake's Lark cigarettes filled my nostrils. He was sitting in one of the lounge chairs with that he had in a circle in the center of the garage. Muller was sitting to his side, not partaking in the smoke or drink his dad had littered about. When he saw us come in, Jake eased up out of his chair and reached for my hand. He smiled big and said, "How are you doin', Younger man?"

I said, "Great." How about you?" We shook hands.

He lied, "Never been better." His smile slipped away, and he sat back down.

I looked over to Muller and said, "Muller."

He replied, "Younger." He smiled and we gave each other a nod.

My thoughts were all over the place. I knew what was in the school, but I didn't quite know how to go about conveying it. I didn't want to have my idea shot down. I needed clarification and support. And now I would get it. Not only from Jake, but also from the most trusted source I could get anything from—my dad.

We sat in the garage and shot the shit for a few minutes. Then Muller spoke up, "First off, I want to say that I really screwed up thinking I could go in the school and kick whatever that thing is out of there."

My dad said, "I hear you two thought it was a good idea to break into the school last spring, too." My stomach sank. At least he was staring at Muller.

"How did you know that?," I asked, glancing over to Muller hoping my good friend hadn't ratted us out.

My dad turned to me and said, "Your grandfather heard the bell ringing in the old schoolhouse last year. He skulked up Center Street to try and catch a glimpse of the vandals who had broken into it. Then he saw the both of you run out the front door of the elementary school. He said you ran like little sissies all the way down to the tunnel." He just stared at me, and he wasn't smiling. "Go ahead, Jake, tell them."

Jake took a long double-draw on his cigarette and started in as he exhaled, "We hear you fellas felt and heard some stuff in the school." He looked from Muller to me. I just nodded my head. He got going, "You see, it all started a long time ago." He's not a chain smoker by any means, and the story he laid out was a three-cigarette story.

He, my dad, Muller, and I went back and forth taking turns talking. I couldn't believe that Jake and my dad knew a lot of this stuff that I had spent so much time and effort figuring out on my own. But then again, I had never asked them. The stories I got were from my grandpa and Grandpa Johnny. When it was my turn, I laid out the history of The Witch.

I went through the whole story I had compiled from all the notes and articles from Peter Ertz, and my talk with Judge Giles. Then I went into the discussions I had with the Wiccans. How it isn't a ghost, it's some sort of a demon. It had at one time been alive and then got buried in the old, abandoned salt mine by the flood of Noah.

Then I explained how it can't move around, but it uses mental telepathy to impose its will onto others—into others—influencing people to harm themselves and those around them. The only way it can move around is by possessing a person, which used to be its preference, but not anymore. It entered Hazel in the salt mine and possessed her for the rest of her life. Helping her or causing her to do the evil deeds that she had done.

Jake agreed and told of how the superstitious vigilantes had thought they corralled The Witch for eternity. But they hadn't. Grandpa Johnny was there the day they hanged Hazel. He told Jake the exact order of events. She dropped. Her neck snapped. She screamed. A whoosh of air blew over them. Grandpa Johnny said that he didn't want to believe that was what actually took place, so he told himself that it was all in his mind.

218

It wasn't till much later that Grandpa Johnny remembered the whoosh of air had blown out over their heads and then back toward the Town Hall. The way he figured it, when Hazel was hanged, the entity that had possessed her left her body and entered the Town Hall. Many strange things started happening in and around the building after that.

Numerous earthquakes were reported in Valley Center. It was presumed that Old John got buried by the old Maple Street hill from an earthquake.

Art Gunther's tractor exploded. He knew how to handle that tractor; he was an expert operator. Something caused that incident. It was no accident; it was an incident.

Dr. Morse got ground up in the gristmill while searching for a crying baby. Horses would go wild while riding past the Town Hall.

My dad told us about the Ungrich brothers being buried beneath the boiler room of the school. He and Jake attended school in the Town Hall while the addition was being built onto Valley Center Elementary School. Lots of crazy things went on in the Town Hall when they went to school there.

Some kid climbed up the rope for the bell and somehow got the rope wrapped around his neck. He was hanging by it. The teacher and some older boys lifted up his legs and got the rope off of him. He ended up being okay. A lot of kids would cut themselves with knives or scissors and pierce their own ears with paperclips. They would hear giggling as their blood spattered on the floor. The teacher was a wreck trying to keep control of the kids, and herself. Richard Shroder fell to his death from the roof when the bell tower was being moved.

They brought up Lottie. Jake was convinced that she became possessed by The Witch. It was well known that she acted like a horse in Sunday school and around her home. But something got inside of her when she grew up that made her go bonkers. She acted like a horse all the time—all of the sudden— when she got older. He talked with her one day and she told Jake that she *was* a horse. She snorted and grunted. He saw her eyes move around. Just like Grandpa Johnny said that Hazel's eyes moved.

Jake was looking off into the distance at a memory. He said, "Believe you me, when she was a kid she was nutty, but she was harmless. The Lottie I knew would never attempt to burn down a house or try to kill anyone. Not without some internal influence." He took a long drag of his cigarette.

I looked to Muller and said, "We heard the Legend of Lottie from the older boys in town." Muller agreed. I admired Jake as he did a double draw on his cigarette. His left eye squinted as a bit of smoke curled into it. I went on, "We heard she was a witch, not just another one of the old, crazy people that somehow were attracted to Valley Center."

My dad said, "She wasn't that old." He thought for second then continued, "She looked old. She had a lot of miles on her. Most of those people were down on their luck. It wasn't that they were crazy, it was the demon that kept harassing them, tormenting them, keeping them down. But Lottie was possessed by it." Jake nodded as he finished off his cigarette and mashed it out in the ashtray.

They brought up James Hadcock and Jeffery Bottum and the rumors that Lottie had burned their house down, killing James. Then Bottum offed himself on Hadcock's grave in Hollow Hill Cemetery.

My understanding of The Witch was growing deeper by the minute. I said, "When Lottie got run over by that truck the entity that possessed her infested Valley Center Elementary School. It has been in there ever since."

Muller's countenance changed. He said, "I got goosebumps when you said that. That explains a lot. The Witch is very powerful, indeed." We were all nodding our heads. Muller thought we heard everything about The Witch from Grandpa Johnny. So much of this he had never heard before.

Jake and my dad went on and told us many more things. But at this point, everyone was convinced that something needed to be done. We talked about all the weird happenings in the school and around The Valley. When asked what they thought should be done they had no idea.

That's when I explained my meeting the Wiccans. Telling them how Trudy can reach these entities. How The Witch was more powerful and stronger than it was before because it draws great energy from an ancient ziggurat that is buried beneath the school. From the school, its reach extends further. I mentioned how The Witch had reached into my mind, giving me evil thoughts when Muller and I were in the school. One thought was telling me to jump over the railing. Another was to let it in. Then yesterday, it entered my mind at the cemetery, enticing me to walk onto the road. I snapped to, and a van sped by. If my grandpa hadn't called for me, I would have been splattered on the road just like Lottie.

Muller said, "I got those same thoughts when we were in the school," he was looking at me. "When Bensen jumped over the railing, I had that same thought then, too." He looked ill. "You don't scare easy. After we came out of the school I pretended to go back in there. I walked home. After I met Father Patrick I knew something had to be done with whatever it is that's in the school, but I couldn't go back in there alone. That's why I went back in with Brian, Bonson, and Bensen."

I said, "Now is the time to act. We can catch it off guard. While The Witch is reaching out to harass everyone in The Valley because the school is empty, we'll hit it right in its wheelhouse. I've already gotten ahold of the Wiccans. They will come here and help us get rid of this thing once and for all. Trudy and Bishop Charles can exorcise these entities." I looked to Muller, "Once I find out when they'll be here, you get ahold of Father Patrick, and we'll set up a meeting at our house." In truth, I didn't know a thing about getting this accomplished. I looked to my dad and asked, "We can do that, right?"

My dad said, "We'll see to it."

Muller said, "We've got to try something." He didn't finish, but I knew what he was thinking, because I was thinking it.

I finished it for him, "For Grandpa Johnny."

He gave me a stern look. He said, "Yeah. For Grandpa Johnny." He reached out and grabbed my right hand with his left in our blood brother oath grip.

My dad and I went back home. I called Doreen and left a message for her to call me back.

Doreen called me back the next day. She said the three of them would be coming to The Valley the following day with Bishop Charles. I said, "I can hardly wait. My mom told me to tell you that you gals are always welcome at our house." I couldn't wait to see them again. To see Doreen again.

Muller arrived at about five o'clock. We sat at the kitchen table talking with my mom. It was about six o'clock when I looked out the window and saw the gals pulling up to the driveway in Trudy's Montego. I walked out to greet them. Olivia was driving. I could see Doreen's beautiful smile lighting up from the passenger seat. Bishop Charles pulled in behind them driving a blue 1973 AMC Rambler.

I jogged out to the car. As they exited the car I gave them a tip of an imaginary hat, bowed my head, and said, "Ladies."

Doreen popped out of the car and said as she smiled, "Preacher Boy." I smiled. Trudy and Olivia chuckled. Doreen was wearing a light-yellow sun dress with bright orange and yellow flowers that suited her well. Her green eyes were aglow.

Doreen slid right into my arms, and I gave her a big hug. "It's great to see you." I remembered those beautiful eyes. That was what I missed the most. Her eyes would glow when I looked into them. I had noticed that same glow wasn't there whenever she met someone else's gaze.

"It's great to be seen." She smiled and gave me a kiss. I walked around and gave Trudy and Olivia each a hug. Olivia was wearing a dark blue sundress. Trudy was wearing a multi-colored flowing sundress that floated around her as she moved. Her long, dark hair now had tiny grey streaks in it.

Muller had followed me out. I heard him say, "It's nice to see that you two finally got to meet in person, and I'm honored to meet you, Bishop Charles." I looked over and saw Bishop Charles exiting his car smiling. Muller walked over and shook the Bishop's hand.

Bishop Charles said, "It's a pleasure meeting you in the flesh, also, Mr. Muller."

I hadn't noticed, but he had a passenger that exited the car on the other side. Muller walked around and gave Father Patrick a big hug. Hmm. Muller seems to know him. I wondered what other secrets he was keeping to himself.

I walked over and extended my hand. I said, "It's an honor to meet you Bishop Charles." I was introduced to Father Patrick, and we exchanged pleasantries.

I said, "So, Father Patrick, I see you already know Bishop Charles." I looked over to the gals and asked, "Have you also met my Wiccan friends?"

Father Patrick said, "Yes, we talked on the phone several times and met in person earlier today. I work with Bishop Thompson around this area doing exorcisms. I told him of Muller's adventures and desperation. When I asked him about extracting entities from buildings, he told me about Bishop Charles. He, in turn, introduced me to them. Together, they asked me to join them here today."

I said, "Wow, it's a small world."

"Indeed, it is," he said smiling.

I looked to Olivia and said, "I'll grab your gear and bring it in while you relax and get situated."

Olivia tilted her head and shot me a grin. She said, "We've got no gear to grab."

Trudy said, "We just need to walk around a bit, get our land-legs back under us and shake off the road dust. Then we can get down to business."

We stood around in the driveway talking. My mom came out to see the gals. I introduced her to Bishop Charles and Father Patrick. She shook their hands and asked, "Who'd like some coffee?"

Trudy said, "I could go for a cup."

Olivia said, "Me too."

I looked at Doreen and she gave me a look that said, 'of course.' I said, "I'll get us all a cup."

My mom and I brought out coffee for everyone. As I passed cups out to everyone I heard Trudy saying to Muller, "I met with Bishop Charles and we both felt an urgent need to get here as soon as possible. We had other obligations to attend to before we could come here. That is why we were not here sooner." She had the most serious look on her face that I had ever seen. "Mrs. Younger, please let us talk in private." My mom went back inside.

Trudy said, "Thank you, Mrs. Younger." Then she continued, "You two are key to extracting the demons from the school." She looked from Muller to me. "You have to agree to do what we propose. This is the only way that it can be done. In order to be rid of The Witch, once and for all, we will go into the school this evening."

Bishop Charles said, "We have permission from the Town Council to enter the school. They want to be rid of the demons, pronto." He looked to me. "You," he looked to Muller, "and you, are going to be the bait to attract it. You are the magnets, the two blood brothers."

Muller said, "You said demons. I don't know. If this thing goes sideways, we might have a permanent roommate living in our heads. And let me tell you, I do not need any input in my life from a demon. Besides, I look terrible in red, and I couldn't imagine walking around with a pitchfork all the time."

Trudy said, "You will not have to worry about any demonic cliches. The oath you made in blood has connected the two of you to The Witch already, making you the only ones we could possibly use to draw it out of the school and away from the ziggurat. When it comes after you, it will split itself in half to possess you both. Each of you will have a finger pricked to get a little of your blood to draw the entity to you. The blood will bring it, I guarantee it. Then you both must invite it in."

I protested, "Are you out of your mind? We can't do that. I figured you would just get rid of it. Exorcise it from the school. Why don't *you* invite it in and then work your magic to get rid of it?"

"I assure that it is not magic. This is the only way," she insisted. "Getting it into a host weakens it. And getting it into two hosts will weaken it even more. Then removing the hosts from the school will weaken it further."

I pleaded, "There's got to be a better way. Another way."

Bishop Charles said, "There is no other way." He was stern and to the point. "You both must accept it in. It's simply too powerful over the ziggurat."

Trudy said, "In order to deal with this entity, it needs to be drawn away from the school, and the only way to extract The Witch from the school is through possession. But you must agree to do this. If not, it will not be able to be accomplished."

Bishop Charles said, "It must be done tonight." He and Father Patrick walked to his car and they drove away.

Trudy glided towards her car. She said, "We are leaving now. Either to prepare to enter the school or to our next assignment. It is your and Muller's choice." Olivia followed Trudy.

I looked to Doreen. She came up to me and said, "Trudy knows what she's doing. It's up to you two." She looked to Muller and back to me. "She would never let you down, and neither will I. Olivia and I will help you. We can do this." Doreen kissed my cheek and followed after them.

As she walked away I said, "Give us a minute to talk."

I turned back to see Muller standing there looking at me with doubt in his eyes, tears welling up in them. He said, "I'm scared. That thing is scary."

I said, "If we're gonna stick by our blood brother oath, we're gonna have to go back in the school."

Muller looked down. His lips were quivering. He said, "We have to do it for Grandpa Johnny."

"Yes, we do. It ain't gonna be easy. If it was easy, anybody could do it, right? We can do it. Let's get rid of that thing." I poured some coffee in a cup and handed it to Muller. I lifted my cup. "For Grandpa Johnny."

He raised his head and then his cup, and looked me dead in the eyes. Muller said, "For Grandpa Johnny." We clicked our cups and drank to the toast.

We went over to Trudy's car. They all turned toward us when we approached. I said, "We decided to go through with it."

My mom had come outside. Trudy, Olivia, and Doreen walked over to my mom and said goodbye to her. I could see tears in my mom's eyes. Somehow she knew what we were up to. She was looking at me like it would be the last time she would see me alive.

I said, "Don't worry mom, we're in good hands." I would be lying if I said that I wasn't wondering if that was going to be the last time I saw her.

Trudy said, "Do not drive to the school. We will park behind the Town Hall and walk to the school from there. We will follow you." They got into their car, and we climbed into Muller's truck. We drove to the Town Hall. I didn't say a word the whole way there. I was scared to death and did my best to hide it from Muller.

We parked in the back of the Town Hall next to Bishop Charles's Rambler. Neither he nor Father Patrick were anywhere to be seen. I figured they must have already went to the school. Trudy got out of her car and stared at the back of the building. After a few minutes she turned and started walking. Muller and I followed the Wiccans to the intersection of West River Road and crossed it. We stopped next to the tunnel entrance across the street from the school.

I said, "This was the tunnel we used to run through when we were kids." No one paid me any mind; they were all staring at the school. The school looked down on us with a cold, somber glare as the sun was setting behind it. The orange glow made it appear that flames were flashing in the windows. The eyes are the windows to the soul, and for the first time I could see it. The school itself was alive, and the flashing in the windows looked just like dancing eyes. Those same dancing eyes I saw in Lone Star.

Trudy held the palms of her hands out toward the school. After a minute, Trudy said, "We must go. All is in place." No one said a word on the walk up the two little sets of steps to the front door of the school.

We were greeted at the door by Father Patrick who was already in the school. He opened the door for us, and let us in. Muller and I went back into the school. Right into the belly of the beast.

Chapter 23

Kicked Out of School

When we entered the school, I looked up the staircase where Muller and I had made our escape and pictured Bensen leaping from high above. It's a miracle he survived such a fall. We walked across the floor where Bensen had landed and followed Father Patrick to the gym. I realized that The Witch had been watching us and hounding us from this building for all of our lives. My stomach sank as my heart raced.

The memory on the playground when the older boy and I were standing up on the swings came flashing back to Muller. He remembered the voice telling him to walk into the swing and a chill ran up his spine. Feeling a sense of doom, he knew, too, that The Witch had been pestering us for years.

We entered the gym. Trudy and Father Patrick led Muller and I to center court. Father Patrick stayed with us there. Trudy glided backwards to the stage at the north of the gym. Doreen stood to our left and Olivia to our right. The Wiccans began chanting.

I was looking around wondering where Bishop Charles was. Father Patrick said, "Madness has no purpose or reason, but does have a goal; to see the blood of every living soul." He pricked one of my fingers with a pin, then he pricked one of Muller's. He lit an urn of incense and began chanting along with the gals. He waved the burning incense back and forth, back, and forth. First to the north, then to the west, then to the east. Back and forth, back, and forth.

I was trying to hear what it was they were chanting. It seemed to be some foreign language. I looked to Muller. He shot me a look that was both panicked and scared. I was scared, too, and hoped to lighten the situation. I whispered to him, "I wouldn't be surprised if Mr. Barlow and Miss Wesson came walking through the door—*'Let me in—*"

I was slapped a thousand times harder than either of them had ever hit me. My body wrenched. My head tilted back. A massive hurricane crashed into me. It felt like when I was knocked out for surgery by sodium pentothal. I heaved forth the total contents of my stomach. A guttural scream came out of me.

I spun with the force of the whirlwind that roiled inside of me. My mouth was foaming. My eyes were burning. My skin was crawling. My flesh was rippling from the ravenous raging lion roaring through my veins. Father Patrick and Doreen held me back as I clawed at Muller trying to attack him. I was spinning inside so fast that I lost my moorings. Storms were clashing and bashing inside of me. I spun around, fell down and rolled around on the gym floor. I heard The Witch screaming above me. It sounded like a giant horse was trying to trample me where I lay on the floor.

I flopped around in convulsions. I was here, I was gone. I was going back and forth, around, and around; screaming and dry heaving as the turbulent waves crashed inside of me. I tried to stay in control. Fighting with these things that were inside of me. Fighting to get away from The Witch that was trying to trample me.

Through the smoldering coals in my spinning eyes, I saw Trudy and Olivia holding onto Muller's arms. Between the ebb and flow of the rip current tearing away my mind, I saw the emergency exit sign above the outer door of the gym. I wrestled away from the grip of Father Patrick and Doreen. I sprang to my feet and sprinted for the door. I crashed through it, running from the school and down the little hills. It seemed like only moments before we had entered the school, but it was dark outside.

I had to get away from The Witch. But The Witch was in me. And The Witch was chasing me. I could hear it coming for me. I had to find a place to hide. The tunnel. I had to make it to the tunnel. I was running at full speed when I crossed School Street. I leapt off the stone ledge by the tunnel and across the creek. Then I jumped back across the creek and into the tunnel and ran for my life.

I had never run through it at night before, but here I was, running by feel back and forth, back, and forth, through the tunnel. One, two, three—jump. One, two, three—jump. Stepping across the slimy creek water as gravity brought me to the bottom of the cylindrical shape of the tube. Running like there was no tomorrow. I fought against the whirlwind inside of me that was whizzing around. Boiling up and then receding. Sloshing back and forth. Lashing at my brain. Tearing me apart.

I wasn't halfway to the outlet when I heard the monstrous blare of what seemed like ten horses braying all at once behind me in the tunnel. The Witch was coming for me. Galloping hooves echoed through the tunnel. It was gaining on me. I could feel claws swiping at me, and hear them scraping along the walls of the tunnel. The Witch was trying to slash me to pieces. My back felt like it was on fire. I could see the end of the tunnel. I had to go faster in order to make it out alive.

A deafening screech rang out. My left foot stepped in the slimy water and slipped out from under me. I went down hard, face first, in the creek water. I slid on the algae laden bottom of the tunnel like a bullet through a barrel. My right wrist scraped across glass from a broken beer bottle that was stuck in the mud at the outlet of the tunnel.

I sprang to my feet, looked down and saw blood squirting from my wrist. I latched onto it with my left hand and squeezed it as tightly as I could. Blood continued pouring out from between my fingers.

I remembered the Parson brothers teaching me how to run through the tunnel. One of the competitions we used to do was climbing up the stone slab wall at each end of the tunnel—with no hands. I hadn't done it in forever, but the memory of it all came to me in an instant. Right foot first about two feet up to the little ledge on the left of the second stone out from the tunnel. Then left foot up two feet to the little ledge on the right side of the first stone slab. Right foot up one foot to that ledge, left foot up two feet, right foot up one foot, left foot to the top and done. I scurried up the stone slab as quick as a cat. I remembered every step as if I had just done it earlier that day.

I could hear the foaming mouth of The Witch gnawing and gurgling in the tunnel outlet beneath me. The storm was raging within me. Up and down, back, and forth. My insides were being torn apart. My mind was being ripped away from me. I could barely think. Doreen came rushing up to me and grabbed me by my bloody wrist while Father Patrick grabbed my other.

I wrestled with them to get away. Blood spilled out. Doreen clamped her hand over my wound, and they pulled me along. They dragged me across the street. I saw the front door of the Town Hall was open. I was fighting them. I had to get away from the thing that had invaded me. I had to flee The Witch that was chasing me.

They took me up the steps and into the Town Hall. Father Patrick said, "Hurry. Come with us, you'll be safe in here." They led me through the door and into the Town Hall. Father Patrick and Doreen hauled me into the back room. Through the turbulent flames in my eyes, I noticed Bishop Charles standing next to a marble baptismal font in the middle of the room.

As I was dragged to the center of the room, an enormous howl came out of Muller as Trudy and Olivia pulled him in. Hooves were crashing and thrashing. It sounded as if the room was being torn to shreds.

The Witch was following my blood trail. It was coming for me. I had to get out of there. I fought with Father Patrick and Doreen to let me go. I couldn't get away. Olivia and Trudy wrestled Muller into the back room. He was stomping on the floor, growling, and snorting. Foam was flying from his gnawing mouth.

Doreen and Father Patrick held my bleeding wrist over the marble baptismal font. Trudy and Olivia held Muller's hands out over the baptismal font next to mine. Father Patrick called out, "The time is at hand."

Bishop Charles came forward holding a dagger. He saw my profusely bleeding wrist and proclaimed, "You're one step ahead of us." He grabbed Muller's left hand and sliced it. Bishop Charles stepped back into position to the east of the baptismal font and began chanting. The three Wiccans and Father Patrick grabbed Muller's hand and my wrist and squeezed. Our blood poured into the font.

Father Patrick wrapped Muller's left hand around my right wrist. He pressed our grips together—our blood brother bond was renewed. Then he got in position to the west of the font. He began chanting along with Bishop Charles. Trudy glided backwards to the center of the outer north wall. She stood with her back to the wall and her arms outstretched making the shape of a cross. When she did this, we all four slid backwards against the walls. Olivia to the east wall. Doreen to the west wall. Muller and I to the south wall. All of our hands were stretched out to our sides just like Trudy's. Muller's left hand was squeezing my right wrist in an Indian wrestling grip— our blood brother grip.

Trudy began chanting along with Bishop Charles and Father Patrick. Neither Muller nor I could move. The thought that death was the only way

229

The Witch had been extracted from a body ran through my mind. I knew I would bleed out and die in this room. The same room where sixty some-odd years earlier, Hazel's fate was decided. Then she dangled from a rope about three feet behind where Trudy was standing.

The sounds the whirlwind was making within me were terrifying. It sounded like thousands of mouths screaming at one another. Teeth grinding and gnashing. Each mouth trying to feed itself. They were consuming one another in a huge roiling cloud of smoke and fire. Like magma churning in a volcano, heaving forth, then collapsing in on itself—devouring itself. I thought, 'How could I have invited this thing in? How can I withstand this thing within me?'

The noise coming from Muller was excruciating. Intense flames were rolling within the clouds of his eyes. The sounds of a thousand voices clamoring, thundering, laughing, screaming, arguing, and yelling all at once. Our hearts were thumping like huge bass drums. Our ears were ringing, our heads were pounding. I felt each beat of my heart in my throbbing, aching wrist. I told myself to keep my focus. It felt as if I would explode. There was no way for this thing to be conquered.

Bishop Charles began dousing us with holy water from an aspergillum. Over and over, he sprinkled us with holy water as he chanted.

The aura that surrounded Trudy was emanating from her, and around her, in a bright, white glow. My eyes were fixed on her as she pierced my mind with her gaze and stated with force, "The blood brothers are the fourth," then continued chanting.

I tried to make out what they were chanting. It sounded like Latin, but it wasn't Latin. I had taken Latin in school and had been to a number of Latin masses in church. It sounded like a language from another world that I can't describe. Over and over again she chanted as she rocked back and forth, back, and forth. Bishop Charles, Father Patrick, Trudy, Olivia, and Doreen all chanted and rocked, chanted, and rocked as holy water rained down on Muller and me.

The bright, white glow of Trudy's aura began to pulsate. With each word they chanted, streaks of the resplendent light of her aura oozed out of her outstretched hands further and further. Like fingertips, her aura crawled around the wall, reaching to touch Olivia on the east wall, and Doreen on the west wall. When the streaks of light touched them, their auras began to glow.

Olivia's glowed whitish red; Doreen's glowed whitish yellow. All three auras combined and shot to Muller and I around the wall like bolts of lightning. We all began glowing purple, like a black light. The whole room was aglow like a black light room. Energy flowed through us. We were like batteries feeding a circuit.

Muller and I were fighting against the entities inside of us. We struggled for control. The pitter patter of the holy water was tapping our heads. It reminded me of all the rainouts we had for baseball games. It came to me. That was it—The rain—The rain! I put all of my effort into a thought. I had to convey my thoughts to Muller. Hazel confessed because The Witch broke from her because of its fear of drowning.

The mental telepathy that The Witch utilized worked in our favor. I was able to reach Muller's mind. He understood my thoughts. It was God's wrath that The Witch feared. He said, "Yes! The rain." Our hair was soaked with holy water. Our faces were wet. We felt the entities breaking from us. With the sound of a thousand angry voices The Witch screamed from within the both of us, *"Never again!"* Our bodies lurched forward—then back—as The Witch leaped out. It felt as if we were thrust from a hurricane into the calm eye of the storm. We were overcome with joy and relief as the entities left us.

A thick, heavy fog filled the room. It hovered over the marble baptismal font that held holy water, mixed with our blood. A burst of energy zapped forth from the Wiccans' auras onto the fog. Bishop Charles raised his hands up high. He and Trudy had total control. A splashing sound echoed throughout the room as The Witch was driven with force into the font.

The contents of the baptismal font boiled and swirled. Choking and gurgling noises bubbled up from the font—then—there was silence. The surface of the font became as smooth as a mirror. The lust for blood took down The Witch.

Muller and I looked down into the baptismal font. What started out as clear holy water, then holy water mixed with our blood, was now pitch-black. It looked like the darkest night you could ever imagine, with no moon and not a star in the sky. We could feel gravity pulling from another dimension like a black hole. We had to look away for fear of being pulled in there with The Witch.

Our interlocked Indian grip loosened. Our hands came down to our sides. I looked at my wrist. It wasn't bleeding anymore. There was a healed scar where my wound had been. That couldn't be, I must have run out of blood. With that thought, I slid down the wall and collapsed onto the floor.

Bishop Charles and Father Patrick drained the contents of the baptismal font into a light brown marble urn that Trudy brought forth. Not one drop was lost. Bishop Charles wiped the font clean with a large white cloth. He stuffed the cloth into the urn. Trudy stuck a lead plug into the opening of the urn. The plug melded into the sides of the urn, sealing it, as they all continued to chant. The urn's color turned to dark black. It looked just like the Witch's Ball. Olivia and Doreen came forward. They wove a silver cord around the marble urn and backed away. Bishop Charles said, "It is done."

Father Patrick and Doreen pulled me up to my feet. I stood there staring at the urn and rubbing my wrist. I looked down to my wrist. All I saw was a healed scar where there wasn't a scar before. I looked back to the urn. Bishop Charles handed the urn to Muller. I could see that the cut on Muller's hand was healed as he took the urn. It was heavy. Muller guessed it to weigh about fifty pounds. I was completely drained.

Trudy looked spent. She said, "Our work here is finished." She glided to the door of the back room and waited as Muller walked out with the urn. She slipped out the door behind him, followed by Olivia.

Doreen looked me in the eyes and smiled. She said, "It's nice seeing you again, Preacher Boy." She gave me a huge hug.

I said, "It's nice to be seen, rather than viewed." She kissed my cheek.

We walked out together behind Muller, Trudy, and Olivia.

It seemed like we had been in there for only a half hour or so, but when we walked outside we could see the sun was about to rise. Birds were chirping. The air smelled fresh and clean. It brought back the memory of the day after the storm tore down my favorite climbing tree when I was a boy.

We walked around to the back parking lot. I looked down the street to where the tree used to stand. Trudy and Olivia stopped at the car. Muller put the urn in his truck. Father Patrick helped Bishop Charles carry the baptismal font out to his car. They put it in the trunk.

Trudy looked to me. In the morning light I could see that she had even more tiny streaks of grey in her frazzled hair. Her face was drawn. Her eyes were sunken in their sockets. She looked beautiful to me. Tears fell out of my eyes. I don't know how I had any water left in me. She mustered a smile. I took her in my arms and picked her up. I hugged her tighter than I have ever

232

hugged anyone. Tears ran down my cheeks. I said, "I don't know how to thank you."

I set her down and she wiped away the tears and held my face in her hands. She said, "You do not have to thank us. You are our friend. Friends help each other." She smiled. "We must go now. We have work to do elsewhere."

I said, "You're leaving already? I was hoping you gals would stick around for a few days."

She glanced to me with a wry smile and winked. She said, "We have got bigger fish to fry." As if the fish that was just fried wasn't a doozy.

I hugged Olivia and thanked her. She said, "I bet you never thought we'd see each other like this, did ya?" She smiled as she pecked my cheek.

"No, I most definitely didn't." I smiled. Our eyes were smiling at each other.

I turned back to Doreen. I said, "Thank you. You are the one I can always count on. I wish you could stay here with me." I choked up and began to cry.

She said, "I'll be back soon." She wiped my tears and smiled. Then gave me a kiss, and a big hug. "We'll get together soon. I'll call you when we get back home." I smiled.

Muller came over and nudged me in the side. He said, "M&M brothers don't cry." That made me chortle. He hugged all three of the women and said his goodbyes.

Bishop Charles and Father Patrick came over and hugged it out with all of us. Muller and I thanked them and the Wiccans for their great service to the community of Valley Center.

Bishop Charles looked to Trudy and said, "Those were some strong ones."

Trudy said, "Had we taken them on any sooner, I am not so sure we would have prevailed. I do not think I would have been ready."

Bishop Charles said, "Imagine if we would have waited any longer." He thought for a moment and added, "We would have prevailed." He gave Trudy a smile and a hug. "However, we couldn't have done it without you. See you at the next one." He and Father Patrick got into his car.

Trudy blushed. She was humbled. She said, "I know you could have. But we do make a great team. See you there." Then she crawled in the back of her car and fell fast asleep. Olivia got in behind the wheel. I held the passenger door open for Doreen. She kissed me and hopped in the car. I closed the door.

We watched them drive away, following Bishop Charles's Rambler.

Doreen smiled and waved. I waved till I couldn't see them anymore.

Muller and I got in his truck. He looked like death warmed over. And that's exactly how I felt. I was afraid to look at myself in the mirror of the truck. What a sight I must be.

When we pulled onto the street, Muller said, "I can't even believe it. We did it. Well, we didn't, I guess. They did." He glanced back to the Town Hall where it all took place.

"I can't believe it either." I rubbed the healed scar on my wrist. I reached my hand out to him, and said, "The blood brother bond."

Muller stopped the truck. He reached over and grabbed my right hand with his left in the Indian wrestling grip. He said, "The blood brother bond." We still shake hands in this manner to this day.

I stared at the urn. I said, "It's so hard to fathom. I never would have thought that it would end in the back room of the Town Hall." I was thinking of Bishop Charles, Father Patrick, Trudy, Olivia, and especially Doreen. Thinking about all the stories we had heard from my grandpa and Grandpa Johnny.

Muller looked at the urn and said, "And it's going to really end when we bury this bitch for good." He started driving. "We'll figure that out after we get some sleep."

I said, "That sounds like a plan. Go past the school. I want to see if it looks any different now."

We drove to the corner at my grandpa's house. We saw his big rock was in the street. I figured someone must have driven on his lawn and dragged it out there, but there were no tire marks. We stopped. Muller and I got out and rolled the rock back to its place. We got back in and drove past the school. It looked cold and empty. He dropped me off at home. My mom came running out and about squeezed the life out of me with a hug. She cried. I would have too if I had any water left in me. We waved to Muller as he drove away.

I went into the kitchen and downed about a half-gallon of milk right out of the jug. Then I got cleaned up, went to my room and fell onto my bed—and into a deep sleep.

Chapter 24

The Last Puzzle Piece and the Afterglow

I was walking up the steps to the elementary school. Throngs of children were going into the school. My feet left the ground as they carried me along with them. They were all talking and laughing. I saw Muller standing on the top of the steps in the new section of the school. He had his arms around two young women who were crying—but they were smiling.

Muller waved to me and said, "Come up here. You can see the whole Valley from here.

The kids carried me up the steps to where Muller was standing. The young women were Hazel and Lottie. They had tears of joy streaming down their cheeks. Their faces looked old, but they were young. They brought their hands up to their faces and slid behind Muller to hide from me.

Muller said, "Look," as he pointed out with his open hands.

We were no longer in the school. We were on top the ancient ziggurat. All around in every direction there was a multitude of people and creatures of every kind. The sun was shining. Everyone was laughing and cheering.

I asked Muller, "What's the celebration?"

I heard the first bell ringing for the school day to start. I was all alone back in the new section of the school on top of the steps. First bell stopped ringing. The doors to the school were open. Fresh air flowed through the building.

Second bell rang. I smelled flowers, green leaves, and apple blossoms in the fresh spring air. Bright light from the shining sun filled the school. No children were scurrying to beat the final bell. That was odd.

Final bell rang. I was going to be late for class. But I don't go to school anymore—

I opened my eyes. The phone was ringing. I heard my mom say, "I'll check and see if he's awake."

I called out, "I'm awake."

She said, "Phone's for you." I got out of bed and went to the phone. It was Muller.

He asked, "Did you hear?"

"Hear what? I just woke up."

"There was an earthquake last night. Probably while we were doing our civic duty."

"That's probably what moved the rock at my grandpa's."

"And it's probably what collapsed the base of the Witch's Ball."

"You don't say."

"I do say. It looks like it was dropped from fifty feet in the air. The base is gone and it's sitting in its own ball mark. Monday morning, we are going to pour a new base for it. Dad asked me to ask you to help. He'll pay you and all."

"Sure thing."

"I'll pick you up first thing in the morning. Before seven. We've got to stop at the Builder's Supply to pick up some stone."

"Okay. See you then." We got off the phone.

Bright and early on Monday morning Muller picked me up in his dad's flatbed dump truck. I got in the dump truck and saw the urn buckled up in the center seat. Muller gave it a pat and said, "Good girl."

I said, "What are we going to do with that?"

Muller said, "You'll see." He was smiling like the cat that ate the canary.

I grinned and said, "Let's rock and roll." Muller backed out of our driveway and off we went.

We arrived at the Valley Center Builder's Supply a few minutes before it was to open. We waited in the lot for our buddy Arnold Stanton to open up for the day. He had been working there for as long as we could remember. After a few minutes, he came pulling into the yard of the Builder's Supply and parked out back. Muller drove around to his vehicle. Arnie hopped out, raised his hand, gave us the peace sign, and said, "Peace, guys," smiling like a guy that got a good night's sleep. Then he scratched himself behind his ear.

I had been exchanging peace signs with him since I was a kid. He was about ten years older than me. We lived across the street from the Builder's

Supply when I was growing up. When he saw me out in the yard he would call out, "Hey Mike."

I would look over and he would start singing the song from The Wizard of Oz, "Ding-dong the witch is dead." I would sing it with him, and we would laugh. That was our favorite movie.

I smiled, gave him the peace sign, and said, "Peace. Peace on earth, guy." I knew he would like that.

He said, "Yeah. Peace on the earth." and he motioned like he was peeing on the entire planet, which I had seen him do a hundred times. Muller and I chuckled.

He laughed, looked back to Muller grinning and scratching away at his upper arm. He asked, "What do you fellas need on this fine morning?"

Muller said, "We need a load of number fifty-seven limestone."

He scratched the side of his smooth, clean-shaven face and looked over at the side of the building. I pictured little puffs of smoke rolling out of his ears as he was thinking. He looked back and said, "I think we can do that."

Muller said, "No rush, take your lunch in to the office and get situated first. Where do you want me to park my truck?"

He looked over to the side of the building again. While scratching his ass he pointed with his lunch pail and said, "Park on the scale." He gave us a quick glance and a smile and said, "Let me go in and take a peace, I'll get the weight of your truck and I'll be right out." He chuckled and walked into the building.

Muller moved his truck onto the scale, and we waited. No more than five minutes later the big overhead door opened. Out came Arnie driving the front-end loader. He scooped up a load of fifty-seven stone and dropped it onto the bed of Muller's flatbed dump truck. He parked the loader. We hopped out of the truck and followed him into the building to the cash register. He wasn't expecting us to come in, we startled him when we walked up behind him. He looked over to the cash register and thought for a few seconds as he was scratching the side of his leg. Then he said, "You fellas were supposed to stay in the truck. I weighed it with you guys in it. Right Mike." He looked to me and grinned.

I said, "Right. Just guess our weights and add it on. We weren't trying to rip you off." We really weren't either. We didn't want him to see the urn.

He lifted the brim of his baseball cap as he stared at the cash register. He scratched the top of his head, pulled his hat back down, looked my way and said, "Get back in the truck, you guys. I'll bring the bill out and you just sign for it." He looked to Muller and smiled.

Muller said, "We sure will. The next time I see you at the saloon, I'll buy you a beer." He knew he'd like that.

He nodded at the prospect, looked over at the cash register, then back to Muller and me. He asked, "Got a big job today?," while he scratched both his arms, one with the other in unison.

Muller said, "Not really. Younger and I got something to take care of." We walked back out and got into Muller's truck.

Arnie came walking out a few minutes later. The building was on my side, so he came up to my window. He was grinning from ear to ear. He had a look about him as if he knew my shoulder was itching and he was going to reach in and start scratching it for me. He handed the bill to Muller for him to sign. He looked between Muller and I and saw the urn. It was glowing like a black diamond. He asked, "What's that? Your date?" He chuckled as he scratched both elbows.

Muller handed the signed bill back to Arnie and said in a serious tone, "It was. She beat us up pretty bad, so we cremated her." The way Arnie was staring at the urn, I thought for sure he was going to reach inside the truck and try to touch it, or scratch it, but he didn't. He stepped back as we pulled away.

I said, "See ya later, alligator."

Arnie followed along beside the truck. He said, "See you crocodiles in a while." He was grinning like an opossum.

I said, "Peace guy." He stopped walking as we pulled onto School Street.

We heard him say, "Peace, guys." We both gave him the peace sign out the window. In the sideview mirror I could see him acting like he was peeing all around in a circle, laughing.

I told Muller, "That guy's a riot. He always cracks me up."

"That, he is." He grinned.

It was seven thirty in the morning. We drove to Hollow Hill Cemetery. It was quite the interesting ride to the cemetery. Muller filled me in on some of what he knew, but hadn't let on to me that he knew it. Jake had told Muller before he called me the night before.

Jake and my dad got the rest of the township officials to agree to block off the driveways to the cemetery for the day of the repair work. The reason for this was to dig up what was buried under the Gunther family marker and place it where it belongs. After that, we would pour a new base for the marker. They were waiting for us at the cemetery. They had everything in place to complete the job.

I had no idea what was buried there—till that day. They were waiting for us at the cemetery. Jake's grandfather, Old John, and Art Gunther were members of the Town Council in Hazel's day. They knew the evil workings of The Witch. In their superstitious minds, in order to be rid of The Witch once and for all, their plan was to bind her dead body in the afterlife—for eternity. And the only way to accomplish that was to do the job themselves. So, they took Hazel's body from the coffin in her grave and buried her in a make-shift coffin under the Gunther family marker; beneath the so-called, Witch's Ball.

When we arrived at the cemetery, I told Muller to stop at the well so I could get a drink of water. I was dying of thirst. Muller pumped and I indulged. He said, "You sound like a cow sucking water out of a trough." I kept going. "Save some for me, Younger." I must have downed a gallon of water. Then I pumped for him. That hit the spot.

I met my dad at the Dill's burial plots. He and Jake had moved the Witch's Ball out of the collapsed base, then dug up the empty grave where Hazel was supposedly laid to rest next to her husband. My dad and I extracted the empty coffin out of the ground. We slid it in the bed of his pickup truck and drove around to the back of the storage shed. We threw it on the burn pile. He lit the pile on fire and stayed there to keep an eye on it. I went over and helped Muller and Jake. They had torn out the old foundation for the Gunther family marker and were digging up the dirt around Hazel's coffin.

Jake went over to his truck, reached into the toolbox, grabbed a rope and said, "That's my daddy's rope." We smiled at each other. It seemed I heard him say that a dozen times before about that rope. He tied a noose in the rope to use as a lasso, and dropped it over and around Hazel's coffin. Jake pulled the rope to snug it up. Muller and I grabbed the rope with him, and we hoisted her up and out from the makeshift grave. Muddy water and a stinky, black ooze drained from the coffin.

Muller and I were met with the rancid stench of decay as we reached down to lift the coffin off the ground. I turned my head to the side; Muller had his face over the coffin. He took in a breath and gagged. I chuckled. We picked up the coffin a few inches and held it off the ground while Jake loosened the noose and pulled the rope off of it. We set it down and backed away from it. Jake waved my dad to bring his truck over and get Hazel's coffin.

Jake said, "Mike," he was looking at me, "Grab that end. And Mike," he was looking at Muller, "You get over there." Muller moved to the opposite side of his dad.

My dad got out of his truck and said, "Smells like we're having something good for dinner." He smiled and got on the other side of the coffin across from me.

Jake said, "My God, this is nasty."

My dad asked, "Are we ready?" We all nodded yes. We reached down and grabbed ahold of the coffin. My dad's face was right over the coffin. He smiled at me. I turned my head to the side.

Jake said, "On three. One, two. Ooot," I heard him gag, and then puke. My dad cracked up laughing. Jake said, "I don't know how I'm going to do this." He stood and wiped his mouth on the sleeve of his shirt. He got it together. "Okay." We grabbed the coffin a second time. "One, two, three." We lifted the coffin up and pushed it onto the bed of my dad's truck.

Jake said, "That was the worst smell I ever smelled in my life. Ben, move the truck over a ways. Mike, go and get that urn."

My dad said, "It's no worse than Limburger cheese." He smiled at Jake and moved his truck. My dad and Jake's wife loved Limburger cheese. Nobody else in either one of our families did. Those two would break some out to eat at a party. It stunk so bad that everybody in the whole house would clear out till they put it away.

Jake gave my dad a long hard look and said, "I'm not so sure which one is worse." He shook his head and smiled.

Muller came back with the urn. Jake said, "Before we get going here, let's have a look at that thing." He and my dad gazed upon the dim glow of the shiny, black, marble urn. Jake said, "Hold that up next to the Gunther's marker." Muller walked over and held it against the Witch's Ball. Jake said, "It looks like the carpet will match the drapes. Don't it Ben?"

My dad chuckled. He said, "It sure does. Let's get rid of that thing and put it in the ground where it belongs."

I asked, "In the ground where?"

"Why, right there." Jake pointed to the hole where Hazel had been.

I said, "I've got a better idea. I think we should take this thing out on Lake Erie with your boat, to the deepest spot, and drop it in there like an anchor and leave it there."

Jake said, "That would be a good place for it, but we're trying to somewhat right a wrong here. The plan is to put Hazel in her proper place. And we feel that in order to quell the superstitions from the past of those that went before us; we should bury that thing here." He pointed from the urn to the empty hole where the superstitious vigilantes had buried what they thought was The Witch.

My dad said, "This is the least we can do for them. They thought they knew what they were dealing with. They didn't. They also thought they were doing what was right. We can't undo every wrong that was done, but we can at least put that thing where they felt it belonged, and put Hazel where she should have been all along."

That was that. I couldn't argue with that reasoning. So, Muller and I shoveled fifty-seven limestone to fill the bottom two feet of the hole. Jake slipped the noose around the urn, and pulled on the rope to secure it. He handed the urn to Muller. Muller carried the urn to the hole and took good care as he lowered it into its new grave.

I took out my pocketknife and said, "Your daddy's rope, it's your honor to cut it" and I handed it to him.

He said, "My grand-daddy's rope," and grinned as he laid down next to the hole.

I grabbed his legs as he reached down as far as he could, pulled the rope tight, and cut it off. I helped him to get up and out of the hole. Muller wrapped up the rope and put it back in the toolbox on the backhoe. Jake loaded up some sand and stone into the bucket of his front-end loader. Muller plopped a bag of cement on top and cut it open with my knife. Muller handed my knife back to me. Jake drove to the well and met my dad there. He had just doused the burned-out fire pit with water.

My dad pumped water into the bucket of the front-end loader. Jake drove back to the hole where Muller and I mixed up a cement, stone slurry in the

241

bucket of the loader. My dad came over with a flashlight. He, Muller, and I looked down into the hole as Jake tilted the bucket forward, nice and slow. We watched the mixture carefully pour in the hole around the urn. The urn disappeared in the mire. My dad motioned to Jake. He tilted the bucket all the way forward, then Muller and I scraped out the remaining muck.

Muller lifted the bed of the dump truck to about a forty-five-degree angle. He and I raked the limestone with shovels to fill the hole to three feet below the surface. While Muller and I were filling the hole with stone, Jake and my dad were mixing a good batch of concrete in the bucket of the front-end loader.

They poured a new base for the Witch's Ball, while Muller and I took Hazel over to her proper place of burial—at long last—in her own grave. It went much smoother over there. The coffin was sitting on straps that we used to lower Hazel into the ground. We wouldn't have to get our faces close to the unpleasant odor.

Jake and my dad met us there. We used the straps to pull the coffin off the bed of the truck and lower it into the ground. They went back to work on the base of the Gunther family marker. Muller filled in the grave with the backhoe. I scraped as much loose dirt as possible onto Hazel's grave with a shovel. Then Muller tamped the dirt down with the bucket of the backhoe. We laid the sods of grass that had been removed to start the process back down on top of Hazel's grave. Muller drove over them to compress them down the best he could. It looked pretty good when we were done.

We drove back to the Gunther plots. Jake and my dad had just finished troweling the new base. As we got out of the truck, Jake said, "If The Witch gets out of this, we'll call it 'Houdini.'" We cleaned up the site. Monday June 2nd, 1980, The Witch of The Valley was laid to rest.

We stood over our finished work. No words needed to be said. We each had a look of relief on our faces. I put my arm around Muller. I said, "Grandpa Johnny is proud of us." We were both thinking of him.

Muller cleared his throat and said, "I know he is." He smiled.

Muller and I walked back over to Hazel's grave. Looking down at her headstone, I prayed in silence that she may now rest in peace.

Muller told me months later that no one ever asked about the ground of Hazel's grave being disturbed. No one noticed because no one ever visited her.

The new foundation was allowed to cure for two weeks. It was time to put the black marble marker back on its base. I went to the cemetery to help Jake and Muller. There wasn't much to it. Jake had some slings that he wrapped around the ball. He lifted it with his backhoe, swung it around and set it down. The world was back in order.

I had brought some flowers with me. I wandered over and placed them on Hazel's grave. Muller walked up to me there and put his hand on my shoulder.

He said, "Ya know, Younger, I bet you're the first person to ever put flowers on Hazel's grave."

My head started spinning and my knees began knocking. Then they became wobbly and buckled. Vertigo drove me to the ground. I dropped to my knees on her grave. My whole body was shaking. I was freezing cold. I bawled out loud, "How could she have handled that thing within her? She was just a child. How could she withstand it for all those years?" Tears were flowing down my cheeks. I only maintained half of what she carried for a short time; Muller held the other half.

"I know what you mean." Muller rubbed the top of my head. "M&M brothers don't cry, remember?" He grinned. I came around and Muller helped me to my feet. He gave me a hug. We both wept.

How do you feel sorry for someone who had done such things? We walked in her shoes for a day. It's not that we condoned the evil deeds that Hazel had done. We wept for the poor little girl that Hazel once was. The lonely, unwanted, unloved, ugly duckling that longed to be loved and accepted; the tortured soul that life drove into the salt mine to find a friend.

From then on, that became part of our yearly tradition. Every year we meet on the Saturday after Memorial Day weekend at the Salty Dog Saloon. We order a drink, his a sarsaparilla, mine a beer. He doesn't drink anymore, and I don't drink any less. We make a toast to Grandpa Johnny, drink to it, and then go to Hollow Hill Cemetery. Just to make sure that everything is in order we drive past the Witch's Ball, to see for ourselves that it's still seated on its base. Then we loop around to visit Hazel, where I place flowers on her grave.

Muller found Lottie's grave. She's buried in one of the small cemeteries in The Valley. After we leave Hollow Hill Cemetery, we then drive there. Muller places flowers on her grave.

You see, Hazel and Lottie were no more a witch than you or I. They had lost their focus and allowed themselves to be used by an evil entity.

After that night of being possessed by The Witch I found it hard to focus. When I got back to college for football practice I couldn't handle it. Every time I tried to get into a three point stance my head would start to spin. Then gravity would pull me to the ground. I couldn't concentrate. In baseball, I couldn't handle focusing on a spinning ball all the way into my glove or hitting my bat. My head would start spinning like the ball. I would be overcome by vertigo and fall to the ground.

To this day I still get episodes of vertigo every now and again, when I'm reminded of the turbulence that overcame me. If I would have known then what I know now, I have serious doubts that I could have gone along with it. Muller feels the same way. The brain fog was lifted from The Valley, but it felt as if it were entirely directed at the both of us.

It took years for me to keep my focus on any task at hand. I would drift away into a daydream about The Witch, get a dizzy spell and have to sit down. Little by little, over many years, I was able to persevere. The brain fog faded, and things went back to normal, save for bouts of vertigo.

It was Doreen who really helped Muller and I along, though. She knew what it was that we had gone through, and she performed healing cleanses on us for well over a year. She became my wife and still helps me. We started a non-profit called Younger, M.D. We treat people in need and help them to heal.

Once in a while we run across people who need the expertise of Bishop Charles and Trudy. That's when Doreen steps up to the plate. Her and Olivia still help them expel evil spirits all across the Great Lake states. Apparently, this whole area is rife with demonic activity both new and ancient. Bishop Charles and the Wiccans have their hands full with no shortage of work to be done.

See, there is an evil ruler of this world that sends storms into our lives. Hoping to disrupt and destroy all of creation. One must learn to focus on the calm, quiet voice of the Great, Holy Spirit of God that rules the universe to guide you through the storms.

There is something that is much bigger than ourselves. There are other dimensions that are beyond our reach. We are destined to join all who have gone before us—each and every one of us.

My grandpa lived to the ripe old age of ninety eight. No matter what age a loved one is when they are taken away, it's always too soon for those who they left behind.

Muller entered the seminary and became a priest. I asked him if he ever did any more exorcisms. He replied, "I tried once, and you know how that went. And after what we went through—no—I've had my fill."

If you ever find yourself walking through the woods of Ohio and a strange, swirling wind comes whispering your way, and the breeze murmurs thoughts in your ears. Don't be surprised to have a foreign idea pop into your head. Or maybe you'll have dreams of a little girl that wants to be your friend; or of an old, wise woman who offers to help you; or a favorite animal, like a horse, enticing you to join them. Luring you to a place of darkness, where shadows dart and demons dwell. Don't go!

Do not fall victim to these forces of darkness. Malevolent forces tempting you to drink of the cup of bitterness; the cup from which they drink. They are wicked, spiteful spirits preying on those who believe that such things are mere superstitions.

Well, I can tell you this. Just like the superstition says, there is a Witch's Ball in The Valley. It's located in Hollow Hill Cemetery. Naysayers may say the ball is just a family marker, but what it really marks is the final resting place of The Witch of The Valley.

You don't have to worry, though. The Witch has been entombed for eternity, safely secured beneath the marker. Encircled by the four spirits surrounding it in all four cardinal directions. There it shall stay, sealed away under the center star of the Star Chamber, guarded by members of the old Town Council.

West
Reiner Wolfe

North
Old John Muller

The historic Star Chamber ceiling, with its bright gold stars, along with four tapestries depicting the four seasons.

South
Art Gunther

East
Heinrich Gunther

Made in the USA
Monee, IL
18 March 2024

55243200R00144